PRAISE FOR

The Darkness Surrounds Us

❧

"Lukasik (*White Like Her*) delivers a gripping ghost story of pandemics past in this well-crafted gothic mystery . . . Readers will sympathize with Nellie's fears and frustrations, and Lukasik maintains a deliciously dark tension throughout. With unpredictable plotting and superior atmospherics, this is an early-autumn treat fit for late-night devouring." ***—Publishers Weekly***

"Moody and atmospheric, *The Darkness Surrounds Us* by Gail Lukasik is a taut gothic mystery with an intriguing twist . . . Readers will enjoy the romantic undertones and the unrelenting suspense in this classically imagined tale." **—Susanna Calkins, award-winning author of the Lucy Campion Mysteries and the Speakeasy Murders**

"Lukasik blends all the elements needed for a dark suspense novel: a forbidding mansion, ghostly presences, secret passages, a hostile housekeeper, a temperamental employer, and residents unwilling to talk to outsiders. For fans of *Rebecca*, *The Woman in White*, and *The Death of Mrs. Westaway*." ***—Library Journal***

"[A] solid tale with appeal for fans of Midwestern gothics, like those by Wendy Webb and Jaime Jo Wright." **—Historical Novel Society**

The
Darkness
Surrounds
Us

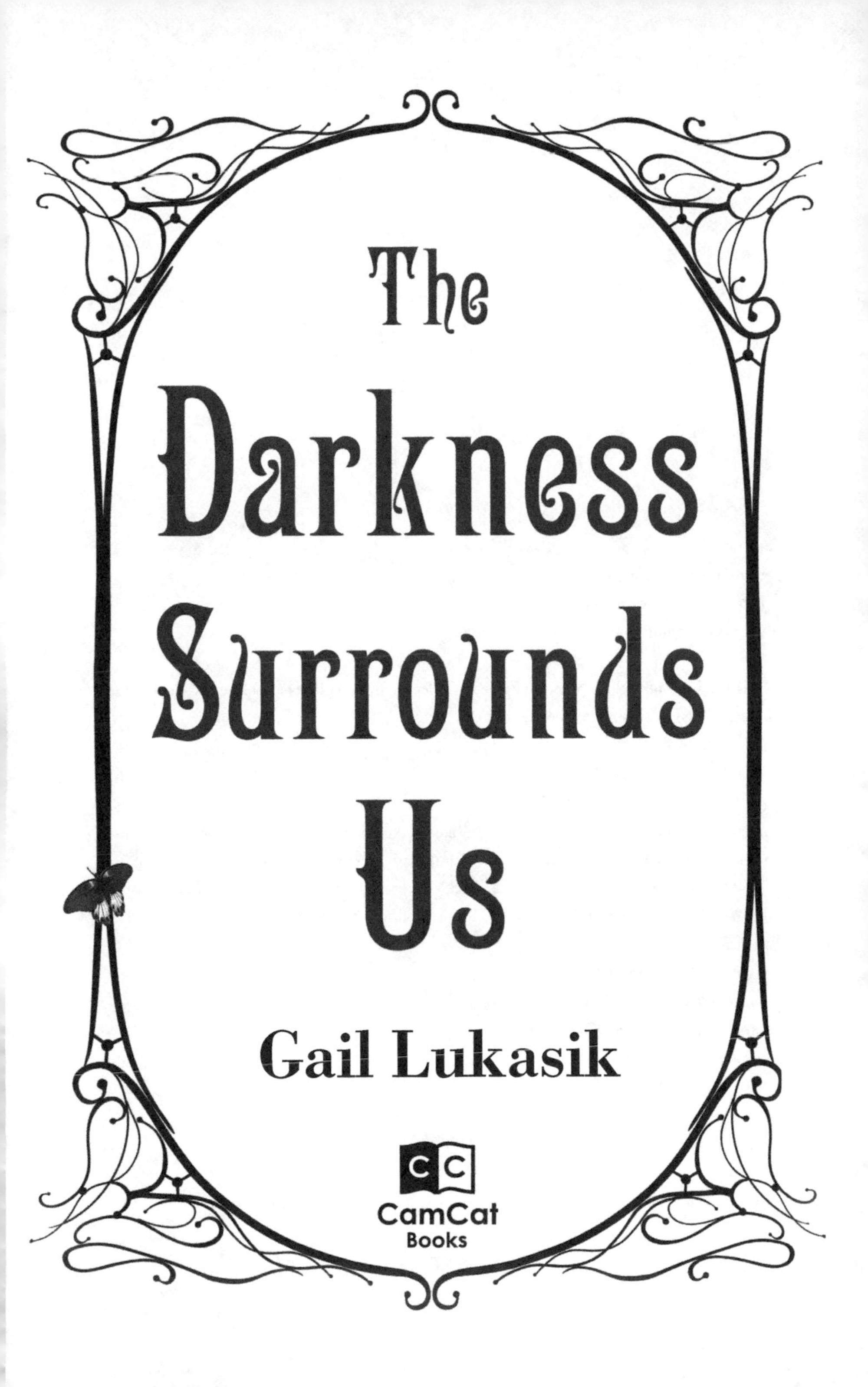

The Darkness Surrounds Us

Gail Lukasik

CamCat Books

CamCat Publishing, LLC
Fort Collins, Colorado 80524
camcatpublishing.com

Hardcover 9780744302899
Paperback 9780744305418
Large-Print Paperback 9780744305647
eBook 9780744305654
Audiobook 9780744305715

Library of Congress Control Number: 2023932288

Cover and book design by Olivia M. Hammerman (Indigo: Editing, Design, and More)

5 3 1 2 4

To the healthcare workers and teachers who bravely stood on the front lines of the Covid-19 pandemic.

"Dead people always seem to get in the way of the living."
Helen Sclair, Chicago's "Cemetery Lady"

PROLOGUE

1918

We are running through the snow. The moon lost among the trees. Black and skeletal, their branches lash my face. But it's the dog I fear the most. His frantic howls coming closer and closer. My mother grips my small hand so tightly it hurts.

Her terror-filled voice keeps saying: "God will protect us. God will protect us."

I stumble and fall. The snow is cold and unforgiving.

When my mother reaches for me, her face is as rigid as stone. It's then I know she's dead.

CHAPTER ONE

November 30, 1918

On the night my mother died, she took her secrets with her.

That's what I thought when I found the photograph and the gold pendant she'd hidden in her dresser drawer.

In the photograph, a couple stands side-by-side, stern and resolute. Behind them a small house, too many trees to count. My mother wears a plain, checked dress, hair spun into a tight bun low on her neck, neat white bonnet on her head. The pendant around her neck clashes with her severe clothes. The man wears a white shirt, dark trousers, and looks a little like me–same pale skin and wide-set eyes. I hold his hand and rest my head against his arm. My loose frock looks too big on my small frame. I'm three, maybe four years old.

On the back of the photograph, written in an exuberant hand, are a time and a place I don't remember.

Harmony, Michigan 1894: Mary, John, and Anna.

Am I Mary or am I Anna? Neither name conjures a memory.

And who is this man I seem so close to? Surely not my father.

My mother had told me my father's name was Paul Lester. That he'd died in a factory accident in Chicago before I was born. There'd been no photographs of him–no likeness to compare myself to. No photographs of any family for that matter.

The man must be my mother's second husband. That's what I told myself. But my mother never spoke of a second husband. I could fathom no reason for her secrecy. And I loved her too much to be angry. But I was sad and confused.

Adding to my confusion was one line, near the bottom of the photograph, so small it's almost illegible.

Our last happy day together before they took John from us.

What happened to this man? And who were the "they" who took him from us?

For months after my mother's death, those questions plagued me, as did the nightmare. Always the same: a cloudless, snowy night, my mother and me running through the woods, her frightened voice saying, "God will protect us."

The nightmare so real, I was beginning to think it might be a memory.

Then the unexpected happened. When I saw the "Help Wanted" ad, I had to answer it. Was it fate?

The ad had been terse.

Needed: nurse and companion. Above going wage. Three months guaranteed. All travel expenses paid. Write to: Mr. William Thiery, Ravenwood Manor, New Harmony, Michigan.

New Harmony, not Harmony. But it was the same place.

I had to apply. It was as if my mother were speaking to me, telling me to go there and find out about her past.

William Thiery's letter offering me the position had been as terse as his ad.

"Take the ferry boat from Charlevoix to New Harmony. Go to The Carp. It's across from the boat dock. Matthew will fetch you," he'd written in his precise hand. No last name. No description. Just Matthew.

The sudden lurch of the ferry boat broke into my thoughts. I picked up my pen, opened my journal, and began to write.

My name is Nellie Lester. I'm twenty-eight years old. I write this aboard the Mersey as it crosses the turbulent lake. It's the 30th of November 1918. The Great War has ended, but the Spanish flu rages on. I've left everything behind–my nursing position on the contagion ward, the Taylor Street apartment where my mother died, and a failed love affair.

It's been twenty-four years since the photograph was taken. Someone on the island must remember my parents. My medical bag is my passport. I've come to deliver the Thierys' baby. I've come to uncover my mother's secrets.

CHAPTER TWO

I don't know if I believe in omens.

But I shuddered when I stepped off the boat and saw the pine coffin and the six men beside it, waiting in the freezing rain. The darkness of their clothes matched the darkness of my thoughts.

Even here I couldn't escape death.

The men took no notice of me as I hurried past them, struggling with my suitcase and medical bag, my boots slipping on the icy dock. I was anxious to find The Carp and escape the sleet and the incessant banging of the fishing boats, which mirrored the thrumming of my heart.

When I reached the end of the dock, my shoulders slumped at the sight of the desolate and forlorn town. St. John's was a scattering of decrepit buildings and houses along a muddy road, anchored by a white church, post office, general store, and The Carp, a moss-covered stone tavern, where I'd been instructed to go.

For a moment I faltered, looking back at the Mersey. The men were boarding the boat, balancing the coffin on their broad shoulders.

I could still change my mind, return to Chicago, and beg the contagion ward matron to give me my job back. After twenty-four years, did I really believe I could find out who the man in the photograph was and why my mother never spoke of him?

The low moan of the foghorn broke through my thoughts pulling me back to the ramshackle town. If there was even a chance, I had to try. There was nothing for me in Chicago except misery and loneliness.

❧

The Carp was a dingy, shadowy place that smelled of old fires and dampness. I sat at the table nearest the door, nursing a cup of coffee, anxious and worried. Matthew was over two hours late and the coffin bearers were drunk.

Loud and raucous, they huddled near the hearth. With each pitcher of beer, they toasted the dead man, Sam, a fellow logger. Their glances had gone from furtive to leering.

They probably thought I was trade. A prostitute. Why else would a woman sit alone in a bar for hours unless she was selling her goods?

I was the only female in the establishment, except for the barkeeper, a tall sturdy woman as disheveled looking as the tavern, who only emerged from a back room when one of the men called for another pitcher of beer.

Where was Matthew? Had I mistaken the day? I pulled out Mr. Thiery's letter. No, it said November 30. And there was only one ferry that ran from Charlevoix to New Harmony.

"Hey, Bernie, another round," shouted the clean-shaven logger. The other loggers boasted thick mustaches or generous beards. One logger's mustache was waxed and curled up at the ends.

The barkeeper emerged from the back room. Though plain faced like me, her luxurious brown hair glimmered in the shadowy tavern light, unlike my frizzy red mess.

She plopped the pitcher on the table. The clean-shaven logger grabbed her around her waist and pulled her toward him.

"I'm having none of that, Abe." She swatted him on the head with her dirty rag. He let go. "Now you louts keep it down. There's a lady present." She jerked her head in my direction.

"More like trade," Abe answered.

That set off a volley of bawdy laughter.

Heat flooded my face. I looked away, fidgeting with my spoon.

"Miss," the barkeeper said, towering over me, holding the empty beer pitcher. "I'm going to have to ask you to leave. I don't know what you're about, but you're upsetting the men. I don't want any trouble." She glanced back at the loggers. "They need to let off some steam. One of their friends died yesterday in a logging accident."

The bitter taste of panic rose into my mouth. "I'm sorry about their friend. But I have nowhere else to go. Matthew was supposed to pick me up hours ago. I don't know where he is. He's to take me to the Thiery house." I was on the verge of tears.

"Ravenwood Manor? Why didn't you say so?" Her whole demeanor changed from suspicious to friendly. "Let me get you a refill on that coffee?"

Before I could answer, she disappeared into the back room. Suddenly, the room went quiet. I glanced at the drunken men. They were staring at me, smirking. Then they ran their tongues around their lips.

I didn't think my face could get any hotter. Humiliated, I buried my face in my journal, blocking out their drunken laughter. I turned to the drawing of New Harmony that I'd copied from a map hanging on the ferry's cabin wall.

Kidney shaped and amazingly small, I probably could walk from one end to the other in less than a day. Most of the island was forested. Ravenwood Manor overlooked Lake Michigan. St. John's was nestled in a cove on Ascension Bay.

Looking at the tiny island surrounded by nothing but water, a wave of claustrophobia washed over me.

The men seemed to have lost interest in me. I closed my journal, letting my thoughts tumble back to my mother.

What had brought her to this desolate island? Had she been so distraught by my father's sudden death, she'd married the man in the photograph and started a new life here?

Whatever her reasons, she would have been thinking of me, wanting a better life for us. I picked up my pen and sketched her face—the dimpled cheeks, broad features, and thick curly hair so black it had a blue sheen.

"How about we go upstairs, honey?"

I'd been so lost in my thoughts that I hadn't noticed the clean-shaven logger standing by my table. His dark eyes traveled my body. I shut my journal and rested my hand on it protectively.

"Did you hear me? I'm inviting you to go upstairs with me for a bit of fun," he said loudly, drawing hoots and snickers from the inebriated loggers.

"I'm sorry, but I'm expected at Ravenwood." Why was I apologizing?

He stumbled back, his lascivious expression gone. For a moment he struggled for words. "I wouldn't be caught dead sleeping at Ravenwood. Strange things go on up there."

His sudden somberness sent a shiver up my spine. "What do you mean? What kind of strange things?"

"Well, for one thing—" He stopped and glanced over his shoulder. "For one thing, no one seems to stay long. If you catch my drift."

"I don't understand." Was he implying no one wanted to work for the Thierys? Maybe Mr. Thiery's curt, unwelcoming letter wasn't a sign of a busy man but a sign of an unreasonable and difficult one.

"Stop bothering the woman." The barkeeper swatted him again with her dirty rag. In her other hand, she held the white enamel coffeepot.

"Just making her acquaintance." He shrugged.

"Get back to your friends and stop your nonsense."

He slunk away, mumbling under his breath.

As the barkeeper refilled my chipped cup, she said, "Don't pay any mind to Abe. When he gets drunk, he likes to stir the pot. Nothing strange going on at Ravenwood. It's just old and creaky, like everything else on this island. I should know."

She seemed so sincere; I wanted to believe her. "Have you lived here long?"

She took my question as an invitation, put the coffeepot on the splintery table, sat down, and rested her thick arms on the table.

"About twenty years or so. Up until last year my pa and I ran The Carp. Now it's just me. He's too infirm."

Twenty years? She'd come to the island four years after the photograph had been taken. Still, she might know someone on the island who had been here when my mother and I lived here.

I ladled a heaping teaspoon of sugar into my coffee, stirred it slowly as I considered my next question. I didn't want to appear nosy. But there was an openness about her that made me want to trust her.

"Someone told me the island used to be called Harmony. Do you know why the name was changed to New Harmony?

"That would be because of Henry Thiery, William Thiery's uncle. He lived at Ravenwood when he wasn't in Chicago. I'd tell you to ask him, but he died some years back." She smiled, revealing two missing lower teeth.

I returned her smile. "Do you know who lived at Ravenwood before Henry Thiery?" I had to be careful. If William Thiery discovered my real reason for coming here, I could be dismissed.

"Can't say I do." She looked away toward the men, as though one of them had called her. When she turned back, her soft brown eyes were narrowed with suspicion.

She picked at a splinter. Though chapped and red, her fingers were surprisingly small and delicate. "You should ask Doctor Proctor. He's our island historian."

"There's a doctor on the island?" I blurted. If the island had a doctor, why did William Thiery hire me?

She laughed. "He's not a real doctor, as such, more of a healer. He's a newspaperman from Chicago. People go to him with their medical troubles."

A newspaperman turned healer? I just prayed he wasn't like the fake healers, who since the pandemic hawked bogus medicines and false hopes.

The barkeeper pressed the splinter back into place with her thumb. "Since we're asking questions. What's your business with the Thierys?"

Though I suspected she knew my business with the Thierys, I answered. I really liked the woman and wanted to ally her fears about me. And I could use a friend. "Mr. Thiery hired me to deliver Mrs. Thiery's baby and care for her afterwards."

She nodded her head. "That's what I figured."

I sensed she was going to say something else but then thought better of it.

"I'm Bernice." She held out her delicate hand to me. "But everyone calls me Bernie."

I shook her rough hand, felt the strength of her grip. "Nellie Lester."

"Nice meeting ya." She stood, grabbed the coffeepot, and started to walk away, then turned back. "Just some advice. I'd be careful asking too many questions, Nellie. Most islanders aren't as friendly as me."

Though she'd delivered her warning kindly, her intention was clear. Outsiders should mind their own business. I felt hurt by her reprimand.

After she returned to the bar, I gazed out the window. The snow had stopped, but the wind was gusty.

I opened my journal and wrote: *Doctor Proctor, Chicago newspaperman, not a real doctor.* Then drew a question mark.

The loud crash of a chair hitting the stone floor startled me. My hand jerked and ink streaked the paper.

Abe was rocking drunkenly on his feet as he jabbed his finger at the logger with the curled mustache sitting across from him. "You're a liar. A damn liar."

The accused man put up his hands defensively. "I'm not saying it's true. I'm only saying that's what Peterman said. He swore he tightened those straps. He thinks someone messed with them."

The man's words enraged Abe even more. "Peterman is looking to put the blame on someone else. A good man is dead because of his carelessness. I'm telling you. He didn't tighten those straps."

The man next to Abe grabbed his arm. "Sit the hell down, will you? If anyone's to blame, it's Thiery; hiring men who know shit about logging and paying us dirt wages. You don't need a crystal ball to see this place is almost logged out."

Abe yanked his arm away. "Yeah, and you don't need a crystal ball to see this place is cursed."

He downed his beer, banged his glass so hard on the table that it shattered, sending shards everywhere. Then he stormed out of the tavern.

I watched him disappear into the dark wondering about the logger's death. Was it due to carelessness, as Abe insisted? Or had someone messed with the straps? If so, why would someone purposely loosen the straps?

The overwhelming smell of whiskey and animal musk pulled me from my musings. I turned around. Looming over me was a powerfully built man with broad shoulders that strained against his black wool jacket. He had the same weathered face and calloused hands of the loggers. But unlike them, his hair was long and unkempt, as was his unruly black beard. His square jaw and crooked nose gave him a combative appearance. His eyes were so deep set, I couldn't see their color. He'd be a hard man to read.

"You Nellie Lester?" he asked impatiently, as if he'd been waiting hours for me.

"Yes. You must be Matthew." I stared at the dried blood on his hands.

"This your gear?" He gestured at my medical bag and suitcase, which rested on the muddy stone floor.

Before I could answer, he scooped up my bag and suitcase and limped toward the door.

I shoved my journal into my purse, fished out a penny and left it on the table.

The cold air was like a tonic after the tavern's smothering miasma. I hurried toward the horse-drawn wagon.

Then I stopped. In the back of the wagon stood a cur, more wolf than dog. A low growl rumbled from the mammoth creature.

"What you waiting for?" he called, tossing my suitcase and medical bag in the back of the wagon. "He doesn't bite."

CHAPTER THREE

The lighthouse's beam pierced the intense darkness, illuminating a snowy landscape so bleak and lonely, I might as well be on the moon.

The cur sat attentive and alert behind me, sniffing the air; or was it me it was sniffing? The gruff man had offered no apology for his lateness. After helping me into the wagon, he'd handed me a carriage blanket. His one concession to courtesy, then he fell silent.

Besides the persistent foghorn, the only other sound was his rifle bumping against my suitcase and medical bag in the back of the wagon, where five skinned rabbits lay. Though inured to blood, the denuded rabbits' vulnerability made my stomach turn.

As the rutted road narrowed, the dark forest closed in. A low tree branch brushed across my cheek. That claustrophobic feeling I'd felt in the tavern returned.

I made another attempt at conversation, anything to break the silence. "What do you do for Mr. Thiery?"

He shook the reins, urging the horse forward. "Whatever he wants."

I sighed with frustration.

It had been a long journey to New Harmony–the crowded train from Chicago to Charlevoix, the turbulent boat ride across Lake Michigan to the island, the long wait in the tavern with the drunken men, and Abe's cautionary words about Ravenwood Manor and strange doings.

As much as I wanted to ascribe Abe's comments to inebriation, they scared me.

"No one seems to stay long," he'd said. But Bernie had dismissed his warning.

The lighthouse beam passed over. No house visible yet, just the dark forest.

"Is it much farther?" I asked, anything to keep my doubts at bay.

"Not far," he answered, as though each word cost him something.

I shifted on the hard wagon seat. The cur shifted with me.

The man's silence was maddening. "I heard one of the loggers died yesterday," I began, ignoring Bernie's well-intentioned advice. "One of the men in the tavern, his name was Abe, he didn't think it was an accident. Do you know anything about it?"

For the first time, he turned toward me. I felt the weight of his eyes. "You ask too many questions. The last one was nosy like you."

"What last one?" Had there been a nurse before me? Is this what Abe meant by no one seemed to stay long? I must have moved too suddenly because the cur let out a deep growl, his warm breath on my cheek. I shrunk down into my coat.

"Didn't last but a few months. She was a nurse from Chicago, like you, though younger. And better put together." He looked me up and down.

Despite myself, I flushed. Did he think I didn't know my own plain face? But it still hurt.

"She didn't take to the island," he continued, savoring his story. "Too nervous and flighty. You the nervous sort?"

It was clear the surly man wanted to frighten me, and it was working. "Why are you telling me this?"

"I don't want Mrs. Thiery counting on you, and then you up and leave like the other one. Mrs. Thiery hasn't been well of late." When he said Mrs. Thiery's name, his voice softened.

"What's wrong with her?" I asked. In Thiery's letter, he'd told me his wife was in good health, just anxious about the birth. There'd been no mention of a prior nurse.

"What I'm saying is you'd better not run off in the middle of the night, like she did."

Run off in the middle of the night? What would make a nurse abandon her pregnant patient?

"I would never do that," I assured him.

"Then we'll have no problems, you and me. Just know I'll be watching to make sure you don't."

The path veered left for a few feet and then curved right. The moon righted itself above the trees and the house came into view.

Perched on a promontory, overlooking Lake Michigan, Ravenwood Manor was a dark, hulking structure.

"Easy, girl." Matthew pulled on the reins as he maneuvered the skittish horse through the deep snow to the front of the manor.

I shivered as I gaped at the three-story brick mansion. It seemed to swallow the land, sprawling over it, and reaching upward toward the unreachable sky—turrets, gables, balconies, and windows too numerous to count. It was as though the manor didn't know its own limitations.

I hadn't expected such a grand house on a remote Michigan island, especially after viewing the shabby town.

Matthew must have seen my astonishment.

"Did you think Mr. Thiery lived in a hovel? He owns most of the island, including the lumber mill." He appeared inordinately proud of Mr. Thiery. "But I expect you know that, or you wouldn't have come."

I didn't know that. That explains Bernie's change of attitude toward me. The islanders must be beholden to him.

Who had built Ravenwood Manor? I wondered. Henry Thiery or whoever owned the island before him, when my mother and I lived here?

Before climbing down from the wagon, Matthew stretched out his left leg, rearranging his trousers over it. I wondered if his limp was recent and what had caused it. Was this what had soured him? For surely he was nursing a grievance.

He came around the wagon to help me down. As he grabbed my waist, he held me suspended above the ground a moment too long, studying me like a pinned insect.

The memory of being restrained by another man returned. I started to tremble.

"Please, let me go," I whispered.

He smiled, then released me.

"Better hurry," he said. "Mrs. Thiery's pains started this morning."

This morning? Why hadn't he come for me sooner?

Worried for Mrs. Thiery, I stumbled through the heavy snow to the back of the wagon.

A first baby. A long labor. So many things could go wrong.

Grasping the wagon's gate, I stepped up onto the floorboard and reached for my luggage.

The cur lunged at me, teeth bared.

I stood still. My heart pounded so loud I'm sure the beast could hear it.

Matthew chuckled. "Better let me get your things."

Reluctantly, I stepped down into a deep snowdrift, almost tumbling backwards.

With a deftness I didn't think he possessed, Matthew reached into the wagon, slung the rabbits over his shoulder, and grabbed his rifle. Then he tossed my suitcase and medical bag into the snow. My bag landed on its side, the medical instruments and bottles jangled inside.

"Please be careful," I said. "There are medicines and medical devices in my bag."

He gave me a sharp look but righted the bag. "Sorry, miss."

I didn't think he was the least bit sorry, but I said nothing, remembering the tightness of his hands on my waist.

"Now get yourself inside," Matthew directed. "I have to get these rabbits to the kitchen or none of us will be eating tonight." He limped away toward the back of the manor, the strung rabbits bouncing off his massive back, the dog at his heels.

His insolence, his warning about the last nurse, his tossing my things in the snow, it couldn't just be about the runaway nurse. It felt personal. But what could he possibly have against me? He knew nothing of my real reason for coming to the island.

As I slogged through the snow toward Ravenwood Manor, the plaintive cry of the cur reverberated through the woods. I stopped. The nightmare was back–the trees lashing my face, the dog coming closer and closer.

Then I thought of the laboring Mrs. Thiery and plunged ahead toward the brooding manor.

CHAPTER FOUR

There was no one to greet me when I stepped inside the cold foyer. A shadowy light spilled across the red-veined marble floor from a kerosene lamp perched on a gilt entry table. Beside it was a blue damask chair. Though the high domed ceiling and wood-paneled walls were meant to lend an air of grandeur, the foyer felt hollow and cheerless. A strange incense-like smell prickled my nose.

"Hello," I called into the cavernous corridor.

No one answered. I looked down the long hallway, dimly lit by flickering candle sconces. At the end of the hallway a faint light glimmered. The house felt empty.

Overhead I heard footsteps. I glanced toward the wide, erratic staircase, debating if I should go upstairs where Mrs. Thiery was probably lying in.

First, I needed to shed my wet coat and hat. I walked to the table and chair, placed my suitcase and medical bag on the floor, and started to take off my wool tam.

"Miss Lester."

I jumped.

When I turned around, a woman was standing behind me. She seemed to have appeared out of nowhere. Birdlike, thin to a fault with a beaky nose, she reminded me of a raven. Her black satiny dress and her gray hair lacquered into a tight bun added to that impression. I imagined her sprouting wings.

"You gave me a fright," I said, putting my hand on my wildly beating heart.

"I'm Mrs. Bucheim, the housekeeper. Let me take your things," she said, scrutinizing my shabby clothes and wet, snowy boots.

As I handed her my hat and coat, I tried not to stare at the smear of blood on her cheek, hoping it wasn't Mrs. Thiery's. Though the woman's face was creased with age, her spine was steely straight. Her age near impossible to guess. Then I saw her hands, knotted with arthritis and resembling tree burls. A jolt of pity rushed through me. She was sixty if a day.

"How is Mrs. Thiery?" I asked, trying to regain my composure.

She glanced at the staircase.

"Doctor Proctor is with her now," she whispered.

"Doctor Proctor?" I said, alarmed, not sure what the journalist turned healer knew about childbirth.

"We thought you missed the boat," she explained, placing my hat and coat on the chair. "Mr. William sent for him. The missus is in a terrible way. She's been laboring since early this morning. Poor dear."

As much as I wanted to explain my lateness, now wasn't the time. "Please show me to her room."

Already, a sense of foreboding was overtaking me. Though first babies were notoriously late, a long labor sapped the mother's strength. And if Matthew was to be believed, Mrs. Thiery was not well.

"Upstairs." She gestured toward the wide and winding staircase.

As I moved toward it, a disembodied voice boomed from the room at the end of the hallway. "Is that the nurse?"

"Yes, Mr. William. I don't know what the delay was." She gave me a sharp look.

"Tell Proctor he can leave now," Mr. Thiery commanded.

"Don't worry, everything will be fine now that the nurse is here," Mrs. Bucheim reassured him.

I started toward the room, wanting to introduce myself to Mr. Thiery. Mrs. Bucheim grabbed my arm.

"The missus is waiting," she said firmly, her black eyes the color of onyx and just as hard looking.

I pulled my arm from her grasp. She said nothing, took the lamp from the table, and started toward the stairs, leaving me in the thickening darkness.

Quickly, I picked up my medical bag and followed her.

As we made our way up the stairs, the kerosene lamp threw eerie shadows on the portraits lining the staircase wall. Men and women, ornately dressed with grim expressions, some holding guns, some holding flowers. Briefly, I saw a blond child woodenly posed with a wilted rose in her hand. Was that a death portrait? But the light moved away too quickly for me to be sure.

The house was strangely quiet, which worried me. Even the most stoic of women cry out in the throes of labor.

When we reached the landing, Mrs. Bucheim led me to the first door on the right.

As I entered the cluttered bedroom, I saw a man standing beside a mammoth four-poster bed fit for royalty. His back was to me, so I couldn't see what he was doing. This must be Proctor–the island healer.

I placed my bag on the settee and walked toward him. In his hand was a spoon. Its brownish-red liquid glittered in the faint light like a ruby. On the bedside table was a bottle–half full, clearly labeled. I didn't need to read the label to know it was laudanum.

I was alarmed that he was giving a woman in labor laudanum. Normally I wouldn't question a doctor, but he wasn't a doctor. "Mr. Proctor," I said, keeping my voice calm. "Please let me help with that."

Carefully, I took the spoon from him. He didn't protest, just shrugged his shoulders. Then I poured the contents back into the glass bottle. If Proctor was surprised, he didn't show it.

"I take it you're the nurse, Nellie Lester? I'm Theo Proctor." He had a quizzical look on his face.

"I am. May I ask how much you have given her?" I asked him politely.

Mrs. Thiery let out a shuddered groan as a contraction rolled over her. I was grateful she was conscious. But her large, hazel eyes were unfocused. Her auburn hair, damp with sweat, was plastered to her forehead. Even at her worst, her beauty was stunning–heart-shaped face, pouty mouth, and tiny nose. Three dark moles dotted her porcelain cheek. Her only imperfection, if you could call them that.

I placed my hand on her forehead. She wasn't feverish.

"One teaspoon." He seemed amused by my directness. "It's helped with her pains. She's been laboring since early this morning."

Where had he gotten laudanum? Only licensed doctors could obtain the drug legally.

"I see." That's one too many, I thought, as I picked up the stopper from the table and pushed it back into the bottle firmly.

Mrs. Bucheim came around to the other side of the bed. "Missus, tell the nurse that the medicine is helping you. You're having such a hard time of it." She stroked the woman's head, a piteous expression on her face.

"Don't be cross with the Doc," Mrs. Thiery pleaded, her voice frail. "It was me who asked him for it. He didn't want to give it to me. But it *has* helped with the pains."

And slowed the birthing process, I thought, but didn't say.

I was in a spot. If Mrs. Thiery's labor were to progress, she couldn't take any more laudanum. Clearly, Proctor and Mrs. Bucheim believed the laudanum was helping her. I needed to get them to leave the room.

"Mrs. Bucheim, would you see Mr. Proctor out please, as Mr. Thiery requested?" I just couldn't address him as doctor. "And please bring me clean towels, a basin of hot water, and tea," I said quietly.

Neither moved. They stood there, looking at me as if I had two heads. In my position at the hospital, I was used to following orders, not giving them.

What would matron do? I asked myself.

"Mrs. Bucheim, the towels, hot water, and tea, please." I imitated the matron's stern tone when dealing with contrary people. It must have worked because she left the room in a huff.

But Proctor remained, a sardonic smile on his face.

Scruffy yet handsome, his blond hair was in need of a cut, his beard of a trim, and his shirt of a wash. He looked like the newspaperman he used to be, right down to his arched eyebrows that made him appear perpetually curious and questioning.

Despite my annoyance with his continued presence, I felt instantly drawn to him.

I turned up the five kerosene lamps, flooding the room with much-needed light. Then I grabbed my medical bag, placed it on the dresser, where a few towels, an ewer, and a basin sat beside a tray of perfumes, hairbrushes, pins, and combs. From the bag, I extracted gloves, carbolic disinfectant, and my instruments and placed them on a fresh towel. Then I sprayed the instruments and my hands with the disinfectant before donning the gloves.

Since he hadn't left yet, I asked, "Have you examined her internally?"

His smile faded. "Not yet."

Another contraction seized Mrs. Thiery. Two in the course of the short time I'd been in the room.

"Mrs. Thiery," I said, "I'm sorry I couldn't get here sooner. But everything is going to be fine." If Proctor hasn't given you too much laudanum, I thought, not sure I believed the man.

"Now, let's see how far along you are."

I sat down on the silk-covered ottoman at the foot of the bed.

"This may be a bit uncomfortable," I warned her.

With a flourish, I lifted the sheet. "Mrs. Thiery, please move to the edge of the bed, knees bent, legs apart."

Whether he saw me insert my two fingers inside her cervical opening, I didn't know. But when I was done, he was gone.

I was grateful Mrs. Bucheim hadn't returned with the towels, hot water, and tea until after I'd broken Mrs. Thiery's water with the amniotic hook.

Her hovering anxiety would have only added to the woman's distress.

After Mrs. Bucheim brought the items, I asked her to leave. With an uncertain and disapproving look, she did.

CHAPTER FIVE

The baby was born just before midnight. A girl, still as stone, skin blue-tinged. She'd yet to take a breath. My panic was so fierce I could taste it. Then my training took over. With haste, I clamped the cord.

"It's a girl," I said, keeping my voice steady as I wrapped the infant in a blanket and moved to the other side of the room, where Mrs. Thiery couldn't see me. Delicately, I rubbed the baby's chest and blew into her tiny mouth.

Nothing.

I did it again, and then again. Still nothing.

"Is something wrong with the baby?" Mrs. Thiery asked, propping herself up on her elbows. "Can I see her?"

I didn't answer, said a silent prayer instead. Then I tried one more time, aware that at least a minute had passed. After another minute, if the baby lived, it would have brain damage.

Then I felt her heart start, her lungs inflate. She let out a shuddered cry.

She was tiny but well formed with a blazing fluff of red hair, not unlike mine. How strange, how fitting.

After swaddling her, I went to the bed and handed her to Mrs. Thiery. "She's healthy. She just needed a little prompting," I reassured her.

Mrs. Thiery held the baby awkwardly, a confused look on her face I contributed to the length of her labor and the lingering effects of the laudanum.

"Am I holding her right?" she asked. I could see exhaustion roll over her.

I nodded. "Have you chosen a name?"

"Hannah."

"A lovely name," I said.

After I washed my hands, I gathered my instruments, bathed them in hot water, and arranged them in my medical bag. The orderliness of the task soothed my jangled nerves. From the bag, I withdrew a tincture. Her bleeding was heavier than I liked. The tincture would stanch it. I mixed it into the tea and urged her to drink it.

"I'll hold the baby while you drink."

Mrs. Thiery seemed relieved to hand me the baby. First time mother jitters, I thought.

After giving me the baby, she drank the tea in two gulps.

"Thank you, Miss Lester."

"Nellie, please."

"And you must call me Catherine."

"Catherine, if you experience any heavy bleeding or pain, please send someone for me, no matter the time. That's what I'm here for."

Her eyes were starting to close.

"I'll stay until you fall asleep." I took the baby and placed her snuggly in the cradle. I also wanted to keep an eye on the baby a while longer.

There'd be time tomorrow to question Catherine about the laudanum. Warn her not to take it. Tell her how it would infect her milk. Just to be safe, I took the bottle and slipped it into my bag.

While I waited for her to fall asleep, I looked around the disquieting bedroom. Dark heavy furniture choked every space. But what was most unsettling was the wallpaper–thick emerald vines twisted around enormous blood red flowers, whose erect stamens were phallic-like and threatening. I would find sleeping difficult in here.

Before making my way down the stairs, I left my medical bag on the landing. If Mr. Thiery were like most new fathers, he'd be waiting anxiously for news.

When I reached the threshold to the drawing room, I hesitated. Sensing someone behind me, I looked over my shoulder but saw nothing.

Taking in a deep breath, I ventured into the grand drawing room, holding the kerosene bedroom lamp aloft. The room's only source of light was the massive hearth and the moonlight streaming in from the wall of windows. Like the Thierys' bedroom, the drawing room was a maze of dark furniture, and at first, I didn't see him. Then I did.

William Thiery was sprawled on a brown leather chesterfield sofa, head back, legs outstretched, and his arms loose at his sides as though sleep had caught him in a moment of weakness. A soft snore escaped him. He was a large man, well over six feet tall, with a wild shock of black hair and a thick mustache. He looked more like the loggers I'd seen in the tavern than a timber baron.

He wasn't the man I'd imagined from his precise handwriting–refined, sporting a smart, trim mustache, a waistcoat, and a gold watch that he liked to check on the hour.

A snifter of brandy rested on a highly polished wood table where a cigar smoldered in an ashtray, which accounted for that incense-like smell.

I envied his deep sleep. Since my mother's sudden death and the discovery of the photograph, sleep had come in fits and starts, peppered with that frightening nightmare.

Placing the lamp on a nearby table, I whispered, "Mr. Thiery." He didn't move. "Mr. Thiery," I said louder, gently shaking his shoulder, feeling its muscularity.

He bolted up as though I'd slapped him. "Who the devil are you?"

"I'm the nurse, Nellie Lester."

"My wife and the baby? Are they all right?" His voice was tight with fear.

"They're both fine," I said. "You have a baby girl."

"Then there were no complications?" He stumbled on the word as though it were unfamiliar to him.

"Were you expecting complications?"

"The other nurse thought there might be." He looked away toward the windows, where the moon nudged the clouds. "Our first one was stillborn. A boy. Catherine was so anxious, the nurse put her on bed rest."

That explained his worry. "I'm sorry about your son. But your baby girl is healthy. They're sleeping, but you can go up and see them."

"Thank you." He rose from the couch, smoothed his hair back from his high forehead and walked toward the hallway.

I called after him. "Mr. Thiery, my room? Where is it?"

He stopped and turned toward me, his gaze lingering on my flaming hair. I resisted the urge to touch it like an apology.

"In one of the turrets. To the left of the stairs at the end of the hallway, you'll see another set of stairs. Take those. And Mrs. Bucheim left you supper in the kitchen. We don't stand on formality here. So call me William."

Before I could ask where the kitchen was, he'd disappeared. I heard his footfalls bounding up the stairs eager to see his new baby.

Taking the lamp, I went in search of the kitchen, my stomach aching with hunger. It was at the back of the house–a cheery room with a hearth, wood plank floors, iron pipe stove, a tall cabinet bursting with dishes, and a worn oak table and chairs. A covered iron pot rested on the stove next to a teakettle.

I lifted the lid. A greasy film floated on the surface of the pungent rabbit stew, carrots and onions bobbed around the white meat. My stomach turned. I replaced the lid and went to the larder–a chilly place crammed with shelves of meats, cheeses, and preserved goods. I wasn't a picky eater, but the memory of the skinned rabbits lingered.

A cutting board and knife sat on the marble-topped table. As I picked up the knife, the image of the baby's blue-tinged skin, its horrifying stillness, flashed before me. Quickly replaced by another image, rows and rows of patients, their skin purpling, as they gasped for air.

My hand shook so badly I put the knife down and grasped the edge of the table to steady myself.

Breathe, I told myself, *breathe. The baby didn't die. This isn't Chicago.*

Finally, the panic seeped away. Still shaky, I carefully cut a chunk of cheddar cheese and returned to the kitchen. In the breadbox was a half loaf of dark rye. I tore off a piece and grabbed a plate from the cabinet. On the oak table Mrs. Bucheim had left me a pot of tea, which was still warm.

Sitting at the table, I ate slowly, exhaustion overtaking me, my mind edging back to the tenuousness of the baby's birth and the laudanum. Where had Proctor gotten the drug? It had been outlawed four years ago, available only to licensed doctors.

Another dark thought came to me. Had Catherine taken the drug before tonight? If so, that could explain her first child being stillborn.

My eyes were starting to close. I wanted to rest my head on the table, bask in the warmth of the hearth. Instead, I washed my dish and cup in the cast-iron sink and headed for the stairs.

When I reached the landing, I heard the low growl before I saw the dog.

"Shoo," I whispered, holding the lamp toward its menacing presence. The dog didn't move.

"So, is it a girl or a boy?" Matthew stepped out of the shadows, startling me.

"A girl," I answered, keeping my eyes on the dog.

"Is Mrs. Thiery well?" he asked.

"Mother and baby are both fine. Please, I'd like to go to my room."

"No one's stopping you," he said, making a wide gesture with his arm.

As I started to move toward him, the dog bared its teeth and snarled.

"Could you curb your dog?" I pleaded. All my energy spent. "I'm sure you don't want to wake Mrs. Thiery and the baby."

I was shaking so hard, I had to steady the lamp with both hands.

"Samson, settle," he said, ruffling the dog's fur. The dog relaxed. "Your things are in your room. Mind the stairs. They're tricky. You wouldn't want to fall."

As I passed him, I felt a slight tug on my skirt. When I turned around, Matthew and the cur were walking away.

CHAPTER SIX

The cold was like a presence. There was no fire in the grate. No wood to start one.

I'd counted four bedrooms as I'd made my way down the hallway to the spiral staircase. Why had I been put in this one? It felt like a punishment.

I shut the door firmly behind me, wondering if this had been the runaway nurse's room. If so, had she felt the same trepidation I was feeling now, after seeing the key dangling on a peg outside the turret room, realizing the door only locked from the outside?

My encounter with Matthew and the cur had left me anxious. I would not sleep tonight if I didn't secure the door in some way. I placed the key and the lamp on the massive oak dresser, then dragged the spindly chair across the worn wood floor and shoved it under the doorknob. It would have to do.

The paucity of the room's furnishings clashed with the manor's faded opulence–a slender, wrought iron bed, one chair, now under the door; an oak bedside table; rough, unpapered walls; and a thin woven rug like an island of color in the drab room. The room felt lonely and forgotten, a reminder of my position in the house, as if I needed reminding.

Matthew's disdain for me was evident in the unlit fireplace and the careless way he'd thrown my purse, suitcase, and medical bag atop my coat. He must have picked up my medical bag from the landing where I'd left it. What grudge was he harboring? Had the other nurse tainted him so much he couldn't show the simplest courtesy of a lit fire to the new nurse?

I slipped into my coat, eyeing the three large stained-glass windows that faced the rear of the house, the most likely source of the cold draft that inhabited the room.

As I walked across the room, it felt tilted as though the floor sloped toward the windows, where a waning moon illuminated their diamond patterning and the golden roses that bloomed at their centers. A mesmerizing design that was too beautiful for this shabby prison. The roses reminded me of my mother's rose pendant, except the windows' roses had leaflets and stems. I pulled the pendant out from under my dress and studied the design.

Was my mother's pendant somehow associated with this house?

Go to bed, I told myself. Nothing unusual about a rose design.

I shut the heavy blue damask curtains against the cold air seeping in through the windows' iron-soldered joints. Though the room was so frigid, I doubted it would do much good.

Looking up at the high-peaked ceiling, I saw spider webs swaying. There must be another draft. But I was too tired to search for it.

As weary as I was, I couldn't settle. I took out my journal and did a quick sketch of the turret room. Instead of settling me, my drawing only emphasized my loneliness. Then I unpacked my clothes, arranging my hairbrush, comb, and pins on the dresser. I hid the photograph and my journal among my undergarments.

It was too cold to undress.

Before crawling under the thin quilt that reeked of musk and damp, I put on my gloves, tied my woolen scarf around my head, and pulled my coat over the quilt.

I turned off the lamp, pitching the room into utter darkness. But sleep didn't come. Images flashed through my brain—the baby's blue skin, the bottle of laudanum, Matthew's iron grip on my waist, the cur's sharp teeth, and that feeling of claustrophobia and being watched.

"No one seems to stay long." Abe's words rang in my head.

You're here to find out about your mother's past, I reminded myself. The rest has nothing to do with you. I rolled onto my left side. Then I gasped in fright. A dark shadow hovered near the hulking dresser. Its long dark hair so like hers.

"Mother?" I whispered so as not to chase her away.

Then I blinked. There was nothing there. A waking dream? My overwrought mind playing tricks on me?

The house groaned and shuddered around me as if it were alive. Then the room's oppression deepened, as did my grief.

CHAPTER SEVEN

Even the bright day couldn't dispel my disquiet or the cold that had settled into my bones. As I dressed, I glanced furtively at the corner where the shadowy presence had appeared.

A trick of the senses, I told myself, caused by exhaustion and grief. And yet the presence had seemed so real and so comforting.

Before making my way to the kitchen, I checked on Catherine and Hannah. Both asleep. I'd examine them after breakfast.

Like a dull toothache, that feeling of being watched returned as I walked past the ancestors' paintings lining the staircase. I stopped at the child's picture. It *was* a death portrait. Perched on the girl's shoulder was a butterfly, a symbol of transformation. The wilted rose had blackened. Her rigid grimace and unformed hands indicated she'd crossed the veil between the living and the dead.

I shivered and moved away, thinking how close Hannah had come last night to joining this grim bunch.

After the dark night, the sunlight streaming through the doors at the end of the hallway was impossible to resist. Breakfast could wait. I strode toward the French doors. Behind the manor, tucked into the bleak, snowy landscape were a barn, stables, and a caretaker's cottage.

Restless, I went into the grand drawing room. Last night in the dying firelight with the trauma of Hannah's birth still fresh, I'd missed the room's masculine aggressiveness. Animal heads gazed down on me as if I were prey–glassy-eyed deer, antlered bucks, and two wolves with teeth bared.

Over the fireplace was a large portrait. The gold plate affixed to it read: *Henry Thiery*. William looked nothing like his uncle, who had a round, robust face, not William's long angular one.

As I gazed around the overly furnished room, I saw nothing of a woman's touch here.

My stomach groaned. I tightened my shawl around me, making sure the moth-eaten hole wasn't visible, and went in search of breakfast. Three months guaranteed gave me ample time to search the rest of the manor.

⸙

"There are honey biscuits and hardboiled eggs. Nothing fancy," Mrs. Bucheim said, pointing to the table where a blue bowl of eggs, a white plate of honey biscuits, and a brick of butter sat. "I didn't think you'd want to eat in the dining room alone."

I was grateful for the kitchen's warmth after the cold night. "Will you sit with me while I eat?"

In answer, she brought the coffeepot to the table, poured me a cup, and then one for herself.

I took a bite of the honey biscuit. "This is delicious."

"My mother's recipe from the old country." She sliced into the butter, then lathered her biscuit.

I didn't ask where her people were from, fearing it would lead to the inevitable question of where my people were from. My mother claimed her family was dead, as were my father's.

"I saw Henry Thiery's portrait over the mantle," I said. "Did you know him?"

"Worked for him for twenty years. He was a kind man, no matter what people say." Her fierce loyalty was evident in the set of her square jaw. "After William lost his father, Mr. Henry invited him to spend summers here as a boy."

"Why would people speak ill of Mr. Thiery if he was kind?" I took a sip of coffee. It was so bitter and strong I thought it capable of holding my spoon upright in the cup. I lightened it with cream and sugar under Mrs. Bucheim's watchful eye.

"People thought he was too harsh. But he was always fair. And what would some of them do if it weren't for the logging business? The fishermen were barely getting by, same for the farmers."

"Maybe they were envious. After all, he built this grand house and owned the town." I cracked open an egg, peeled and salted it, then took a bite. The center was hard and greenish, like the eyes of the dead child in the portrait. I put the egg down.

"It wasn't him that built the house or the town."

I sat up straighter. "What do you mean?"

"All I know is, it was here before Mr. Henry bought the island twenty-two years ago. Why are you so interested in Henry Thiery?" The photograph was dated 1894. That meant Henry Thiery purchased the island two years after the photograph I'd found hidden in my mother's dresser was taken.

I shrugged my shoulders. "Just making conversation. I noticed the death portrait of that blond child on the stairs. Was she a relative of Henry Thiery?"

"What are you going on about portraits for?" Mrs. Bucheim got up from the table, went to the stove, and started stirring a pot. I could see from the rigidity of her spine that something I'd said had upset her.

"These biscuits really are delicious," I said, trying to cajole her.

She turned from the stove, her arms folded over her bony chest. "I'll fix you a tin. You can take it to Doc Proctor by way of an apology for your rudeness last night."

It was as if she'd slapped me. I gathered my dishes and brought them to the sink.

"Let me clean up," I said, taking one of the rags from the wood counter.

Her black eyebrows were like a gathering storm. "I can manage. Shouldn't you be seeing to the missus and the baby? That's why you're here, isn't it?"

She must have seen the hurt in my eyes, because she added, "Thank you, though, for offering."

Her hands were clumsy as she ran the rag over a dish. The gnarled knobs of her knuckles red and inflamed. "I can give you something for your arthritis. It's a tincture that'll ease the pain and help with the inflammation."

Her face softened, and for a moment I thought she might accept my offer. "Doc Proctor's treating me."

I started to leave, then remembered my cold room. "I'm guessing in last night's confusion, someone forgot to light the fire in my room."

She seemed surprised. "I'll see to it."

"Is that where the other nurse slept?" I couldn't help myself.

She grabbed a tin from the cabinet shelf, lined it with waxed paper and began filling it with biscuits. "The missus thought you'd like your privacy."

It was clear she was done answering my questions.

"Where is Mr. Proctor's cottage? I'd be happy to bring him the biscuits." This would give me a chance to ask him about the laudanum–and the island; after all, Bernie had called him the island's historian.

Her directions came with a warning she seemed to relish. "Follow the path at the back of the manor. You'll see a maze before you reach the cottages. Don't go inside. You might walk for hours in there and never find your way out. Some say there's a house at its center."

I was intrigued. "Is there a house at its center?"

"How would I know?"

"You've never been tempted to find out?"

"Some things are best left a mystery," she replied pointedly, handing me the biscuit tin.

I took the tin from her.

"Doctor Proctor may not be a proper doctor, but we trust him." Her smile was weak and insincere.

As I exited the kitchen, it was clear to me Mrs. Bucheim didn't trust me. I'd have to find a way to win her over.

CHAPTER EIGHT

After my morning examination of Catherine, I realized that Mrs. Bucheim wasn't the only one who didn't trust me. Catherine had found fault with everything I did.

Your hands are too cold. You're hurting me. I don't like the taste of that medicine.

Finally, I'd stopped listening. Her complaints felt personal, aimed to wound me. Was I being compared to the other nurse and found wanting?

Now, as I made my way down the spiral stairs, I readied myself for whatever complaints Catherine might sling at me.

When I reached the first-floor landing, I heard Catherine's raised voice. Worried, I hurried to her room. The door was shut.

Before I could knock, Catherine shouted, "Just go to your precious logging camp."

"I can't talk to you when you're like this," William fired back.

Rather than return to my room, I put my ear to the door. Whatever the Thierys were arguing about, I needed to know. Maybe there was something else behind Catherine's excessive complaints that had nothing to do with me.

"This isn't the first time you've broken a promise," Catherine accused.

What promise had he broken?

"You knew what you were getting into when you married me. As I remember it, you were eager to live in this grand house," William snapped.

"That was before I knew what it was like living on this godforsaken island. I'm lonely. I have no one to talk to. There's nothing to do. Nowhere to go. I can't do it anymore. I won't." Her voice was shaky with tears. She was on the verge of hysterics.

"I told you, once I get the mill profitable so I can sell it, we'll go back to Chicago," he said.

"I want you to fire the nurse. I don't trust her."

I jerked back from the door. Fire me?

"I'm not firing the nurse. And I'm not discussing this with you when you're like this," William said wearily.

I almost felt sorry for him. Catherine's emotions were like a roller coaster that left you both exhilarated and shaky.

"Just go, then," she cried.

His angry footsteps alerted me. I hurried past the landing, to the other side of the hallway.

"Good afternoon," I said, smiling as I walked toward him, swinging my medical bag as if I didn't have a care in the world.

"Is it?" he fired back as he dashed down the stairs.

I hurried after him. "William, if I could have a word." I needed to make him see that Catherine's behavior had nothing to do with me.

"Make it quick."

"You have to be patient with Catherine. After a woman gives birth, her emotions are unsteady. She may say things she doesn't mean."

"Save your breath. I know all about Catherine's emotions." William ran his hand through his black hair. He was beyond agitated. "I have to go."

The loud slam of the front door shuddered through the house.

"Miss Lester, what are you doing standing here? Shouldn't you be seeing to Mrs. Thiery?" Mrs. Bucheim accused.

Where had she come from?

"Mrs. Bucheim, I didn't see you." I glanced down at her raw and inflamed hands. "Please, if you won't take the tincture, let me give you a salve for your hands," I offered, hoping to win her over.

"What good would that do? Unless I stop cooking and cleaning?"

"It'll soothe the pain and help with the healing."

She humphed. "Don't forget the tin for Doc Proctor. And the apology."

CHAPTER NINE

The sky was as troubled as my mind as I trudged down the path behind Ravenwood Manor to Proctor's cottage. William and Catherine's bitter words spun in my head. There was something else at play here that had nothing to do with me. Something to do with a promise he'd broken.

Though free of the dreary manor, its long shadow darkened the path. I glanced back at the house. A cluster of ravens perched along the roofline like sentries, their glossy black bodies glistening and ominous. In the wintry daylight, the house was even gloomier with its chipped and worn red brick, weather-stained shingles, and missing masonry. It was a house in need of repair—a house of secrets.

A movement caught my eye. Someone was standing in the turret window, watching me. They moved away so quickly I only caught a fleeting glimpse of a woman dressed in black. What was Mrs. Bucheim doing in my room?

I patted the pocket where I'd sequestered the photograph of my mother, me, and the unknown man and moved on. If she searched my things, she'd find nothing.

After I passed the caretaker's cottage, where Mrs. Bucheim told me Matthew lived, I came upon an assortment of abandoned structures whose purpose I couldn't discern.

As the path jogged left and the maze came into view, Mrs. Bucheim's warning rang in my head. "You'll see a maze before you reach the cottages. Don't go inside. You might walk for hours and never find your way out. It's rumored there's a house at its center."

My curiosity overcame my fear. I stepped off the path and headed to the maze's entrance trudging through deep snowdrifts.

Surrounded by towering evergreens, the maze looked like something from a Grimm's Fairy Tale. Shadowy and foreboding, its treed walls tilted inward. I felt drawn to it.

Clutching the biscuit tin to my chest like a shield, I stepped inside. The temperature dropped, the light disappeared, the evergreens closed in on me.

Though the path was precarious, I kept walking, compelled to see what was at the maze's center. When the path diverged, I stopped. Not sure whether to go right or left. I looked over my shoulder. The entrance was no longer visible, just trees choking the air with a piney scent. It was hard to breathe.

An image arose. My mother squeezing my hand too tightly, her face a pale moon as we ran through the darkness. For the first time I was convinced that my nightmare was a memory.

A raven squawked overhead. The image left—vaporous as last night's presence in my room.

Trembling, I turned around and hurried back toward the entrance, stumbling through the deep snow.

When I emerged from the maze, Matthew was standing there, a rifle cradled in his arms, a scowl on his rugged face. The cur wasn't with him.

"What were you doing in there?" It sounded like an accusation.

"I'm on my way to Mr. Proctor's cottage."

"You won't find his cottage in there." He laughed, and his whole appearance changed. "You know there's no house at the center, if that's what you were looking for. That's just Mrs. Bucheim having her fun."

"I didn't think there was," I said, embarrassed.

He glanced up at the sky that had turned threatening. "You'd better get going. Looks like more snow. You wouldn't want to get stranded at Proctor's cottage." He smirked, then headed in the opposite direction.

A feeling of desolation overcame me when I saw the dilapidated cottages in the clearing–caved-in roofs, broken windows, doors hanging open, and oddly arranged in a circle. Only one wasn't run down. Though in need of fresh paint, its shake roof was mended, the windows unbroken. Smoke puffed from its chimney.

I started toward Proctor's cottage, then stopped, my heart racing wildly. Suddenly it hit me. *This is the place.*

Tucking the tin under my arm, I reached into my pocket for the leather holder. My hands trembled as I slipped the photograph out of the holder.

The roofline, the two windows, the door so neatly centered–this was where we stood when the photograph was taken. Though it was impossible to tell which cottage it was, they were all so alike.

A thousand questions swirled in my head that I had no answers for.

Maybe Proctor could answer them.

The photograph secure in my coat pocket, I tromped to Proctor's cottage.

"Mr. Proctor," I called out as I knocked on his door. "It's Nellie Lester."

Nothing. I knocked again, louder. Still no answer.

Curious, I went to the side of the house and peeked in the window. Clothes, books, and papers were strewn across his bed and on the floor. Embers glowed in the hearth. Wherever he was, he hadn't been gone long.

The light was starting to go and the cold wind was swirling the snow. I was chilled to the bone. I'd leave the biscuits on the doorstep and come back tomorrow.

Then I heard a thrashing coming from the forest. I hurried to the front of the house.

Proctor burst from the woods, a stricken look on his face. When he saw me, he stopped. It was like watching a chameleon change color. His pace slowed and a smile spread across his handsome face. He was hatless and his wavy blond hair was wet with snow.

"Miss Lester," he said. "Did you bring me a gift?" He gestured toward the tin.

"Biscuits," I said, raising the tin.

"Ah," he said. "Mrs. Bucheim's honey biscuits. Come inside. You look frozen. I'll make coffee. Then you can tell me what brings you to my humble dwelling."

CHAPTER TEN

Sitting in the tiny parlor, I wondered. Was this the cottage where we'd lived?

Nothing nudged my memory. Though the whitewashed walls, simple furniture, and cozy hearth reminded me of our tiny apartment on Taylor Street—our haven from the hardships of the outside world.

But that was where the similarities ended. Fragrant herbs hung from the low ceiling, books and newspapers scattered across the plank floor that was covered with a rag rug whose bright colors had faded. I caught one title: *The Favorite Medical Receipt Book and Home Doctor*.

"I'm told you used to be a journalist. But now you're a healer." My eyes traveled from the herbs to the two shelves lined with bottles.

Proctor put his coffee mug on the wooden crate that served as a table and leaned forward in his ladder-back chair as though he needed to get a better look at me. He was tall and lean limbed like an athlete. His white shirt was open at the neck, revealing a smooth chest.

It was hard not to stare.

"I'm still a journalist. I make no claims of being a healer," he defended himself, his blue gaze fixed on me. "If this is about last night, I told William there was nothing I could do for Catherine. But he insisted I treat her. You can't tell William anything once his mind is made up. He's used to getting his way."

"Mr. Proctor, you must know that giving her laudanum would slow her labor and affect the baby?" The herbs and the home medical book troubled me. Contrary to his protestations, he was practicing medicine.

His wind-burned face reddened even more. He put up his hands in surrender. "I didn't want to give it to her. I'm aware of the drug's effects. But she begged me. I meant no harm."

"How did you come by it? The laudanum." My back ached from sitting in the ladder-back chair and trying to resist the pull of his handsomeness. He seemed so open and honest, I wanted to abandon my inquiry. But for the sake of his patients, I couldn't.

"Call me Theo. And can I call you Nellie?"

"Theo, where did you get the laudanum?" I persisted.

"Someone left it in the back of the cottage's kitchen cupboard. I found it when I moved in. I use it sparingly." He jerked his thumb toward the kitchen. "Hey, why all the questions? You'd think you were the journalist."

Though he seemed sincere, I wasn't sure I believed him. But I let it go. I was an interloper on the island. Why would he listen to me? I took a sip of his bitter coffee. It seemed it was a day of bitter drinks.

"It's also part of my profession, asking questions," I said, smiling despite myself.

Proctor reached into the tin and pulled out another biscuit, took a large bite, then put his feet on the crate. Crumbs scattered on his white shirt, melted snow dripped on the crate from his boots.

"Go ahead," he said, chewing around the biscuit, "ask your questions. Though I can guess what you want to know. Why am I here? Why aren't I back in Chicago working at the *Times* writing stories about the flu and the armistice? Why am I hiding myself away on a desolate island practicing the healing arts? Taking handouts from a logger baron? I've asked myself the same questions."

Now I flushed, waiting for him to continue. When he didn't, I said, "So why are you here?" I was genuinely curious.

"Look, you end up in a dead-end place like this because you're either running away from something or running toward something. I'm a little of both. What about you, Nellie Lester? Why would a girl like you leave Chicago? What are you running away from?"

I looked past him, up at the painting over the hearth mantle. A boat rested in a harbor, serene and picturesque. Like Proctor. I could see why people trusted him, why they came to him. His openness was intoxicating. Or was his openness an act, a way of disarming people?

Despite my misgivings, I decided to trust him. What choice did I have? He knew the island and its history. He was the logical person to ask. And I trusted myself to know if he was telling me the truth. I had to take the chance. From my coat pocket, I fished out the photograph. "This is why I'm here," I said, handing it to him.

His face remained passive as he studied the photograph. Then he turned it over and read: "Harmony, Michigan 1894: Mary, John, and Anna."

His genial smile evaporated. He held the photograph toward me. "Is this you as a child? The wide eyes, upturned nose, and generous mouth are the same. Even the hair."

I nodded. He'd recognized the little girl as me.

"So who are you? Mary or Anna? And why the name change?"

"I wish I knew. That's my mother. But," I hesitated, uncertain what to say about the man in the photograph. "I'm not sure who the man is. Maybe her second husband. My mother told me my father died before I was born."

Under his unrelenting gaze, I shifted in my chair. Men seldom looked at me with such interest. "I believe we're standing in front of one of these cottages."

He raised a skeptical eyebrow. "So, you and your mother lived here before Henry Thiery laid siege to the island and started hacking down trees like a man possessed." He paused. "Why are you showing me this?"

"After my mother died, I found the photograph and this rose pendant." [illegible]lled out the pendant from under my dress. "The pendant may have nothing to do with my mother's time on the island. But, for some reason, she never wore it."

He glanced at the pendant but said nothing.

"I need to find out why she was here. And who this man is. Bernice from The Carp told me you're the island's historian. I was hoping you could help me."

"Did she now?" That seemed to amuse him.

Still holding the photograph, he got up and walked to the window, as if he needed to get a better look at it.

I turned in my chair. Proctor's back was to me, his wide shoulders hunched. But he wasn't looking at the photograph. He was staring out the window.

"What I know about Harmony, you could fit in a one-inch newspaper column. Indians were here first. Then in 1832 a Catholic priest brought Christianity to the savages, as some people like to call them." His voice dripped with sarcasm. "Around 1887 Caleb Engel and a group of his friends, followers, who knows what they were, came here, built the manor, the cottages, the buildings in town, and the sawmill. Quite an industrious lot. Then, one day, they left. No one knows why. No one knows what they were doing here. Religious sect? Utopian community? Locals claim they disappeared in the middle of the night. But locals claim a lot of things, like how wolves still roam the island. Makes for a good story though, doesn't it?"

I'd never heard of Caleb Engel. But my mother and this man must have been part of his group. The dates matched.

"Do you know when Engel and his group left the island?" I wished he'd turn around so I could see his face.

"Sometime in 1894. Henry Thiery laid claim to the island in 1896. Though he didn't live here until 1898 when he started his timber business."

1894. The year the photograph had been taken.

A gust of wind rattled the windows, rushed down the chimney, igniting the embers. A few fell on the plank floor.

Proctor left the window and sat down, placing the photograph on the stone hearth, too close to the fire. "You're wasting your time if you think you're going to find out anything about Engel's group. Or this man."

My stomach clinched, the acrid coffee rising up into my throat. "This photograph is the only thing I have to go on. As a journalist, didn't you follow your instincts? My instincts tell me the answers to my mother's past and this man's identity are still here. Someone must know something. Just tell me who to talk to." Desperate for some validation, I was on the verge of tears.

He picked up the photograph from the stone hearth and looked at the inscriptions again. "You were what, three or four when this was taken? You don't remember anything about being here?"

A headache was forming behind my eyes, an insistent throbbing like something wanting to escape my brain.

"No, nothing." I wasn't going to confide in him my disturbing visions last night and today inside the maze.

He placed the photograph on the crate, then took a gulp of coffee. "My guess is the community fell apart and they went their separate ways. No mystery."

"What about this man and the inscription on the back?"

"I have no idea who he is. Before my time. As to the inscription, he wouldn't be the first man to leave his wife and his stepchild for some cockamamie community."

Proctor saw the crushed look on my face. "Look, your mother probably had a good reason for hiding this from you. Maybe you should just let it go."

"I can't."

I snatched the photograph from the crate, shoved it inside the leather holder, and made for the door. I wasn't going to cry in front of him.

"Thank you for the coffee," I said in a tight voice.

"You should search the manor's library," he suggested.

I turned from the door, struggling to keep my emotions in check. "The library? Why?"

"I once asked William if the books were his uncle's. He found that particularly humorous. He said his uncle would sooner burn them than read them. The books were Engel's. If you do search the library, don't let William catch you. He doesn't like anyone touching what's his. I found that out the hard way."

I wondered what he meant by that.

"I'll keep that in mind."

"One more thing. Don't show anyone else that photograph," he warned.

"Why's that?" I challenged.

"You don't want William and Catherine thinking that's the reason you came here."

Feeling exposed, I slammed the door and stepped out into the cold, swiping at the tears I could no longer hold back. If Proctor was right, I'd never know why my mother came to the island or who the man in the photograph was. That secret part of her would be lost to me forever. But at least he'd given me a path to pursue—the library.

The light was dying. A few snowflakes fluttered down. I strode across the snowy circle, past the abandoned cottages to the path leading to the manor. If Proctor was watching me, I wanted him to think that's where I was going.

For all his congeniality, I didn't know if I could trust him. He'd blanched when he saw the photograph's inscriptions, then moved to the window, calculating what he was going to tell me.

A utopian community? A religious sect? My mother abhorred organized religion, forbidding me to attend any church. But maybe her experience on the island explained her aversion? And maybe the man in the photograph felt otherwise. That's why she'd written, *they took John from us*.

I glanced back at Proctor's cottage. The curtain twitched. He was watching me. I kept walking. Once I passed the last cottage, I circled behind it, determined to discover what Proctor had been doing in the deep woods. There was no trail. But his footprints wove through the trees. I followed them.

Dusk was turning the trees into menacing shapes. Even the birds were quiet. A person could get lost in here at night. I was about to turn back when I saw something through the trees. I moved toward it, not sure what it was.

When I reached it, I was astonished.

My first thought was—an angel in the forest.

She was young, beautiful, winged, and made of stone. With eyes downcast, she towered over me, a heavenly expression on her face.

My second thought was—an angel guarding the dead.

Behind her, in rows, some covered with snow, some not, were flat, stone grave markers. I bent down to read one. Abigail, daughter of Jeremiah and Esther Strong, born 1888 died 1888.

Like a woman possessed, I moved from stone to stone, brushing away the snow and reading each inscription. All had died while Caleb Engel and his followers lived on the island. There were eleven graves. None bore the name John. I sat back on my heels as the snow swirled around me.

Why hadn't Proctor mentioned the cemetery to me?

CHAPTER ELEVEN

"*The Return of the Hunters*," I whispered. That's what the three men resembled as they struggled through the deepening snow behind Ravenwood Manor, lugging what looked like a body wrapped in a blanket.

My mind refused what I saw.

Instead, I thought of that Brueghel painting Francis had showed me when I thought love would save me. It hadn't. It had nearly destroyed me.

His slender surgeon's fingers had traced the painting as though he'd painted it.

"The artist is Pieter Brueghel the Elder," he'd explained in his condescending way that I refused to recognize until it was too late. "He's depicting . . ."

I'd put my finger to his lips to stop him talking, a little tipsy from the wine. "He's depicting men returning from the hunt." I'd laughed as though it were all a joke.

Then I wasn't laughing as he'd held me down, ignoring my pleas, until I finally whimpered into silence.

I shook myself free of the memory. I wasn't watching men returning from a hunt, unless their prey was human.

Against the white snow the men's black silhouettes were eerie and recognizable. The unreasonably tall William Thiery, leading the way; the limping Matthew, grasping one end of the wrapped corpse; the other end held by a man I didn't recognize.

As they made their way through the snowdrifts, the cur circled them, jumping and sniffing at the bundle.

I watched in horror as the cur yanked the blanket's edge free, exposing a woman's torso.

Thiery kicked the dog, sending it howling away into the storm. It darted past me.

"William," I shouted, suddenly seized with foreboding–the men's furtiveness, the blanketed body. Something horrible had happened. Had the flu reached the island? And this woman was its first victim?

"William," I shouted again, hurrying toward them, fighting the buffeting wind, the snow's coldness in my mouth.

Either they didn't hear me over the wind's howl, or they chose not to.

By the time I reached them, they were already inside the icehouse, a round brick building not far from Ravenwood Manor and adjacent to the inland lake, as impressively fashioned as the manor. From inside, the lantern's light stained the snow a sick yellow.

I stepped inside. Immediately I felt a drop in temperature. Packed in straw and sawdust, ice was stacked around the large room like an inverse igloo. The lantern rested on a stack of ice and backlit the space with eerie shadows.

Someone had rewrapped the corpse, which had been placed on a table in the center of the spacious room.

As I moved closer to view the body, William looked up, his face hollowed and strained in the uncertain light. "This doesn't concern you, Nellie."

"Who is this? Did she die of influenza?" I asked.

Matthew glared at me, chewing on the corner of his mouth. He jerked his head toward the door, indicating I should leave.

The other man studied his boots, his watch cap in his hand. It was Abe, the logger who'd warned me about Ravenwood Manor. He shifted from foot to foot. Whether from the cold or nervousness, I didn't know.

"Go back to the manor," William ordered.

I knew I should do as William asked. But I couldn't. I had to know what the woman died of. If it was the flu, certain precautions needed to be taken.

"Did the woman die of influenza?" I persisted.

When no one answered, I jerked the blanket from the corpse's face with a swiftness that surprised them.

The men recoiled at the sight.

Her frozen face had a gray pallor, her eyes a milky hue. Only the dirt etched into her skin's crevices detracted from her beauty. She had fine features, dark lashes, and long dark hair that had frozen into ringlets. One of her gold hoop earrings was missing.

"Damn you, woman. She didn't die of no flu," Matthew swore. "There was no call for that." But he didn't move to cover her face.

"Who is she?" I asked again, coming around the table to better view the body.

"Irene Hayes." William paused, struggling with what he wanted to tell me. "The nurse before you."

I looked at Matthew. "But you told me she left the island. Disappeared in the middle of the night."

William shot Matthew an angry scowl, and said, "Her things were cleared out. We thought she'd gone back to Chicago." He'd regained his composure, his words carefully measured.

The woman before me, who'd slept in the turret room, was now a frozen corpse on a warped table in an icehouse. What had happened to this poor girl?

The bitter coffee and the honey biscuits rose in my throat. I swallowed hard. It was not like me to be squeamish. I'd viewed countless dead bodies in worse shape than her. But I'd never viewed a corpse whose place I'd taken.

Hoping to discover what killed her, I lifted the blanket away from the rest of her body, which like her face was scattered with dirt. No one stopped me.

I could see no signs of trauma on the front of her body, no blood on her green silk dress with its lace shawl collar frozen forever in place. She'd been a woman who'd taken pride in her appearance, probably aware of the power of her beauty.

Gently, I rolled her over. Her dark hair was matted with blood and dirt, as was her neck and the top of her dress. I ran my fingers over the back of her head and felt an indentation. Part of her skull was caved in.

"Did you see this?" I asked.

"She probably fell and hit her head," William answered impatiently.

"Can't you leave the girl in peace?" Matthew accused.

Shivering, I rolled her onto her back. The intact condition of her body was perplexing. If she'd died from a skull fracture, why weren't there signs of predator damage?

Abe had yet to say a word. His forehead shined with sweat, though it was frigidly cold in the icehouse.

"Where was she found?" I directed my question to William.

"In the new section, where we're supposed to work tomorrow," Abe answered, finally meeting my eyes. His were so dark, I couldn't see the irises. "It was me that found her. It was kinda peculiar."

"What was pecu–"

William interrupted me. "There's nothing we can do for her now. I'll send word to Sheriff Wilkins. Let him know there's been an accident. Until then, we'll leave her in here." He grabbed the lantern and moved toward the door. Matthew and Abe followed.

"Wait. Where are her things? You said she took them when she left," I questioned.

"We'll look for them tomorrow," William said, exasperated.

When I didn't move to leave, he lifted the lantern toward me. "Nellie, let's go."

With care, I arranged the blanket around the dead woman. She was so stiff and cold.

Once outside, the men quickly dispersed. William and Matthew strode toward the manor's rear entrance. I followed behind them. Abe hurried past us, probably headed to the logging camp. Wherever that was. It would be a tough trek through the snow.

Cold as I was, I was in no hurry to return to Ravenwood. Whether Irene fell and hit her head or not, I wasn't sure. I'm no coroner. But the frozen condition of her body, where it was found, and the dirt troubled me. The only explanation that made sense was that her body had been buried, which meant her death hadn't been an accident as William insisted.

I wondered what Abe thought was peculiar.

CHAPTER TWELVE

"William, was it you who found her?" Catherine asked, as she poured herself a glass of claret from the etched-glass decanter. Her eyes were fixed on her husband, as though daring him to stop her. It was her second glass. Her cheeks burned with an intensity akin to fever.

"One of the men," William answered, stabbing at a boiled potato, then popping it whole in his mouth. Dark circles ringed his eyes. His tie was askew. Tied in anger or carelessness?

Upon hearing of Irene's death, Catherine had insisted we all dine together in the formal dining room, another masculine-charged room of hard surfaces, stiff-backed chairs, animal heads, and wall-paper strewn with English hunting scenes. Only the silver chandelier blazing with candles and the kerosene sconces offered any softness.

Catherine gave no reason for her request. I feared the news of Irene's death had incited another of her mood shifts. I worried for her and Hannah.

Sitting at one end of the massive table, Catherine appeared undone. Her pink, lacy silk robe had slipped open, revealing a satin nightgown as white as her skin. Her auburn hair wasn't dressed and fell wildly over her shoulders.

I, on the other hand, was wearing my one good dress, made of black wool with a white lacy bib that always made me feel like a schoolmarm.

My only jewelry the gold pendant and seed pearl earrings, a gift from my mother for my twenty-first birthday.

"I wonder what she was doing in those woods?" Catherine twirled the glass, the wine tipping the edge.

"And to think she was here all the time." Mrs. Bucheim shook her head. "Poor girl."

I didn't know if it was customary to eat with the help, but no one wanted to question Catherine's wishes. In the great Chicago houses, the help resided downstairs.

Matthew seemed unreasonably uncomfortable. His eyes riveted to his plate, he was tugging at his shirt collar as if it were strangling him, unsure of what utensil to use.

"Did Irene have family?" I asked Mrs. Bucheim, moving the gamey meat around in my mouth, its sweet taste turning my stomach.

"If she did, she never mentioned any." Her chin was slick with grease.

"Maybe that's why no one's come looking for her," I suggested. I couldn't understand how no one knew she hadn't left the island.

Matthew looked up from his plate. He'd been gobbling down his food like a lodger in a Chicago boardinghouse. "No one came looking, because they thought she was still here."

"Did she receive or send any letters?" The image of her frozen body in the icehouse haunted me.

"Not that I remember." Catherine swallowed a generous gulp of her claret. "William, do you remember Irene receiving letters from family? You were always so attentive to her." Was she taunting him?

William hit the table with his fist so hard the plates jumped. "I don't want any of you talking about this. Do you understand me? Especially you." He thrust his finger at me. "Ezra Wilkins will see to this business. That's his job."

Rather than answer him, I dropped my gaze and concentrated on the meat congealing on my plate.

"I'm going upstairs," Catherine said. "Mrs. Bucheim, will you send up my food, please?"

A milk stain the size of a dime had blossomed on her silk robe, the responsibility of motherhood writ large on her body.

"Mrs. Bucheim, you'll do no such thing," William stated firmly. "Catherine wanted this dinner and she's staying here until we're done." This was the side of William that Proctor had warned me about. *He always gets his way.*

Unsure what to do, Mrs. Bucheim looked from Catherine to William, her loyalties torn.

Finally, it was Catherine who relented. "It's fine, Mrs. Bucheim. No need to fuss over me. William's right, I should finish what I started."

She picked up her knife and fork and started cutting her meat over and over into smaller and smaller pieces, until blood puddled the plate. But she didn't eat. Instead, she reached for her glass and drank the rest of her claret, then poured herself another.

With a shaky hand, she raised her glass. "To Irene Hayes. God rest her troubled soul."

No one raised their glasses to meet her toast. The milk stain was now the size of a quarter.

Pity coursed through me, for Irene, for Catherine. "To Miss Hayes," I said, lifting my glass. "May she rest in peace."

How many such prayers had I said over the bodies of the dead since the flu outbreak? How many times had I questioned the sense of it? Had the bereaved even heard me, already wondering if they were next? The young stricken down, leaving the old behind to grieve.

"Will you help me upstairs?" she asked me, then rose from the table and left the dining room.

When I stood, I saw William's harsh expression, the retracted lips, and his flinty green eyes. Surely, he wasn't angry with me for helping Catherine. Wasn't that why I'd been hired? To take care of his wife? The woman was shattering. Did he not see that?

"She's exhausted," I explained.

"When you're done with her, see me in the drawing room." William's fisted hands rested on the white linen tablecloth.

CHAPTER THIRTEEN

When I entered the Thierys' bedroom, Catherine was pacing, walking around the furniture as though they were an obstacle course. Sensing her mother's agitation, Hannah had begun to stir.

"Are you all right?" I said, lifting Hannah from the cradle. As I nuzzled her, taking in her sweet baby smell like a balm, the horrid day fell away.

"I need to feed her." Catherine stopped pacing, threw off her robe, climbed into bed, and untied her nightgown, exposing her breasts.

I hesitated. Hannah felt so warm and solid in my arms. And Catherine blazed with resentment and alcohol. Intertwined with her milk would be strong emotions and wine, maybe the lingering laudanum, the things of colic and nightmares.

"What are you waiting for, Nellie? Give her to me." She gestured with her small hands.

"Catherine," I began. What could I say? You're too upset to nurse your baby. You've had too much to drink. The laudanum may still be coursing through you. In her frazzled state, I doubted she'd listen to me. I was just a lowly nurse and she was mistress of the manor. I placed Hannah in her arms.

As if day had flipped to night in one stroke, a serene look overcame Catherine, her anger gone. Transfixed, she stroked the baby's head. "Where did this red hair come from, little one?" she asked.

Under the lamp's glow, Hannah's fluff of red hair shone brightly.

"Do you think it'll change?" Her words were slow and heavy with sleep.

"It's hard to say," I said nonchalantly. Mine hadn't changed–still the color of copper pennies.

Catherine stared at me, her hazel eyes more golden than brown–cat like. "Were you teased as a child because of your hair?"

Carrot head, witch, demon girl. I've never forgotten the taunts. Though their jibes had stung, I'd pretended not to care.

I'd asked my mother if my father's hair had been red.

"You could say that," my mother had answered, her eyes drifting away. Another of her vague answers I hadn't questioned. Though sensing my disappointment at not telling me more about my father's appearance, she'd added, "But like you, he loved to draw."

As a child, I learned that questions about family distressed my mother. So eventually I'd stopped asking them.

All I knew of my grandparents was they were from a small southern town whose name she couldn't remember.

"Nellie, are you listening?" Catherine's voice broke into my thoughts. "I asked you if were teased as a child."

"I think Hannah's hair is beautiful," I answered with conviction.

"So you were teased. Well, that's not going to happen to Hannah. I'll see to it."

Not wanting to answer any more questions about me, I changed the subject.

"Were you and Irene close? You seem very upset by her death."

"She was my dearest friend. The only person I could talk to on this accursed island." She started to cry. "I was bereft when she left."

Hannah stirred, opened her eyes, and gazed up at her mother. A quizzical expression on her face.

"I'm sorry," I said. She looked so lost and forlorn in the big bed with Hannah at her breast. Though a wife and a mother, she was spoiled and naïve, still a child at twenty, married to a man ten years older than her who had no patience for her rippling emotions.

She reached out for my hand. "Maybe we can be friends."

This morning, she'd demanded William fire me. Now, she wanted my friendship.

"That would be lovely," I answered, taking her hand and squeezing it, knowing how difficult that would be. A city-hardened nurse on a mission to discover her mother's past and a young, spoiled heiress. An impossible gulf but one I was willing to try to cross.

When Hannah finished nursing, I took her and placed her in her cradle, tucking the blanket around her, lingering on her sweet face.

When I turned around, Catherine was already asleep.

I dimmed the lamp and left the room, slowly descending the stairs. I'd won Catherine over, but I feared I'd lost William.

⁂

"You can't give in to her petty whims." William lounged in a brown leather chesterfield chair, strategically placed by the fireplace, so that he could stretch out his long legs and feel its warmth.

I sat forward in the matching chair that seemed to engulf me, ready to defend myself. Before I could begin, he cut me off.

"And don't give me that claptrap about childbirth. Catherine's been like this since she lost the first baby. Don't coddle her. That's the mistake Irene made."

"What are you saying?" If what he said was true, then her instability had another cause than giving birth—a festering grief over losing her first child.

"Catherine became too attached to Irene. They were close in age and Irene was too agreeable when it came to Catherine. Hysteria. That's what Irene called it."

So, William and Irene had discussed Catherine's mood shifts. Probably in this same room, late at night, after the pregnant Catherine had gone to bed.

"I don't think Catherine's a hysteric. I think she's grieving the loss of her first baby. She probably thought having Irene near her would prevent that happening again."

He plucked a cigar from the humidor on the marble-topped table, cut its end, lit it and puffed. The pungent scent mingled with the burning wood in a heady blend.

"She wants you fired." He flicked his cigar in the ashtray, inhaled, then blew a perfect ring of smoke.

"Did I do something to displease her?" I asked, directing my attention to the collapsing logs and the sparking embers, how ardently the fire burned.

"You tell me." He released another ring of smoke. This one hovered around his dark head.

I coughed as I inhaled the smoke. I felt as though I were smoking his cigar. What would it be like, I mused, to sit in a grand drawing room, in a mansion, with servants and wealth, casually smoking and interrogating a lowly nurse?

Then I smiled to myself and leaned back in the stiff leather chair, stretched out my legs, not caring if he saw my worn shoes. Sometimes the rich see only what's in front of them and, even then, they're blind to reality, cocooned in their wealth. He had no idea who I was. Or why I was here.

"If she's displeased because I took the laudanum, it was for her own good. Hannah could have died."

He bolted up in his chair. "Died?"

He needed to understand the seriousness of the laudanum, an insidious drug that doctors for decades had given patients for everything from headaches to menstrual cramps to diseases of a nervous character. I'd seen too many men and women in the throes of addiction die.

"Hannah wasn't breathing at birth. I breathed life back into her, rubbed her heart, and got it beating. The laudanum could have killed her." I was weaving my way back into his good graces with truths and half-truths. "I don't know where Theo–Doctor Proctor–got it. But Catherine shouldn't take it. It'll pass through her milk to the baby."

"Where's the laudanum now?" He sounded worried.

I'd gotten his attention, finally broke through to what was important. He was seeing me, weighing my importance in his life.

"Secure in my medical bag." I took in a deep breath and forged ahead. "Are you firing me? I'd like to know, so I can make arrangements to leave the island."

I was bluffing. Even if he fired me, I had no intention of leaving the island. Though where I'd live, I had no idea. Maybe Bernie would put me up at the inn in exchange for working at the tavern?

"I fire people who don't do their jobs. Far as I can see, you're doing yours." He paused. "There's something I'd like you to do." He rested his elbows on his knees and stared at me. "Sheriff Wilkins will be here in a few days to collect the body. Before that, I want you to take another look at it."

"For what reason?" My mind raced. Why had he changed his mind about my being involved? He'd been so adamant.

"Will you do it or not?"

"Yes, of course. Then you're thinking her death wasn't accidental?"

"I don't think anything. Examine the body and get back to me."

For all his protests to the contrary, something wasn't sitting right with him about Irene's death. Nor was it sitting right with me.

"What troubles me is why she left in the middle of the night. And why no one noticed." Other things were troubling me, but I held back, until I reexamined the body. If only I could talk to Abe.

He sat back in his chair, his legs spread wide. "It wasn't the middle of the night. We discovered she was missing around dinnertime. That's when Mrs. Bucheim found the note in her room and her things missing. She'd gone into town that afternoon and never returned."

"What did the note say?" If she was leaving, how did she end up in the forest?

"I don't recall. You'll have to ask Mrs. Bucheim."

I felt his lie in the stillness of his body.

Another question pushed at me. "Why did no one notice Irene leaving with her belongings?" Nothing escaped Mrs. Bucheim's alert bird eyes.

William smashed his cigar in the ashtray, sending up a swirl of smoke. "That's what I want to know."

Chapter Fourteen

Though the fire had been lit, the turret room was no more welcoming than it had been last night. But at least it was warm. I undressed in front of the iron fireplace, carefully placing my good dress, chemise, and stockings in the top dresser drawer. There was a run in my stocking I'd have to mend. It was a relief to untie my corset and breathe deeply.

Once in my flannel nightgown, I stood before the cloudy dresser mirror and unpinned my hair, brushing my tight curls, while my mind whirled with questions. Why had Irene left a good-paying position? What was she doing in the forest? Meeting someone? If she had been running away, where were her things? And why was her body still intact? No evidence of wild animals disturbing her, although she'd been missing over a month.

I plaited my thick hair, crawled under the quilt, and turned off the lamp. The room resolved into shadows. With trepidation and anticipation, I turned toward the dresser. No apparition wavered there. I should have been relieved, but I wasn't. I longed to see my mother. I'd never felt so alone and lonely.

A floorboard creaked. My eyes flew open, my chest pounding. Someone was on the landing outside my door. The key!

Thoughts of being locked inside invaded my mind. Quietly, I slipped out of bed, slid open the bottom drawer, and reached under my clothes for the key. It wasn't in the corner where I'd put it.

Frantically, I ran my hand over the drawer's bottom. When I felt the key's cold roughness, I sighed with relief.

Mrs. Bucheim had been in my room this afternoon, probably going through my things. Assessing who I was, so she could report back to Catherine or William. I'd have to find a better hiding place for the key.

As I stood, I heard the creaking again. Key in hand, I went to the door, unhooked the chair, and opened it tentatively. No one was there.

I shut the door and stood with my back to it, listening. Faint but unmistakable, I heard footsteps descending the stairs.

Who had been outside my door? And why?

The only person who'd been openly hostile to me was Matthew.

My wild imagination pumped dark thoughts into my brain. Had Irene been harassed by him? Had she lain awake at night, listening to the house move around her, as if the turret room rotated above it?

On the cold tortuous ride from the town to the manor, Matthew had warned me about being too nosy like Irene. He'd described her as nervous and flighty, which contradicted William's description of her as too agreeable, and Catherine's description of her as an ardent friend.

What had Matthew said about her reason for leaving? "She didn't take to the island." Was he the reason she didn't take to the island? Had he done more than harass her? I shuddered thinking about it.

But William said she hadn't left in the middle of the night; she had left a note and had taken her belongings. Why had Matthew lied?

I pushed away from the door and turned on the lamp. I'd been holding the key so tightly it had left an impression in the palm of my hand.

From the top dresser drawer, I took out the black mourning ribbon. Its frayed edges a reminder of the grief I'd carried for months after my mother's death. Nimbly, I threaded the ribbon through the key's bow, knotted it, and slipped it over my head. No one would be locking me in this room.

All thoughts of sleep gone, I searched the room and my things for anything out of place or missing. When I was done, I sat down on the bed, satisfied that nothing was amiss.

Then, my eyes lit on my medical bag. I got up, lifted the bag from the floor, and peered inside. The laudanum was gone. I remembered seeing it this morning when I'd examined Catherine.

I sat back on the bed, clutching the bag. Is this what Mrs. Bucheim was doing in my room? Looking for the drug? For what purpose? Did she think I wouldn't notice it missing?

The wind shook the windows furiously, moving the damask curtains with each gust. I rose from the bed and pulled back the curtains. The windows were etched with ice, air funneling through the gaps. Winter was here in earnest.

A dark figure moved across the snow-crusted grounds, heading in the direction of the icehouse. It was Matthew, the cur close on his heels.

I stood and watched for a long time, but he never returned to his caretaker's cottage. What was he doing wandering around outside on such an unforgiving night?

Cold and dread had settled in my bones. I closed the curtains and stoked the fire. The circular room seemed to swirl around me. I could feel Irene here in this place, her fear and her longing.

I would not give into it. I had a purpose that went beyond caring for Catherine and the baby or the mysterious Irene Hayes: to discover why my mother had come to the island and who the man in the photograph was.

Quietly, I shoved the chair back under the doorknob. It was the best I could do.

Digging my journal from my purse, I sketched Irene's frozen body–the stiff black hair, the green dress, milky eyes, and the one earring, trying my best to capture her beauty. Then I turned my pencil to darker things–the jagged indentation in the back of her head and the blood that had frozen on her neck and dress.

Death had surprised her. Whether she fell backward or someone smashed in her skull, her death had been quick. A small blessing.

With a swiftness that took my breath away, my dying patients rose before me with their horrible, blue-black faces, choking and clawing the air, begging me to save them.

I shut my journal and closed my eyes against them.

After extinguishing the lamp, I crawled under the chilly sheet, watching the room settle into darkness.

I turned to my left side, with anticipation.

"Mother," I called into the night, like I used to, as a child afraid of the dark.

Then, she was there, as she always was when I called. Hovering near the dresser. More shadow than self.

"She needed me," I whispered. "You understand."

Her shadow slipped behind the dresser, taking my words with her.

When I dreamed, I dreamed of the dead woman–her frozen corpse and her gray pallor. She, too, was whispering, "Nellie, Nellie."

When I reached out to comfort her, she shattered into pieces at my feet. Bereft, I knelt down and one-by-one began putting her back together.

CHAPTER FIFTEEN

The fried eggs were cold, the coffee bitter, and the salt pork overcooked. Another night of troubled sleep left me restless and irritable, with a thudding headache, the nightmare too real, the shadowy presence not easily explained.

Mrs. Bucheim stood at the stove, catatonically stirring the colorless oatmeal. Her mind was elsewhere. She'd barely acknowledged my greeting when I sat down to breakfast. Stray gray hairs escaped her usually tightly fashioned knot.

"Don't you think it strange," I said, trying to pull her attention from the stove, craving the sound of a human voice, "that Irene never wrote or received any letters?"

She slopped the oatmeal into a brown bowl, sprinkled it with sugar, and placed it on the oak table in front of me. Then, she returned to the stove, as though she were guarding it.

"She was a strange girl," she murmured, as if Irene were in the adjacent room.

Already a crust was forming on the top. I pushed the crust aside and took a spoonful. It tasted like paste. But I forced myself to swallow another mouthful, not wanting to insult Mrs. Bucheim. At least it was warm.

"Strange in what way?" I gulped the coffee to dislodge the gruel stuck in my throat.

She turned from the stove, holding the ladle. A large drop of oatmeal plopped on the wood floor. She didn't seem to notice.

"When she wasn't seeing to the missus, she was wandering the woods. I told her not to, because of the logging and the men." She lowered her voice, out of a sense of propriety. "But she didn't listen. And look what happened."

"Do you think one of the loggers killed her?"

Her drawn face flushed. "It was an accident, like Mr. William said."

Her blind loyalty to William would be admirable if it wasn't so misguided.

"And before you ask about her belongings," Mrs. Bucheim continued. "They were cleared out of her room. Not a hair ribbon or a pin to be found. And she left a note. We all thought she'd left the island." She plunged the ladle back into the pot of oatmeal.

"The same room I'm in?" She'd evaded my question before. I had to be sure.

"What other room would I be talking about?" If only for a moment, she'd emerged from her gloom and was her old prickly self.

"William told me about the note. Do you remember what it said?"

She hesitated, seemingly considering whether to tell me. "Something about being sorry and having no choice."

"What do you think she meant by having no choice?" I was like a runaway train.

"How would I know," she answered, stirring the pot with vigor.

Not able to swallow any more of the dreadful gruel, I put my spoon on the oak table and considered how to broach the topic of the stolen laudanum. There was no good way.

"When I left Ravenwood yesterday, I saw you at my bedroom window."

If her spine got any straighter, it would snap in two. "I wasn't in your room yesterday," she answered indignantly.

"I can't be sure who it was. But someone was in my room. And since then . . ." I hesitated. "The laudanum in my medical bag is missing."

She banged the spoon on the side of the pot so hard, I jumped. When she turned to face me, her black brows were knitted in anger.

"You probably misplaced it. If I were you, I'd watch who I was accusing of stealing."

Though her eyes never left mine, I wasn't sure I believed her. How far would she go to please Catherine?

"Mrs. Bucheim, I wasn't accusing you of stealing." Not directly. "But I didn't misplace it. I'm very careful with my medicines." I took a breath to steady myself. "We wouldn't want Catherine taking an addictive medicine, would we? It's not good for her or the baby." Someone took the laudanum, and my money was on the evasive and loyal Mrs. Bucheim.

Matthew took that moment to enter the kitchen from the mudroom, the cur by his side, bringing in a gust of cold air with him.

"Don't bring that dog in here. It's filthy," warned Mrs. Bucheim, her bad humor falling on him.

For the first time, I saw Matthew cowed, his insolence gone, a sheepish expression on his face.

"Come here, boy." From his woolen trousers pocket, he took out a red bandana and wiped the dog's paws. When he was done, he patted its enormous head, as though its feelings had been hurt.

My stomach turned as he sat next to me, reaching over me to grab a slice of bread. To my dismay, the cur settled under the table. Its mammoth head rested on my foot.

"What have you misplaced?" he asked. This close I smelled his coarse soap and the musky scent of his clothes.

"When I was visiting Mr. Proctor yesterday, someone went into my room and took the bottle of laudanum from my medical bag."

"What you bothering the doc for? Aren't you supposed to be looking after the missus?" Matthew stopped chewing and frowned.

I ignored his barb. "If either of you should find the laudanum, please bring it to me. It's a potent medicine that could be dangerous in the wrong hands." I had no doubt he'd been outside my door last night.

"This isn't Chicago, where there's a thief on every corner and a hand in every pocket." He grinned. "No one took the laudanum. Like Mrs. Bucheim said, you probably misplaced it."

Something passed between them that I couldn't decipher. There was no penetrating their wall of solidarity.

Mrs. Bucheim turned away, busying herself with preparing Catherine's breakfast tray.

Matthew swiped at his mouth with his shirtsleeve, grabbed the remaining bread, and a chunk of cheese.

"I gotta go. We're working on that new section we opened yesterday."

"Was that where Irene's body was found?" I asked.

"What of it?"

"Nothing. It's just, well, William wanted me to examine Irene's body." I hesitated. "If I could see where her body was found, it might help explain what happened to her."

He found this amusing, grinning from ear to ear like a Cheshire cat. "A logging camp is nowhere for a woman. Am I right, Mrs. B.?"

She seemed miles away as she spooned oatmeal into a blue bowl for Catherine's breakfast.

"Mrs. B.," he said, louder. "What do you think of nurse Nellie going to see where Irene's body was found? Tell her what kind of women hang out at logging camps."

She looked at us, a stricken expression on her face. "Isn't it bad enough the poor girl is dead. Do we have to talk about it?"

Something was eating at her.

Matthew pushed back his chair and went to Mrs. Bucheim. "I'm sorry if we upset you. I know you were fond of Irene." He patted her shoulder caringly.

Though she went back to preparing the tray, I could see her body relax. "Mr. William will be fit to be tied if you're late again," she blustered at him.

"Yes, ma'am," he said, doing a mock salute. "C'mon, Samson."

As if poked with a stick, the dog darted from under the table and faced me, teeth bared and growling.

Mrs. Bucheim swatted it with her dishcloth. "Get out of my kitchen, you mangy mutt."

With its tail between its legs, the cur ran into the mudroom and clawed at the back door, whining. So, the beast could be tamed.

"There was no need for that, Mrs. B.," Matthew said.

He limped into the mudroom, took his coat from the peg, and left.

The cold air that rushed into the kitchen stirred me. I rose from the table with my dishes and placed them in the sink, holding back my offer to help.

"You've known Matthew a long time, haven't you?" I said, fingering the edge of the checkered dishcloth. The tenderness Matthew had shown Mrs. Bucheim spoke of a deep relationship.

She picked up the crammed breakfast tray and held it out to me—a bowl of oatmeal, bread, butter, several slices of salt pork, and freshly fried eggs. "Tell the missus that I'll bring her tea shortly."

Reluctantly, I took the tray. "I'm sorry if I offended you. I'm just worried about Catherine—"

She interrupted my apology. "Better get a move on. The missus doesn't like her eggs cold."

As I made my way up the winding staircase, balancing the tray, I thought about the relationship between Matthew and Mrs. Bucheim. His tenderness toward her had a familial feel. And there was a physical resemblance I hadn't noticed before. Both had sharp features and similar coloring. But he referred to her as Mrs. B., not mother or aunt.

But why would they hide a family relationship? And how could they keep that secret for so long? Or maybe I was the only one who didn't know.

When I reached the child's death portrait, a sliver of fear ran through me. Something was different. It was her face. In the shadowy light, her skin appeared slack, her one eye drooping, the other one pleading. It was as if she was decomposing.

Then a burst of light chased the gloom. Her face was as before, except for an unnatural sheen I hadn't noticed.

I couldn't shake the sensation that the child *hadn't* crossed over and was trapped between this life and the next.

CHAPTER SIXTEEN

After lunch, Catherine was bright as a penny and just as brittle.

To my every inquiry about her health, she chirped *fine*, like some addled bird. She looked anything but fine, still pale, her eyes ringed with lack of sleep, hair in disarray, yet buzzing with energy.

Something was off.

Though I suspected the laudanum, other than her euphoria, her pupils weren't dilated, and her pulse was only slightly elevated.

"Catherine, I have to ask you something that might upset you." I moved to the large expanse of windows, where she was rocking Hannah, and sat down on the ottoman.

She stopped rocking. "If it's about Irene, I don't know if I can bear talking about her."

That derailed me for a moment. "Well, actually, it is about Irene. But if you don't want to talk about her, I understand."

"No, it's all right. How else can we be friends, if we can't talk openly."

Her desire to be friends touched me. But her sudden shift in mood toward me made me leery. "Did Irene ever mention where she trained as a nurse?"

"I don't remember the name of the school. But it was in Chicago."

"Was it the Illinois Training School?" That was the school where I trained.

"That might be it. Why?"

"I could write the school and find out if Irene had any family." It troubled me that no one seemed concerned about informing Irene's next of kin of her death.

"I don't think she had family. We were very close. I'm sure she would have told me if she did." Her rocking became more insistent, no longer soothing. Hannah stared up at her mother in alarm.

"Did you ask her?" I carefully nudged.

Catherine's gaze went to the windows where three ravens were circling the trees in some bizarre dance. And beyond them lay the vast lake that stretched to the horizon.

"I don't remember. Really, Nellie, you're as curious as Irene, with all your questions. She'd go on and on. 'Is the business doing well? Do you like living on an island?' 'Do you miss Chicago?' It was tedious." She stopped rocking and stood.

"Here, take her." She thrust Hannah into my arms and started pacing the room, back and forth and around the furniture, like a caged lioness.

I nestled Hannah on my shoulder and rubbed her back. She was as restless as her mother. I needed to calm her.

"Catherine, why don't you get dressed. I think a change of scenery would be good for you."

She stopped pacing. "I thought you said it was too soon for me to go to town?"

"It is. But maybe you'd like to sit in the solarium. The sun will do you good. You could get a book from the library to read."

Before lunch, I'd explored the first-floor rooms and discovered that adjacent to the library was a solarium lush with ferns and other plants I couldn't name.

Hannah's head went heavy on my shoulder. Carefully, I got up from the ottoman and put her in her cradle. Instantly missing her warmth.

"If you think it's alright," Catherine said, coyly tilting her auburn head.

"We'll bring Hannah, as well," I suggested.

She rushed to me and hugged me with unexpected strength. I was enveloped in her expensive perfume, a cloud of exotic flowers. "You are a good friend, Nellie. I don't care what the others say."

Impishly, she put her hand to her lips. "Oops."

That gave me pause. "What others?"

She waved her delicate hand dismissively. "I don't know why I said that. Everyone thinks you're very competent."

⸎

After settling Catherine in the solarium with *Bleak House* by Charles Dickens, I returned to her bedroom. This was my opportunity to search for the laudanum. Matthew and William were at the logging camp and Mrs. Bucheim was banging around in the kitchen, whipping up another bleak meal I'd find hard to swallow. At this rate, my generous stalwart figure would be as gaunt as Mrs. Bucheim's.

I started with the two nightstands. A few lace handkerchiefs, a rosary, and half a roll of Pep-O-Mint Life Savers were all I found. But the bottom drawer was stained with a suspicious dark color. I rubbed my finger over it and sniffed. Though faint, I detected a bitter scent that could be laudanum. Or it could be something else.

Then I riffled through her two armoires, amazed by the abundance and fineness of her clothes–two fur coats, dresses for every occasion in silk, satin, wool, and velvet, some elaborately embroidered, some beaded, all expensive and tailor-made. Dresses meant for another lifestyle, another place. Catherine didn't belong on a desolate island, bereft of female companionship.

Though time was of the essence, I couldn't resist taking out the scarlet velvet dress. Standing in front of the full-length mirror, I held the dress against my body, imaging myself wearing it.

The color enhanced my pale skin and dark brown eyes but clashed with my flaming red hair. It pleased me. What must it feel like to own a fleet of tailor-made dresses?

Pricked with envy, I returned it to the armoire and continued my search. No laudanum.

Finally, I knelt by the bed, lifted the cream satin bed skirt, and peeked under it.

"What are you doing?"

Startled, I jolted up.

Bernie seemed to fill the doorway. Ensconced in a black dress with a starched white collar, she looked very different from the rough-and-tumble proprietor of The Carp. Her unruly brown hair was restrained in a generous chignon at the base of her neck.

Her transformation was so striking I don't think I would have recognized her if I'd passed her on the street.

With what dignity I could muster, I stood and smoothed my black serge skirt.

"I lost one of my instruments. I thought it might have rolled under the bed," I stammered, my face as red as Bernie's hands.

She seemed to accept my excuse. "Did you find it?" she said, marching into the room, toting a metal pail bursting with rags, a jar of beeswax, and the unmistakable dark bottle of Lysol.

The sight of the Lysol made me nauseous. A memory of scrubbing the contagion ward with the pungent disinfectant washed over me. No matter how hard I'd scrubbed, the young kept dying like leaves shed from a tree. Lysol smelled like death to me.

I shook my head, floundering to regain my composure.

"I didn't realize you worked here," I said, praying Bernie wouldn't go tattling to Mrs. Bucheim about my losing a medical instrument. Which would only support her belief that I'd misplaced the laudanum.

"Twice a week for Henry Thiery. For Mr. William, once a week. Only way I can keep kit and caboodle together. The Carp barely makes ends meet. How are you settling in?"

She was the first person to ask me that. I felt tears prick my eyes. "It takes some getting used to. But I'm managing."

I wanted to tell her everything–my mother's nightly visitations, Matthew's threatening presence, Catherine's instability, my certainty that Irene Hayes had been murdered, and why I was really here. But I didn't. Loneliness was clouding my judgment.

"I wouldn't worry about getting used to it. Now that the baby's here, I imagine you'll be going home before the island ices up."

"Ices up?" I asked, not sure of her meaning.

"Most winters, by February, the lake freezes up from here to the mainland. Isn't passable until spring. Did no one tell you that?" She opened the jar of beeswax, took a rag, and scooped out a generous portion.

I shook my head. My contract ended at the end of February. I'd be stranded here until spring. Would the Thierys keep me on that long? My position was precarious, dependent on Catherine's whims.

"How do you get supplies?" My throat felt like it was closing. Suddenly, I understood the clutch of panic in Catherine's plea to William. "I can't do it anymore. I won't."

"We know how to put up provisions for the winter. You won't starve. If that's what you're worried about. But we're cut off from the outside world. Except for the Swede who snowshoes across the lake with the mail once a week."

"Like you said, I'll probably be gone by then." Once I know why my mother came here and who the man in the photograph was, I'll leave. The prospect of being marooned on this island, imprisoned in Ravenwood Manor and the turret room, terrified me.

"I heard about Irene," Bernie said, as she polished the large ornate dresser. "Do you know what happened?"

I decided to stick to William's story. The Carp was the hub of rumors and idle gossip. "It seems she fell and hit her head."

"Well, I'm sure Sheriff Wilkins will sort it out."

"Did you know Irene very well?"

Bernie moved on to one of the armoires, with another scoop of beeswax. "Oh, sure. Nice girl. Always asked how I was. I know Mrs. Thiery was very fond of her, as was Mr. Thiery. Too clever for her own good, if you ask me though."

"In what way?" No one had mentioned Irene's cleverness.

She straightened up and stretched her back. "She had Mrs. Thiery wrapped around her little finger, catering to her every whim like she did, and the missus being susceptible on account of losing the baby. And Irene knew when to bat those big green eyes of hers at Mr. Thiery to get her way." There was no rancor in her words.

"Are you saying there was something going on between Irene and Mr. Thiery?"

She put her hands on her hips. "I never saw anything like that. Now, I'd better get back to work or Mrs. B. will be madder than a wet hen in winter."

CHAPTER SEVENTEEN

Hannah wasn't crying, she was wailing, full-throated cries of distress that sent me running to the solarium. Where was Catherine?

A cacophony of anguish greeted me as I burst into the room.

Catherine was huddled in a corner, her arms around her knees, sobbing and rocking.

But it was Hannah I was most concerned with. Her wailing was at a fevered pitch. I went to her. She was beet red with fury, kicking her legs, her fists clenched, her blanket bunched around her feet. After checking her diaper, which was dry, I picked her up, wrapped the blanket around her, and held her.

"There, there," I lulled. "It's all right. It's all right."

As I soothed Hannah, I watched Catherine rocking back and forth, seemingly catatonic. Her hair was in disarray, pins sticking out like quills.

After a few minutes, Hannah started to settle, her cries subsiding into hiccups. She let out a deep sigh. I put her back in her cradle, tucked her blanket around her, then crossed the room to where Catherine cowered.

I knelt on the cold stone floor beside her. "Catherine, what's wrong?"

She didn't look up, just kept rocking. I'd seen patients at the hospital with similar symptoms. Inevitably, they'd be sent to Dunning, the state mental hospital. A fate I wouldn't wish on anyone.

For all her mood shifts, I didn't believe Catherine was mad. Though I was beginning to worry if she was emotionally fit to care for Hannah.

"Catherine, look at me," I demanded, needing to get through to her.

Slowly she raised her tear-stained face.

"Why are you crying? Tell me what's wrong."

She blinked, as though she'd just realized I was there.

With a shaking finger, she pointed to one of the rattan chairs.

Thrown across the chair was a shawl I'd noticed earlier. It was made of finely woven silk, with a colorful peacock motif.

"I don't understand," I said.

"It's hers. It's Irene's. She would have never left it behind. It was her mother's. She would have never left it."

"Maybe in her hurry to leave, she forgot it," I reasoned.

"No, no, no." She shook her head vehemently. Her hairpins pinged the floor. "You didn't know her. She would never leave it. She's haunting me." Frantically, she looked around the solarium as if Irene were hiding somewhere in the room.

It was an irrational question that would play into her neurosis, but I had to ask it if I was to understand Catherine's terror. "Why would Irene haunt you?"

"Because I cast her out. And now she's dead. It's my fault." Her eyes dared me to disagree. "Get away from me, you harpy."

She shoved me so hard I fell sideways onto the stone floor. The room suddenly off-kilter–the peacock shawl; the rattan's obscene flowers, as big as babies' heads; and Catherine's catlike eyes fixed on me. We were in a jungle of Catherine's making.

"I'm not leaving you," I said, pushing myself up from the floor and standing.

"What's going on here? What have you done to the missus?" Mrs. Bucheim hurried into the room, a disapproving look on her gaunt face.

"Come here, you poor girl," she said, reaching for Catherine's arm and helping her to her feet. Like a scolded child, Catherine stood, her head down, her loose hair covering her face.

"Mrs. Bucheim, did you see it?" Catherine voice was wobbly and child-like. "Irene's shawl, on the chair. She wouldn't have left it."

"Never you mind about that. That's none of your concern. Now, let's get you upstairs. I don't know what the nurse was thinking, having you come in here." She glared at me.

"I told her I didn't want to. But she made me," Catherine said.

"You just need rest. I'll take you to your room." Mrs. Bucheim shot me a withering look. "Nurse Lester will bring you a pot of tea after she brings Hannah upstairs."

An angry flush crawled up my neck and into my face. "Mrs. Bucheim, you know I would never hurt Catherine or abandon her like Irene did." Why was I defending myself? I'd done nothing wrong.

"Don't you disparage Irene," she snapped. "You didn't know her. She did the best she could. And now, she's dead. Mark my words, Mr. William will hear of this."

Mrs. Bucheim shepherded the now tranquil Catherine from the solarium, leaving me to collect Hannah.

Though her rebuke was undeserved, she was right about one thing. I didn't know Irene. And as much as I wanted to know what happened to her, I knew I should let it go.

My mother's cautionary words came back to me. "Stay out of things that don't concern you. It only leads to trouble."

Until coming to this desolate island, I'd lived my life by that philosophy—ruffling no feathers, making no waves. I was the quiet girl who obeyed the rules, who acquiesced. Even when the man I trusted violated me, I said nothing.

Was that the life I still wanted? Did I have the courage to live a bolder life?

Even my mother had broken her own rule once. I was maybe twelve years old. We were on the North State Street streetcar being jostled with people as diverse as Chicago.

A blustering white man had demanded that an old colored woman give up her seat to him.

"You, darkie, get out of that seat," he'd said.

With a look of resignation, the old colored woman had struggled to her feet balancing her groceries and clutching her purse. Everyone had looked away, even the few colored people standing nearby.

Then my mother had stood. "Ma'am," she'd said. "Please take my seat."

When we exited the streetcar, the white man had hissed at us, "Nigger lover."

Later, when I asked my mother why she'd done that, she'd said, "It wasn't right what that man did. Doesn't matter that she was colored."

Back then I wondered what made my mother speak up that day. It wasn't the first time we'd seen colored people treated with disdain on the streets, on public transportation, and in stores.

Weeks before the streetcar incident, Mr. Cox, the corner market's shopkeeper, had refused to wait on a colored man, commenting to my mother afterward that too many coons were moving to Chicago.

She'd said nothing, merely nodded her head as if she agreed.

Newspapers talked about the increase in the colored population who'd moved to Chicago from the South as the reason for these hateful incidents.

But what made my mother risk her life that day to give a colored woman her seat? I'll never know.

Since finding the photograph and coming to the island, I'd questioned who my mother really was–the subdued woman who'd kept to herself? Or the brave woman who'd stood up for an injustice?

I wanted to see her as that brave woman.

I wanted to be a brave woman.

I decided I wasn't going to let Irene's death go. But first I had to talk to Mrs. Bucheim about Catherine.

§

After Catherine fell into a restful sleep, thanks to the sleeping tincture I'd slipped into her tea, I made my way downstairs to the kitchen, looking for Mrs. Bucheim. If I was to help Catherine, she and I needed to make peace or at least come to an understanding.

To my surprise Mrs. Bucheim wasn't there. The kitchen was squeaky clean, dishes put away, and the floor swept. A gamey stew simmered on the woodstove. Rabbit, deer, squirrel? For all her faults, Mrs. Bucheim was a paragon of efficiency, even with her arthritic hands.

She'd probably gone to her room, which was in the other turret on the southwest side of the manor, accessible by a different staircase. Catherine had mentioned that sometimes Mrs. Bucheim took an afternoon nap.

I knew Bernie hadn't left yet, because I spied her coat hanging on a peg in the mudroom. If I hurried, I'd have enough time to search the kitchen and larder. More than ever, I was certain Catherine's bizarre behavior stemmed from the laudanum. Either she was taking it knowingly or someone was giving it to her.

Not sure how much time I had, I tried to move quickly, but it was slow going. The cupboards were crammed with dishes, pots, pans, glasses, cups, herbs and spices, and all manner of kitchen utensils.

When I finished scouring the kitchen, I moved to the larder, which proved just as fruitless as the kitchen. I rattled the door that led from the larder to the cellar. Locked. No key hanging on a peg. If Mrs. Bucheim had taken the laudanum and was giving it to Catherine, she'd hidden the drug elsewhere.

Frustrated, I plopped down on one of the kitchen chairs, staring at the window over the sink, where winter sunlight filtered into the room. It was another chilly winter day of changeable weather. The island seemed to exist in an atmosphere singular to itself.

As I sat there, I thought about Catherine's hysterical reaction to Irene's shawl. Laudanum induced? Mental instability? Guilt?

"I cast her out," Catherine had said. "And now she's dead."

Mrs. Bucheim's version of Irene's note supported that Irene had no choice but to leave. But why dismiss Irene? Catherine lauded her as a friend. And why had no one seen the shawl, so blatantly displayed in the solarium, until now?

The sound of footsteps drew me back to the warm, fragrant kitchen.

"Wool gathering?" Bernie said, as she strode into the room, lugging the metal pail and cleaning products. My eyes flicked away from the Lysol and concentrated on the window's wavering sunlight.

"Are you done for the day?" I asked. It was going on four o'clock.

"As my dad likes to say, another day, another dollar." She walked past me and into the mudroom, where she deposited her pail and supplies.

Rising from the chair, I followed her into the cold room, a thought percolating in my head. "Bernie, can I ride into town with you? I have to mail a letter."

Though I'd promised William I'd examine Irene's body this afternoon, it could wait until tomorrow. I needed to write to the nursing school about Irene, and the sooner the better. Someone should inquire about her family.

"Sure. Just have to hitch up the horse to the wagon. It'll take about twenty minutes or so."

That should give me enough time to write the letter. "Thank you."

"You're in luck," she said, as she shrugged on her black wool coat that looked like a man's coat and pulled on her boots.

"How's that?"

"Only day the post office is open till five."

I dashed up the staircase to my room and hurriedly wrote my letter to my former teacher and friend, Eleanor Lawrence. She still taught at the Illinois Training School for Nurses. If Irene had attended the school, Eleanor would have known her.

When I came downstairs and went to the kitchen, Mrs. Bucheim was standing by the stove stirring her dinner concoction.

"Where do you think you're going?" she asked, scrutinizing my coat.

"Catherine and Hannah are sleeping. I'm going to town with Bernie to mail a letter. I'll be back before dinner. When I get back, I'd like to talk to you about Catherine's health."

She raised her shoulders and huffed. "And how do you expect to get back?"

In my excitement to leave, I hadn't considered that. "I'll walk. I know the way."

"Suit yourself," she huffed.

CHAPTER EIGHTEEN

The town didn't fare much better in sunlight than it did in sleet and fog. Instead of chasing its gloomy shabbiness, the bright sunlight only made it more evident–ramshackle houses on short, snowy streets going nowhere; weathered wood buildings in need of paint. Only the white stone church, with its bell tower, shone brightly.

When I'd asked Bernie about the church's denomination, she'd said, "St. Michael's is Catholic. Father Quinn, our island priest, is as tough and hard a drinker as the loggers. Most nights you'll find him bellied up to the bar, trading stories with the loggers and fishermen. And Sundays, he's spewing fire and brimstone. But a kinder man, you'll never meet. He'll loan you money in a pinch. You a churchgoer?"

I'd answered vaguely. She'd let it drop.

From the way she'd sung Father Quinn's praises, I suspected she was a churchgoer.

Though Bernie assured me it was a short distance from the tavern to the post office, it felt longer, and not just because of the buffeting wind off the lake. Accustomed to the cramped Chicago streets, their noise and hustle and bustle, I found the town's quiet spaciousness dispiriting and the clanging of the fishing boats in the harbor eerie. There were fewer fishing boats today. But a tall sailing sloop bobbed in the water beside a long boat named The Spray.

Once the lake iced up, the fishing boats would also be gone. Then, the town and the island would be a prison.

It had only been a few days since I'd stepped off the Mersey, but it seemed like ages. Though I'd escaped the horrors of the contagion ward, I had not escaped death but inadvertently stumbled upon one. And I was no closer to finding out who the man in the photograph was or why my mother had come here. I had to find a way to search the library undetected.

No surprise, the two-story clapboard post office was another shabby building. Facing the road, it was connected to the town market by an enclosed breezeway. At the rear of the post office hung a sign, "Jail," probably a one-cell room, where the occasional drunk spent a night. Market, post office, and jail—the structure's multifunction compactness spoke to the town's economy.

I pushed open the post office's heavy wood door and stepped inside the snug room. No one was at the counter.

"Hello," I called.

No answer.

Shivering with cold, I went to the woodstove in the center of the room. The wood gave off a pleasant piney scent reminiscent of Christmas trees.

As I warmed my hands, I noticed the rows of cubbies festooning the wall behind the counter, some containing letters.

Was I too late? Had the mail boat already come and gone?

I left the stove and went to the bulletin board near the door that displayed a plethora of flyers and notices. Someone had neglected to take down the all-too-familiar war poster: *I want you for the US Army.*

There were no instructional flyers about the flu that had papered Chicago. *Go Home and Go to Bed Until You Are Well. Help Us Keep Chicago the Healthiest City in the World*, one had read. So many had ignored the instructions and paid for it with their lives, and the lives of their loved ones.

Shaking off my dark thoughts, I went to the counter and called out again.

From a back room, someone shouted, "Stop your caterwauling. Didn't you see the bell?"

How had I missed the bell on the counter?

A man, as weathered as the town, emerged from a side room off the enclosed breezeway, carrying a sack.

He tossed the sack on the counter, sending up a swirl of dust motes. Sharp blue eyes and stark white hair suggested his advanced age, but he appeared robust in his red plaid flannel shirt. An unlit pipe was planted between his teeth, a pencil behind his furry ear.

With an unnecessary flourish, he pinged the bell. We weren't off to a good start.

Then, he took his pipe from his mouth and smiled. I relaxed.

"I'd like to mail a letter," I said, retrieving the letter from my purse.

He seemed to find that amusing. "Well, miss, then you've come to the right place. I'm George Orr, postmaster. Also proprietor of the market, and sometimes jailer."

A man who wore many hats.

I smiled as I slid the letter across the counter, enjoying his humor. Since arriving on the island, I'd had little reason to smile.

He picked up the letter and perused it. Then he stared at my red hair as if he'd never seen red hair before. "You must be the Thierys' nurse."

It wasn't a question. I suspected he'd known who I was the moment he'd seen me. He didn't need to read my name written on the envelope.

He seemed such an affable man, I decided to play along. "That's right. My name's Nellie Lester. I replaced the other nurse, Irene Hayes. I'm sure you heard what happened to her."

He nodded. "I sent the telegram to the sheriff."

Another hat the man wore. I cleared my throat and pushed forward. "Mr. Orr, I'm trying to locate Irene's family. As postmaster on a small island,

I'm sure you're quite familiar with people's mail. And I was wondering if Irene ever mailed or received any letters?"

"That'll be three cents. Should get to Chicago sometime next week. What do you want me to do with your mail?" Ignoring my question, he continued. "I only ask, because the Hayes gal had me hold her letters. She didn't want anyone from the manor picking up her mail."

So, Irene had received letters but hadn't trusted anyone at Ravenwood Manor with her mail.

"Who usually picks up the mail for Ravenwood Manor?" I asked, digging in my purse for the three pennies. I would need to ask William for my first week's pay. I had only one penny left.

"No one in particular. Depends who's in town. Which means Matthew mostly, when he picks up supplies from the market."

He dropped the coins into a slotted drawer under the counter, then opened a ledger book and noted the transaction.

"I see you keep detailed records of transactions." I decided to take a different tack with the reluctant Mr. Orr concerning Irene's letters.

The compliment seemed to please him. He grinned around the pipe stem. "That I do. Though my memory's still pretty good." He tapped the side of his head.

"And as postmaster, you probably have to keep an eye on where the letters go and where they come from." I really was poor at dissembling.

"That's not for public knowledge," he said sharply. "Thought you'd get the idea when I didn't answer you the first time."

My face burned with humiliation, but I wasn't giving up. If Irene had a family, they needed to know she was dead. "Like I said, I'm–I mean, we're trying to locate Irene's next of kin. It would be helpful if you could tell me if she received or sent any letters."

He reached into his trousers' pocket, pulled out a match, struck it on the counter, and lit his pipe. As he puffed on his pipe, he stared at me, considering whether to answer me.

I smiled at him as the cherry-scented tobacco filled my lungs. Finally, he looked away. He'd decided something about me.

"About a week before she took off, she mailed a letter. Only letter she ever sent. It was to the same place where your letter's going. This nursing school."

My heart thudded in my chest. "Do you remember the person she sent it to?"

"A matter of fact I do. Miss Eileen Parker. Only reason I remember the name is my cousin married a Parker, though her first name was Barbara."

"Did Irene get a reply?" I gazed at the cubbies behind him. Could the letter still be there?

"Came after she left the island."

"Do you still have it?" I was finding it hard to stand still.

"I gave it to Matthew. He said he'd take care of it."

Why hadn't he returned the letter to Eileen Parker, instead of giving it to Matthew? Wasn't that post office policy? As unpleasant as it was, I'd have to ask Matthew about the letter.

Instead of accusing him of breeching policy, I continued my left-footed finesse. "With your sharp memory, I'll bet you remember the letter's sender."

He puffed on his pipe, sending out a billow of smoke that circled his head. "Now, missy, I may be old, but I'm not stupid. You don't have to flatter me. Seeing as you're trying to find that girl's folks, I'm going to tell you. The letter was from the same gal Irene had written to, Eileen Parker."

"Sorry, but I need my letter back," I said.

"What for?" he asked.

"I need to add a footnote. Please. It's very important." I didn't know an Eileen Parker but maybe Eleanor did.

"I don't usually do this," he said, handing me the letter. "But seeing as it's your letter, I don't see the harm."

Carefully, I inched open the envelope flap with my finger and took out the letter. "Can I borrow your pencil?"

On the bottom of the letter, I wrote a short paragraph. *Ask Eileen Parker about Irene Hayes. Irene wrote to her before she went missing, and she wrote back. I need to know why. Irene disappeared before the letter arrived. It was intercepted by Mr. Thiery's caretaker.*

When I looked up, Orr quickly looked away. He'd been trying to read what I'd written.

After I slipped the letter back into the envelope, I said, "Do you have anything I can seal the envelope with?"

"I'll take care of it," he said, holding his hand out for the letter.

Though a seemingly nice man, I didn't trust his helpfulness. Living on the island was like living in a fishbowl. "I'd like to do it myself, if you don't mind."

One furry eyebrow went up. But he reached under the counter and pulled out a jar of glue. I sealed the letter and gave it back to him.

"Thank you, Mr. Orr. You've been most kind."

I started toward the door, then turned back, realizing I hadn't answered his question.

"If I receive any mail, please hold it for me. I'll come by for it. And please, don't tell anyone about the letter I just sent. Even Mr. Thiery. Can I trust you to do that?"

He took the pipe out of his mouth, rested it on the counter, put his thumb and index finger together, and ran them over his mouth. "It'll be our little secret."

I stepped out into the bitterly cold day. The sun had set, and it was a long walk to Ravenwood Manor.

As the town faded in the distance, I suspected my letter wouldn't be a secret for long. I didn't trust Orr's promise. He'd given Irene's letter to Matthew when he should have returned it to Eileen Parker. Had Matthew given Irene's letter to William? If so, what had he done with it, and what was in the letter?

The wind shivered through my clothes. I felt the island's sway like a gravitational pull I couldn't resist, dragging me downward into an abyss of lies and secrets.

CHAPTER NINETEEN

The lighthouse beam circled overhead, as I trudged down the snowy path through the dense forest, my mind swirling with speculations about Irene's death.

Whether accidental or purposeful, Irene was killed by someone. The maelstrom of the Thierys' marriage provided a strong motive. I could see how William might succumb to Irene's charms. She was bright, beautiful, and, if I believed Bernie, manipulative–a dangerous combination in the face of an unhappy marriage.

If William and Irene had had an affair and William feared discovery, would he murder to keep that secret? Maybe Irene expected marriage and threatened to tell Catherine?

How easy it would have been for William to lure Irene into these woods and murder her. But then, why would he ask me to examine the body?

A tree brushed against my cheek. Snow shimmered down on me.

I stopped. The trees had closed in overhead. I looked down. The path was too narrow for a wagon. I'd been so engrossed in my musings; I'd missed the turn north to Ravenwood Manor. I was lost.

Suddenly, a high-pitched shriek, like the wailing of a baby, echoed through the forest, then another and another. Each growing weaker, until there was silence.

Whatever it was, it was dead now.

Then, a chorus of howls erupted, followed by something thrashing through the woods. Coyotes? Wolves?

I turned back and started to run, stumbling, slipping, and sliding. The thrashing sounds were coming closer and closer.

As I rounded a bend, I heard a shout. But I didn't stop.

My side ached. Trees lashed my face. I didn't care. I had to escape whatever wild creatures were chasing me.

When I reached where the path diverged, I quickly turned around, fully expecting to see a pack of animals running toward me.

Nothing. Just darkness and trees. As I turned back, the lighthouse beam passed over the path ahead of me.

I froze, too frightened to scream.

A dark, shadowy figure blocked the way. It didn't move, just stood there, looking at me.

"What do you want?" I cried.

As the light disappeared, so did the figure. As though it had never been there.

I listened to the night. I heard nothing but the screeching of an owl.

❧

I was still shaken when I entered the mudroom—chilled to the bone, hollow with hunger, my feet and hands blocks of ice. I touched my cheeks, felt the scratches.

After I hung my wet coat and hat on one of the pegs, I took off my snow-crusted boots, then walked into the kitchen in my stocking feet, not caring that my big toe stuck out of one.

Like a fixture, Mrs. Bucheim hovered over the stove, stirring her gamey concoction.

"Mr. William is waiting for you in the drawing room." She smiled smugly, staring at my scratched face.

I didn't have the strength to ask why.

But she seemed eager to tell me. "I didn't tell him anything that wasn't true."

❧

William looked like a man stretched to his limits. A bottle of whiskey and a half-filled glass rested on the table beside him.

"Do you have anything to say for yourself?" he asked in a weary voice.

Hungry, tired, and aggrieved, I'd stood like a penitent in my stocking feet as he listed my faults. I could strangle Mrs. Bucheim. For all I knew, she was lurking in a dark corner listening, savoring my humiliation.

Struggling to control my hurt and anger, I gazed up at the dead animals, then at the hearth, and then at him.

"Mrs. Bucheim is right about one thing," I conceded. "I did ask her about the laudanum. Asked her, not accused her. The laudanum went missing yesterday. And I thought I saw her in my room that day. I made a logical conclusion. But I suppose I could have been wrong." The shadowy presence in the woods had left me uncertain of my senses.

I took in a deep breath and blew it out, preparing for his next onslaught. He wasn't going to like what I was about to say.

"William," I kept my voice level. "It's possible Catherine is taking the laudanum. And if she is, so is Hannah. It's transferred through Catherine's breast milk. Do you know if your wife has taken the drug in the past?"

"Possible? So, you have no proof Catherine's taking the laudanum." His long, angular face looked hollow in the shadowy firelight.

He'd ignored my question.

"No, I don't. But the drug's effects are consistent with her changeable behavior."

His face remained passive. "Didn't you tell me her mood changes were because of childbirth?"

"That was before the laudanum was stolen," I said, my legs trembling with fatigue.

"Then it's all speculation. Catherine would never endanger Hannah."

I could see my words were falling on deaf ears.

"Mrs. Bucheim believes Catherine needs rest to calm her nerves," William said. "I tend to agree with her. It was irresponsible of you taking her to the solarium."

I took in a steadying breath. "I don't know what Mrs. Bucheim told you. And I know she means well. But it was Irene's shawl that sent Catherine into hysterics. Not the solarium. Don't you find it odd no one noticed it before now? Irene's been gone over a month." I sounded as desperate as I felt. *Please don't fire me. Please don't fire me.*

He downed the whiskey in one gulp, then brushed at his luxurious mustache with the back of his hand. "I promised Mrs. Bucheim I'd talk to you and I did. As to the laudanum, let me know if you discover any evidence Catherine's taking it."

He'd been persuaded. I was seeing another side to the cutthroat logger baron. Though stern, he was fair like his uncle.

"Thank you, I will," I said.

"Sheriff Wilkins will be here in a day or two. Have you examined Irene's body?"

"I will tomorrow." Another strike against me. I should leave now and count myself fortunate. But I didn't.

"William, I need to ask you something concerning Irene."

He raised his tired head. "What about Irene?"

"I was at the post office this afternoon and Mr. Orr mentioned that a letter came for Irene, after she disappeared. And that Matthew picked up that letter."

"Matthew never said anything to me about a letter for Irene. Orr is certain of this?"

"He seemed quite sure. The letter was from a teacher at the nursing school Irene attended, a Miss Eileen Parker. Irene had written to her before her disappearance."

He stared through me. I wasn't sure he was listening.

"If Matthew has the letter, it could help us find Irene's family."

William poured himself another whiskey. "I'll look into it. You confine yourself to caring for Catherine and Hannah. Leave the rest to Wilkins."

He chugged the whiskey, then left the room.

Before making my way to the kitchen. I went to the solarium in search of Irene's shawl, the cause of Catherine's hysterics. It was still there, crumpled on the chair, where Catherine had thrown it. The finely woven garment shimmered with its peacock feather design. It still held a faint trace of a flowery perfume, something a young girl would favor, too frivolous for my taste.

Catherine's words came back to me. "She's haunting me."

She's haunting all of us, I thought, gazing around the dark room, as though Irene were here.

I gasped. Quick and indecipherable, a tall, dark shape dashed past the solarium.

Clutching the shawl, I walked to the glass wall and peered into the snow-lit night. Nothing. Whatever it was, it was as ethereal as the hulking presence in the woods.

Unnerved, I was still clutching the shawl when I entered the kitchen.

❧

After a cold supper of weak tea, cheese, sliced ham, and bread, I made my way to the turret room. Despite the fire, it felt as lonely and desolate as the two nights before. I shut the curtains against the chill draft, undressed, and crawled under the meager quilt, putting the dead woman's shawl over me for warmth. Unlike Catherine, I wasn't afraid of a dead woman haunting me.

My mother once told me, after I'd awakened crying from a dreadful dream of a dead neighbor, "It's not the dead you have to be afraid of. It's the living."

Now, thinking back on her words, I wondered what in her life had brought her to that conclusion. Had something on the island made her leery of the living? Or was it something that happened before she came here and might have been the catalyst to her joining Engel's mysterious group.

Tomorrow, if I could escape Mrs. Bucheim's vengeful eye, I'd search the library to see if Engel's books might hold clues to my mother's past.

Exhausted, I turned off the lamp. The house ticked around me. Gingerly, I shifted to my left side. No presence hovered near the dresser.

"Mother?" I coaxed. But the apparition didn't come. I turned away and closed my eyes against the threat of tears.

When I turned back, she was there, more light than substance. I said nothing, just watched until she faded away.

Then like a fierce undertow, sleep pulled me down.

⚘

I can't see him only feel his hands circling my neck, the weight of his body crushing me, his breath whispering my name like a curse. Gasping for air, I claw at him. My throat closes. I'm dying.

⚘

I shook myself awake, still clawing at his hands. But it wasn't his hands around my neck. It was Irene's shawl.

Sobbing, I untangled it and flung it to the floor.

The dark too intense for my fevered mind, I turned on the kerosene lamp and went to the smoky mirror. There were no bruises on my neck, only scratch marks from the trees. It had seemed so real.

After returning to the hard bed, I watched the curtains move in and out. *Just like breathing*, my last thought as I drifted off to sleep.

CHAPTER TWENTY

I stealthily made my way down the dark hallway, the clattering of dishes, pots, and pans assuring me that Mrs. Bucheim was occupied in the kitchen. For how long, I didn't know. But I had to take the chance. My position was precarious.

This morning a livid Catherine had accused me of stealing Irene's shawl, demanded I bring it to her, then carelessly tossed it on the settee, letting me know she didn't want it, she just didn't want me to have it.

I hurried through the grand drawing room, aware of the staring eyes of the dead animals, slid open the pocket doors, and quietly closed them behind me.

The library was so dark and dusty an intense melancholy overcame me, making me want to escape the dreary room. Instead, I flung open the draperies, covering the west-facing windows. Dust motes swirled in the arcing wintry light.

Modestly furnished, the library contained a walnut trestle table with matching chairs, a rolling library ladder, a kerosene lamp, and on either side of the hearth two oddly shaped, black Victorian chairs. Nothing looked inviting or comfortable.

Gazing at the walls of books, I sighed at the enormity of my task. Hundreds filled the elaborately carved walnut bookcases. It would take me days to go through all of them. Days I might not have. But if Theo was right, and the books were Caleb Engel's, they might reveal something about Engel and the community.

Even with the draperies open, the gray day offered scant light. I lit the lamp and began perusing the books. After a few trips up and down the library ladder, I realized the books weren't organized alphabetically by author's name. Similar to a public library, Engel had organized the books by subject matter–philosophy, science, medicine, literature, and theology. Within each discipline, the books were arranged by author. Some books were printed, others were handwritten. All were leather bound. Caleb Engel had amassed an amazing library.

On a whim I decided to start with science, my field.

Since I didn't know what I was looking for, I scanned the various titles and authors, impressed with the variety of scientific subjects from medicine to natural history to astrology. When I reached the authors' names beginning with *E*, I was reading so fast, I almost read past the name.

John Engel.

My hand trembled as I slid out the book. It was heavy and beautifully bound in Moroccan leather. The title was etched in gold across the front: *Ornithology or the Natural History of Birds of the United States*.

I opened the book, releasing a musty unpleasant smell. The full color sketchbook of birds and flowers was done in two dimensions. As I leafed through the pages, each more magnificent than the next, I wondered who John Engel was in relation to Caleb. Brother, son, cousin? I looked at the back of the book for a biography. There was none.

After replacing the book on the shelf, I started scanning the other sections for books by John Engel.

The slam of a door startled me. I didn't move; my eyes riveted on the closed library doors. Then, the house went quiet again.

With growing anxiety, I moved on to the theology section. I had to hurry. Mrs. Bucheim would soon notice my absence, another tick against me if she caught me dawdling in the library.

With my finger I traced the names on the book spines. When I came to the name Caleb Engel, I stopped, the raised gold letters of his name tingling on my skin.

Ideas on the Fate of Man, pertaining to the Present Times and the Second Coming. His book title was as impressive as his library.

As I removed the weighty tome, I heard voices coming from the drawing room. Hugging the book to my chest, I tiptoed to the pocket doors and listened. It was Mrs. Bucheim and Theo Proctor. I couldn't hear what they were saying, only the tenor of their voices, Theo cajoling, Mrs. Bucheim friendly. She'd never used that tone with me.

What was Theo Proctor doing at the manor? Had I already been replaced by him?

Gradually, their voices faded.

Still holding Engel's book, I went to the trestle table. A leather bookmark protruded from its pages. I opened to the marked page and started to read. Alert to every sound, in case Mrs. Bucheim or Proctor returned.

"Harmonie is the essence of God's earthly kingdom and can only be obtained by the pursuit of Christian perfection," Engel wrote. "Only those of untainted blood are deemed worthy of being Harmonites and residing in God's earthly kingdom of Harmony."

I read on. Engel laid out his belief in Christ's imminent Second Coming. Stress on imminent, meaning in their lifetime. To be worthy, the Harmonites had to strive for purity and perfection, which could only be achieved by living communally under strict adherence to certain tenets set out by Engel, who had been ordained by God as a prophet.

So, Harmony had been a religious community, not a utopia.

When I reached Engel's last religious tenet, I was stunned. The Harmonites, as he called his community, were to be celibate. Anyone not adhering to celibacy would be admonished before the community. Whatever that meant.

In addition to the religious doctrines, there were unbendable laws regulating every aspect of their lives, from when they worshipped to what they wore.

The photograph of us in front of the cottage sprung into my mind. Now I understood our strange clothes.

I continued reading. For serious transgressions, a meeting of the brethren, ominously named the reckoning, meted out punishment.

The Harmonites' one concession to the feminine was a virgin spirit named Sophia. Depicted as a winged woman, she was analogous to the human soul.

Engel noted: "Only to the purest does she appear." Then he added, "She's appeared to me on numerous occasions."

The winged stone angel guarding the dead had to be a statue of Sophia.

I collapsed back into the chair, my mind whirling, like the dust motes in the somber light.

Though I now knew what my mother was doing in Harmony, it gave me no comfort. She'd been an ardent follower of a religious fanatic, who believed Christ's Second Coming would be in her lifetime, which, to my practical mind, was delusional.

What had possessed my mother to join such a strict and unyielding religious sect? This was not the mother I knew. Leery of religion, she'd kept to herself. She'd lived like a woman in hiding. Her only friend was Mildred, a woman she worked with at the embroidery company.

Was coming to Harmony the man in the photograph's doing? This man I couldn't remember. Was he trying to escape something in his own life? Maybe living in a community of like-minded people with a common belief, even if that belief was suspect and the sacrifice extreme, offered him and my mother a sense of comfort and belonging.

And yet the community had failed. "They took John from us," my mother had written.

John. Was the John in the photograph John Engel?

My thoughts scattered, I rose and put the book back on the shelf, then returned to the science section. I pulled out John Engel's beautiful book and turned to the drawing of the blue jay I'd found so arresting, with its delicate grays and blues. As though I could conjure John Engel, I ran my fingers over the drawing.

Then I closed my eyes and inhaled deeply, letting my mind wander. A vision snagged me.

"Hush, daughter," the man whispered, pointing to a jay in the tree–the open sketchbook on his lap, his slender freckled fingers deft as he drew, smell of cedar, the tingling of the grass on my legs, the bird's ardent cry.

As suddenly as it had come, the memory left.

I shook my head, wanting to dismiss the memory as fantasy. I'd never been an imaginative person, preferring the stability of the scientific world. Even my sketches were mostly utilitarian, records of places, skillful renderings, but not beautiful.

But since coming to the island, my mind had played tricks on me: the presence in my room, the vision in the maze, the previous night's strange figure in the forest, and now this latest vision of a young girl and her father, a father with coppery hair like mine.

Afraid, I closed the book. What was happening to me? Why would I want my father to be a relative of a religious zealot who believed he was God's prophet on earth, filling their receptive minds with the misguided belief that Christ was returning to them? Because he'd drawn such precise, yet beautiful illustrations? Or because I was desperate for a father, even a flawed one?

The afternoon light had dimmed. My practical self returned. I needed to examine Irene's body, as William requested.

I started toward the bookshelf, then changed my mind. The nights were long and sleep difficult. The book would be a good distraction. Maybe it would conjure more visions.

As I pushed open the pocket doors, Mrs. Bucheim was standing in the drawing room, gazing out the windows. Rare to see her daydreaming.

At the sound of my footsteps, she turned abruptly. "What were you doing in there? And what's that you're holding?"

Grasping John Engel's book to my chest, I felt emboldened. "It's an ornithology book written by John Engel. He was a relative of Caleb Engel." *And my father*, I whispered to myself, suddenly sure of it. As I was sure that the presence in my room was my mother. Like the dead girl in the portrait, I was caught between two worlds–the real and the unreal.

She stared at me as if I'd told her the moon was made of cheese. "I don't know what you're babbling about. Who's Caleb Engel?"

"Mrs. Bucheim, I find it hard to believe that you don't know who Caleb Engel was. He owned the island before Henry Thiery. You're living in his house. That's his library." I pointed to the pocket doors.

She stepped back, as though afraid I'd gone mad. "That was before my time. I've never heard of Caleb Engel."

"So you say. By the way, I'm heading to the icehouse to examine Irene's body. No need to tell William, he already knows."

I strode out of the room, my mother's words chiming in my head, "You may have won the battle, but you probably lost the war."

I didn't care. That look of astonishment and fear on Mrs. Bucheim's shriveled face was worth it.

I clutched the book tighter. *So this is what it feels like to have a father.*

CHAPTER TWENTY-ONE

The slate sky promised more snow as I made my way to the icehouse, lugging a lantern, still shaky with the awareness that John Engel was my father. My mind nattered at me: What happened to him? Could he still be alive? And why had my mother lied to me?

Suddenly, raucous kraaing noises filled the sky. I looked up. Throngs of ravens were darting from tree to tree in frantic agitation. It was as if they sensed what lay inside the icehouse, and what I was about to do.

I quickened my pace, dreading my task.

It wasn't the prospect of examining a decimated corpse that filled me with dread. I'd seen worse at the hospital—bodies burnt beyond recognition, wives' faces beaten to a pulp by miscreant husbands, and maggot-infested corpses. It was the evidence I might find, proving with certainty that Irene had been murdered. Telling William, who'd been adamant that her death was accidental, might cause my dismissal. Or should I keep silent and hope Sheriff Wilkins does his job?

A sketchy portrait of Irene Hayes was taking shape in my mind: nosy, devoted, flighty, flirtatious, manipulative, and adventuresome, possibly an adulteress.

Not until I reached the icehouse door did I see the footprints in the snow. A sliver of light stained the snow. Someone was inside.

I pulled open the door. Theo was bent over the body, lantern in hand, using what looked like a pencil to pry a fragment of frozen clothing away from Irene's chest.

The sight of his blond handsomeness flustered me. "Theo, I didn't expect to see you here," I blurted out.

He didn't look up. "Come to have another look, have you?"

So Mrs. Bucheim had told him I'd already examined the corpse. What else had she said about me?

As cold as it was, I left the door open, rather than be entombed with the body and Theo. I lit my lantern and put it on the ice shelf nearest the corpse, flaring the room with much needed extra light.

"I'd like to show you something. If you could hold your lantern close to her head, please," I said, as I approached the icy table.

He obliged.

With my gloved hands, I grasped the fragile skull and turned it, so he could see the wound. Her head was a mess of dark frozen blood spangled with ice crystals. Her neck and dress were stained with blood, where it had seeped from her wound.

"What do you make of this?" Our heads were so close I could smell the coffee on his breath and the fresh soap from his morning ministrations. Was it the arctic cold that was robbing me of breath or being so close to Theo?

An avidness I hadn't expected overtook him, as he circled the wound with his pencil. "Three theories. She fell and hit her head. She was pushed. Or someone smashed her skull in with a heavy object."

Wanting to assess the wound more carefully, I pried her stiff hair aside and ran my gloved fingers around the edges, then pressed inward. The frozen blood cracked like ice on a pond. The wound was mostly smooth with some jaggedness. My guess, a rock had crushed her skull.

But there was nothing to indicate if this was an accident or murder. If it wasn't an accident, someone had hit her from behind. She wouldn't have seen it coming. I repositioned her head and gazed at her gray face, frozen in time. If only she could tell us.

"What do you think caused this wound?" I asked.

He put the pencil behind his ear and ran his bare hand around the gash. Then he took a handkerchief from his coat pocket and wiped his hands. "More than likely a rock. And there was force behind it."

"What do you make of the dirt and the lack of decomposition?" I wanted to see if he agreed with my initial assessment, that someone had buried Irene.

His blue-eyed stare was disarming. "Considering she went missing over a month ago, there should be more decomposition, not to mention the critters. She should be a pile of bones. Then there's the dirt. Only explanation is she was buried. Someone was there when she died. That's what you're getting at, isn't it?"

"It's only an educated guess. I can't prove it." Our eyes held a moment too long. I broke my gaze first.

"C'mon, Nellie. Say what we're both thinking. What are you afraid of?" He flashed the lantern in my face, making me step back from its intensity. I bumped against one of the jagged ice piles.

What was I afraid of? I'd come to the island seeking the truth about my mother's past, thinking I'd escaped the death I'd left behind. But it followed me here. Before me on this icy table was a young woman, whose place I'd taken. A young woman who I believed was murdered.

Why was I afraid to say that to him? Was it that I didn't trust him? Or was it that saying it aloud brought the terror of her death too near.

I took in a deep breath, the cold air stinging my lungs. "Someone was there when she died and buried her in a shallow grave," I whispered. "And the logging disturbed the grave."

"And?"

"And what?"

"She was murdered. Why else bury her?" His face flared with anger.

"I'm not sure. It could have been an accident," I answered, confused by his anger. "Someone could have shoved her. She hit her head. They panicked and buried her."

"Shoved her or bashed her head in. Someone killed her," he retorted. "And I'm going to find out who did it. She didn't deserve to die like this." He touched her dark, stiff hair so lovingly, I half expected her eyes to open.

"You were close, weren't you?"

He put the lantern down on an ice shelf behind him. "Irene had a naiveté about her I found refreshing. Sometimes she'd visit me. Ask my advice about certain herbal remedies or about island life."

A needle of jealousy pricked me.

Irene had found a way to belong, a way to wend herself into everyone's heart, even the truculent Mrs. Bucheim. I'd yet to do that. My woundedness kept me from trusting people.

"I don't think you should play detective," I said, looking down at Irene's body. "Perhaps you should leave the investigation to Sheriff Wilkins."

He laughed. "Ezra Wilkins couldn't find his way out of a paper bag. What are you going to tell William? That's why you're here, isn't it? He asked you to examine the body again. You know he's using you. Covering his bets."

Where was all this vitriol toward William coming from? "What do you mean, covering his bets?"

He was so agitated he took the pencil from his ear and broke it in two. "Let me handle William."

"And what will I tell him when he asks me about my findings?"

"Tell him what he wants to hear. She fell. It was an accident. Or tell him you're not a medical examiner. Tell him anything but the truth."

"I don't know if I can do that." I was never a good liar. My face betrayed me.

"Nellie, I'm trying to protect you. You don't want to end up like Irene, a frozen corpse in an icehouse."

"Are you saying William had something to do with her death?" Did he really believe that?

"All I know is something spooked Irene."

The way his eyes wouldn't meet mine, the abruptness of his explanation—there was something he wasn't telling me.

"Thank you for your concern. But I think I can take care of myself." The pull I felt toward him was intoxicating and dangerous.

He exhaled deeply, clouding the air. "Have it your way, then. Have you searched the library?"

"I have."

"Did you find out anything about Caleb Engel?"

Neither of us saw Matthew standing in the doorway. How much had he heard?

"Doc, you have to come now," he said, panting. "There's been an accident at the camp."

Though he was looking at Theo, I was the one who asked, "What kind of accident?"

"You should bring your medical things. It's a bad one. A tree crushed his leg."

"Maybe I can help," I said, trailing behind the two men as they left the icehouse and Irene's forlorn corpse.

CHAPTER TWENTY-TWO

The woods hummed with activity as we neared the logging camp. Matthew had made it clear that I wasn't welcome. But Theo insisted I come. Bumping along the rough road, his level of scorn was evident in his silence.

All Matthew would say about the man's injury was that it was bad and the hurt logger's name was Charlie. Theo had remained silent as well, clutching his leather medical bag like a lifeline. I imagined the hodge-podge of herbs, ointments, remedies, splints, bandages, and various instruments in his bag. All of which would be useless if he didn't know what to do with them.

When I'd asked Theo if he'd ever treated a crushed limb, he'd answered, "Plenty of broken bones."

A wide trail off the main road led to the camp, set deep in the forest, as though it had been dropped there. The rough-hewn buildings looked as rugged and sturdy as the loggers, made of massive logs held together with chinking–bunkhouse, cook shanty, outhouses, stable, smithy, and a few other buildings I couldn't name.

William greeted us as we stepped down from the wagon, his face flushed with cold and worry. "I'm glad you're here," he said to me. "I'm sure the doc could use an extra pair of hands."

His greeting pleased and surprised me. I shot Matthew a withering look.

"I want you back on the line with the men," he ordered Matthew. "Take the gray horse. We need that section cleared today. And keep a sharp eye on them. We don't want any more accidents."

"I'm not babysitting them men," Matthew said, sharply. "It's no one's fault. The tree fell the wrong way."

Again, I wondered at the nature of their relationship. His insubordination hinted at a familiarity beyond boss and foreman.

William's jaw tightened. "That's the second accident this week. I can't afford to lose any more men. You're to keep a close eye on things. Don't make me regret making you foreman."

"Aye, aye, boss," Matthew said sarcastically, then turned on his heel and limped angrily toward the lean-to shed, where two horses were tied up.

"Charlie's in the bunkhouse," William said, striding in the direction of the largest building.

The snow was dirty and trampled, the forest alive with the ringing of axes and the gnawing of saws. I inhaled the overwhelming scent of pine. It was as though the trees were bleeding sap, and in a way they were. I felt the weighty gloom of Ravenwood Manor lifted from me.

When we reached the bunkhouse, William stopped. "You go on in. I've got some business I need to see to. When you're done, I'll be in my office at the mill. Abe will take Charlie to the marina, where a boat to Charlevoix is waiting."

Theo nodded, then opened the bunkhouse door and went inside. I trailed after him.

The only light in the bunkhouse came from an overhead kerosene lamp and one window at the rear of the structure. A cast-iron stove dominated the room. Along both sides of the space were rows of bunks, with low benches in front of them. Trousers and shirts hung from long wooden poles under the low ceiling. The place reeked of tobacco, sweat, and smoke. The room was cramped and uncomfortable, the bedding primitive. I couldn't imagine spending one night here, let alone months.

There was a calendar nailed to one of the wood slats, the days Xed out like a prison sentence. On one of the tables was a small Victrola, the only luxury I could see.

Abe was sitting next to the injured man. Charlie was sprawled on one of the benches, writhing in pain; a dirty blanket covered his torso. A half-empty bottle of whiskey was on the floor.

Theo seemed to come alive at the sight of the hurt man. "We're going to have to move him, so I can get a better look at his leg," he said. "Abe, move that large table to the center of the room under the lamp. I'll also need the smaller table for my instruments."

After Abe dragged the two tables across the crude wood floor, Theo placed his medical bag on the small table and directed me to do the same with mine.

"Let's get him on the table," he told Abe. "Try not to jostle him too much."

"Should I give him more whiskey, Doc?" Abe asked.

"Let's move him first."

As they lifted Charlie from the bench, he cried out in agony. Blood had seeped through his trousers. I shuddered at the sight of the dirty blanket and the filthy table. Infection was almost certain.

Under the kerosene lamp, I saw that the bottom half of his right trouser leg was a mess of blood, bone, and tissue. His foot rested at an odd angle. Someone had had the forethought to tie a tourniquet above the injury to stanch the bleeding. From Charlie's paleness, I surmised he'd lost a lot of blood.

I opened my medical bag and took out an assortment of instruments–gauze, bandages, disinfectant, and the bottle of ether. I didn't need to see the leg. I already knew it was past saving.

"Do you want me to cut away his trousers?" I asked Theo.

In answer, Theo shed his coat and rolled up his shirtsleeves, then disinfected his hands and his instruments. I followed suit. With one of the instruments, he tried to pry up the trouser leg, but it wouldn't budge.

"Am I going to lose my leg, Doc?" Charlie cried.

I prayed Theo wouldn't tell him the truth. I picked up my scissors and handed them to Theo.

"Let me get a good look first," Theo answered.

Carefully, he cut away the man's trousers from the damaged leg, exposing the pulpy mass of crushed bone and tissue.

Just as I thought, there was no saving the leg. Now it was a matter of saving Charlie's life.

"We'll need hot water, clean towels, and more whiskey," I said to Abe, who rocked side to side, staring at the destroyed leg.

"Jesus," Abe whispered, ignoring my request.

In a panic, Charlie raised himself up on his elbows. "Mother of God," he cried. "I can't lose my leg. You have to save it." He gripped Theo's arm. "Promise me, you'll save it."

"Doc Proctor will see to it. Right, Doc?" Abe insisted, his fists tight by his side.

"At least it's only your leg."

I didn't think that was much consolation to Charlie, who lay back, his eyes focused on the beamed ceiling.

Theo was still holding the scissors and gazing at the mangled limb, a look of bewilderment on his face.

I moved closer to get a better look and to assess where to make the incision.

"Tell him, nurse," Abe coaxed me. "Tell him it's going to be all right."

It was not going to be all right. It would never be all right.

"Theo," I said, "can I speak to you outside?" This was a complex surgery, requiring skills I knew he didn't possess.

Theo put the scissors on the table and followed me outside.

After the stifling miasma of the bunkhouse with its smell of desperation, the cold air hit me like a tonic.

"If we're to save his life, his leg has to be amputated," I stated. "You can see that, right? You've never done an amputation. I doubt you've ever watched one either." I didn't wait for his reply. "I've never done one either, but I've assisted at quite a few."

Theo emerged from his trance. "What are you talking about? No one's doing an amputation. We'll get him stable. You heard William. Charlie's to be taken to the mainland, where's there's a doctor who can handle it."

"Who knows how much blood he's lost. Not to mention the risk of infection. He may not survive the journey."

He looked at me as if I'd lost my mind. "You're not suggesting you amputate his leg?"

Adrenaline spiked through me as images of amputations at which I'd assisted flooded my mind–the importance of cutting away dead tissue and cleaning the area, where to make the incision, cauterizing the blood vessels and nerves.

"If you help me, I think I can do it." I was convincing myself, as well as him.

He shook his head emphatically, his wavy blond hair falling over his forehead. I wanted to reach up and push it back, reassure him that we could do this, if we worked together.

"It's a bad idea," he countered. "If he dies, William will blame you and send you back to Chicago. Is that what you want?"

I knew he was right. Everything Theo said made sense. It was too risky. Charlie could die on the table and I'd be blamed. I hated that he was right. And yet I wanted to take the risk to save the man's life.

My entire life I'd been shoved into corners–dismissed and overlooked. My homespun face, my gnawing poverty, my fatherlessness had always held me down like chains. Here on this island, those chains had fallen away. Though the outside world continued to see me as a lowly woman, for once I didn't. For the first time in my life, I felt a wildness, impossible to resist.

I struck back at him. "If the man dies, William will also blame you for not stopping me. That's what you're afraid of."

"I don't care what William Thiery thinks of me. I'm not helping you amputate Charlie's leg. It's too risky." Theo reached for the door. "Let's get this over with."

For a moment, I stood looking at the camp, the crude buildings, and the smoke from the chimneys, making the gray sky grayer. I looked down at the trail of blood in the snow from the injured man–the red stark against the white.

A gust of cold air slithered down my back with its snakelike tongue. I'd never felt so free.

Dutifully, I opened the door and stepped inside, assuming my role of nurse and helpmate.

"Nellie," Theo called to me, "the ether, please."

❧

Theo and Abe carried the unconscious Charlie on a pallet to the waiting wagon. His breathing was heavy and his pulse weak, but we'd cleaned his leg, cut away the dead tissue, and cauterized the blood vessels. He'd yet to wake. I wasn't sure he ever would.

The woods were quieting, as dusk approached and the cold descended, adding to my bone-chilling weariness. I pulled my wool tam over my ears, shoved my hands in my coat pockets, and ignored the loggers returning to the camp for their evening meal. Some stared boldly at me, whispering, then laughing. I'd heard it all before, the crude jokes about my plain face and generous body.

My attention was focused elsewhere.

As Theo settled Charlie in the back of the wagon, I approached Abe who was bouncing on his feet, shivering with cold.

"I have to ask you something," I said.

He stopped moving and tilted his head, looking at me questioningly.

"In the icehouse, you said there was something peculiar when you found Irene's body."

He pushed back his watch cap and scratched his head, his stiff black hair in disarray. "I never said that. I gotta get Charlie to the boat."

He started to walk away.

I followed him. "C'mon, Abe. Please tell me what you meant. What was peculiar?"

He leaned in and whispered, "Listen, lady, keep out of it." His pungent breath smelled of onions and tobacco.

Theo jumped down from the wagon and joined us. "Keep out of what?" he asked.

"Abe noticed something peculiar about Irene's body when he found it."

"I never said that." He walked to the front of the wagon. "We better get going, Doc. The boat's waiting on us."

"Theo, you know what we talked about in the icehouse. Don't you think one of us should see where Irene's body was found? Can you manage the wagon alone?"

Abe was bouncing on his feet again, unable to contain his pent-up energy.

Theo took my arm and walked me away from the wagon. "What are you doing?"

I took in a deep breath, thinking how to convince him. "When William, Matthew, and Abe brought Irene's body to the icehouse, Abe started to say there was something peculiar about Irene's body when he found it. William cut him off. I thought if Abe showed me where he found her, I might find evidence to support our theory that she was buried. And maybe, Abe would tell me what was so peculiar."

"Why didn't you tell me this before?" He looked offended.

"Does it matter? I'm telling you now. Please, Theo, help me do this." He hadn't trusted me to amputate Charlie's leg. Would he trust me with this?

"I don't like it, but all right. After I drop Charlie off at the dock, I'll come back for you."

He returned to Abe. "I want you to take Nurse Lester to where you found Irene's body."

"Mr. Thiery's not going to like it," Abe protested, yanking down his cap over his ears. "And what do I tell Matthew when he sees me traipsing through the woods with her?" He jerked his thumb toward me.

"I'll take care of Mr. Thiery." Theo smiled at me. "And as to Matthew, you tell him I asked her to do it."

Before getting up on the wagon seat, Theo squeezed my arm reassuringly. "We made the right decision not amputating Charlie's leg."

I wanted to say, "That's yet to be seen," but I nodded instead, not wanting to sound ungrateful.

CHAPTER TWENTY-THREE

A crescent moon cut the black sky with a precision as sharp as the cold night. Occasionally, an animal stirred, breaking the utter stillness. As I slogged down the deeply rutted logging road, I struggled to keep up with Abe, who'd lapsed into a resentful silence.

On both sides of the road were open tracks of land where there'd once been lush forest. What will the island look like when William is done with it? When he's wrung every bit of profit from the land? I wondered. I felt the loss keenly.

After about a mile, the road narrowed. Up ahead, I saw a solid wall of trees. Their fate probably sealed already.

Turning right, Abe abruptly left the road. I scurried after him. All around me was devastation. Uneven tree stumps punctuated the trampled ground—snow-packed and scattered with the debris of felled trees and discarded scrub trees. I lifted my skirts as I maneuvered the rough terrain, stepping cautiously, careful not to turn an ankle.

On a hill in the distance stood a small stand of fir trees, looking lonely and desolate. The area reminded me of the newspaper photographs of No Man's Land on the Western Front, that place of war and death, where so many soldiers had died.

Abe stopped in the middle of the cleared area. "This is where I found her."

"You're sure this is the place?" How could he know? It all looked so alike in its destruction.

"Can't tell you the exact spot. But somewhere in here." He swung his arm out, encompassing the entire destroyed landscape.

I stared at him, making him look me in the eye. His dark eyes were like pools of obsidian. "What did you think was peculiar?"

In the slump of his shoulders, in the way his eyes danced away, I knew he didn't want to tell me. "Her body was covered with leaves and dirt."

"And what did you make of that?"

"Nothing." He shrugged his shoulders. "Maybe the wind blew them there."

"The wind blew leaves and dirt over her entire body?" I said, incredulously.

"Well, not over the whole body. Scattered like." He was moving from foot to foot again, his nerves getting the better of him. "Look, that's all I know."

My suspicion was that the logging had exposed part of Irene's body. Abe had seen it and had gone to investigate. Probably he'd dug around and unearthed more of Irene's corpse. But for some reason, he didn't want to tell me that.

"And what did you do after you found her?"

"Why you giving me the third degree? I had nothing to do with this."

"If you had nothing to do with it, why can't you answer my question? Why are you so nervous? What did you do after you found Irene's body?"

He let out a deep sigh. "It was obvious she was dead. So, I ran and got Matthew."

I wanted to make him play out this charade he'd concocted.

"And what was Matthew's reaction when he saw her body?"

"Looked like he was going to puke." He smiled nervously.

"And Mr. Thiery?"

"Same as always—all business. Man's got a poker face. Never know what he's thinking. He seemed more annoyed than anything."

That assessment didn't totally jibe with what I knew of William, but until this afternoon, I'd never seen him at work, only at home, dealing with a mentally unstable wife.

"Listen, I told you what I know. Let's go. I'm about starved."

"Was there anything else at the gravesite?"

He gave me a queer look when I said gravesite.

"I never said it was a grave. Don't put words in my mouth. Nothing was there but her body. Now let's head back to the camp."

Though it was dark and cold, and I didn't relish being here alone, especially after my unnerving experience in the forest last night, this would be my only chance to survey the place where Irene was found.

"You go ahead. I want to check out the area."

For a moment he hesitated, probably weighing the trouble he'd be in for leaving me alone.

"Okay, then," he said with some reluctance. "Just keep to the road."

After he disappeared, I tentatively moved across the uneven land, pushing over spent logs and other debris, finding nothing but empty tin cans and cigarette butts, occasionally startling small animals that scampered away into the night, their homes upended.

As I worked, I was keenly aware that Abe might have lied to me about where he'd found Irene's body, as well as his obvious lie that her body wasn't buried but left in the open. Scavengers would have ravaged an unburied body left outside that long. Irene's body was pristinely preserved. Then there was the dirt. Someone had buried her in a shallow grave. Someone had killed her. Who that someone was, I didn't know.

When I reached the small stand of trees atop the hill at the edge of the clearing, I was shivering, my face burning with cold. I plopped down on a rock atop the hill. I'd found nothing.

Trembling with cold and disappointment, I gazed down at the flattened earth. As the lighthouse beam traveled overhead, a glint caught my eye. It was on the far western edge of the clear-cut area.

Heart thumping, I hurried down the hill.

Something shiny protruded from under a downed shrub tree. I knelt and pulled it out. To my astonishment it was a gold locket on a thin gold chain. The chain was broken.

I tore off my right glove and opened the locket. Inside were two photographs. As the lighthouse beam passed over again, I saw a fresh-faced soldier, smiling broadly, unaware of what was ahead for him. The other was of Irene in her nurse's attire, her beauty startling. Her large, knowing eyes looked back at me. I sat back on my heels, gazing at her face. In life, her eyes had been her most beautiful feature, seductive and alluring.

I closed the locket and stood, then slipped it into my coat pocket. Abe hadn't lied about everything. Irene had died here.

As I started walking back toward the logging road, it began to snow. My mind was so enmeshed with thoughts of Irene, I didn't hear the footsteps until it was too late. The blow pitched me forward. Then everything went black.

❧

I woke up under a blanket of snow. Disoriented, I lay on the hard ground, watching the large loopy flakes fall. Then I remembered–the footsteps, the crushing blow to my head, and then nothing.

I had to get out of here. My attacker could still be lurking nearby. I sat up quickly and instantly regretted it. A roiling shuddered through my stomach. I leaned over and vomited. That's when I saw the footprints, disappearing into the snowy night, leading to the logging road.

There was no other way back to the camp. I had to chance it. If the attacker had wanted to kill me, I'd already be dead. I patted my right pocket. The locket was still there.

Slowly, I rose to my feet, my head thudding mercilessly. I probed the wound. The swelling was the size of a marble. When I took my hand away, my glove was wet with blood.

Unsteady, I started walking toward the logging road, stumbling over the uneven snowy ground. I wanted to lie down and let the snow cover me, like it was covering the ugliness of the clear-cut land. But I kept walking.

When I reached the logging road, I stopped, certain I'd heard the whinny of a horse. Heedless of my wooziness and pounding head, I hurried down the road, feeling the warm blood trickle down my neck. The image of Irene's neck and dress, stained with frozen blood, flashed through my mind.

Up ahead a wagon appeared, as though sent to banish all my thoughts of death and dying. I quickened my steps and waved my arms.

Matthew was urging the horse forward. Theo was saying something to him, while gesturing toward me.

It was going to be all right. I was going to be okay.

When the wagon reached me, Theo jumped down. I took a few steps, then collapsed into his arms, my vision tunneling.

"You're bleeding," he said, bolstering me up. "What happened?"

The last thing I remembered was his handsome face too close to mine, my jumbled words, and then a slow drift into unconsciousness.

CHAPTER TWENTY-FOUR

I woke to a confusion of smells and sounds—a sharp odor of raw wood, a high-pitched screech of a saw, and a steady grinding noise that intensified my splintering headache.

I was sprawled on an uncomfortable couch, covered by a wool blanket that stunk of tobacco and body odor. For some unfathomable reason, I'd been brought to the sawmill office.

The roller shade was drawn and a lamp lit the snug room. Light spilled in from an open doorway, which probably led to William's office.

My coat and hat were thrown on one of the two chairs. My worn boots under the other. With trepidation, I lifted the blanket. I was still dressed.

Gingerly, I turned my head and felt the wound. Though Theo had dressed it with gauze, my fingers were sticky with blood.

Head wounds bleed profusely, I assured myself. It was a good sign I was conscious.

Aware of my stomach's instability, I slowly eased myself up onto my elbows. No nausea. Another good sign.

"Hello," I called. "Is anyone here?"

Theo's worried face appeared in the doorway. "You're awake."

"How long have I been out?" I asked, as he came into the room, carrying his medical bag and closing the door behind him.

"Not long. About twenty minutes." He scraped the empty chair over, sat down, and brushed his hair from his forehead. "That was a nasty fall you took. How's your head?"

"I didn't fall." Carefully, I turned toward him, not wanting that churning in my gut to return.

His light blue eyes darkened. "What do you mean?"

I took in slow, calming breaths before answering. "Someone came up behind me and hit me on the head, probably with a rock. Like Irene."

"Did you get a look at him?"

"No, it happened too fast."

He took my hand in his. His hand was hard and warm, the heat spreading through me like a blanket. "I should have never let you go off with Abe. What was he thinking, leaving you alone?"

His misguided chivalrousness made me leery. I'd fallen for a man's flattery once before. I wouldn't do it again. I withdrew my hand.

"Don't blame Abe. I told him to leave." My answer was as chilly as the room.

"The attacker, he didn't . . . You weren't . . ." Embarrassed, he didn't finish his sentence.

I was in too much pain to share his embarrassment. "I wasn't violated, if that's what you're asking me."

"Then, it was a warning. You see that, don't you?"

"A warning? I don't know anything about Irene's death. Why would anyone think I do? The only reason I'm here is to find out about my mother and the man in the photograph." With no concrete proof, only a memory, I wasn't going to tell him I was almost certain that the man in the photograph was John Engel and my father.

I glanced over at my coat, where the locket was stowed. If I wasn't attacked for the locket, then maybe Theo was right and it was a warning. Someone didn't want me looking into Irene's death.

"Yeah, but no one knows that but me, right?" His quizzical look was full of doubt.

"No one else knows," I assured him.

"Good. From now on, you focus on your mother and that man. I'll look into Irene's death."

I gritted my teeth, making my headache worse. I knew he meant well, but I resented his telling me what to do.

"I want to go home," I said petulantly. I couldn't believe I'd called Ravenwood Manor home. But right now, it was the only home I had, as sad as that was.

Looking hurt, he stood and went to the table and opened his medical bag. "You'll need something for the pain."

"Why did you bring me here? Why didn't you take me to Ravenwood?"

"You were unconscious, and I needed to stop the bleeding. What would you have done?"

I'd upset him. "I'm sorry. I didn't mean to question your care."

"Yes, you did. Just like you questioned my treatment of Charlie. It's obvious what you think of me and my medical skills."

"I know you care about your patients," I said.

"Save it."

From his medical bag, he took out a bottle and held it up so I could see it.

"Does this meet with your approval?"

Like a scolded child, I nodded. Aspirin was written across the bottle in bold letters.

He poured water from the pitcher into one of the enamel mugs, unstoppered the bottle, and shook out two tablets.

Chided, I took the tablets and the mug from him, put the tablets in my mouth, and washed them down with the water.

"Thank you," I croaked.

He grunted in response.

After taking several deep breaths, I sat up, then swung my stocking feet to the cold plank floor.

Theo watched me as if I were doing an intricate magic trick.

For a few minutes I sat there with my hands on my knees, considering if I should tell Theo about Irene's locket. He seemed sincerely concerned about me and hurt by my questioning his medical treatment.

"Are you feeling sick again?" he asked, handing me my boots.

"No, just taking it slowly." My feeble attempt at amends.

As I struggled into my wet boots, a shiver ran through me. Then I stood, my legs wobbly. Theo got my coat and helped me into it. When he turned away, I slipped my hand into my right pocket. It was empty. As was the left pocket.

Disappointment and anger coursed through me. I'd made the right decision, not sharing what little I knew about who might have killed Irene.

His face remained placid and concerned. "I'll come by Ravenwood tomorrow to check your wound."

"Mrs. Bucheim will be delighted." How false we both sounded.

The wagon bounced along the rutted logging road. Every bump jostled my head, releasing an explosion of pain. It was as though my brain swam inside my skull, loose and untethered.

Matthew and Theo sat on the wagon bench. I caught only a word or two over the rumblings of the cart and the snorts and whinnies of the horse.

When we reached the shoreline, the fog descended and the snow rose up to meet it. The two men seemed to disappear. Under the low murmur of their voices, I wondered which one had stolen the locket. And why?

CHAPTER TWENTY-FIVE

"What did I tell you?" Mrs. Bucheim clucked at me. "Didn't I say a logging camp is no place for a woman? You could have been killed, like poor Irene. Didn't I say that, Matthew?"

Matthew looked up from his plate of beef stew, gravy glistening in his dark beard. "I think she's learned her lesson."

It was Matthew who'd said a logging camp was no place for a woman, but I wasn't about to contradict Mrs. Bucheim, who seemed as agitated as a hive of bees. She'd insisted I eat, and I didn't have the strength to resist. My headache had lessened, but a nauseating dizziness took its place.

The kitchen felt suffocating, rank with smells, some of which I couldn't name, none of which were pleasant.

Like a fixture, the cur slumbered under the table. I was too exhausted to care that his massive head rested on my foot.

Though I had no appetite, I knew I had to eat if I was to heal. I took a sip of tea. Then, I forked a cube of beef, popped it in my mouth, and slowly chewed, as if I'd just learned how. The beef was stringy but savory.

"The stew's very tasty," I complimented Mrs. Bucheim, hoping to quiet her nattering. I just wanted to finish supper and crawl up the winding stairs to the turret room, where I could ponder who had attacked me and who had taken the locket.

A brief smile flickered across her craggy face, and then disappeared. "Are you feeling okay?" she asked.

"Just tired," I answered, then realized she was being sarcastic. The woman had no pity.

"Go easy, Mrs. B.," Matthew said. "She helped save one of the guys today."

He'd defended me. I looked at him in disbelief. His face wavered. I blinked several times, trying to focus.

"Did Charlie make it?" I spoke slowly, as though tasting every word.

Matthew's frown seemed to swallow his face that kept splitting apart and coming back together. I stared down at my plate, the one stable thing in the room that wasn't spinning around me.

"Doc says he came to when they got to the dock. Was talking up a storm, then went out again."

I looked up, watching his mouth move around his straggly mustache. "Did you say there was a storm?"

"Are you okay?" he asked.

"I don't know." I clutched the table with both hands. I was on the Mersey again, my stomach lurching with every roll of the waves.

Matthew stood up so quickly his chair fell to the floor.

I shrunk away from him. "Get away from me," I said, covering my face with my hands to ward off a blow. "It was you, wasn't it?"

His large hands reached for me. I pulled away. It was then I realized I was falling. The cur barked. Mrs. Bucheim let out a shriek. The plank floor was hard and unforgiving. The crash of dishes was the last thing I heard.

⸙

I was weightless. The flickering of the light was like the flickering in my mind. An earthly scent stirred me awake. His flannel shirt too soft against my face. Round and round I went. My hand touched the cold air that wafted down on me. I was in my body and out of it, watching as Matthew struggled up the spiral stairs, his breath hard but determined.

Mrs. Bucheim's dark shadow stoked the fire, sending embers flying up into the netherworld where I wanted to go.

"Who are you?" I thought I said. But no one answered.

My body on the stiff bed, hands on my clothes, taking them away from me.

"No," I whispered, the cold shocking me. I wanted to sleep.

Her gnarled hands guided my nightgown into place, the thin quilt, as gossamer as the draft that inhabited the room with its secrets.

❧

My mother stands over me. Her faint, sad smile says so much, says so little. When did she get so old?

"Tell me, is my father alive?" I beg her.

"There's nothing to tell. You know everything already."

"I don't," I cry.

"It's all here."

Then the dream faded and with it my mother.

CHAPTER TWENTY-SIX

Light hovered around the drapes, wanting in. I rose into the gray morning convinced my mother had been here the night before. Then pain slammed me back to the turret room, the cold fire, the warning I'd been given.

Cautioning myself as I would a patient, I slowly got out of bed. Though groggy and muddled, at least my vision wasn't blurred. From my medical bag, I retrieved two aspirin and a healing salve, then walked to the blurry mirror.

My wild, blazing hair crested my shoulders, under my brown eyes dark smudges, my skin paler than milk. I shivered at the thought of Mrs. Bucheim undressing me.

Standing in my bare feet, I unwound the bandage. It was soaked with dried blood. The bleeding had stopped. I turned trying to see the wound, then gave up and felt it with my fingers. It wasn't deep. It was the force of the blow shaking my brain inside my skull that had caused my loss of consciousness and last night's hallucinations. Gently, I applied the salve to my wound, wincing. Then I took the two aspirin. It would ease the headache but not eliminate it. It was all I could do.

"The attack was a warning," Theo had said.

It gave me little comfort.

As I slipped out of my nightgown and started to dress, a fragment of last night's dream lingered in the cold air,

"It's all here," my mother had said.

Here, where? In this room? In this house? On this island?

Will you never say what you mean, mother?

I fastened my corset, once again horrified at the thought of Mrs. Bucheim's knotted fingers unfastening it. It wasn't false modesty that made me blanch but my vulnerability before this woman who clearly did not wish me well.

I cringed, remembering Matthew carrying me to my room, the intimacy of his closeness, his musky scent invading my nose. The humiliation stung.

Like a reprimand, John Engel's book, my father's book, was splayed open on the chair. Finding out my father's fate is what I should be concentrating on. I picked it up and sat on the bed, admiring his artistic ability.

A flamboyant male cardinal stared at me, his proud gaze captured, the red so similar to the color of my hair. The bird was so faithfully rendered, it looked as though it could fly off the page.

In a feral act, I brought the book to my face and inhaled deeply. Even after all these years, a trace of the wash he'd used remained.

The quickness of the vision took my breath away.

A man turning toward me with such warmth in his pale face, it outshines his red hair.

Just as swiftly the vision dissipated, leaving me with the weighted book and no answers.

"Father," I whispered. "Where are you?"

With care, I put the book on the chair and arranged my nightgown over it.

There was no putting it off any longer.

I moved toward the door with my heart thundering in my chest, dreading facing Mrs. Bucheim and Matthew. I placed my hand over my heart and felt the gold pendant, but nothing else. The key to the turret room wasn't around my neck.

Frantic, I searched the dresser, peered under the bed, and went through my medical bag. It wasn't there.

I rushed to the door and turned the knob. It opened.

Sighing with relief, I stepped onto the landing. Maybe Mrs. Bucheim, the house stickler, put it on the peg. The peg was empty.

Where was the key? And who had taken it?

As I made my way down the twisting stairs, I felt sick.

§

"No one took your key. Just as no one took that laudanum," Mrs. Bucheim protested, as she slopped oatmeal into my bowl. A thick gob slid down the outside and puddled on the wood table. It looked like vomit. "Though why the key was around your neck, I don't know. You city girls have strange ideas. Did you think someone was going to lock you in your room like Rapunzel?"

Rapunzel? Maybe I was living on an enchanted island where death was swept under the carpet and the fairy princess didn't die but lay frozen on a bed of ice?

Mrs. Bucheim was on a tear this morning, fluttering around the kitchen like an exotic butterfly, the kind you don't want landing on you. When I told her Theo would be making a visit, you would have thought I said President Wilson was coming.

I wasn't sure if her jaunty mood was because of Theo's visit or her seeing me last night in a helpless and vulnerable state.

"If no one took my key, then where is it?" I asked, a shiver of dizziness passing through me.

Mrs. Bucheim slapped down a large mound of dough on the floured counter and started kneading it, like she had a grudge against it.

"In all the to-do of last night, I put it in my pocket." She pounded the dough so hard the dishes in the wash pan rattled.

After sprinkling sugar on the oatmeal, I took a few spoonfuls to keep her happy, then pushed the bowl away, settling on her dark, bitter coffee, which was what I craved this morning to sharpen my senses. No milk, no sugar.

"Can I have it back, please?" The coffee burnt my tongue. Its bitterness sent ripples of sick through my gut.

"As you can see, I got my hands full right now."

I didn't like that answer. "Mrs. Bucheim, I'm not sleeping in that room without that key." I'd sleep in the grand drawing room if I had to.

She brushed a stray gray hair from her forehead with her hand, leaving a smudge of flour. "What's your worry? No one's locking you in your room," she scoffed.

"Why is the lock on the outside anyway?" I pursued her like a dog its tail, knowing that this was going nowhere.

Her fist made a mean hole in the dough. "Probably was a storage room once upon a time. The key is in my room. I'll get it when I'm done. I think that blow to your head rattled your brain. Maybe you should rest today. I'll tell the missus what happened."

"I'm fine, really. Why don't I get the key for you?" I'd never been to Mrs. Bucheim's room. This would give me an excuse to search it for the laudanum.

"No one goes in my room but me."

A loud banging on the mudroom door startled me.

"That can't be the doc already. I haven't got the biscuits baking."

The person banged again, only this time louder. I went to the mudroom and opened the door. A stocky middle-aged man dressed entirely in black, wearing a red-checkered hunter's cap, stood there looking annoyed.

"Thought you'd never answer. Colder than a witch's rump out here." The gruff man walked past me and into the kitchen, tracking snow and mud on the plank floors. I trailed behind wondering who he was.

"Mrs. Bucheim," he said warmly. "Are you baking those biscuits for me? I wouldn't say no to a coffee either."

"Sheriff Wilkins," Mrs. Bucheim beamed, her gaunt cheeks splotched with two red circles of color, like a dance hall girl's makeup. "Help yourself to coffee. The biscuits will be ready shortly. It's good to see you. I just wish it were under different circumstances. We're all heartsick over Irene. Such a lovely girl."

"Life and death, Mrs. B. Life and death." He poured himself a cup of coffee, then pulled out a chair and sat down across from me. "You must be her replacement."

His face was burnt from the cold and etched with lines. Except for his hunter's cap, his black attire made him look like an undertaker, not a sheriff. He took off his hat and rested it on the table. He was as bald as an egg.

"I'm Nellie Lester," I said. "Nice to meet you, Sheriff Wilkins. When you're ready, I can show you where her body is." Though the prospect of viewing Irene's eerily preserved corpse again turned my stomach, I needed to persuade him that Irene's death wasn't accidental.

His thick brown mustache disappeared into his coffee mug as he drank. "No need. I know where the bodies are kept." He laughed at his joke. "Meaning no disrespect."

"There are a few things I'd like to talk to you about," I insisted. What had Theo said about the sheriff? He couldn't find his way out of a paper bag?

He narrowed his beady eyes as he took me in. "No skin off my nose, miss. But from what William said in his telegram, the girl died from a fall. You know something different?"

Mrs. Bucheim stopped kneading the dough and was staring at me. I didn't want to discuss my suppositions in front of her.

I shook my head, causing a swell of pain that made me wince. "It's about Irene's next of kin."

That seemed to satisfy him. He gulped down the rest of his coffee. "Grab a lantern and your coat then. I want to get back to the mainland before dark."

❧

"Now, what did you want to tell me that you couldn't say in front of Mrs. B.?"

Maybe he wasn't as dense as Theo said.

We stood on either side of Irene's shrouded body. Our breath mingling in the frigid air, the lantern's eerie light adding to the macabre scene. As I stared down at the blanketed corpse, my resolve faltered.

"Miss Lester?" Wilkins prompted.

"It's better if I show you." I lifted the blanket.

At the sight of Irene's perfectly preserved body, that horrifying dream rose up—Irene's frozen body shattering into pieces and me trying to put her back together.

"Geez," Wilkins exclaimed. "She's as frozen as a carp. Look at those ice crystals. Even so, she was a beaut of a gal." He crossed himself, as though that gesture could erase his thoughtless comment.

His crude words seemed to ground me. "That's what I want to talk to you about. I've examined Irene's body twice. Once when she was first brought to the icehouse and then with Theo." A confused look passed over his face. "Doc Proctor."

"What were you poking around a dead body for? Aren't you the midwife? The doc should handle this." He looked around the icehouse. "In fact, why isn't he here?"

My head was starting to throb. "Mr. Wilkins, if you like, we can wait for Theo. He's coming by later today. But he'll just repeat what I'm going to say." Maybe he'd take me seriously if I told him that Theo and I agreed Irene's death wasn't accidental.

"Don't get yourself in a snit, miss. Spit it out."

Patiently, I explained my theory that Irene hadn't fallen but had been killed, possibly murdered. The intact state of her body and the dirt adhering to it proved she'd been buried in a shallow grave. I turned her head and showed him the wound. When I was done, he pushed his hunter's cap back on his shiny dome and scratched it.

"Well, now, William's telegram said the girl died from a fall."

"Think about it, Sheriff. She disappeared over a month ago. If she'd fallen, her body would have been in the open all that time. Animals would have scavenged it. As you can see, there's no damage."

"William didn't say anything about a shallow grave. But I see your point. The critters would have made quick work of her if she'd been out in the open. Where exactly was she found?"

I'd finally gotten through his shiny, thick skull. "Abe, one of the loggers, found her in the forest." Here's where my story fell apart. "He claims her body was under a pile of leaves and dirt."

"Did he now?" He ran his stubby fingers over his chin.

"I think he was lying," I pressed.

"Lying? Why would he do that?"

"I don't know. Maybe William asked him to." I was skating on thin ice, accusing William, who Wilkins probably viewed as a powerful and important businessman.

"I'd be careful if I were you, making accusations about William Thiery. Most of the islanders are beholden to him for their livelihoods."

I'd lost him. I could see it in his ink-drop eyes and the set of his jaw.

"Maybe William didn't tell Abe to lie, but it's obvious, isn't it, that he did." I gestured toward Irene's body, so still, so full of secrets. "I just want you to consider the possibility that Irene's death wasn't accidental."

"It isn't up to me. It's up to the coroner. But I'll tell him what you said." He pulled the blanket over Irene's corpse with the finality of a curtain being closed.

"There's one more thing." I had to convince him.

He let out a loud sigh of impatience.

"Yesterday I was attacked near the logging camp in the area where Irene's body was found. Someone hit me in the back of the head." I turned and showed him my head wound.

"What were you doing at the logging camp?" he asked.

"A logger was hurt. After I helped Doc Proctor treat him, I asked Abe to show me where he'd found Irene's body. That's when I was attacked."

He cleared his throat, and his face went red. "Sorry to ask you this, miss. But were you interfered with?"

Blood rushed into my face. "No. I think the attack was a warning. Someone doesn't want me looking into Irene's death." I didn't mention the locket, since I no longer had it.

"Seems to me you're lucky that's all he did. Unless you can identify him, there's nothing I can do. Take my advice, stay away from the logging camp. It's not safe for a female."

The man seemed incapable of focusing on the obvious.

With more strength than I thought him capable of, he slid his beefy arms under Irene's body and picked her up. His legs bowed under her weight, as he shuffled out of the icehouse and walked to the pushcart he'd retrieved from the barn. With a staggering grace, he placed her body on the cart.

Though my head felt like it was splitting in two, I tagged along bombarding him with questions. This was my last chance to convince him that Irene had been murdered. Once Wilkins saw William, who would push for an accidental death verdict, and once Wilkins boarded the boat to the mainland, the case would be closed.

"Don't you want to talk to Doc Proctor? He also thinks Irene was killed. Have you found any next of kin? Don't you think there's a possibility Irene was murdered?"

At the word *murder*, he stopped abruptly. I stumbled backward, almost falling into the snow.

"No, no, and maybe," he said sternly, his patience at an end. "This is a small island, miss. Everyone knows everyone. There's no crime here to speak of, except for the occasional missing horse, which usually turns up in a day or two. As to your attack, I'll ask around the camp. See if anyone knows anything. But don't hold your breath. Loggers stick together."

Unexpectantly, he touched my arm. "I'm not totally discounting your theory. But I'm not counting it either. If the doc were standing here, I'd tell him the same thing. But the coroner has the final word."

His answer gave me no comfort.

"What will happen to her body?" I asked. Though I hadn't known Irene, I felt a sense of loss and obligation. No one was standing up for her.

"If we can't find any kin, the county will bury her."

She'd be buried in a pauper's grave with the other unclaimed lost souls. The thought troubled me greatly. "Please hold off on her burial. I've written to one of her teachers at the nursing school. She may know if Irene had any family."

His face wrinkled with annoyance. It was another request adding to his work.

"Please. For her family's sake." I prayed Irene had family and that I could find them.

"You've got two weeks. If she's not claimed by then, I have no choice but to turn her body over to the county for burial."

"I expect to hear by next week." I hoped.

For all his claims of being in a hurry, he didn't leave. "How long do you intend staying on the island?"

"My contract is up in February." There was something behind his question that made me uneasy.

He nodded his head. "I'm only saying this for your own good, but the sooner you get off the island the better. Happens to some sensitive types like you. We call it island fever. You start to feel like the walls are closing in? That people are watching you? Are you seeing things that aren't there?"

"What? Are you serious?" I asked, thinking he was joking.

"As a bullet." He touched the brim of his cap. "Now I gotta get moving. I'd like to get back to the mainland today."

I watched him struggle with the heavy pushcart over the snowy, uneven ground. When he reached the barn, he transferred Irene's body to the waiting wagon.

Mrs. Bucheim emerged from the mudroom waving her arms, a tin of her biscuits in one hand, the other holding a black shawl around her bony, gaunt shoulders.

As he and the wagon disappeared around the east side of the manor, Theo's words came back to me. "William always gets what he wants."

CHAPTER TWENTY-SEVEN

As I gazed at the desolate cottages, that feeling of isolation overtook me again. The Harmonites had lived here. And now they were gone, disappeared in the night, possibly taking my father with them. I could almost hear their words in the gusting wind, feel their spirits all around me in the snow that was falling too hard and too fast.

It had been an impulsive decision to come here, telling no one where I was going. But I needed to speak to Theo, ask him to waylay Wilkins before his boat left in hopes that he could convince him to investigate Irene's murder.

This impulsiveness was unlike me. Was I suffering from island fever, as Wilkins suggested?

No. My concussion was to blame for my cloudy thinking and impulsiveness.

A blast of snow pushed me backward. Though I was dressed warmly, the unrelenting cold penetrated my clothes. My head felt splintered.

Before I could knock, Theo swung open the door, letting a gust of snow into the cottage. He wore a white fisherman's sweater and brown corduroy trousers.

"Nellie?" The astonishment in his voice threw me. "What are you doing here?"

"You have to come now," I pleaded. "Wilkins is going to let the coroner decide Irene's cause of death. Do you know anything about the coroner? Is he in William's pocket? Can we trust him to be impartial?"

"Slow down," he said, pulling me inside and shutting the door. The parlor blazed with warmth and smelled of hot cider and pinewood. "Sit down. How's your head? Let me take a look at it."

He guided me to the two-arm settee and sat me down like a child.

"Didn't you hear what I said? You have to convince Wilkins that Irene was killed, maybe murdered."

"You look like you could use a warm drink. Cider, coffee, tea? Or something stronger? Have you taken anything for your head?"

"What's wrong with you? Aren't you listening?"

"Nellie, you're overwrought. What makes you think Wilkins would listen to me, if he didn't listen to you?"

"Because everyone around here thinks your word is gospel. And I'm an outsider."

He laughed. I wanted to slap him. I was trembling so hard; I shoved my hands between my legs to stop the shaking.

"I thought we were on the same side," I said. "You agreed Irene's death wasn't accidental. That sheriff is going to bury her in a pauper's grave." Tears sprang into my eyes. I swiped at them angrily.

He sat next to me. His closeness made me angrier. I inched away.

"And I thought we agreed I was going to do the investigating. You could have been killed yesterday."

I hadn't agreed to anything. His blue-eyed concern was smothering, as was his musky scent, the piles of books, and the hanging herbs.

I jumped up. My head brushed against one of the herbs, sending down a shower of seeds.

It was then I saw it. Lying on the table beside the hearth.

"It was you who took it," I accused him, grabbing the locket, fear rushing through me.

He looked puzzled. “You asked me to take it.”

“What are you talking about?” He was trying to confuse me.

“By the wagon, right before you lost consciousness, you whispered, ‘Irene’s locket is in my pocket. Take it.’”

I rubbed my throbbing head. “I never said that.”

“Look, I don’t have to tell you that a concussion messes with your memory.”

I was holding the locket so tight, I smelled its metallic scent.

Did I ask him to take it? I vaguely remembered whispering something to him, but I couldn’t recall what it was. Something about Matthew. Nothing about the locket.

“Why would I ask you to keep it?” I lashed out.

“You think I stole it from you? When are you going to trust me?”

Snow crested the windows. I tugged at my scarf, suddenly too tight around my neck. I was finding it hard to breathe.

“I have to get out of here.”

“Not a good idea.” He rose from the sofa and came toward me, a blue bottle in his hands.

Panicked, I sidestepped him and ran for the door, still holding the locket. It was as though I could see Irene’s beautiful face, those large limpid eyes, hear her voice say–run.

Surprise was on my side, as I dashed outside into the blinding snow, not looking back. I could hear nothing above the fierce wind. Ravenwood Manor seemed impossibly far away.

&

I slammed the mudroom door and leaned against it, panting heavily, the locket still clutched in my hand. Theo hadn’t followed me.

As if pulled by gravity, I slid to the floor, waiting for the room to stop spinning. Everything felt tilted. With my eyes fixed on my snow-crusted black boots, I concentrated on unlacing them, watching my clumsiness. As if order could replace chaos, I put the boots side by side on the rug beside the door, lined up like soldiers.

My hands were numb and useless. It took me several attempts to unbutton my coat. I hung it and my wet tam on a peg and slipped the locket into my dress pocket.

When I entered the kitchen, Mrs. Bucheim was sitting at the table chopping carrots. She didn't look up, just kept chopping, then putting the carrots in a white bowl, which was already brimming with onions and potatoes.

Chop, chop, chop like the pounding in my head.

Her hands were ugly with pain. For a moment, I felt sorry for the old woman, struggling with her deformed hands. Every stroke of the knife must be agony.

Then she spoke and my pity evaporated. "The missus has been asking for you. And she's none too happy."

"Where did you say I was?" I asked, warming my frozen hands over the wood-burning stove.

"With the sheriff. After that I didn't know where you were." She looked up, took in my wet skirts, flushed face, and stocking feet. Then went back to her chopping.

Mrs. Bucheim, the enumerator of my faults and failings, had probably incited Catherine.

There was no need to ask her where Catherine was. The gentle notes of a Brahms's lullaby floated into the kitchen. With dread, I walked through the dining room to the front parlor.

Catherine sat at the mahogany piano lost in the music, her delicate fingers moving across the keys with grace and lightness. Her scarlet day dress clashed with the quiet song, as did her auburn hair. Undone, it tumbled to her shoulders. Hannah slept in her cradle near the fireplace.

It was a serene picture of motherhood. One that rang false.

I'd only briefly glimpsed the front parlor. Now upon closer inspection, the room appeared shabbier than the others. The rich royal blue curtains were frayed at the edges, the cream-colored damask settees and chairs threadbare, and the Oriental carpet's reds and navy blues faded. Once this must have been a stunning space to receive guests, especially with its view of the lake and the endless horizon. And unlike the ardently masculine drawing room, this room bespoke of a refinement that seemed counter to Engel's strict religiosity. But maybe Henry Thiery had decorated the parlor, not Caleb Engel.

Catherine stopped playing when she saw me standing in the doorway, a scowl on her pretty face. "The sheriff left over an hour ago. Where have you been?" she barked.

"I was visiting Mr. Proctor about a . . . medical matter," I stammered. I was cold and my head hurt. I wasn't thinking straight.

She slammed the lid down so hard the keys jangled. Hannah stirred but didn't wake. "You were hired to take care of Hannah and me. You didn't check on us this morning. Then you went traipsing off to who knows where."

"I'm sorry. You're right. I should have seen to you and Hannah first." Good sense overcame my indignation.

"You still haven't told me where you were."

"I took a walk along the path behind the manor."

She tilted her pretty head, considering whether to believe me.

"Mrs. Bucheim told me you were attacked yesterday. I would have thought that would deter you from venturing down wooded paths by yourself. What were you thinking, roaming around the logging camp?"

"I thought if I could see where Irene's body was found, it might explain what happened to her."

"Really, Nellie, what did you think you'd find? Irene's belongings?" She laughed shrilly. "I'm sorry you were hurt. But Irene's death is none of your concern."

That was the second time today I'd been told that.

She got up from the piano bench and moved to the settee by the windows, her silk dress the brightest thing in the tired room.

"Come. Sit with me." She patted the damask seat. "I have something important to discuss with you."

Reluctantly, I joined her on the settee. Her eyes were bright but clear, a healthy glow on her face. I didn't see any traces of drug use.

She leaned in and whispered, "You understand I had to reprimand you. Mrs. B. is listening. If I hadn't, she would have gone tattling to William. He thinks I'm not strict enough with the staff. I really wasn't that upset with you."

Surprised, I drew back. Hadn't she wanted me fired a few days ago? I never felt surefooted with her.

"What did you want to talk to me about?" I asked, craving the solitude of my room.

"Tomorrow afternoon I want you to go with me when I visit Father Quinn to make plans for Hannah's baptism." She squeezed my hand. "Before you say no, it's been a week since Hannah's birth. My bleeding is scant. And I'm dying to get out of the house."

It hadn't been a week, but her bleeding was minimal, and physically she was in good health. But I didn't want her to have a setback. I'd seen it before. Women so anxious to resume their lives, they overexert themselves to the detriment of their health.

"Can't the baptism be postponed until you're fully recovered? Or can't it be done here? You need at least two weeks rest," I reasoned.

"Babies have to be baptized in church and as soon as possible. If they die before being baptized, they spend eternity in limbo. That can't happen to Hannah. I won't let it." Her foot was tapping anxiously.

I wasn't about to discuss theology with Catherine. Though that seemed a harsh judgment for an innocent child. My only concern was her health. What was worse? I asked myself. A short trip to the church or Catherine in hysterics? Against my better judgment, I said, "I suppose it's all right if it's a brief trip."

She clapped her hands. "I knew you'd see it my way." She stared at my worn black day dress with its wet hem. "Do you have another dress you could wear?"

"The one I wore at the dinner party." The one that made me look like a schoolmarm.

"Oh, dear, no. That won't do." Her eyes roamed over my body.

"Let's see. You're taller and wider than me. But maybe one of my maternity dresses would fit you. Mrs. B. could let out the hem and the sides."

Like a sudden fever, shame rose to my face.

"Oh, don't be embarrassed, Nellie. No one cares but you."

"Why do I need a special dress to visit the priest?" The prospect of being hemmed into one of her maternity dresses by the prickly Mrs. Bucheim made me nauseous.

"Not for tomorrow. For the baptism. I want you to be Hannah's godmother."

Godmother? I was practically a stranger.

"Has William agreed to this?" I couldn't imagine him consenting to such a preposterous idea. Nor could I imagine myself as Hannah's godmother.

"William told me to choose who I like. And I like you. It was to be Irene. But, oh, well." She looked past me as if Irene were standing behind me.

"Shouldn't the godmother be a family member or a close friend?" I was desperate to change her mind.

She frowned and tugged at her dress. "My family can't come. There's no one else. And you did save Hannah's life. So, in a way, you're already responsible for her."

"Catherine," I said calmly. "Not only am I not a Catholic, but I don't expect to be here past February. Isn't a godmother expected to be in a child's life?" I knew little of godmother duties.

"Father Quinn won't object. William is very generous to the church. And if it weren't for his uncle, Father Quinn wouldn't have a rectory.

Besides William and I don't expect to be dying anytime soon. It's merely ceremonial. So, it's settled."

She took my silence as a yes.

Pleased, she bounced up from the settee. "Will you be a dear and bring Hannah upstairs for me. You can check on us then."

She moved to a chair and picked up a shawl. With a dramatic flourish, she wrapped it around her shoulders, then glanced back at me, a mischievous expression on her face. It was Irene's shawl.

I said nothing, mesmerized by the rows of peacock feathers, their iridescent ends, like eyes, mocking me.

Peacock feathers are bad luck, I once heard, harbingers of misfortune, illness, and death.

Feathers, I reminded myself, not a shawl with a peacock design.

Still, I was troubled. Not until I reached the staircase did I know why. When Catherine donned the shawl, it was as if she'd slipped inside Irene's skin. Her expression so like Irene's in the locket's photograph, it was frightening.

Catherine's perfume lingered in the air as I walked up the main staircase. When I reached the child's death portrait, I stopped, not believing what I saw. In the shadowy light, again her flesh appeared to be loosening, her one eye drooping, the other fixed on me.

I stepped closer, then jerked back, horrified.

It wasn't the shadowy light. The girl's face was decomposing, her flesh green and slack, her eye hanging down. I hurried up the stairs, away from the gruesome portrait.

CHAPTER TWENTY-EIGHT

The key wasn't on the peg or in my room. For a careless moment, I considered letting it go until tomorrow. Did I really believe someone would lock me in my room? But I wouldn't sleep without the key.

I started down the spiral staircase, my shadow moving along the wall, like another version of myself, growing and receding. When I reached the second floor, I stopped and listened. The house felt empty.

As I neared the Thierys' bedroom door, I heard Catherine crooning a lullaby to Hannah. Her voice sweet and steady. Maybe the trauma of Irene's death, the shock of giving birth, and the responsibility of motherhood explained her instability, not the laudanum. Then, there was the burden of living on an island in the winter.

I tiptoed past and made my way toward the stairway on the other side of the manor. It, too, wound around and around. How did the arthritic Mrs. Bucheim manage it?

When I reached the turret landing, I saw light under her door. She was still awake.

I knocked softly. "Mrs. Bucheim, I need the key to my room."

There was a rustling, the creak of a chair, and the scratchy sound of music.

The door flung open with such force I stepped backward. "What's wrong?" Mrs. Bucheim asked. "Is it the missus?" Her frothy white nightgown was in opposition to her thin braid that snaked over her shoulder.

"I came for the key," I said, peering over her shoulder into the handsomely furnished room. Upholstered chairs, a four-poster bed with a silky quilt, a pedal sewing machine, a thick Oriental rug, and a Victrola, which was starting to lose speed, the music as discordant as Mrs. Bucheim's expression.

"This couldn't wait until morning?" She put her hands on her narrow hips.

"If you wouldn't mind getting it for me." I folded my arms over my chest, letting her know I wasn't leaving without it.

"Since you're here anyway," she huffed her displeasure. "But I don't like you coming to my room and bothering me at night."

"That's a lovely Victrola," I said.

She glanced over her shoulder. "Mr. William bought it for me on one of his trips to Chicago," she preened. "I'll get the key."

Though she hadn't invited me in, I trailed after her, curious to see her room.

While she rummaged in her desk for the key, I sat down in the dark walnut rocker. Its emerald velvet seat and intricately carved leaves mimicked the bedposts.

Though identical in size and design, Mrs. Bucheim's room was a far cry from my meager bedroom. Hers was crammed with furniture all highly polished and finely made. It would have been a cozy bedroom, if not for the wallpaper. Oversized green leaves and sad, drooping white flowers crawled up the walls. In one place the pattern didn't match, creating an off-kilter effect. It looked like the flowers and vines were escaping the walls.

"Was the furniture here when you came to work for Henry Thiery?" I asked, wondering why this room was lavishly furnished and mine wasn't.

"Except for the sewing machine and Victrola. What of it?" She thrust the key at me. The grief ribbon was missing.

"It's just interesting that the other turret bedroom is so sparing in its furnishings."

"Are you complaining about your room again?"

"Just an observation." Key in hand, I rose from the rocker. "Can I also have the ribbon that was tied around the key?"

"I don't know about any ribbon. Now it's late and I'd like you to leave."

I didn't believe her. Was she being vindictive because I'd disturbed her? "Well, if you happen to find it, I'd like it back."

"You know, that's not the only key to your room," she said. Then firmly shut the door.

I stood outside her door shaken.

⸙

When I reached my room, the pounding in my head had become excruciating. I put the now useless key on the dresser beside Irene's locket and retrieved two aspirin from my medical bag. Luckily, the ewer still held water from last night's ministrations. After taking the pills, I changed into my nightgown and braided my hair. But I couldn't settle.

"That's not the only key." Mrs. Bucheim's taunt was laced with triumph. What pleasure it gave her playing on my fears. Had Irene been bedeviled by her? Doubtful. Mrs. Bucheim appeared truly saddened by her death.

For the first time, the room was too warm, the fire radiating heat like an errant sun. I picked up the locket, grabbed the quilt from the bed, and scraped the chair over to the rose-colored stained-glass windows. Instead of closing the curtains, I left them open, savoring the cold air seeping from the joints.

In the dim lamplight, I studied the locket. It was gold plated with a simple filigree design. It probably had cost the soldier a week's wages. Irene must have cherished it. I would have.

Was the locket a token of remembrance? Or was the soldier waiting for her return? No. There'd only been the one letter for her from Eileen Parker. My guess was the soldier had died.

His death might have made Irene vulnerable to a powerful man like William or maybe someone educated like Theo? Surely, not Matthew, who had the manners of a sow and the disposition of a porcupine. Though some women might find his raw ruggedness appealing.

Irene had been wearing the locket when she died, which suggested the soldier was still with her, if only in memory. I clutched the quilt tighter around me. I knew so little of love affairs and their consequences. There'd been Francis and no one else. His forcing himself on me had taught me not to trust men.

I thought Theo would prove me wrong. He hadn't. But he'd been so adamant in proclaiming his innocence, that he hadn't stolen the locket, that instead I'd asked him to take it. Even now I wanted to believe him. In this creepy, ancient house, on this desolate island, I longed for a friend, someone I could trust and confide in, maybe even love.

Fingering the locket's broken chain, I pictured the killer's rage as he ripped it from her neck. But it couldn't have happened that way. I'd seen no marks on her neck.

My headache was easing. I got up, placed the locket on the dresser beside the key, and turned off the kerosene lamp.

With reluctance, I crawled into bed. Once the room settled into darkness, I turned toward the dresser. My loneliness overwhelming me, I waited expectantly for the presence. Nothing shimmered in the dark. Only the dead shadow of the dresser. Had my mother forsaken me?

"Can you forgive me?" I murmured, thinking that would summon her.

The cold swept down on me, robbing the room of its warmth. I stared at the dresser so long, my eyes watered. Nothing. Then I remembered the awful wallpaper in Mrs. Bucheim's room with its disturbing emerald vines and drooping flowers, unlike my room's plain walls.

I lit the kerosene lamp and grabbed my journal. Closing my eyes, I envisioned Mrs. Bucheim's room. Then I opened my eyes and sketched it complete with the dreadful wallpaper.

Where the pattern of vines and drooping flowers broke was the exact place where my mother's spirit had arisen every night, except tonight.

CHAPTER TWENTY-NINE

The morning's fog had burned off and left a dull light that filtered into the chilly solarium.

I sat stiffly on the rattan three-cushion sofa, while Theo applied a healing salve to my wound with too much vigor, clearly agitated.

I'd asked him to use my salve, rather than whatever he'd concocted in his cottage, only adding to his ill humor.

After lunch, he'd arrived at Ravenwood, distracted and seething. Even Mrs. Bucheim's preening hadn't improved his mood.

Under Mrs. Bucheim's watchful eye, I'd reluctantly followed him into the solarium. The only place, he'd insisted, with sufficient light to examine my head wound. Though I thought it was less about the light and more about privacy.

"Why would I take the locket?" He broke the silence.

"I don't know. You tell me." I sat up straighter, tensing my muscles, as though preparing for an attack. I wished he'd stop touching me. My nerves tingled with each touch.

"How are the headaches?" His professional tone masked his seething anger that pulsed from him.

"Bearable. Now please answer my question." I turned and faced him, steeling myself against his fierce, dark blue gaze, like a sky gone wrong—one you can't look away from no matter the impending danger.

"I didn't steal the locket. You asked me to take it. Believe me. Don't believe me. I really don't care." He took in a deep breath and let it out. "I was going to bring the locket to you yesterday, when I checked your wound. But you came to my cottage. And then you ran out like your hair was on fire."

Everything he said made sense. If only I remembered, if only I could be sure.

"Did you talk to Sheriff Wilkins?" I probed.

"For all the good it did. He's letting the coroner have the final say so on Irene's cause of death. When I showed up, William was none too happy to see me or hear what I had to say."

Would William fire me for what I had told Wilkins? Catherine told me this morning that he'd slept at the mill. He'd yet to make an appearance at Ravenwood.

"Thank you." The words stuck in my mouth, like Mrs. Bucheim's oatmeal.

"Just keep it clean and dry. But I don't need to tell you that, do I?" For the first time that day, he smiled.

A truce of sorts settled on us, as soft and precarious as the light.

For all my distrust of him, he had directed me to the library, where I'd learned about Engel and the Harmonites. I decided to take a risk.

"I found out something about the community who lived on the island before Henry Thiery. It's in the library."

He didn't say anything, just followed me into the gloomy room stagnant with the stale smell of old books. I threw open the drapery, releasing a hurricane of dust.

"What did you find?" he said, marveling at the towering shelves of books.

I walked to the theology section, withdrew Caleb Engel's theological book, and went to the trestle table. Theo sat beside me. I opened the book to the title page.

"*Ideas on the Fate of Man, pertaining to the Present Times and the Second Coming*, by Caleb Engel," he recited. "The Second Coming? So, they were a religious community."

"A very peculiar and strict one. In his book, Engel lays out his religious tenets and principles. One of his tenets was celibacy. He believed that the Harmonites, that's what they called themselves, were the chosen people and had to be purified for Christ's Second Coming on earth. His tenets were a way of doing that. They covered every aspect of daily life, even what they wore. Engel stated that he was God's prophet."

"God's prophet, huh?" he scoffed. "It's amazing what people will believe given the right leader. The best of them are misguided idealists. The worst do serious harm, especially when they're under the spell of a megalomaniac, which I'm guessing Engel was. Wasn't it Voltaire who said, 'Those who can make you believe absurdities, can make you commit atrocities'?"

He saw my stricken look. "I'm sorry. But you have to admit that anyone who was a part of Engel's community was deluded. C'mon, chosen people? Second Coming?"

Though Theo was probably right, what he said didn't jibe with my wary, streetwise mother.

Suddenly, the pocket door opened, and Bernie barged into the room, carrying her mop, pail of rags, and cleaning products. "I didn't know anyone was in here. Hello, Doc. Hello, Nellie. I can come back later, if you're busy."

"That's okay. We're done," I said, closing the book.

Theo stood. That charming smile plastered across his face. "Bernie, I was going to bring the elixir to the tavern this afternoon. But since you're here, I'll give it to you now."

"My back's been hurting to beat the band, Doc."

Inwardly, I groaned. Theo's home remedies were probably harmless but also probably useless.

Theo went to the solarium and returned with his medical bag and a small blue bottle, not brown, like the one containing laudanum.

"Thanks, Doc." Bernie took the bottle, put it in her skirt pocket, and began wiping the bookshelves with a fragrant rag. The strong odor of Lysol filled the room, making me queasy. Would the horror of that smell never leave me?

"Gotta get this room shipshape for the party after we come from the church," Bernie explained. "Though why anyone would want to come in here, I don't know. But if that's what the missus wants, that's what she gets."

I picked up the book, returned it to the bookshelf, and hurried out of the library, sick to my stomach.

"Hold up," Theo said, as he darted after me.

I stopped in the grand drawing room. "We shouldn't talk about it here," I whispered, nodding my head toward the library, and desperate for a curative powder for my stomach.

"It's not about that." He came so close I stepped back.

"It's about the baptism. Do you think Catherine's well enough?" he probed. "It hasn't been a week since she gave birth."

Though I agreed with him, I bristled at his questioning my medical skills. "If she doesn't tire herself, she should be fine. Now, I have to get ready. We're meeting with the priest this afternoon."

"Yeah, sure." He hesitated. Something was on his mind.

"What?" I asked.

"Don't take this the wrong way. Matthew, I can understand, but you? Did Catherine explain why?"

My jaw must have dropped open. "Matthew?"

"I thought you knew."

"Catherine said her family wouldn't come to the island. And there was no one else. She never said Matthew was the godfather." Matthew as godfather seemed as incongruent as me as godmother.

He shook his head knowingly. "She didn't tell you, then."

"Tell me what? Is there a rift between her and her family?" That was the only reason I could think of for them not attending the baptism. The lake hadn't frozen over. There was plenty of room for guests.

He pulled me away from the library door toward the expanse of windows. "Catherine's family cut her off when she married William. She's from old Chicago money."

"And Matthew? Why him? Doesn't William have family he could ask to be godparents?"

"A mother and his uncle Henry, both dead, and a cousin he detests. Matthew and William grew up together on the streets of Chicago. Both were fatherless. Mothers worked in factories. They got into a lot of trouble. Petty stuff like shoplifting and brawling. Henry Thiery saved William from that life. He spent summers on the island, learning the logging business. Matthew tagged along. There's nothing Matthew wouldn't do for William. I'd say the same for William, but self-interest trumps everything for him, even loyalty."

And yet William tolerated Matthew's insubordination and hunting when he should be overseeing the loggers.

"Why do you dislike William so much? He lets you live in the cottage rent-free. Am I right?"

"Lets me?" Anger reddened his face. "He doesn't let me do anything. I pay for that privilege by being at his beck and call."

"Then why don't you leave?" Maybe he'd confide in me his real reason for living on this island.

"And go where?"

"Back to Chicago. Back to your newspaper work."

"There's nothing left for me there." His eyes went soft with pain.

What was he running from?

"I have to change before we leave for the church," I said.

He touched my arm. I felt the warmth of his fingers through the thin cloth. "Just be careful, Nellie. Don't get involved in their business."

Hearing my name from his lips caused a shiver that stayed with me longer than I wanted.

❧

After taking a curative powder, I donned my one good dress. I was still fuming with frustration.

The thought of standing in church, vowing fidelity to Hannah, with a man I could barely tolerate and who barely tolerated me, repulsed me.

What was one day in a lifetime of days? I told myself, staring at my wavy image in the warped mirror. Theo's ministrations had loosened my hair. I refastened my unruly mop, coiling it into a topknot. My hair was so like my mother's, thick and tightly curled, nearly impossible to tame. Except hers was black as night. My coppery hair was like my father's, if my vision in the library was to be trusted.

What had Irene's thoughts been as she stared at her image in the distorted mirror? I picked up the locket and opened it, gazing at her brilliant face.

Where would I be if Irene hadn't been murdered? In Chicago nursing the dying, watching them take their last breaths, as they clawed the air, turning blue, then black.

And wondering who my father was and why my mother came to an island named for what it wanted to be, not what it was—Harmony.

CHAPTER THIRTY

Matthew brooded as he flicked the reins, urging the horse over the snow-packed road.

If it weren't for the plug of chewing tobacco bulging from his cheek, he'd look like a proper gentleman in his black suit and overcoat, white starched shirt, and black tie. Apparently, he, like Mrs. Bucheim, would do anything for Catherine.

Catherine hadn't said a word since we left Ravenwood. Swaddled in a beaver coat and hat, she gazed at the bleak landscape with an anxious expression.

I, too, felt anxious. I'd agreed to tell the priest I'd recently converted to Catholicism. A poor liar, I feared he'd see through my deception.

Why hadn't I objected more vehemently?

As the church came into view, I gazed at the tall steeple, its spire lost in the thick gray clouds, portending more snow. A feeling of vertigo swept over me. I concentrated on my gloved hands until the sensation passed.

Matthew tied the horse to the post in front of the church, then put a blanket over the animal, before helping Catherine and me from the sleigh.

When we reached the church's door, I stared transfixed at the lintel above it. Chiseled into the white marble was the date 1889. The Harmonites had built this church. Not that I needed proof. Theo had told me they'd built the entire town.

What held me was the carved rose below the date, so distinctive I couldn't miss the resemblance. The rose's design matched the turret windows' roses, right down to their three-leafed stems. Father, son, and Holy Ghost?

Suddenly afraid, I whispered, "I can't go in there."

A memory, swift and sure, arose. *My mother sobbing. Bonneted birds flapping around her. I'm calling for my father. Where is he?*

"Nellie, c'mon. Father Quinn's waiting for us," Catherine's impatient voice lashed through the memory.

"You heard the missus." Matthew's breath was warm on my neck. I swatted at him.

"I'm going to be sick."

I ran stumbling through the snow to the side of the church. Crouching over, I vomited. When I was done, I wiped my mouth with my handkerchief, then slowly made my way to the church door. My head ached and my mouth tasted sour.

"Something the matter?" Matthew asked, with more compassion than I expected.

I shook my head afraid to speak, afraid to invoke the memory still pulsing under my skin. I stepped under the marble lintel, under the date that floated above the rose, as though time had no place here.

The church's simplicity confused me–whitewashed walls, rows of dark pews, and a plain altar. A crucifix hung behind the altar. Weren't Catholic churches crowded with saints and stained-glass windows? I caught the tinge of incense, spicy and disturbing.

A black-frocked stout man hurried unsteadily toward us. He was younger than I expected. Maybe in his forties. Whether it was his unsteady gait or the black stubble on his face, he looked unkempt.

"Catherine, you're looking none the worse for wear. How is the little one?" He took her hands in his.

"She's fine, Father. And you're looking your usual hearty self."

"That I am." He let go of Catherine's hands and turned toward Matthew.

"Matthew, it's good to see you in church." He smiled slyly, his message none too subtle.

Matthew shrugged. "Don't get used to it, Father."

Then, the priest turned to me. "You must be Nellie Lester," he said, his black eyes blacker than his hair, than his clothes. The white collar snapped me present, kept me from running out of the church into the cold air where I could breathe. As did his ruddy complexion and bulbous nose, splattered with broken capillaries–Bernie's description of the priest as a hard drinker visible.

"I'm pleased to meet me you," I answered, squirming under his gaze.

"Likewise. Now, if you would all follow me, please," he said. His black cassock flared, as he led us to the front of the church, veering left to an alcove that held the baptismal font.

"This is where Hannah's baptism will take place," he explained needlessly.

The priest turned his dark eyes on me. "Nellie, Catherine tells me you've recently converted. What church do you attend in Chicago?"

I gave Catherine a sharp look. "St. Joseph's." I named the only Catholic Church I'd ever been to. One of the ward nurses had married at St. Joseph's last spring.

I didn't think I fooled the priest. But he let it go and continued his instructions, talking quickly as though he was eager to be done.

"During the ceremony the parents and godparents will take vows. I'll ask you to renounce Satan and all evil. Then, you'll profess your faith and vow before God to raise the child as Catholic. Do you think you can do that?"

His black eyes fixed on me. I hesitated, aware of Catherine's stare. "Yes," I answered reluctantly. I assured myself that there was little chance I'd have to raise Hannah. As to the profession of faith, I viewed it as an acceptable white lie.

"Well, that's it, folks. I'll expect everyone here on Sunday for Mass, baptism to follow."

As we shuffled out of the alcove, the priest said, "Catherine, I need to speak to Nellie for a moment. Alone."

"Of course, Father. I'll be waiting in the sleigh. And remember what we talked about, Nellie."

He guided me to the front pew. "Father," I began, fully intending to confess my deceit and bow out of the baptism.

His hand trembled, as he put his finger to his full lips. "Wait until they leave." Was it alcohol or another disease that caused his tremors?

While we waited, I gazed at the gruesome image of Christ on the cross. Had Engel and the Harmonites erected the crucifix? Had my parents and I sat in this very pew, staring at Christ's agony? The memory of my calling for my father flickered. Something dreadful had happened in this church.

The door closed.

"If you're going to confess that you're not a Catholic, save your breath. Catherine is an awful liar. And you're worse." His bluntness surprised me.

"What could I do, Father? She has no one else," I pleaded.

"Just don't go blabbing about it and everything will be fine. Keep to your conversion story."

Though I bristled at the deception, I said, "So my not being Catholic isn't against your rules?"

"Sometimes rules have to be broken. But that's not what I want to talk to you about." He looked over his shoulder again. Satisfied we were alone, he leaned in. The faint scent of alcohol colored the air.

"Did you find anything of Irene's at the manor?"

Why was he concerned about Irene's belongings? "Just her peacock shawl."

"I see." He rubbed his whiskery chin. "And nothing else?"

"Why are you asking me this?"

"Did they put you in the turret room? The one with the lock on the outside?"

He knew about the lock on the outside of my room? I stared into his dark, fathomless eyes. Had Irene confided in him?

"Yes, that's the room I'm in. What's this about? If you know something about Irene, please tell me. I'm certain she was killed," I said impulsively.

"I heard it was an accident. What makes you think she was killed?"

I explained my theory that Irene hadn't fallen but had been pushed or bludgeoned with a rock. How the state of her body proved the perpetrator had buried her in a shallow grave.

"Hmm. I see what you mean."

I hadn't expected him to accept my explanation so readily. "Irene confided something in you, didn't she?" I probed.

He looked away, deciding whether to trust me with whatever Irene had told him. When he turned back, he said, "I'm only telling you this because if she was murdered, that changes things. But you have to promise me that what I tell you stays between us. Understand?"

I nodded.

"There was a diary." He pulled at his stiff collar.

"Irene kept a diary?"

"It wasn't hers. She found this diary at Ravenwood. She didn't say where. But something about the diary frightened her. The week before she disappeared, she came to see me to tell me she was leaving. She couldn't stay at Ravenwood any longer. She said it was an evil house. I told her I'd perform an exorcism. She laughed. 'It's not just the house, Father,' she said. 'It's the island. It's cursed. It's like there's a darkness surrounding it.' That was the last time I saw her. And if she was murdered, as you claim, maybe this diary had something to do with it."

What the priest said went contrary to what Catherine told me, that Irene left because she cast her out. Which was the truth?

"Did she say anything else? Like whose diary it was?"

At the creak of the church door, we both looked back. Matthew strode up the aisle. "Father, the missus is feeling poorly. We have to go."

Father Quinn sprung up from the pew, as though he'd been caught drinking the communion wine. "Of course. We can't have the mother sick before the baptism."

When I stepped up into the sleigh, Catherine didn't look poorly. "What did Father Quinn want?" she asked suspiciously.

"My reassurance that I'd converted."

"And did you give it to him?"

"What do you think?" *You're not the only one who can dissemble,* I thought.

Satisfied, she sat back on the leather seat and closed her eyes.

As the sleigh moved through the wintery landscape, I ruminated over what the priest had told me. What was in this mysterious diary that had frightened Irene? And that made her believe Ravenwood Manor was evil and the island cursed? *It's like there's a darkness surrounding it.*

When we arrived at the manor, a letter and a telegram rested on the hall table. All I glimpsed was a Chicago address and the name Mrs. Margaret Newell. Catherine snatched the letter and telegram and bustled up the stairs, still wearing her snowy boots.

I headed for the kitchen, wanting a warm drink before I headed to my room in search of this diary.

"Keep your coat on," Mrs. Bucheim said, as she lowered a covered dish into a large basket. "Mr. William sent a logger to bring you to the mill. He's in the barn waiting on you."

"Did he say why? Is someone hurt?"

"I guess you'll find out when you get there." She placed a white cloth over the basket. "Give Mr. William the basket. And tell him the missus would like him home tonight."

"Let me get my medical bag." I dashed to my room to grab it. My search for the diary would have to wait.

The logger was seated at the kitchen table when I entered the kitchen. Mrs. Bucheim must have summoned him from the barn. I recognized him from the tavern. He was the logger who'd tried to calm Abe.

He tipped his hat and stood. "The wagon's out back, miss," he said.

CHAPTER THIRTY-ONE

From William's aggressive stare, my summoning to his office had nothing to do with an injured logger and everything to do with me.

Sensing William's displeasure, the logger stood sheepishly by the door.

"Put the basket on the table in the other room," William barked at him. "Then head back to the camp. I'll see to Miss Lester."

I didn't like the way he spoke. Nor did I like the nearly empty whiskey bottle on his desk and the smudged glass beside it.

Once the logger left, I sat down in one of the bank chairs, holding the medical bag on my lap. Something was different. No grinding noise, no high-pitched saw. The sawmill was quiet and there was a faint burning smell.

"Is someone hurt?" I asked. "I noticed the sawmill isn't running."

He put his elbows on the desk and lurched forward. "I'd sack you right now, if it wasn't for this damn baptism."

I wasn't sure what I'd done to garner firing. I thought we'd settled our differences.

"Sack me? I don't understand," I answered, my eyes drawn to the small portrait of Henry Thiery that hung on the wall behind William. It was impossible to escape the man's image. Did William feel his beady eyes judging him every day?

The last time I was here, I'd been unconscious in the adjacent room and had little memory of William's office. A crowded, smoky place littered with William's possessions–tin coffeepot, enamel cups, ashtray, pipe, file cabinets, newspapers, charts, ledgers, and a rifle standing in the corner.

"You don't understand? You must think I'm an idiot. Is that what you think, Miss Lester. That I'm an idiot? I asked you to examine Irene's body and report back to me. Not go shooting off your mouth to Wilkins about your murder theories. And what the hell were you doing snooping around the logging site? You could have been killed."

His usual self-control was gone, most likely attributable to the whiskey. Not the first of the day judging by his nasty flush, unsteady hand, and blurry eyes. William didn't strike me as a heavy drinker. Something had set him off. I hoped that something wasn't me.

I bit my lip so hard I tasted blood. Then I said what was on my mind anyway. "Theo agrees with me," I told him, purposely not mentioning my discovery of Irene's locket.

"I should send him packing too. That meddling weasel–always sniffing around Catherine with his potions."

Never argue with a drunk. Matron's words came back to me.

"I admit it was wrong of me not to come to you first." I shooed away matron's words. I had to make William see reason. "But you can't argue with the facts. Irene's body was intact. For that to be the case, she had to have been buried. Whoever buried her killed her."

He was holding the glass so tightly his knuckles were white. "Wilkins thinks that's hogwash. Did you find anything else in your examination of her body?"

So, Wilkins had dismissed my theory. "No, but it was a cursory examination. An autopsy might reveal more."

"No one's cutting her up. Wilkins assured me of that."

Why was he so set against an autopsy? Then it hit me. Was he afraid Irene had been pregnant? Or did he know she was? Even if she was, there was no way to prove the child was his.

I tried to hide the tidal wave of emotions churning inside me. An inconvenient pregnancy was a stronger motive for murder than an affair. Now I understood his anger. Not only had I called into question Irene's manner of death, I'd pleaded with Wilkins to investigate it.

"Nellie." His raised voice broke through my thoughts. "Did you hear what I said?"

"I'm sorry, no."

"I'm giving you two weeks' notice." He finished the whiskey in his glass.

The unfairness of it rankled me. "I've done everything you've asked of me, even lying to a priest, so you could have a godmother for Hannah. Please, let me stay until February." I had to stay. Two weeks wasn't enough time to find out what happened to John Engel, my father.

He went quiet.

The only sounds were the wind rattling the windows and the fire crackling in the woodstove. Slowly, he got up and walked around the desk.

His large body loomed over me, blocking my way to the door. I shifted in my chair, calculating if I could make it to the door before he grabbed me.

But he didn't grab me.

He sat on the edge of the desk, a nasty grin on his handsome face, so close I could smell his musky odor.

"I knew girls like you in school. Always lording it over the rest of us chumps, with your brains and smart answers. Well, this isn't school." He lifted my chin, so I had to look into his hard green eyes.

This was the street thug Theo had described. I thought of Irene's shattered skull. For the first time, I was afraid of him.

"Don't look so scared. I'm not going to hurt you."

Someone knocked on the door. He pulled his hand away and returned to his chair behind the desk.

"Yeah, come in."

A grizzled logger sauntered into the room. His skin was as gray as his hair.

"Should be up and running by morning, Mr. Thiery," he said.

"What was wrong with it?" William asked impatiently.

"The blade got loose. The problem is, it's damaged. Lucky no one was hurt."

"Didn't you check the blade?"

"Yes, sir. Checked it this morning. It was nice and tight." He put his head down. "Only way this could have happened was if someone messed with the blade."

William slammed his fist down on the desk so hard, some of the papers slid onto the floor. "Find out who did it. And the mill better be up and running by morning."

The logger couldn't get out the door fast enough.

I was about to deliver Catherine's message, but William spoke first.

"Lyman will take you back to Ravenwood. Tell Catherine there's a problem at the mill. I won't be home tonight."

"Is there anything I can do to help?" He looked so defeated, my heart softened toward him.

"You've done enough," he replied sarcastically. "You've got two weeks."

My sympathy faded.

As I moved toward the door, he said, "By the way, Charlie made it. But his logging days are over. The doc on the mainland amputated his leg."

Did I really expect a modicum of gratitude? Two weeks had to be enough.

CHAPTER THIRTY-TWO

Weary and discouraged, I dragged myself into the kitchen. Though it was not quite nine, the manor seemed preternaturally quiet.

Mrs. Bucheim had left a note on the kitchen table. *Dinner is on the stove. Turn off the lamp when you're done. I'll clean the dishes in the morning.*

"Yes, ma'am," I murmured, moving toward the woodstove, surprised by her note's thoughtfulness. A crack in her stern façade or duty? I was too tired to care.

When I raised the pot's lid, I was pleasantly surprised. It was chicken stew. Floating in the golden gravy were chunks of chicken, carrots, onions, turnips, and potatoes.

I stoked the woodstove's fire and warmed the stew. While I waited, I tore off a piece of wheat bread. As I chewed, I ruminated on my predicament. I had two weeks. There was nothing more I could do to find Irene's killer.

I'd come to the island to find out about my mother's past and her relationship to the man in the photograph. If my visions were memories, and I had come to believe they were, then that man was my father, John Engel. From now on, I was going to devote my every minute to finding out what happened to him. If I could discover his fate, then maybe I'd understand why my mother had kept his identity from me. Though, I wasn't sure what my next step should be.

The aroma of the stew filled the kitchen, interrupting my thoughts. I ate with relish. It was the first meal I'd enjoyed since arriving at Ravenwood. Not just because the stew was savory, but because I ate alone, without Mrs. Bucheim's watchful presence and Matthew's barely contained hostility.

Hang Mrs. Bucheim and her rules, I mused, gathering my dirty dishes. No one wants to face dirty dishes in the morning—the image of her gnarled hands rising. I pumped water into the washbasin and washed and dried my dishes.

The mindlessness of the domestic act shifted my thoughts to the diary. Whose was it? And why had it frightened Irene? Could it possibly have belonged to one of the Harmonites?

Logic told me it was unlikely it was Catherine's or Mrs. Bucheim's. Neither would leave a diary lying around for Irene to find. That left someone from Henry Thiery's or Caleb Engel's time. If it was from Engel's time, it might reveal something about the fate of the Harmonites and my father.

I'd start with the turret room. If that proved fruitless, I'd return to the library. After that, I wasn't sure where I'd look. There were so many places a diary could be hidden in this immense house.

❧

My room was as I'd left it—bed unmade, my clothes on the chair covering my father's book, the useless key on the dresser. I placed my medical bag on the thin carpet, shut the drapes, and began my search.

As I scoured the room, I wondered what made the priest think the diary was still in the house? Irene could have taken it with her when she left. Her belongings had yet to be found. Considering what she told Father Quinn about the diary's disturbing contents, she could have also left it behind.

There were no hidden compartments in the dresser drawers, no loose floorboards, and nothing under the mattress. That left under the bed. I placed the lamp on the floor, knelt beside the bed, and peered underneath. The thick layer of dust covering the wood floor had been disturbed, and not by a broom nor by me.

I got up and moved the bed, then walked over the floorboards. One creaked. Grabbing one of my medical tools, I pried the floorboard up. A hidden compartment appeared. It was large enough to hide several diaries, but it was empty. Sitting back on my heels, I wondered if this was where Irene had found the diary? A shiver ran through me as I gazed at the empty compartment. Only desperation or fear would compel someone to hide a diary here.

I replaced the floorboard, moved the bed back and paced the room, my mind too anxious to settle. Two more weeks, barely enough time to sift through the vast library, let alone the entire manor for a diary that may or may not have belonged to a Harmonite, that may or may not reveal my father's fate, that may or may not even be here.

I opened the curtains. Matthew's cottage was dark. William was at the mill, and Catherine and Mrs. Bucheim were asleep. No chance of being caught.

Holding the lamp aloft, I tiptoed down the steep spiral stairs to the landing. I waited. All quiet. Then I made my way down the main staircase, through the hallway, past the drawing room, and into the library.

The cold room seemed omniscient, the books sentient with secrets. Had my parents been in this room? In this house? I was beginning to see Ravenwood as a palimpsest, layered in the past, each layer telling a different story. I only had to strip away the layers to lay bare the truth.

Strumming with energy, I pulled the library ladder to the arts section and started my search. I reasoned that the diary was most likely a thin leather book, no bigger than ten inches by eight inches, and with no title on its spine.

Surprisingly, there were many such books: sketchbooks, handwritten books of poetry, and books containing sheet music.

Curious, I pulled out one, expecting to see hymns. Instead, I found music by Schubert, Debussy, Chopin, and Beethoven. Music Engel deemed worthy of Christ's kingdom on earth?

My enthusiasm and energy were starting to lag. It was well after midnight. I had one more wall of books. I climbed the ladder and resumed my search.

As I slid a promising looking book from the top shelf, a growl startled me. I dropped the book and twisted around too quickly, causing the ladder to sway.

Matthew and the cur lurked in the doorway, their dark shadows thrown across the library floor.

"What do you think you're doing?" Matthew asked menacingly. "William doesn't like anyone going through his things." He'd dressed hastily. His shirttail hung out of his trousers, his boots were unlaced, and his hair stuck up around his head.

"Please curb your dog." At the sound of my voice, the dog lunged at the ladder, jumping frantically, trying to get at me. I clung to the bookshelves, as the ladder teetered.

"Samson, come." The dog obeyed and slunk to his side but remained alert.

Cautiously, I descended the ladder, keeping my eye on the dog. When I reached the bottom, I picked up the scattered papers and shoved them into the leather binder.

"I couldn't sleep. I wanted something to read," I explained.

From his smirk, I knew he didn't believe me.

"Now, if you don't mind, I'm going to bed." I picked up the lamp and walked toward the door.

"Not so fast," he said, moving in front of me. The dog snarled. "I don't know what you're doing in here at this hour. But if you don't want to get fired, you'd better quit it. I'm telling you this for your own good." A note of sincerity I hadn't expected tinged his words.

"I'm afraid it's too late for that," I replied, not trusting his sudden change in attitude toward me.

"What do you mean?"

"William sacked me this evening. I've got two weeks."

"And you thought you'd help yourself to his books?" He gazed at the book I was holding to my chest.

I knew it was a mistake to trust him.

"I'm not a thief. I can buy my own books."

He held out his hand. I thrust the binder at him. "Why do you dislike me?" I asked, my face burning with shame.

"You're too much like the other one. Sticking her nose where it doesn't belong. Look what happened to her."

Was that a veiled threat? I wondered as I walked around him, my heart wild in my chest.

Once inside the turret room, I inhaled deeply as though emerging from under water. My hands trembled as I undressed, washed, and donned my nightgown. With care I brushed and braided my difficult hair, careful not to touch my wound.

As a nurse, I'd faced many difficult and menacing men. But Matthew terrorized me. How far would he go to protect the Thierys? Would it include murder?

After I turned off the lamp, I closed my eyes and kept my back to the dresser, afraid to evoke the presence. Afraid it wouldn't come if I did.

In my dream I hear footsteps on the spiral staircase, coming closer and closer. With a panic akin to drowning, I realize I've forgotten to shove the chair under the door. Before I can grab the chair, a woman walks in and hovers by my bed.

Her blond hair flows down her back like a sun-touched river, glistening with yellow leaves, Irene's locket around her neck. She's ethereal in her white hospital gown.

"Clara?" I say, astonished she's alive.

"Don't give up on me," she says. Specks of blood dot her chin and mouth.

I can still save her. I rise from my bed and take her hand.

Cold, she's so cold.

"I won't give up," I whisper, afraid someone will hear me and warn me of the dangers of false hope.

Her large eyes won't leave me, as I fetch my medical bag.

"You're too late," she gasps, blood now frothing from her mouth, her face turning blue, as she rakes the air in that macabre dance I know too well.

"It's not too late," I say, desperate to save her.

But I fumble with the bag. My hands gnarled like Mrs. Bucheim's. I'm breathing too hard as I dive into the bag and grab a glass bottle. It shatters in my hands. There's blood everywhere. I can't stop bleeding. The bitter odor of laudanum fills my lungs.

Clara turns her back to me.

"No," I say.

But it's no longer Clara, her blond hair now dark like Irene's. Blood oozes from her skull, down her neck and onto the white hospital gown that's now crimson.

When she turns around, I brace myself, expecting to see Irene's face.

It's not Irene. It's my mother.

"Why did you leave me alone?" she says, her dark eyes kinder than I deserve.

§

The dream dissolved and my mother with it. I opened my eyes and lay on the hard bed, sobbing.

Did I really think I could escape the memory of that awful night?

In the quivering light of the contagion ward, I'd sat by Clara's bedside, spooning laudanum into her gasping mouth, believing I could save her or at least ease her death. While at that same time in our tiny apartment on Taylor Street, my mother had clutched at her heart and died alone.

CHAPTER THIRTY-THREE

I'd overslept. Last night's dream still with me as I fashioned my hair into a chignon, I couldn't shake the disturbing image of Clara, transforming into Irene and Irene into my mother. Each transformation more terrifying than the last.

"Don't give up on me," Clara had pleaded. I hadn't.

Maybe the dream was telling me not to give up on finding Irene's killer. If I didn't give up, if I pursued Irene's killer, could I atone for the guilt plaguing me over my mother's lonely death?

"Why did you leave me alone?" My mother's words like a slender knife in my heart.

But then, Clara had said, "You're too late." Too late for what?

I shook my achy head. When did I start putting stock in dreams? And when did I start believing in visions and nightly apparitions, expecting a presence I believed was my mother? Since coming to this island that Irene called cursed.

I gazed at my blurry image in the tarnished mirror. Like the image, I was starting to dissolve, my edges no longer sharp and defined.

Dreading the day ahead, I rubbed at a stain on the bodice of my good black dress. It would have to do for the baptism. Before leaving the room, I took a jar of healing salve from my medical bag. A peace offering for Mrs. Bucheim. I'd wear her down with kindness.

Then I made my way down the spiral stairs. When I reached the landing, I heard the soft murmur of voices coming from the Thierys' bedroom. I hurried down the main staircase.

Despite my best intentions, I glanced at the girl's death portrait. My heart thundered in my chest. Her face was gone, only her hair remained. I looked up and down the stairs. No one was watching. I ran my finger over the empty space. The canvas felt damp and had a putrid smell. Someone was trying to frighten me. But for what purpose?

Unsettled, I headed to the kitchen.

A flushed and frantic Mrs. Bucheim was stirring a pan of eggs. Another pan was sizzling with potatoes, and biscuits were baking.

From the empty plates in the sink, I guessed she and Matthew had already eaten. Was the altered portrait Matthew's work?

"I'm just going to have coffee and a biscuit this morning," I said, dropping in a chair, exhausted from lack of sleep, and still shaken by the portrait.

"The missus wants you in the dining room. You're to have breakfast with her and her cousin, Mrs. Newell," she barked at me, emptying the potatoes onto a silver platter. "She arrived last night. Watch yourself with that one."

That explained yesterday's telegram. I was glad that Catherine would have family with her on this momentous day.

"What do you mean?" I inquired.

"You'll see soon enough. But knowing you, maybe I should be warning her."

Before I left the kitchen, I placed the jar of healing salve on the counter.

"For your hands." I fully expected her to reject my offering.

She directed her raven eyes on it, humphed, and continued stirring the eggs.

Maternal cousins, Margaret Newell was as different from Catherine as salt is from pepper—Margaret being the pepper and Catherine the salt.

Though Mrs. Newell shared Catherine's wavy auburn hair, hazel eyes, and petite frame, the resemblance ended there. Her clothes were as direct and unvarnished as her manner. She wore a deep burgundy walking suit, a single strand of pearls, and sturdy boots. She took her coffee black, declared herself a suffragette within the first thirty minutes of conversation, and thankfully had rescued me from being Hannah's godmother.

I liked her instantly.

"So, you're the other nurse," Mrs. Newell said, as she spooned scrambled eggs onto her plate.

Blue-patterned china, silver cutlery, and linen napkins graced the table. Probably Catherine's way of impressing her cousin, who would report back to Catherine's family.

How was I to answer that? I nodded.

"Did Cathy tell you I recommended Irene to her? She nursed my mother in her last days. A lovely girl, though a little on the fanciful side for my tastes. But her heart was in the right place. A tragedy what happened to her."

"Madge, do we have to talk about her on Hannah's day?" Catherine fidgeted with her silverware. She'd yet to touch her food. She kept sipping her coffee and stirring in more cream.

"I don't want to spoil your day. But I do feel some responsibility for her death." She turned toward me. "How did she die? Cathy was rather vague on the details."

If Catherine stared at me any harder, I'd turn into a pillar of salt. "I don't know that it's my place to say."

Mrs. Newell looked from me to Catherine, whose glare could cut through metal. "Cathy? What's going on?"

"Why do you have to be this way?" Catherine accused Mrs. Newell. "I'm glad you're here. But can we not talk about Irene?" She pushed back her chair and stood. "Please finish your breakfast. I must feed Hannah and get ready."

"Cathy, I'm sorry if I upset you. I didn't mean to," Mrs. Newell called after her.

We listened to Catherine's footsteps as they retreated down the hallway.

"I sometimes forget how sensitive and high-strung Cathy is," Mrs. Newell said. "I expect you know that about her."

I nodded again, not sure what to say. I'd only seen the neurotic, unstable side of Catherine.

Mrs. Newell leaned in as if someone was lurking in the hallway. "How did Irene die? Cathy said it was an accidental fall. Something about her walking in the woods and her leaving a note saying she was returning to Chicago. That doesn't sound like Irene. She never shirked her responsibility to my mother. Even after her fiancé died, she showed up the next day. I was impressed by what she said when I told her to take the day off. 'We must tend to the living. They need us more than the dead.' The Irene I knew would never leave her patient."

What difference did it make if I told Mrs. Newell my suspicions about Irene's death? I'd already been fired. There was nothing more Catherine or William could do to me.

"I believe Irene was killed. It might have been accidental. Someone could have shoved her and she fell and hit her head on a rock. Or," I hesitated, what Pandora's box was I opening? Mrs. Newell was a harridan, a crusader. Maybe I could get her on my side, Irene's side. "Or someone attacked her, hit her on the back of the head. One of the loggers found her body when they opened a new logging section."

"You think she was murdered, don't you?"

Her discerning gaze was unnerving.

"Yes. That's what I think."

"And you've told William but not Cathy?" She was assessing the situation.

"Since Hannah's birth, Catherine has been in a fragile state. Irene's death hit her very hard."

"And what did William say?"

"He believes it was an accident. And the sheriff is leaning that way too." I explained to her the condition of Irene's body and why I thought she'd been buried. She listened attentively.

"Do you know of any reason someone would kill Irene?" she asked.

I wasn't about to share my speculation that William and Irene had had an affair and that she might have been pregnant.

I shook my head.

"Mrs. Newell, you seemed to have known Irene quite well. Do you know if she had any next of kin? Someone needs to tell them of her death and claim her body for burial."

"Irene told me both her parents were dead and she had no siblings. And her fiancé died in the war. I think that was part of the reason she was such a devoted nurse. Her patients were her family."

"I was afraid that was the case." So, no one would claim Irene's body. She'd be buried in a pauper's grave.

"Where's her body now?" Mrs. Newell asked.

"The sheriff took it. The coroner needs to make a final determination about the cause of death. If the body's not claimed in two weeks, she'll be buried in a pauper's grave."

"Oh, no. I can't have that. Give me the name of the sheriff. I'll talk to William about transporting Irene's body to Chicago and burying her there. She deserves better than a pauper's grave."

"Thank you." Relief flooded through me.

"Now, I'd better go see Cathy." Mrs. Newell pushed her empty plate away. "When will you be heading back to Chicago?"

"In two weeks." Sooner than I wanted.

She slipped a card from her suit pocket and handed it to me. "The suffrage movement could use a woman like you. When you return to Chicago, stop by the Women's Equality League. The address is on the card." She smiled broadly.

"I just might do that," I replied, wondering what she meant by a woman like me.

CHAPTER THIRTY-FOUR

As I gazed at the group posed for the baptismal photograph, it struck me that one of them could be a murderer. With the exception of Mrs. Newell, and possibly Father Quinn, they all had a motive to murder Irene.

"Catherine, please tilt Hannah forward so we can see her pretty face," George Orr directed. Besides being the postmaster, market proprietor, and jailer, he was the town photographer. He'd arrived at Ravenwood toting a camera and tripod that looked as weathered as him. His pipe firmly planted in his mouth like an extra appendage.

Orr's seating arrangement resembled a wedding photograph. On William's side were Matthew and Father Quinn. On Catherine's side were Mrs. Newell and Mrs. Bucheim.

Everyone but Catherine wore a look of forbearance. She seemed unusually subdued, which worried me. Was this the calm before the storm?

This morning when I'd examined her, all her vitals were normal. But she had a vacant look as if she'd crawled down a deep dark hole and was content to stay there. Laudanum?

In contrast to Catherine's stillness, William's leg kept bouncing up and down. Twice Mr. Orr had politely asked him to keep still.

After Catherine adjusted Hannah in her arms, Orr said, "Good, now don't move."

Pleased with everyone's pose, he moved to the camera, which was perched on the tripod. Like a magic trick, his head disappeared under the black cloth.

"Mr. Orr is a man of many talents," I whispered to Theo, who stood next to me languidly sipping a whiskey. Despite my misgivings about Theo, I felt pulled to him. For the baptismal celebration, he was decked out like a dandy in a natty suit, complete with a gold pocket square, white stiff-collared shirt, gold stickpin, and polished black boots. Clothes from his former life.

"What's the old saying? 'A jack of all trades is a master of none, but oftentimes better than a master of one.' I guess that applies to many islanders," Theo quipped.

"Do you know how old he is?" With admiration and amazement, I'd watched him set up his camera and haul chairs from the dining room to the great room. He moved like a thirty-year-old.

"If I had to guess. I'd say early fifties."

"Has he always lived on the island?" I asked, none too subtly.

Theo cocked his head and smiled. "He wasn't here when the Harmonites lived here. If that's what you're asking."

Before I could respond, Orr bellowed from under the black cloth. "Everyone hold still." Then he squeezed the black rubber bulb.

My attention was drawn back to the motley group: Catherine beautiful but vacant in her emerald velvet dress, the fine lace collar as fragile as her. Mrs. Newell sturdy and forthright in her burgundy suit. Her finishing school breeding evident in her crossed ankles. Father Quinn's pleasant flushed expression, hands folded as if in prayer. Mrs. Bucheim clad in stern black, barely able to manage a smile. William's and Matthew's dark suits matched their stern and forbearing expressions. William's impatient fury manifested in his curled fist.

"Now one more photograph with everyone," Orr said.

My heart sank, too aware of my shabby schoolmarm dress and hastily done hair.

"I'd like the rest of you to stand behind the baptismal party." Mr. Orr beckoned us with his hand.

Bernie, who'd been observing from the room's threshold, walked toward the seated group, tugging on her black silk dress that was a size too small and several years out of fashion. She'd been helping Mrs. Bucheim set up the food platters in the dining room.

When I didn't move, Theo touched my elbow. A shiver ran through me. "He means you too, Nellie."

Reluctantly, I joined the group, feeling like a fraud. I had no business being in this photograph. I had no deep or lasting relationship with the Thierys. In two weeks, they'd never see me again.

"Miss Lester, I'd like you in the middle," Orr said. "Doc and Bernie on either side of her. Good. Okay, hold that pose."

He dashed back to his camera and snuggled under the black cloth. "Can you manage a wee smile, Miss Lester? It's not a funeral."

He hadn't asked William or Matthew to smile. But I complied.

Hannah let out a hiccup and everyone laughed. "Miss Hannah, no more movements please," Orr joked. "Ready. Hold still." He pressed the black bulb.

When Mr. Orr emerged from under the black cloth, he clapped his hands. "Now let's eat."

"That wasn't so bad, was it?" Theo teased me.

I smiled weakly and walked to the dining room. My head was throbbing and a queer feeling had come over me. Had I just had my photograph taken with a murderer?

❧

Outside, the light was fading. The lamps cast a warm yellow glow around the grand drawing room making the room cozier, as did the burning hearth.

Balancing my plate on my lap, I sat on the leather sofa too cognizant of the dead animals' disconcerting stares. I'd allowed myself one glass of whiskey punch at Bernie's urging.

As though Bernie could read my discomfort, she'd said, "You'll need it. Only way I can abide these shindigs."

After piling her plate with slabs of beef, potatoes, and root vegetables from the buffet table, she'd followed me from the dining room to the drawing room and plopped down next to me on the sofa, causing a whoosh of air to escape.

"Have you been to many parties at Ravenwood?" I asked idly, watching Father Quinn, who was standing by the fireplace, plate in hand, engrossed in a conversation with Mrs. Newell and Theo. I wanted to get him alone to discuss the diary. Mrs. Newell appeared to be doing most of the talking. Like myna birds, the men nodded in unison.

"Not since William took over. When old Henry Thiery ran it, he had a Christmas and New Year's party every year. He invited everyone on the island except the loggers. He drew the line with them. Though many of them spent the holidays with family." Bernie looked around the room. "This room would be decorated to the hilt. Mr. Thiery spared no expense on food. If you know what I mean."

I shrugged my shoulders noncommittally. I wasn't about to comment on Mrs. Bucheim's cooking.

Bernie shifted her bulk. "I heard you were attacked at the logging camp. Do you know who did it?"

I wondered who told her. Mrs. Bucheim, complaining about my careless ways or one of the loggers who frequented The Carp?

If she'd heard I was attacked, then she must know I didn't see the attacker. "I never saw him. He hit me from behind." I placed my half-eaten plate of food on the side table. The heavy meat and potatoes felt like lead in my stomach.

I waited for her to chastise me. "Some of the loggers said you were snooping around where Irene's body was found."

Bernie was pumping me for information, more grist for the tavern's gossip mill.

"I've been thinking about what you said the other day," I said, abruptly changing the subject. "That Irene had William wrapped around her finger. Are you sure you didn't see something between them?"

She barked out a laugh that stopped the conversations momentarily. "No, ma'am. Even if I did, do you think I'd tell you? No offense, but I know what side my bread's buttered on." With much effort, she heaved herself off the sofa. "Are you done with your plate?"

"Yes."

"Let me take it to the kitchen for you."

Before I could protest, she snatched my plate and headed out of the room. Like me, she teetered between staff and invited guest. But unlike me, Bernie knew when to keep her mouth shut.

I had to find a way to get Father Quinn alone. Catherine had already retired with Hannah. Soon the others would be leaving. Empty plates scattered the room. William and Matthew stood by the windows smoking cigars.

As I studied them, I noticed how similar they were–big, dark-haired men with broad chests and shoulders. Though William appeared more refined. I pictured them running the streets of Chicago together. Fatherless boys in need of a steady hand. Each having the other's back.

"Miss Lester, you look a million miles away."

I looked up. I'd been so lost in thought I hadn't seen Father Quinn extricate himself from Mrs. Newell.

"I'm afraid I was. Can I speak with you a moment in the library. It's of a personal nature."

"Of course."

Not wanting to draw undue attention to us, I didn't close the library's pocket doors. Mrs. Bucheim had left a lamp burning on the library table and the fire was stoked.

"Impressive collection," the priest said, taking in the walls of books. "Now what's on your mind?"

"I searched my bedroom and almost all of the library for the diary. But I didn't find it. Was there anything else Irene said about it? Anything that might help me find it?"

He thought for a moment, rubbing his hand over his florid cheeks. "She did say it was a woman's diary. Did I mention that?"

"No, you didn't. Did she say when the diary was written?" He seemed more interested in the books along the walls than answering my questions.

"I guess I should have asked her more questions."

He walked toward the bookshelves on the far wall and pulled out a book. "Moroccan leather, if I'm not mistaken. Quite a handsome book."

I joined him. "Father, is there something you're not telling me?" I was convinced he was holding something back. He'd asked me to search for the diary and now he was being coy.

"I've told you all I could." He returned the book to the shelf.

All he could? Or all he knew?

"I'm going to keep looking for the diary. Whatever you're not telling me, I'll eventually find out."

A sudden commotion of raised voices erupted in the next room. We both looked toward the door where Bernie stood red-faced and panting.

"Nellie, you'd better come quick. Doc says you're to get your medical bag. It's Abe. He's beat awful bad."

CHAPTER THIRTY-FIVE

Abe was unrecognizable, his face a pulpy mess. Blood streamed down from a deep cut over his left eye. His other eye was swollen shut, the lid a nasty purplish blue. From the way he awkwardly held his right arm, I thought it might be broken.

Theo picked up a dishcloth and pressed it to the cut. His coat was thrown over a chair and his sleeves were rolled up. "Give me a hand, Nellie. We'll need hot water."

I placed a pan of water on the stove, then I plucked Mrs. Bucheim's apron from the kitchen hook and put it on.

"What happened?" I asked William, who was glaring at Abe as though he wanted to continue the beating.

"One of the loggers caught him spiking a tree. It was him who was sabotaging our operation. You murdering bastard," William shouted. "You'll hang for this."

Matthew leaned against the sink counter, his hands gripping the counter's edge, his knuckles bruised and bloodied with rage, saying nothing.

"No one was supposed to die," Abe mumbled through his swollen lips. His black coat shined with blood. A metallic smell filled the warm kitchen.

"Can we just concentrate on treating the man?" Theo said in frustration. "There's time for recriminations later. William, why don't you and Matthew wait in the drawing room? I'll let you know when we're finished."

"Just get it done," William snapped, then stomped out of the kitchen.

Matthew pushed away from the counter and headed for the door. When he reached Abe, he sucker punched him in his right shoulder. Abe let out a strangled cry.

"Was that necessary?" I said to Matthew.

"It was him that attacked you, missy. He admitted it," Matthew answered.

"C'mon, Matt," William called from the hallway, where he'd been watching. "He'll get worse than that when the law gets ahold of him."

After they left, Theo said, "Do you have something in your bag to close the wound?"

"I have needles and silk sutures. Have you examined his arm?"

"His shoulder is dislocated."

"It hurts like the devil," Abe replied.

Without a word, Theo moved behind Abe.

"What are you doing?" Abe asked, looking over his shoulder in alarm.

"I'm going to count to three," Theo explained. "Now take in a deep breath, one, two." Before he said three, he popped the shoulder back in place.

"Damn you," Abe cried out.

"Try moving it," Theo directed him.

Gingerly, he moved his arm.

"Okay, let's see to that cut."

"Is it true? Did you attack me?" I asked, as I put the basin of hot water on the table.

He hung his head. "I'm sorry. I saw you pick something up from the ground. I thought you found one of my spikes. I didn't mean to hit you that hard."

"You didn't mean to hit her that hard? You fool, you knocked her unconscious. You could have killed her," Theo answered angrily.

Grudgingly, I took a clean washcloth from the kitchen drawer, submerged it in the hot water, and started cleaning the blood from Abe's face, trying unsuccessfully to tamp down my resentment. Theo was right. He could have killed me.

"Doc, you gotta help me," Abe begged, grabbing Theo's shirtsleeve. "They want to fix me up for the murder of that nurse. I didn't do it. Mr. Thiery and Matthew are saying she saw me spiking trees and I killed her, so she wouldn't talk. That's what they're going to tell the sheriff."

How quickly William had changed his mind about Irene's death being an accident, now that he had someone to blame for her murder.

"Did she see you spiking trees?" I asked, dropping the cloth into the basin. The water turned pink with his blood. He could have panicked, killed her, and buried her body, unaware William would be logging in that area next. He was capable of violence. Even after he'd inadvertently caused Sam's death, he'd continued his sabotage.

"When I found her body, I didn't even know who she was. Scared me to death. Her face all frozen. Eyes staring at me."

Theo reached into my medical bag and started rummaging around.

"Let me get the needle and sutures for you," I said.

My normally organized medical bag was in disarray, so it took me a few minutes to locate the items from the bottom of the bag.

After I prepared the needle, I handed it to Theo.

As I watched him suture Abe's gash, I wondered about Abe's motives for the sabotage.

"Why did you vandalize the logging operation? Did someone pay you?" I asked.

Abe choked out a laugh. His face was a grimace of pain. "Pay me? Yeah, you whites think everything is about money. This island was the Odawas' land first. When the Timber Baron is done with it, there'll be nothing left to it, except dirt."

How had I missed it? It was writ large in his sharp nose, high cheekbones, burnished skin, and thick, black straight hair. Abe was a Native.

Theo wiped his hands on a kitchen cloth, then threw it down in disgust. "You killed Sam. And you almost killed Charlie. You think that justifies what you did?"

"What do you know?" Abe spat at him. "No one killed your people and took your land. The Odawas lived here for hundreds of years. Then you whites came to destroy it. One day your destruction will destroy you."

His fierceness dissolved into profound sorrow.

"Tell me the truth, Abe. Did you kill Irene?" Did I really expect a man so bent on revenge at any cost to answer me truthfully?

"I'm telling you, I never seen her before that day I found her body." He stared at me, his eyes dark and unflinching. "You were right, though. She was buried in a shallow grave. But no one's going to believe me. Just like they don't believe you. William Thiery has everything fit up nice and tight."

"Nellie, the disinfectant," Theo demanded. "I'm sick of listening to his lies."

I dug into my bag, my eyes fixed on Abe, weighing the truthfulness of his denial. My hand grasped a glass bottle. I looked down. I was holding the bottle of laudanum. It was empty.

Shaken, I shoved the laudanum bottle back into the medical bag before Theo saw it, then retrieved the disinfectant. Someone had snuck into my room and slipped the empty bottle back in my bag. Why?

"Are you done with him?" William asked, as he came into the kitchen followed by Matthew and George Orr. "I need to send a telegram to the sheriff tonight. I want him outta here tomorrow."

"He's stitched up. See he doesn't get unstitched on the way to the jail," Theo warned.

"You do your job, Doc, and we'll do ours," William sneered at Theo. "Get up, you lying piece of shit."

Before Abe could stand, Matthew yanked him off the chair so hard it crashed to the floor. Abe pulled his arm free, then bolted for the back door. But Matthew was too quick. He grabbed him by his jacket and threw him against the mudroom wall. Abe grunted in pain.

"Where do you think you're going?" Matthew spat at him.

Holding Abe's right arm, Matthew shoved him through the mudroom door.

The slam of the door was like the sealing of Abe's fate.

After they left, I dumped the bloody water in the sink and wiped down the kitchen table with disinfectant.

Theo picked up the overturned chair, poured himself a mug of coffee, and sat down. "Do you believe him? That he didn't kill Irene?" he asked.

I was about to ask him the same question. "It makes sense that he might have killed her if she'd caught him sabotaging the operation. But I don't think he did it." I was too worked up to sit.

Theo cocked his tired head. "Based on what?" He took a gulp of coffee and wrinkled his nose at its bitter taste. I pushed the sugar bowl toward him.

"I watched his eyes when he denied it. He didn't look away." As a nurse, I'd learned to read people. I'd developed a sense about when they were lying.

"That just means he's a practiced liar. And I don't believe his spiel about protecting his native lands. This is about money. Someone is paying him to vandalize the logging."

His cynicism jarred me and said more about Theo than Abe. "Who would do that?"

"A competing operation. Timber supplies in the Midwest are dwindling. There's more competition from the big Midwest companies. If William's business fails, a bigger company could come in here, buy him out for pennies on the dollar, and harvest the rest of the timber."

"Okay, maybe someone was paying Abe to vandalize the logging," I conceded. "But I don't see him killing Irene."

Theo stood, rolled down his shirtsleeves, and buttoned his cuffs, then shrugged into his suit jacket.

Instead of leaving, he stepped closer to me. His eyes, as they searched my face, were more gray than blue. Slate, I thought, the color of a darkening sky.

The overwhelming heat in the kitchen was the heat between us. I wanted to move away. But I held still, letting the moment be his. A bead of sweat trickled down my spine. The murmur of voices from the grand room faded away. It had been a long time since a man had looked at me this way.

I wanted to tell him about the laudanum's sudden appearance in my medical bag. I wanted to tell him how fear had crept into my nights and now my days. How I'd learned of a diary that could hold the secret of my father's fate. And that I believed my father was John Engel.

But then, he stepped back. A decision made. "I thought you were a better judge of character, Nellie." His words crueler than the moment lost.

The image of Irene's locket on his hearth rose up before me. "I did too," I said, walking past him before he could say anything else I didn't want to hear.

CHAPTER THIRTY-SIX

I was still trembling as I made my way up the winding spiral staircase. That night it felt as if I'd never reach the top, that I would just go on climbing and climbing, round and round, never knowing who killed Irene, never discovering what happened to my father.

It had been a disturbing day and a frightful night.

After everyone had retired, I crept down the stairs intent on searching the library for the illusive diary, purposely not looking at the girl's portrait.

When I stepped into the dark drawing room, a voice called out, "Nellie."

"Who is it?" I said, startled, for an irrational moment fearful it was the presence made corporeal.

Then my eyes adjusted to the darkness. Mrs. Newell was stretched out on the sofa. "I didn't mean to frighten you," she said. "But I need your help."

Before I could ask, "Help with what," she assailed me with a barrage of questions. Did I notice how nervous and erratic Cathy was? Was it too soon for Hannah and Cathy to travel? Would I be her ally in persuading William that Cathy should return to Chicago with her?

To my every objection, she had an answer. She was like a charging bull.

"Then it's settled," she said. "You'll convince William that Cathy needs treatment for her nerves. If he agrees, I want you to accompany us as Cathy's nurse. I'll make it worth your while."

She didn't ask me, just assumed I'd go with them, as though I had no life of my own.

But I relented, knowing any suggestion from me would turn William against the idea.

Frustrated, I left Mrs. Newell lounging on the sofa content as a cat.

When I reached the foyer, Mrs. Bucheim had materialized out of the murky shadows, hissing in my ear, "You stay out of it."

⸙

The empty laudanum bottle sat on the dresser mocking me, as did the useless key, and Irene's locket.

You're not safe here, they jeered. *Look how easily someone could slip in and out of your room without your knowing.*

The most likely culprit was Mrs. Bucheim. The empty bottle a message.

Then there was Abe, my attacker and confessed saboteur. Was he Irene's killer? For all my protestations to Theo, I couldn't totally dismiss him. If he wasn't, then the killer was still loose on the island. Could the killer be living in this house?

Before undressing, I took my father's book from the chair, put it on the dresser with the bottle, the locket, and the key, then slipped the chair under the doorknob. My small measure of safety.

I struggled out of my best dress. There was a small bloodstain from Abe's injuries on the white lace. Disheartened, I poured water from the ewer into the basin and dipped the collar in the water. Taking the bar of Ivory soap, I scrubbed it. The stain faded but was still visible. My best dress ruined.

Unbidden, Father Quinn's words from the baptism chimed in my head. "Do you believe in the resurrection of the body and life everlasting?" Words that stuck with me.

Had my parents said similar words under the mesmerizing command of Caleb Engel? As an Engel, was my father one of the cult leaders? Regardless, my father and mother, like the rest of the Harmonites, were wedded to the resurrection of the body and life everlasting.

Shivering, I slipped the nightgown over my head. The fire was dying and the room had gone cold. I stoked the embers and watched them fly up the chimney. Then I crawled under the meager quilt, pulled my wool coat over it, and turned off the kerosene lamp.

A tumult of emotions pinged inside me as I turned onto my left side.

Last night's dream rose vividly in my mind.

"Why did you leave me alone?"

The kindness in my mother's eyes couldn't mitigate my guilt. Forever, I would be the daughter who didn't come home as she'd promised. The daughter who let her mother die alone on the parlor floor, where she'd crawled, trying to reach the door, trying to get help.

I fought sleep, not wanting to dream, but finally it dragged me under.

❧

Wind tears at my nightgown, unraveling my hair. Rain stings my face. I've never been so cold. I'm teetering on the cliff's edge looking out at the lake. The angry curl of whitecaps smashes against the treacherous rocks below. A cloaked figure walks toward me. I can't see his face only his hands, which hold a rope. Thick and strong like a snake.

I have to make a choice.

Now the cloaked figure is behind me. He whispers my name.

I turn. He raises the rope.

I won't die this way. I step backward into air.

❧

I jerked awake before I hit the rocks.

Like fingernails, snow tapped the windows. My coat lay on the floor. I reached for it and pulled it over me, trembling with fright.

I still felt the air rushing up at me, taking my breath away.

CHAPTER THIRTY-SEVEN

The day was cold but sunny, the snow crisp underfoot. I watched Mrs. Newell walk the jetty to the Mersey. The same boat that brought me to the island a little over a week ago. To my relief, Mrs. Newell's attempt to convince Catherine to leave had ended in a curt goodbye and a promise to write.

Matthew, who'd driven us to town, stomped behind her lugging her suitcases, clearly annoyed at having to play chauffeur once again.

When I asked him this afternoon if I could accompany Mrs. Newell to town to post a letter, he'd predictably said, "I won't be coming back for you."

"I can find my own way," I'd assured him.

Besides the Mersey, a lone fishing boat and a three-masted sloop bobbed in the harbor. Though ice chunks tossed in the turbulent waves, it no longer concerned me. I'd be gone before the lake froze up.

After Mrs. Newell boarded the boat, I made my way to the town. I had no letter to post. I was headed to the church. Father Quinn knew more about the diary and Irene than he'd told me yesterday.

The northeast wind tore at my exposed skin, but I didn't tighten my scarf. I couldn't shake last night's dream—the snake-like rope in the cloaked figure's strong hands.

Though I'd dismissed Wilkins's warning about island fever, now I wondered if there wasn't some truth to it. How else could I explain that feeling of being watched, the disturbing visions and nightmares, the child's death portrait, and the apparition I wanted desperately to believe was my mother?

A hand grabbed my shoulder. I jumped and swung around, stumbling backward into a snowy rut.

"Mr. Orr," I said. "You startled me."

"Sorry, miss. I did call out. But you must not have heard me."

His black watch cap was pulled low over his forehead, emphasizing his white bushy eyebrows and keen blue eyes.

"Is there something you wanted?" I asked, antsy to find Father Quinn. It was after three o'clock and sunset was around 4:45. I wasn't walking back to Ravenwood in the dark again.

"Was that Mrs. Newell I saw boarding the Mersey?"

That's what he chased me down in the street to ask? "Mrs. Newell has urgent business in Chicago she needs to attend to. Have you heard from Sheriff Wilkins?" I said, through chattering teeth.

"Let's get out of the cold," he said. "I've got a fresh pot of coffee on. And a letter came for you today."

I relented. Whoever had sent the letter, it was a letter from home.

⁂

We huddled around the woodstove in the post office. Orr dragged two folding wooden chairs from a back room and explained that he wanted to be within shouting distance of the prisoner.

As I waited for him to fetch the coffees and my letter, I gazed around the room. The same posters festooned the walls and now seemed more like wallpaper than public announcements, visual signs of how slowly time moved here. When my eyes lit on the closed door to the jail, I thought about Abe, sitting in his cell and ruminating on his fate as he waited for Sheriff Wilkins.

Orr strode back into the room, holding two mugs of coffee, the letter sticking out of his navy flannel shirt pocket.

"Thank you," I said, taking the coffee and holding it between my hands, savoring its warmth.

Orr sat down, pulled the letter from his pocket, and handed it me. "Is that the letter you've been expecting?"

Oh, how I longed for the city's anonymity.

"I won't know until I open it, now, will I?" I smiled mischievously, tucking the letter into my purse.

He slapped his leg and laughed. "You're a lively one, aren't you? Though you're good at hiding it. I saw that yesterday when I was sizing up everyone for the photograph."

I covered my embarrassment as I sipped the bracing coffee. "Did you notice anything else when you were looking through your lens?"

He shifted his chair nearer as though someone might be listening. "Mind you, this is between us. But William Thiery looked as nervous as a man being chased by a pack of wolves. His wife, on the other hand, was calm as glass."

His poetic and accurate description of the Thierys surprised me. Orr was an observant man, whose various jobs as town jailer, proprietor, and postmaster had honed his ability to read people.

My curiosity piqued, I asked, "Why do you think William was so agitated and Catherine so calm?"

"It's no secret that the logging business isn't what it was in Henry Thiery's time. And Mrs. Thiery, well, she has a healthy baby."

"Anyone else you care to comment on?" I probed.

His furry eyebrow arched. "Are you asking about Doc Proctor?"

I flamed red and hid behind my coffee cup again. But he'd seen my embarrassment. "Don't worry. I doubt anyone else that day noticed your interest in him."

Flustered, I said the first thing that popped into my head. "Mr. Orr, how long have you lived on the island?"

He looked up at the ceiling. "Going on twenty-three years. Came here from Lake City, Michigan."

I did a rough calculation. "You were here before Henry Thiery. Who was living here then?" Why hadn't I thought of asking Orr about the island's history earlier? As postmaster, he was privy to the island's comings and goings. Maybe he knew something about the Harmonites.

"Fishermen and a few farmers. That's how my wife and I ended up here. The land was cheap. We bought a small tract of farmland. There were a handful of us hearty souls. The Hubers, the Fishers, the Byrnes, and the Smiths. About a year later, Thiery sweeps in and buys most of the island." His words were tinged with bitterness.

"What happened to your farm?"

A cloud passed over his weathered face. "Even in the best of years, it was a struggle. When Henry Thiery decided he was going into logging, he started buying up the farms. That was about 1902. Before that he'd only summered on the island. My wife was ailing and I thought living in town would be an easier life for her. So, I sold him my farm. As part of the deal, he threw in the market with the living quarters upstairs for us. Lucky for me, the postmaster job came vacant."

Why was I not convinced by Orr's story? Something about selling his land troubled him. Or maybe it was the memory of his ailing wife?

"You don't regret giving up your farm?"

"Like I said, it was a struggle. And I wasn't the only one to sell. The rest of the farmers sold off, most left, except for Brig Smith. At least Brig and I stayed. His son logs for Thiery during the winter. Fred Huber, that's Bernie's dad, ended up selling his farm too."

"Did Thiery throw in The Carp as part of Mr. Huber's deal?"

"Another business Thiery was glad to see the back of. Cantankerous old cuss, Fred Huber. His arthritis turned him bitter as a pill. Back in the day, he outworked all of us. Strong as a bull and just as quick-tempered."

"And Bernie's mom?"

"Died. Fred decided to start over here."

All very interesting but not what I wanted to know. "Did you ever hear of Caleb Engel and his religious sect? They lived on the island from 1887 to 1894."

He took a long swallow of coffee. "One of the island's unsolved mysteries."

I knew what he was referring to, but asked anyway. "Unsolved mystery? What happened to them?"

"That's why it's unsolved; nobody knows. What's your interest?"

"Idle curiosity. Theo told me that Engel and his followers built the town and Ravenwood Manor."

"And a fine job they did. I'll say that for them. You don't see craftsmanship like that today. After they left, we swooped in like a bunch of house sparrows and stole their nests." His grin deepened the lines in his craggy face.

My eyes traveled to the jail's door. "When do you expect Sheriff Wilkins?"

"Tomorrow." He reached into his shirt pocket for his pipe, tobacco pouch, and matches. He tamped down the tobacco and lit the pipe, filling the air with its pleasant cherry scent.

"Has Abe admitted to killing Irene?" I asked.

"Swears it wasn't him."

"Do you believe him?"

"They all claim they're innocent." Suddenly, he seemed reticent to talk.

So, he believed Abe had murdered Irene. "I'd like to check on his injuries." I wasn't convinced Abe murdered Irene. And he might know something about who did.

He sent a swirl of smoke up toward the ceiling. "I would have thought you'd be glad to see the back of him."

I had no answer for that. "It doesn't matter who he is or what he might have done. He's my patient and I want to make sure he's healing properly. It'll only take a minute."

He laughed sardonically, probably seeing right through my ruse. "Sure, what the heck. I have to change the waste bucket anyway."

He led me through the locked door and down a short hallway. The overpowering stink of human excrement hit me before we reached the jail cell.

I put my hand over my nose. The smell didn't seem to bother Orr, whose pipe billowed smoke like a steam engine.

"Wait here," Orr said, "while I dump the bucket."

The narrow cell was dirty, dank, and cold. A coppery water stain ran from the small iron-barred window to the stone floor. The dingy walls had chunks of plaster missing.

Orr unlocked the cell, retrieved the bucket, and shut the cell door, then hurried to a door at the rear of the jail.

"Abe," I called, moving closer to the iron bars.

He didn't stir. He was stretched out on a wooden pallet, his arm draped over his face, as though he could shut out the stark cell and the reality of his situation. He looked like a condemned man resigned to his lot.

The back door opened and I stepped back. Orr replaced the bucket in the cell, then shut the door with a loud clink. The stink lingered.

"Get up," Orr said sternly, his affability gone. "The nurse wants to check your injuries."

"Tell her to get out," Abe said. He'd yet to move or acknowledge my presence.

Orr turned to me. "You're wasting your time on this murdering Injun bastard." His blue eyes flared with anger.

I gave Orr a sharp look. This was a side of Orr I hadn't seen before.

"Abe, please," I beseeched. "I just want to make sure you're all right."

Reluctantly, he stood and came to the cell bars. The bruises on his face had purpled. His eye was still swollen shut. His left ear was battered and bruised. It hadn't been yesterday.

"Who did this?" I reached through the iron bars and touched Abe's swollen ear, trying to feel the extent of the cartilage damage.

Orr grabbed my hand with too much force and pulled it back roughly. "Not a good idea, miss."

"Ask him," Abe said, directing his venom toward Orr.

I looked at Orr accusingly. "Mr. Orr, can I speak with Abe alone?"

I expected him to refuse me. Instead, he shrugged, and said, "Make sure you keep your distance. He tried to kill you once before." His words dripped with a hatred I didn't think him capable of. Was it Abe he hated or all Natives?

The door squeaked shut behind him.

"The sheriff is coming for you tomorrow. If you know anything about Irene's murder, please tell me."

His one-eyed stare was unnerving. "Did Thiery send you? Is that why you're here? To try and get me to admit I murdered that nurse?"

"Nobody sent me. And I'm not trying to get you to admit anything."

"Then why are you here? To gloat?" His voice's sadness was in sharp contrast to the violence on his face.

"I'm here because I don't think you killed Irene. And if you didn't, then the murderer is still out there."

"I don't know anything about her murder." He hesitated and looked away, probably deciding if he could trust me. "I'm not the only one who wants the logging stopped."

"There's someone else who's been sabotaging the logging?"

"That's all I got to say." He returned to his pitiful bed, turned his back to me, and curled into a fetal position.

As I reached for the doorknob, I thought he said, "I'm sorry." But when I looked over my shoulder, his back was still turned toward me.

What must it be like, I wondered, having to live your life hiding your true identity, because of bigots like George Orr? Nothing justified Abe's acts of sabotage or his attacking me, but I understood his feeling of helplessness. His people's land had been taken from them, and now he had to watch it being destroyed.

"Did he tell you anything?" Orr asked, when I emerged from the jail.

"Nothing. Thank you, Mr. Orr." I held back my reprimand. Though Orr was contemptuous of Abe and Native people, I had no proof he'd beaten him. It could have been Matthew.

"You heading back to Ravenwood?" He puffed out another cloud of fragrant smoke.

Whether I told him or not, I knew his eager blue eyes would be watching me, filing away another bit of information about me to share with the islanders.

"I thought I'd stop by the church and visit Father Quinn."

Orr pulled his gold pocket watch from his shirt. "It's just after four. I doubt he'll be at the church."

"What do you mean?"

"The tavern opens at four."

CHAPTER THIRTY-EIGHT

A swayback horse shivered outside The Carp. Though still harnessed to a wagon, his owner had at least thrown a blanket over him. I was reminded of the clusters of horse-drawn vehicles jockeying for space on South Water Street in Chicago on market day. How I longed for the bustle of the city, the throng of people. I felt like this horse—alone in the cold, wanting to go home.

When I reached the tavern, trepidation coursed through me, my last visit vivid in my mind. Now I realized that Abe's drunken fury had been a sham, a way to throw the blame on someone else. Though nothing justified what he did, despite myself, I pitied him. He seemed so lost and alone and damaged. They were going to fit him up for Irene's murder.

My former lover's words came back to me, "One day your bleeding heart will be the death of you."

And one day, your cruel heart will turn you to stone, I mused, as I stepped inside the tavern. The yeasty smell of beer, old fires, and unwashed bodies assailed me.

Father Quinn and another man sat at the long wooden bar. Quinn was dressed in dark trousers and a gray wool shirt. I didn't recognize the other man—a big, rough-looking fellow of middle years, who dwarfed the shorter Quinn. They were so entangled in conversation, they didn't notice my entrance.

Bernie was nowhere to be seen.

Though the hearth blazed like a furnace, it did nothing to chase the tavern's dampness. Before I reached the two men, Bernie emerged from a back room, toting a keg of beer on her shoulder like a dockworker, a disgruntled look on her face.

When she saw me, her irritation turned into a smile. "Nellie, what brings you in here?"

The two men shifted in their seats and turned toward me. I was struck again by the carnality of Quinn's appearance—his generous lips, ruddy skin, and fleshy nose.

"Miss Lester," Father Quinn said, rising from the bar stool and walking unsteadily toward me.

It was barely after four. Was he already drunk?

"Is everything all right?" He tilted his head at the bar and shifted his eyes, signaling me to be cautious.

Taking his meaning, I lowered my voice and leaned closer. "I need to speak to you in private."

"Of course," he said. "We can talk at the rectory. Bernie, I'll be back shortly. Don't let that rascal drink my beer." He gestured at his half-finished glass. Though his face flamed a dangerous shade of red, his speech rang clear as a bell.

Bernie nodded. "Sure thing, Father. It'll be just as you left it."

"Got my own beer, you son of a she wolf," the large man joked.

I felt sorry for the horse waiting outside. It looked like it was going to be a while before he'd be bedded down in his stall.

⚘

A feeling of dread clung to me as I went up the creaky, dark stairs to the church's second floor.

"The church wouldn't spring for a rectory," the priest explained, as we stepped inside a sparsely furnished room burdened with tall windows and high ceilings, which made the room cold and unwelcoming.

"Old Henry Thiery, bless his soul, had some of his boys partition the space into separate rooms, so parishioners didn't have to stare at my bed when seeking spiritual counsel."

A massive desk dominated the room. Ledgers and rolled charts were scattered across it, a swivel chair behind it, and a bench in front of it. I recalled Bernie mentioning that the priest had shipping interests. On the other side of the room stood a hearth and two straight-backed chairs, a rickety wood table between them. A mug rested in the center of the table. No fire burned in the hearth. Our breath punctuated the chilly air. How I longed for the cramped but warm apartment on Taylor Street I shared with my mother.

"Do you have many parishioners?" I asked, trying to distract myself from my roiling gut.

"Enough. When they show up." He blew on his red, chapped hands. "I can start a fire, if you like."

I knew he was as anxious to return to the tavern as I was to escape the troubling church. "This won't take long," I replied.

"Can I get you a coffee?"

I said yes, hoping he'd join me. I needed him clearheaded and reasonable.

As he made his way to the kitchen, he swayed slightly, then recovered.

While he was gone, I moved to one of the chairs near the hearth. Though I couldn't see the contents of the priest's mug, which sat on the table, I smelled it—alcohol.

When he returned, to my chagrin, he brought only one mug of coffee—lukewarm and sugarless. A spot of cream floated on top like a grease spill. I noted that his hand shook ever so slightly.

"What's so important that you hunted me down?" He scowled at me.

Hunted? Where was the jovial priest of a few minutes ago? Was he annoyed that I'd interrupted his afternoon libations?

Nervous energy sparked through me, as I placed the coffee on the table next to the priest's mug, careful not to spill it. Having treated many drunken men at the hospital, I knew the precariousness of their moods–jovial one minute, belligerent the next. He'd turned belligerent.

"It's about Irene's diary," I began, abandoning caution, attempting to shake the man into compliance.

"I already told you everything I could." He ran his hands up and down his wool trousers as though his legs had fallen asleep.

"But not everything you know," I pressed. "Am I right?"

His dark eyes bore into me so keenly I shifted in my seat.

"Why are you so interested in this diary?" He picked up his mug, took a generous gulp of alcohol, and then put it back, too close to the table's edge. "I should have never told you about it."

Could I trust this unsteady priest? Irene had. And Irene was dead.

"Father, I think you know why." I centered his mug on the table, ordering the moment that also teetered on the edge. "You asked me to look for the diary. You told me it scared Irene so much, she couldn't stay on the island any longer. And that Ravenwood Manor was evil. Of course, I want to know what's in the diary."

"For a nurse, I thought you'd pay more attention to what people tell you. That wasn't why she was leaving the island," he said sharply. "Don't put words in my mouth."

The light slanted oddly across his face. "I don't mean to put words in your mouth." I took in a shuddered breath. I didn't think I'd misheard him. But I let it go. "If it wasn't the diary, then why was she leaving?" I already suspected Catherine's casting Irene out wasn't the only reason for her departure. "A young woman's been killed. If you know something, you need to tell me."

He got up so quickly, he bumped the table's edge. I snatched the two mugs before they tumbled to the floor.

I thought he was headed out the door. Instead, he went to the windows on the other side of the room. As he stood gazing out into the fading day, a slight tremor went through him. What matter of conscience was he wrestling with?

When he came back, his flushed face had paled, the shadow of his beard like a sooty stain on his face.

"Look," he said, all his belligerence gone. "You're not Catholic, so I don't expect you to understand this. I can't tell you why she was leaving the island, because she spoke to me under the seal of confession. But I can tell you, it had nothing to do with the diary."

His pursed lips were resolute.

I knew little of confessions, but I knew of sin. I'd sat with the dying as they confessed their wrongdoings to me. I'd given them what little comfort I could, so they could die in peace. What transgression had Irene committed that burdened her conscience, making her want to leave New Harmony?

I stared at the conflicted priest. Color had flared back into his face. His hands were folded in his lap so tightly, I felt his resolve. There was no budging him from his religious vow. He wouldn't betray her confession.

"I respect your vow, Father. I know you can't tell me what she confessed. But can you tell me what sins she didn't disclose?" I didn't expect him to agree to my suggestion. It amounted to the same thing. Would he see it that way?

He raised his eyes to the lofty ceiling as though the answer floated above him. Then he spoke. His eyes were fixed on something above our heads as he mechanically began reciting the Ten Commandments. When he was done, he made the sign of the cross, then muttered, "God help me."

He'd listed only nine of the Ten Commandments.

"Adultery?" I whispered.

He neither denied nor confirmed my question.

My hunch about William and Irene was right. They'd had an affair. Their affair had impelled her to leave. But before she could, she was murdered. Only one person wouldn't want that affair made public–William. But if she was leaving, why kill her? An act committed in the heat of the moment? Had she threatened to tell Catherine? And then, there was the possibility of an unwanted pregnancy.

"I know what you're thinking," he said. "There are other married men on the island besides William Thiery. Many of the loggers have wives and families. And Irene had a penchant for roaming the woods. I wouldn't jump to conclusions."

Why was the priest trying to shift the blame? Surely, he knew the likeliest candidate was William.

He held up his trembling hand, then quickly put it down. "Before you ask, she never named the man. If you find that diary, bring it to me."

His abrupt shift from Irene's adultery to the diary made me suspicious. "Why?"

"Because you're not one of us. The diary belongs to the island."

Like me, he had no skill with subterfuge. "Father, what aren't you telling me about the diary? If I find it, I'm going to read it. So, you might as well tell me now."

"You're like a pit bull with a poodle; you don't know when to let go." His jovial mood was back. "Swear before God, you'll bring the diary to me if you find it."

"I'm going to read it first. But all right, I swear."

That seemed to satisfy him. "Irene told me there was something in the diary that someone on the island wouldn't want known."

He stood, signaling our talk was over.

"Someone on the island? Did she say who it was? And what this person didn't want known?" My head was thrumming with the priest's revelation.

"That's all I can tell you. Don't forget your promise."

"I never break a promise," I said too hastily. My mother's twisted face erupted before me, the curl of her hand, her outstretched arm on the shabby parlor rug, as she reached toward the door.

I couldn't escape the dreadful church fast enough.

CHAPTER THIRTY-NINE

Light fluffy flakes fell carelessly as I trudged along the snowy road. A thin sliver of winter light wavered on the horizon. I'd stayed too long with the priest. Soon it would be dark. I needed to keep my wits about me.

But my restless mind churned with Father Quinn's revelations. Irene had been having an affair with a married man, most likely William, and according to the priest, that was her reason for leaving the island. But was William also the killer?

A careless shove, a fateful tumble backward, her skull hitting a rock, a quick burial in a shallow grave. That would explain his insistence that Irene had fallen accidentally. A half-truth he could live with. Though the question remained, why kill her if she intended to leave? Was I too focused on him?

Theo had said William always got what he wanted. He was a dangerous and desperate man. I'd been dismissed because I'd thrown suspicion on Irene's death. Soon I would be gone. No one left to question Irene's death or Abe's culpability, except maybe Theo.

As the road veered left, the wind hit me with such force I was pushed back. I pulled my scarf around my face, lowered my head, and forged into the gusts.

I had to find the diary. Though the priest vehemently claimed he knew nothing else about the diary, his demand that I bring it to him wasn't about me being an outsider. He knew more than he was telling. I was sure of that. After all, he'd said there was something in the diary that someone on the island didn't want known.

If a Harmonite wrote the diary, what possible bearing could it have on someone living here now? The Harmonites left the island twenty-four years ago. Maybe one of the Harmonites returned? Orr had mentioned the stubborn Brig Smith and his son and their unwillingness to sell their land. Did their ties to the island date back to the Harmonites?

The jangle of bells startled me from my ruminations. I twisted around. A black cutter sleigh was coming fast toward me. It was Theo.

He pulled up beside me, holding the reins loosely in his gloved hands. Hatless, his face flushed, his blond, wavy hair wet with snow, he seemed immune to the cold.

"Get in," he said. "You can tell me what you were doing in town."

I walked around the brown bay, stepped up, and sat in the sleigh's red upholstered seat. Not wanting to answer his question, I said, "Where are you coming from?"

"You're shivering." He retrieved a wool blanket from under the seat. As he tucked the heavy blanket around me, I tried not to inhale his earthy, clean scent or stare at his handsome face. Both impossible.

"Bobby Jenkins has the croup," he said, shaking the reins and urging the horse forward. "His father is one of the trawlers. Now your turn."

I patted my purse. "A letter came for me."

His sardonic smile was disarming. "Irene did the same thing. Didn't trust anyone at Ravenwood to pick up her mail. So, who's the letter from?"

"A friend," I said, nonchalantly.

"A friend, huh? Anyone ever tell you, you have a distrustful nature?"

"Only since I've come here."

He laughed a deep-throated laugh, rich and promising. For the first time that day, I relaxed and leaned back into the soft padded seat, savoring the heft and weight of the blanket.

"Do you have to hurry back to Ravenwood?" he asked, fixing his gaze on me.

I did. Catherine would be fitful if I wasn't home by dinner. "Why?"

"Do I need a reason to invite you to my cottage?"

It was an invitation best refused. It was past five. Mrs. Bucheim would be clucking around Catherine, pecking at my tardiness, my irresponsibility, inciting her into a frenzy of emotions I'd have to deal with later.

"Only if you tell me why you came to New Harmony. But I can't stay long."

❧

We said little until we'd settled in the ladder-back chairs in front of the fireplace with our drinks. A cider laced with whiskey for Theo and an herbal tea for me.

Before handing me the tea, he'd recited its ingredients, a sly smile on his face. "Honey and chamomile. I was going to mix mistletoe into warm beer, but you don't seem to be suffering from the bubonic plague."

"I guess I deserve that." I returned his smile. "Did people really believe warm beer and mistletoe could cure the plague?"

"Desperate times, desperate people. But I don't have to tell you about desperate people. I'm sure you've seen your share, working in the city's contagion ward."

Who had told him where I'd worked? William? Catherine?

I'd never talked about my experiences on the contagion ward, even to my mother–the cascade of rank smells like swimming through a cesspool; blood seeping from patients' noses, mouths, eyes, and ears; their skin a frightening dark blue turning black like nightfall, like death. But the worst was watching the dying claw for air.

"Air hunger," the matron had called it, trying to give a name to something that shouldn't be named. Her round, good-natured face flushed with worry.

I shrugged, not wanting to talk about it. "Like you said, desperate times, desperate people."

With trembling hands, I took a generous gulp of the herbal tea, letting its pleasant warmth soothe me. Suddenly I was very tired. My eyes strayed to the rigid straight-back settee with its colorful but faded patchwork seat. It looked more inviting than what waited for me at Ravenwood Manor–a thin mattress, a threadbare quilt, and nightmares that were too real.

"I didn't mean to upset you. I thought maybe you'd want to talk about it."

I fought against the pity in his eyes.

He'd understand. But to tell him would splinter me and make me live it again. I had to just trundle on. That's what the matron had told me when she found me broken and weeping in the supply closet.

"I'm fine," I said, my voice brimming with false lightness. "Weren't you supposed to tell me what brought you to New Harmony? What you're running away from?"

"I was hoping you'd forget." He placed his mug on the hearth's ledge, got up and went in the direction of his bedroom.

As I waited, I studied the nautical painting above the hearth. The lone boat, floating on water as still as glass, was intoxicating. I wanted to crawl inside that boat and let it take me where it would like a deranged Ophelia.

When he walked back into the room, he was wiping a framed photograph with his shirttail. His broad shoulders protectively slumped forward.

Though there was no need to, he pulled his chair closer to mine, then handed me the photograph.

Dark soft hair, an oval face. Not beautiful like Irene, but pretty and impossibly wholesome.

"My wife, Alice," he said.

"What happened to her?" Surely something tragic or he wouldn't be living on this bleak island.

"What happens to so many women. She died in childbirth and my son with her. Some complication." He stared at her image as if he could bring her back to life.

"I'm sorry." What else could I offer him? The grief still there in his eyes.

"She died alone in the hospital while I was running down a story. After that, I couldn't stay in Chicago. Too many memories."

The similarity of our compounded grief struck me. "You can't blame yourself." If only I could heed my own advice.

"Can't I?"

"It doesn't help. Believe me. I know."

"What do you know, Nellie?" He took my hand in his. I let him.

When was the last time someone had touched me so gently?

My story needed no preamble. "My mother died alone while I nursed a patient, who I knew wouldn't live through the night. The patient knew too, and she asked me to stay with her. I did. The next morning, I found my mother dead on the parlor floor. I often wondered if I could have saved her."

"And you think finding out about your mother's past could ease some of your guilt? Bring you some peace?"

I fought my desire to take my hand away, to edge away from him, from his grief, from his understanding. "Something like that. Has it worked for you? Healing others?"

"Today, yes. Other days, no. But after five years, the guilt lessens." He let go of my hand.

That moment of intimacy gone–too sudden, too uncharted. I handed him his wife's photograph, felt its rough edges, a reminder he was still hers. He placed the photograph on the hearth's mantle, lovingly centering it.

When he sat down, I could see he'd crossed back to what we were. Whatever that was. Friends? Colleagues?

It was late. I should go, I told myself, staring into my teacup where leaves floated listlessly. But I didn't want to go.

"I visited Abe this afternoon." I fought my breathlessness like a bad cold, the warmth of his hand still lingering. "He claims someone else, besides him, wants the logging stopped."

He brushed his wavy blond hair off his forehead, a gesture I was too fond of. "C'mon, Nellie. What do you expect him to say? If they pin Irene's murder on him, he'll hang," he said, angrily. "Hell, he'll probably hang for Sam's death."

"I don't think he murdered Irene. I think William did." It was as if I wanted to incite Theo more.

"Based on what? Women's intuition?"

"Based on what I know. They were lovers," I stated, though I didn't know that for sure.

My gaze strayed to his wife's photograph, her doe eyes, too sweet and innocent.

"Who told you?" he asked. I couldn't tell if he was annoyed or amused.

"Does it matter? It's true. That gives William motive. I'm sure he wouldn't want Catherine knowing."

"I considered that," he said, dismissively.

"What do you mean? You knew about the affair?"

"About a week before she disappeared, Irene showed up here distraught. Big surprise, William had made promises to her he had no intention of keeping. The usual crap a man tells a woman when he wants to bed her. Sorry for my bluntness."

"Nothing I haven't heard before." As I suspected, the priest was wrong. There was no lumberjack boyfriend.

"William told Irene he was going to leave Catherine after the baby was born. They were going to run away together and start a new life. Frankly, I was surprised she fell for it. She wasn't inexperienced. She'd had a fiancé."

"The soldier in the locket."

"Yeah, him. He died in some French town no one's ever heard of. Crushed her. It was why she took this job."

"Do you think William killed her?" I wanted to know if I was safe at Ravenwood.

"He had a motive. But I'm not convinced. Don't get me wrong. William's a lot of things. He's a selfish son of a bitch. But I don't see him as a killer."

I did. "Maybe you don't know him as well as you think."

"Is there something you're not telling me? Has he forced himself on you?"

I shook my head, blushing liked a damsel in a dime novel. "There's an undercurrent of ruthlessness and menace about him."

"Still doesn't make him a killer."

I glanced at the photo of his dead wife. "I should go. It's late."

I waited for him to protest. When he didn't, I walked to the door, and took my coat from the peg.

"Thank you for the tea."

"Hold up," he said. "Let me drive you back."

CHAPTER FORTY

It was past midnight. Though bone tired, I made my way to the library determined to continue my search for the diary. Time was running out.

Though the library was freezing, I didn't dare light a fire. After placing the kerosene lamp on the table, I walked toward the windows and closed the drapery against the cold, snowy night. The reflection of my pale drawn face and sunken eyes stopped me.

When was the last time I'd slept through the night? I couldn't remember.

I shut the heavy drapery against my stark image.

With more resolve than I felt, I rolled the ladder to the last section to be searched, reminding myself to look for a book with no title or author on its spine. I decided to peruse the lower shelves first, hoping the diary would be here and I wouldn't have to climb the rickety ladder. As I scanned this section, I realized the books were a hodgepodge of categories and the diary wasn't among them.

I gazed up at the unsearched shelves and sighed. My legs ached, my eyes were scratchy with fatigue, and I was shivering. I blew into my cold hands, then climbed the creaky rungs.

When I reached the top of the ladder, a slim, leather-bound book caught my eye. It was at the end of a row and just out of reach. I stretched toward it. My fingers caught its edge. As I inched it out, the ladder wobbled.

In a panic I grabbed the bookshelf, letting go of the book. It tumbled to the floor, its loose pages strewn everywhere. It wasn't the diary. I finished scanning the rest of the shelves but didn't find the diary.

Disappointed, I climbed down the ladder and started gathering the scattered papers and placing them in the oxblood leather binder. Yellowed and fragile, put away and forgotten, they'd probably rested on that top shelf since Engel's time.

Curious, I carefully unfolded one of the papers. I stared at it in disbelief. I was holding the original sketch of Ravenwood Manor's first floor. Each room was carefully delineated. At the top of the paper was the date 1887. That was the year Engel bought the land. At the bottom of the paper in the right corner were the initials: C.E.–Caleb Engel.

I turned the drawing over, looking for notations. There were none.

A plaintive howl pulled my attention away. I went to the window and peeked around the curtain. Matthew and the cur were tromping through the snow in the direction of the caretaker house. What was he doing out on such a bleak, wintry night?

With haste, I refolded the fragile paper, then collected the rest of the drawings and placed them in the binder.

With the binder secure under my arm, I scurried from the library, my heart hammering in my chest with excitement.

§

Like an archeologist unearthing a buried civilization, one that can only be understood by what it left behind, I studied the faded ink sketches. Harmony's purpose, an Eden on earth, was evident in each drawing. Though Harmony was modest in size, it was generous in ambition.

Sitting on the hard bed, I marveled at Engel's devious and ingenious mind. The community was designed to be totally self-sufficient and by inference isolated–granary, grist mill, school, tavern, post office, church, stables, gardens, orchards, farmland, cottages, cemetery, in-town houses, most now abandoned, and Ravenwood Manor, originally named Eden House. Every structure and plot of land merited its own drawing, even the maze.

Contrary to what Mrs. Bucheim had said, there was no house at the maze's center, rather a raised altar supported by four Doric columns. In front of the altar were rows of half circles, probably benches for the congregants.

I envisioned the Harmonites solemnly walking the intricate maze, chanting and praying, dressed in their somber clothes, the women with their bonneted heads lowered, the men, of course, leading the way. All in servitude to Caleb Engel.

A log fell over in the fireplace, startling me from my reverie. Putting the maze drawing aside, I picked up the two interior drawings of Ravenwood and laid them side-by-side on the bed. Like the other drawings, these were done with great care and attention to detail. Even a piano had been sketched in the front parlor, in the same place where the piano now sat.

I was about to refold the drawings when something odd caught my eye. Along the interior of the manor's east side were stairs that ran from the cellar to a door. If I was reading the drawing correctly, the door connected to my room. But there was only one door to my room. Had the architect drawn the staircase and Caleb abandoned the idea?

I looked up from the drawing to where the door should be. The ponderous dresser covered most of that wall. I could see no door. As I stared at the dresser, a shiver went through me. The presence had appeared to me in the spot where the door should be.

With trepidation, I got up from the bed and moved to the dresser. It was tall and wide enough to cover a small door. I ran my fingers along the narrow space between the dresser and the wall, then pulled them away, as if I'd been burned. There was a draft.

As if I could distance myself from what was behind the dresser, I retreated to the other side of the room, my mind whirling.

Was there a door there? And if there was, maybe what appeared to me in the night wasn't a presence. Maybe someone in this house was sneaking into my room intent on terrorizing me. But I surely would have heard this person moving the heavy piece of furniture?

I glanced at the dresser, then looked away quickly, not liking where my thoughts were taking me.

The presence, my mother, whatever shimmered in the night had stood there beside the unmovable dresser beckoning to me, as if guiding me to whatever was behind it.

Like a banshee wanting in, the wind howled and battered against the windows. I put my hands over my ears, as if that could block the storm of my rampant thoughts.

Go to bed, I told myself. You can't be sure it's there. You can't even trust your own senses.

I wouldn't sleep until I knew.

Once the heavy drawers were removed and piled on the floor, one atop another, I braced myself against the dresser and pushed. It barely moved. I pushed again and again.

Little by little I inched the dresser away from the wall. There was a door.

Though warped, the wood door still retained its red color. Surrounding the tarnished brass doorknob and keyhole were deep gouges. I ran my fingers over them. I felt the person's desperation in the jagged grooves.

Someone had been locked in this room and had frantically tried to escape. An errant Harmonite?

I took the lamp from the bedside table and placed it on the floor in front of the door. I'd come this far. I needed to know if a hidden staircase was on the other side.

Again, I met resistance. The knob turned but the warped door wouldn't open. Was something blocking it? I bent down and peered through the keyhole. Nothing but darkness.

Rolling my achy shoulders, I took a few steps back, then ran at the door. It swung open. I pitched forward, losing my balance, and falling sideways onto a stone landing.

For a moment, I lay there stunned, my heart skittering in my chest, the frigid air wafting up from the house's depths toward me. Then I sat up slowly and gazed down the stone staircase that disappeared into darkness. I'd almost fallen down those dark stairs.

My shoulders and side aching, I struggled to my feet. Then I fetched the lamp from the bedroom floor and returned to the stone landing. Lamp in hand, I shined it down the stone staircase. There was a narrow passageway barely large enough for one person.

This could wait until morning. It was too late to explore. All good reasons to go to bed. None of which I listened to.

As I made my way down the uneven stone steps, the wind swooshed around me. It sounded like breathing. The walls were so close I couldn't stretch out my arms.

When I reached the bottom of the stairs, the confining space made me lightheaded. I could see no door. But I knew from the drawing that there had to be one.

Where I thought the door might be, I pushed against the stony wall. A rattling noise filled the chamber. I pushed harder, and like a magic trick, a section of the wall opened.

I picked up the lamp and held it out. I was standing on the threshold to the cellar. As I stepped inside, I was assaulted by the overwhelming and unpleasant smell of damp earth. Though large, the cellar felt like a tomb.

It had been cut out of bedrock and had a dirt floor. Shelves of preserves, bins of root vegetables, racks of wine, and barrels of apples and kegs filled the enormous space. I looked behind the door I'd come through. It was lined with Mason jars containing beets, onions, and green beans. They accounted for the rattling noise.

As I perused the room, I wondered why Engel had built a hidden staircase that led to the cellar? It seemed unnecessary.

On the far wall was a serviceable door that led from the cellar to the outside. On another wall were steps leading to the larder. I walked the circumference of the room, not sure what I was looking for, but too overwrought to stop.

As I neared the south wall, where barrels were piled haphazardly, I felt a rush of cold air. I shined the lamp into the space. Near the top of the barrels was a gap. Placing the lamp on the dirt floor, I moved the barrels away from the opening.

A tunnel appeared. It was small and arched, supported by rotting wood beams, and frigidly cold. It reminded me of the underground tunnels under No Man's Land I'd seen in the newspaper. But this wasn't No Man's Land.

The tunnel hadn't appeared on the drawing. Who had constructed it? Engel or Thiery? And why? Surely William and the others knew of its existence, but maybe not about the hidden door and staircase.

I needed to know where the tunnel led.

Lamp in hand, I crouched and started down the dark tunnel. I told myself I could always turn back. But I kept walking, stooped low, seeing nothing ahead, the lamplight my only guide.

The cold was brutal, the tunnel endless. I should have worn my coat. My teeth chattered, my head hurt, and my hands and feet were beyond cold.

It couldn't be much farther, I assured myself. Though what it was, I didn't know.

Then I spotted stairs up ahead. I quickened my pace. When I reached them, I lifted the lamp and gazed up. The stairs led to a trap door. But where the trap door led, I didn't know. It was impossible to tell how far I'd walked.

I placed the lamp on the top step and pushed hard against the trap door. It flew open with a thud. Cold air and snow blew down on me. In the dawn light, I saw a long stone slab and the Doric columns of the altar above me. I was in the center of the maze under the ceremonial altar. I crawled out from under the altar and stood. It was like emerging from a womb.

The wind and snow had stopped. Splinters of daylight silvered the whiteness. The tall fir trees bent with snow were like sentries guarding the heart of the maze.

Even the snow-covered stone benches seemed eerily expectant, as if they were waiting for the spirits of the disappeared Harmonites to return.

Whether it was the immense quiet or the stark white snow, I felt like I'd entered another world not of this earth. One I didn't want to linger in.

As I made my way through the tunnel back to Ravenwood, I thought I knew why Engel had constructed the tunnel, the altar, and the maze. There was no longer any question in my mind that he was the tunnel's architect. The tunnel was part of a religious rite, a physical journey, reflecting a spiritual one from darkness to light.

But what awaited the person when they emerged from the darkness into the light? Resurrection or sacrifice?

CHAPTER FORTY-ONE

I have to reach the trapdoor. The tunnel is collapsing around me. On hands and knees I crawl toward it, choking on dirt, my eyes gritty, my heart asunder in my chest. When I reach the door, it won't budge. I watch in horror as the dirt rains down on me. This is how I'm going to die, entombed in a tunnel. And no one will ever know.

Above me loud banging. Someone is out there.

"Help," I rasp.

The banging grows louder, more insistent.

"Help me."

"Nellie, wake up."

I blinked my eyes open. Light seeped around the corners of the drapery. It had been a dream. I lay on the iron bed, fully clothed, where I'd fallen asleep in the early morning hours. My head was fogged with the dream that had been so real, I tasted dirt on my tongue.

"Nellie Lester, open the door," Mrs. Bucheim called again.

"I'm coming," I said, raising myself up on my elbows, my shoulder protesting in pain.

As I eased myself off the bed, I heard crinkling. Eleanor's letter. I remembered reading it before I fell asleep. A chatty missive full of good wishes. No mention of Irene Hayes, but I hadn't expected any. Our letters had probably crossed in the mail.

When I opened the door, Mrs. Bucheim's pinched, worried face greeted me, her gray hair so tightly done, I saw white patches of her skull peeking through.

"Is something wrong? Is Catherine alright?" I asked. Tendrils of the dream still clung to me.

"You overslept," she said, looking past me as though she expected to find a man in my room. The dresser was in its usual place. I'd stowed the binder with the drawings in the compartment under the bed, along with Irene's locket and John Engel's book. Nothing amiss to give away my night explorations.

"Is that what you came to tell me?" I smiled to dispel my annoyance.

She humphed. "No, of course not. Doctor Proctor wants you to go with him to town."

"Did he say why?" I asked, looking away from her dark, judging eyes. It was then I saw my dirty shoe prints on the thin rug. I had to get her out of the room before she noticed them and started asking questions.

"Father Quinn is dead. I'll fix you a cold breakfast. You can eat on the way."

Stunned, I just stood there, watching her turn on her heel and stride out of the room. Her strident footfalls on the steps like the questions knocking around in my achy head.

Quickly, I brushed the dirt from the carpet, then poured water from the ewer into the bowl and washed. My dress was wrinkled from sleep, but I wasn't about to don my good dress. Though Eleanor's letter held nothing of importance, I stashed it under the mattress.

⸙

Theo drove the sleigh as if Father Quinn could still be saved. I felt sorry for the brown bay who, though spirited, seemed to struggle in the deep drifts and had to suffer Theo's impatient whip. Nearly a foot of snow had fallen overnight. Bells jingling wildly, the sleigh rocked from side to side. I wished Theo would slow down, so we didn't end up a casualty of his recklessness.

I had no stomach for breakfast and left Mrs. Bucheim's covered basket on the floor of the sleigh, along with the thermos of coffee. Last night's discovery of the hidden staircase and the tunnel had left me uneasy.

When I asked Theo the circumstances of Quinn's death, he'd answered curtly, "George Orr found him. That's all I know."

His simmering agitation puzzled me and kept me from telling him about my night of discoveries. What would he make of the hidden staircase and the tunnel leading to the altar in the center of the maze?

Orr must have been watching for our sleigh. His horse-drawn cart waited outside the market. As soon as we pulled up, he bustled out bundled in a black coat, watch cap, woolen scarf, and leather gloves, and carrying a shovel. His ever present pipe missing.

"He's behind the church," he said, throwing the shovel in the back of the wagon. "We'll need to dig him out."

Once at the church, Orr tied up his horse and circled around the back entrance, struggling to keep his balance as he tromped through the deep snow.

After Theo tied up the bay, he retrieved a plaid blanket from the sleigh and threw it over the horse. We walked in Orr's footprints. I noticed there were no other footprints, except Orr's. Not even Father Quinn's. The heavy snow had erased them.

By the time we reached the body, my face burned with cold and I was panting with exhaustion. My lack of sleep was catching up with me.

"Is this how you found him?" I asked Orr, whose eyes were averted from the corpse, focused instead on the stand of snow-laden evergreens behind the church. The tranquil wintry scene was in sharp contrast to the dead man at our feet.

The sun's harsh glare made the priest's ghastly visage more vivid. His death grimace sent shivers through me. Not because of his milky eyes that looked upward as if in entreaty to his God, or his gray, crystallized pallor, or his gaping mouth filled with snow, but because of the frozen pool of black blood around his head–a bloody halo that reminded me of Irene's smashed skull.

"I didn't move him. Just brushed the snow off his face." Orr stole a quick glimpse at the priest, then looked away again at the trees. For a man who prided himself on the nuances of human gestures and expressions, studying them with such precision he could characterize a person, it was evident that his curiosity ended with the living.

Near the priest's head was a large indentation in the snow. Where I imagined Orr had fallen back in horror at what he'd uncovered.

Theo's silence was unnerving. Was he thinking what I was thinking? That Quinn's death might be connected to Irene's.

"What were you doing behind the church?" I asked Orr, who still wouldn't meet my eyes, his gloved hand anxiously gripping the shovel.

"We were to meet this morning. When I couldn't find him in the church, I walked around the back and that's when I saw him. Well, I didn't exactly see him. Just this mound of snow. It didn't look right." He shifted the shovel to his other hand. "What I can't understand is why he was wandering around in a snowstorm. We had gale force winds last night."

"He could have come from the tavern. Got disoriented and froze to death. He wouldn't be the first man too drunk to find his way home," Theo piped in angrily.

His condemnation felt personal.

"What about the blood around his head? Any guesses?" I asked Theo, who was glaring with disgust at the priest's horrendous face.

"Let's roll him over," Theo answered.

"You're going to want to get the snow off him first," Orr offered. "It's hard as ice."

Theo took the shovel from Orr and sliced through the snow with the precision of a surgeon. When he was done, he threw the shovel aside, knelt in the snow, and pushed the body over. It was as stiff as a wooden plank.

"Damn it," Orr swore. "That's a lot of blood. Looks like he hit his head on one of them stones."

Jutting up from the pool of blood was a sharp-edged stone matted with hair and brain matter. Based on the amount of blood, Quinn probably hadn't died instantly. But it was unclear if he'd been conscious as his life slipped away. Had he gazed up at the snow as it slowly buried him? Had he heard the banshee winds, knowing he was dying? I prayed not.

I knelt beside Theo to get a closer look at the priest's skull. Like Irene, his skull was caved in. I took off my glove and probed the wound. The edges were jagged just like the stone under his head. There was no mystery here.

I could feel Theo's questioning gaze as he rolled the corpse onto its back, shifting it so the head didn't rest on the stone.

Orr stepped closer and peered down. "You can't see the rest of the stones because of the snow. But there's a stone path that leads from the church to the woods over there. Father Quinn called it the contemplation path. I've seen him walk that path fingering his rosary."

"Can we store him in your icehouse until the sheriff gets here?" Theo asked Orr, as he stood and brushed the snow from his trousers and coat.

"Sure thing. I'm expecting the sheriff this afternoon. He might want to speak to you, Doc."

"He knows where he can find me. Now let's get him to your wagon."

Though the icy snow had seeped through my coat and dress, dampening my stockings, I didn't move. Something was troubling me. All the evidence pointed to an accidental death. As Theo said, the intoxicated Quinn probably had slipped and fallen backward onto one of the path's stones. The wound matched the stone under his head. Though the circumstances of his death were different from Irene's, what were the odds of two deaths from fractured skulls in such a short time?

"Nellie, we need to move the body." Theo offered his hand to help me up.

I took it and struggled to my feet, shaking the snow from my clothes. "I'll meet you at the buggy. There's something I need to do."

Theo raised a quizzical eyebrow but kept silent.

The heft of Quinn's frozen body nearly brought the men to their knees, as they lifted his corpse and stumbled through the deep snow, heading toward Orr's waiting cart.

Once they were out of sight, I took the shovel and cleared some of the snow from the path, looking for stones similar to the one that killed the priest.

After uncovering four, I stopped. All the stones were similar in size and evenly spaced along the contemplation path. It seemed to have been an accident.

Craving the buggy's warmth and Mrs. Buchheim's thermos of coffee, I trudged in the men's footprints, my doubts lingering.

When I reached the buggy, I spotted Theo and George headed behind the market to the icehouse. If I hurried, I'd have enough time to talk to Bernie and be back at the sleigh before Theo. I leaned the shovel against the sleigh, patted the horse, and scurried toward the tavern.

CHAPTER FORTY-TWO

After the bright sunlight, entering the murky tavern was like entering a cave. The only light came from the hearth where an old man sat in a wicker wheelchair, a plaid blanket over his legs. So lost in his thoughts, my entrance went unnoticed. He kept gazing into the fire, as though enchanted.

This had to be Bernie's father, Frederick Huber. Though the white-haired Huber was confined to a wheelchair, the breadth of his shoulders and length of his legs suggested he'd once been a big, powerful man. I recalled George Orr's description of him as a cantankerous old cuss whose arthritis had turned him bitter as a pill, who'd once been strong as a bull and just as quick tempered.

The hearth must have recently been stoked because the room was unusually warm. I took off my gloves, unbuttoned my coat, and loosened my scarf. As I pulled the scarf away from my neck, it caught on the pendant's chain. I pulled the pendant free, then stomped the caked snow from my boots.

The man turned his rheumy eyes toward me. "What you doing in here, girlie?" His sour expression was made more so by his sharp features, hawkish nose, and jutting chin.

"My name's Nellie Lester. I'm here to see Bernie."

"Can't hear you," he said, cupping his ear. "Come closer, I promise not to bite."

As I strode to Mr. Huber, my boots stuck to the dirty stone floor. When I reached him, I leaned over him, so he could hear me. "Is Bernie around? I need to speak to her."

He grabbed the dangling pendant and held it fast in his gnarled hand, keeping me stooped over.

"The golden rose," he said. His cloudy eyes gazed up at me, then back at the pendant. "Where'd you get this, girlie?"

"It was my mother's," I said, endeavoring to pull the pendant from his viselike grip.

"Where'd your mother get it?"

"I don't know. She never wore it. I found it after her death."

My answer seemed to satisfy him. He let go of the pendant and settled back into his chair.

"A shame she never wore it. It's finely made."

I stared at the crotchety old man as the pieces slotted into place. He'd called my mother's pendant *the* golden rose as if it meant something to him. Here was someone who might know about the Harmonites, whose golden rose design adorned the turret windows and was carved above the church door.

"How long have you lived on the island, Mr. Huber?" I asked.

"As long as I've been here. And none of your business."

"Mr. Huber, when did you come to the island?" I persisted.

"Bernie," he bellowed, his voice surprisingly vigorous. This was a man who refused to be brought low by age and infirmity.

"What do you want, Pa?" Bernie answered from a back room. "I'm busy right now."

"You heard her. She's busy." He grinned at me. It was clear he wanted me to leave.

"Bernie," I called. "It's Nellie Lester. I need to talk to you. It'll only take a minute."

He yanked so hard on the sleeve of my coat I almost lost my balance. "You're the other one, aren't ya? Are you looking to stay the night? I got a fine room for you." He grinned mischievously.

"The other one? You mean Irene Hayes?"

"Pa, what are you doing? Let go of her coat." Bernie emerged from the back room with a tray of mugs. She placed the tray on the wooden bar and went to the old man.

Huber released my coat, and I took a step back from his large, gnarled hands and pungent breath.

"I'm sorry, Nellie. My pa's not been himself lately. Pa, this is Nellie Lester, the nurse I told you about. She delivered the Thiery baby."

"I know who she is. I'm not senile yet. Now fetch me a coffee like a good daughter."

Bernie scurried to the back room, but not before I caught her look of annoyance.

I fingered the pendant, deciding on another tactic. "You called my pendant the golden rose. What did you mean by that?"

"It's gold, ain't it?"

Before I could prod him further, Bernie returned.

"Sugar and cream, just like you like it," she said, handing her father a steaming mug of coffee. "Now why don't I get you upstairs?"

"After I finish my coffee." His cloudy eyes shifted toward me. "Got a nice room upstairs for you," he repeated.

"Why don't we sit over here and leave my pa to his coffee." Bernie led me to a corner table far from Huber.

What an ornery old coot. If he knew something about the Harmonites, he wasn't telling me.

"Pay no attention to my pa. He talks a lot of nonsense and thinks it's fun to torment me. So, what brings you in here?" Her strained smile was pasted on.

I rested my forearms on the wobbly table. "I'm afraid I have bad news. It's Father Quinn."

"Has something happened to the Father?"

I glanced down at her delicate red hands, in stark contrast to her bulky form. "This morning George Orr found Father Quinn's body behind the church. It appears he fell and hit his head."

Head bowed, she quickly made the sign of the cross, then kissed her thumb. I felt humbled by her reverence. What must it be like to have the consolation of faith?

"Theo and I were called to examine the body," I explained, bending the truth. "I was wondering when he left the tavern last night?"

She blew out a breath, fluttering her fringe of brown hair that hid her high forehead. "Let's see. I think they left around midnight."

"They?" I asked.

"Brig Smith and Father Quinn. Brig was in the tavern when you came looking for Father Quinn yesterday."

So that was Brig Smith, the farmer, who wouldn't sell to Henry Thiery.

"Then Brig Smith was with him when they left? Would they have been going in the same direction?"

"No. But I asked Brig to walk him to the church. Knowing Father Quinn, he probably waved him off." She shook her head regretfully. "It's my fault. I should have insisted he stay the night. It was blowing something awful. And he was three sheets to it." A guilty flush crept up her neck and into her face.

"It's not your fault." I patted her hand, trying to console her.

"No, it is. When you run a tavern, you get to know the men who come in here. When he came back from meeting with you, I seen he was troubled. Though he said nothing, I could tell. I've never seen him drink like that. And him with the shaking palsy. I should have made him stay the night."

"Please don't blame yourself," I said.

When she didn't answer, I rose from the unsteady chair. "Well, I'd better get back to Ravenwood."

"Thanks for letting me know," Bernie said. "I suppose the church will be taking charge of the funeral arrangements."

"I expect so."

I glanced over at Huber who was staring into the fire. "There's something else I need to ask you. When did you and your pa come to the island?"

"Like I said before, about twenty years or so ago. What's this to do with Father Quinn's death?"

A cup shattered on the hard floor, startling me.

"Pa, what did you do now?" Bernie jumped up from the chair and went to her father.

"Stop your fussing. Just dropped my cup."

As Bernie knelt on the floor gathering pieces of the cup, I said goodbye.

When I reached the door, Huber boomed out, "Nice meeting you, girlie."

CHAPTER FORTY-THREE

"Why did you want me to see the priest's body?" I asked Theo, as he held tightly to the reins, trying to maneuver the bay down the snowy road.

"You know your way around a corpse," he said, a wry smile on his wind-burned face.

I returned his smile. Considering the grizzly morning, his humor was a much-needed tonic. "More so, since I came here."

I retrieved the thermos from the sleigh's floor and unscrewed the cap, releasing the alluring scent of coffee.

"Are you bothered by the similarities between Irene's and Father Quinn's deaths?" I asked as I poured coffee into the thermos cap, my hands unsteady as the sleigh bumped along.

"Is that why you were digging in the snow? I saw you. What were you looking for?"

To chase the cold that had settled into my bones, I took a generous swallow, savoring the coffee's warmth. Coldness seemed to be a constant condition since I'd come to the island.

"Would you like some coffee?" I asked, holding the cap toward him.

"Don't change the subject. And yes, I would. But I'd better keep both hands on the reins."

"I'll hold the cap for you." I brought the cap to his lips and tipped it slightly as he drank. In the fading morning light, I saw glints of blond stubble on his face. A small scar I'd never noticed scissored his right eyebrow.

When he was done, there was a drop on his chin. I blotted it with my finger, thinking of all the men I'd nursed. How many times I'd held glasses or cups to their beseeching mouths. None had stirred me like Theo.

"Thanks," he said, looking at me, his eyes more gray than blue, like the pewter sky, washed and fading.

"What were you doing with the shovel?" he repeated his question.

"Seeing if the stone that smashed Father Quinn's skull was uniformly spaced from the other stones. I wanted to make sure it wasn't put under his head after the fact."

"What a skeptical mind you have. And was it uniformly spaced?"

"Yes."

"You almost sound disappointed that there was no foul play. Quinn's death was an accident. Irene's wasn't."

"Probably." It was on the tip of my tongue wanting release. The secret the priest had told me, the one I swore to keep–Irene's diary.

The road snaked west, the wind picked up. We'd soon be at Ravenwood. The priest was dead. What difference did it make now?

"Did Irene ever mention she'd found a diary at Ravenwood?" I ventured.

"A diary? Who told you this? Quinn?"

His mind was as keen and sharp as the day with its cold edges and deep drifts. It would be fruitless to retreat now. Nor did I want to.

"Yes, it was Quinn. Irene told him about a diary. It's possible one of the Harmonites, a woman, wrote it. But he said there's something disturbing in the diary. And apparently it affects someone living on the island now."

We were at the turnoff to Ravenwood. Theo continued past it. We were headed to his cottage.

Did I want to go to his cottage? Mrs. Bucheim would question what took me so long. Catherine would be agitated by my prolonged absence, fretting and pacing her room like a captured animal.

"I need to get back to the manor," I protested.

He kept going. "And I need to know about this diary and the other things you're keeping from me."

I could have demanded he take me to Ravenwood immediately. I could have pulled back on the reins if he refused. I could have shouted. But I didn't. I sat back against the cold upholstered seat and let myself become part of the wintry landscape–so white it hurt my eyes.

❧

Word for word, I related how Father Quinn asked me to search the turret room for the diary, how something in the diary scared Irene, repeating again that the diary contained something someone living on the island now wouldn't want known.

He'd listened intently, a whiskey-laced coffee in his hand, sitting beside me on the uncomfortable settee as though our closeness was essential to the diary's secrets.

"So, Irene said the diary was written by a woman. And it's harmful to someone living on the island now," he repeated. "Then I doubt it belonged to a Harmonite. They left over twenty years ago."

"Maybe one of them came back," I offered. My untouched coffee mug sat on the crate. My acidic stomach swirled with tension.

"So what if they did?" He paused. "You're not thinking this diary has something to do with Irene's murder? I thought you pegged William as the culprit?"

I envisioned Theo in his other life, his hat pushed back on his blond head, eagerly holding a pencil, ready to jot down my answer in his journalist pad.

"I still believe William killed her, maybe accidentally in the heat of passion. He had motive and opportunity. You confirmed they were having an affair and that William made promises he couldn't keep. Besides, as far as I know, only Irene and the priest knew about the diary." Even as I said it, I questioned my certainty.

"My interest in the diary has to do with my mother and the man in the photograph. If the diary belonged to a Harmonite, which I think likely, then it's also likely one of the Harmonites returned to the island. That person could tell me what happened to the man." With no tangible proof, I still wasn't ready to tell him that I thought John Engel was my father.

"You're grasping at straws. Whatever is in that diary might have nothing to do with your mother, the man in the photograph, or the Harmonites. It could have been written during Henry Thiery's time. And we only have Irene's word that it's harmful to someone living on the island."

He stared into his coffee mug, then at me. "You realize that if William is the killer, you're not safe at Ravenwood."

I balked at his suggestion. "I won't be there much longer. William's given me two weeks' notice." I wasn't sure why I'd held off telling Theo. Maybe saying it made it too real.

"William sacked you? Why?"

"For telling the sheriff my murder theories and for snooping around the logging camp."

He didn't respond. He was considering what to say. "Don't get me wrong, William's a bastard for firing you. But maybe, it's for the best."

"For the best? How can you say that? Finding out how my mother's past is connected to that man is the only reason I took this job. I'm not leaving until I know what happened."

"Like I said before, you may never know." He put his cup on the crate and took my hand in both of his. I felt like a captured bird.

Tear pricked my eyes. I swiped at them with the back of my free hand. "Why are you saying that? I thought you understood." I pulled my hand away. "Do you know something about my mother you're not telling me?"

"All I know is you're putting yourself in danger. And that worries me."

"I'm not leaving. I'm so close, I . . ." I looked away from his intense blue stare, swallowing the unspoken words.

"So close to what? You've found something. Haven't you?"

It was unnerving how he could read me. "An open book, that's what you are," my mother would say. "You'd make a dreadful poker player."

Like Francis, Theo wanted something from me I wasn't sure I wanted to give. But Theo wasn't Francis. I'd given Theo nothing that I didn't want to give. And Francis had taken what he'd wanted by force.

"In the library," I began, "I found the original drawings for Harmony and Eden House. That's what Engel called Ravenwood Manor. They were tucked away in a nondescript binder."

"And?" he prodded.

"And I found a hidden stairway that leads from my room to the cellar. I never saw the door because it was hidden behind a large dresser."

Theo's eyes had that faraway look. "Why would the Harmonites build a hidden staircase from the turret to the cellar? There's a perfectly good door from the outside to the cellar? Unless, they were worried about a fire."

I hadn't thought about the possibility of a fire and the stone stairs acting as a fire escape. I'd been too distracted by the tunnel.

"Maybe. But in the cellar, I found a tunnel. It was behind a wall of barrels. It led to a trapdoor. When I pushed open the trapdoor, I was under an altar at the center of the maze."

He didn't seem surprised. "I wondered what religious hocus-pocus those Harmonites were up to."

"You knew about the altar?" I asked. "Mrs. Bucheim told me a house was at the maze's center."

He shrugged. "She may not look it, but Mrs. Bucheim is quite fanciful in her own Germanic way. After she warned me off the maze with her tales of a mysterious house, I decided to find out for myself. That's when I found the altar. I never told Mrs. Bucheim, because I didn't want to ruin her Brothers Grimm tale."

"There's something else." I took in a shuddered breath, wanting to confide my fears. Desperate to hear his skeptical mind offer a logical explanation for the nightly presence that I wanted to believe was my mother. For the visions I believed were memories of my father. And for the dead child's dissolved face on the portrait that I'd convinced myself someone had altered.

Instead, I said, "I think someone was imprisoned in the turret room. I found gouges and scratches around the lock and doorknob of the door leading to the hidden staircase."

"I can't see Henry Thiery locking anyone away in that room. Must have been the Harmonites. What a sick group they must have been."

He saw the crestfallen look on my face. "Sorry, Nellie, that was thoughtless."

"I'd better get back," I said standing, careful not to brush my head against the hanging herbs. I'd been wise not to reveal the manor's spectral happenings.

Theo rose from the settee and moved so close I felt his breath on my cheek. When he kissed me, I didn't resist. Nor did I think beyond the moment.

CHAPTER FORTY-FOUR

With mounting alarm, I watched Catherine turn from side to side before the full-length mirror like a crazed fashion model.

"What do you think of this one, Nellie?" she asked, her voice jittery with excitement. She held a beaded silk chartreuse dress in front of her, more suited to the opera than to a logging camp.

Determined to surprise William with an impromptu dinner at his mill office, she'd roped Mrs. Bucheim into preparing a basket of food, complete with two bottles of wine, Matthew into playing chauffeur, and me into lady's maid. I thought her plan madness.

"Are you sure this is a good idea? William's probably busy or he'd come home for dinner. I'd hate for you to be disappointed." I feared his wrath would descend on her and she would break into pieces that I'd have to put back together.

"Oh, pooh. You're such an old fuddy-duddy. William will be delighted to see me." She waved her hand dismissively.

At the sound of her mother's raised voice, Hannah stirred in her cradle.

"Catherine, come sit by me. I need to talk to you." I wanted to check her pulse, gaze into her amber eyes for signs of dilation. I didn't like her agitated state or her skin's deep flush.

She carelessly threw the beaded dress atop the pile of other dresses on her mammoth bed, then resentfully stomped over to the damask settee.

"I don't have time for this, Nellie. I have to get ready."

"Please sit. It'll only take a minute."

"Oh, all right. But make it quick."

"Did Mrs. Bucheim tell you where I was today?" I asked, keeping my voice modulated as though I were talking to a child. I found it odd she hadn't asked about Father Quinn. Was his death what had caused her emotional upheaval?

Her eyes danced around the room, her slippered foot tapped to her own internal music. I placed two fingers on her wrist. Her pulse was racing.

"Catherine, look at me." Her eyes were dilated. I glanced at the empty teacup on the side table.

"I don't want to talk about Father Quinn. I'm going to have dinner with my husband tonight. Don't ruin it for me."

"Father Quinn's death was an accident," I persisted, pushing through her haze. "During last night's snowstorm he fell, hit his head, and froze to death."

A tear rolled down her cheek.

"Were you close to the priest?" I asked, surprised by her emotion.

She nodded. "I could always go to him with my problems and he'd listen." She wrung her hands. "First Irene, now Father Quinn. Who's next? I should have listened to Madge and gone to Chicago. Promise me you'll protect Hannah while I'm at the mill."

Protect her from what? "Nothing is going to happen to Hannah."

She laughed sardonically. "Like nothing happened to Irene or Father Quinn? Sometimes I think this island is cursed."

Irene had said the same thing to Father Quinn.

Catherine jumped up from the settee and went to the cradle.

"My sweet, sweet girl," she cooed, then she moved to the bed and fumbled through the array of dresses that I now saw as a diversion, her way of not wanting to face the priest's death.

"Why not wear that burgundy wool day dress? It's a cold night. It'll keep you warm," I suggested.

"Oh, Nellie, did no one ever teach you how to charm a man?" Her words were tinged with pity I didn't want or deserve.

My face flamed as red as Catherine's, remembering Theo's mouth on mine. How his hands had traveled my body and mine his. How I'd finally pulled away. It's not always about dresses, I wanted to tell her, but I held back. She was spinning in her own world of romantic dinners with her husband.

She picked up the beaded chartreuse and stepped into it, then slipped her arms into the sheer gauze sleeves. It was a spectacular dress that enhanced her auburn hair and amber eyes.

"Help me with the buttons."

Reluctantly, I rose from the settee and fastened the silk-covered buttons.

"What do you think?" she asked, admiring herself in the mirror.

"Lovely," I said. "I'm sure William will be charmed." More like angry that you invaded his male domain. Or maybe she was right. Maybe I knew nothing about how to charm men.

As she rummaged in her armoire for shoes, I returned to the settee and surreptitiously picked up the teacup. Holding it to my nose, I sniffed deeply, then sipped the dregs. Even the tea couldn't hide the bitter taste of laudanum.

So, the empty laudanum bottle had been a taunt. Whoever had taken the bottle had kept the drug. But was Catherine knowingly taking it or was someone dosing her? Either way, she had to stop.

"Catherine," I said, as I glanced at Hannah, sleeping so peacefully, too peacefully. "There's laudanum in your tea. I tasted it."

Holding onto the bedpost, she put on the fragile-looking satin shoes. "It's none of your concern what's in my tea."

"Listen to me. I know you love Hannah. You can't take laudanum while you're nursing."

"Don't ever question me about Hannah. You hear me?" Her face was scarlet, her voice steely. She strode to the dresser and absently plucked one of her perfume bottles from the array on the mirrored tray. She looked at it, and then quickly put it back, selecting another one. With shaking hands, she squeezed the atomizer, releasing a heavy scent that wafted toward me like a fog rolling in off the lake.

Without a word, she rummaged through her coats, chose the fox fur, yanked it off its hanger, and tossed it on the bed. "No need for frumpy dresses. This will keep me warm tonight," she declared caustically.

I ignored her mocking remark and went to the dresser. It was only a hunch. I picked up the rejected perfume, took out the stopper and sniffed–laudanum. I held the bottle up to the light. It was a third full. It was impossible to tell how much she'd taken since Hannah's birth.

When I turned toward Catherine, her eyes were riveted on me.

"What are you doing? Put that down," she demanded, a sliver of fear in her voice.

"Who gave this to you?" I retorted.

"No one. I found it," she said indignantly, her arms crossed over her generous bosom.

"Where did you find it?" I was having trouble controlling my temper. I wanted to shake her silly.

"In the larder on one of the shelves. What of it?"

I'd searched the larder and found nothing. She was covering for someone.

"Who gave you the bottle, Catherine?"

"I told you I found it in the larder. Now stop badgering me."

"It was Mrs. Bucheim, wasn't it? She gave it to you. William needs to know about this."

"Go ahead, tell him. He's not going to believe you. He thinks you're nothing but trouble. Why do you think he fired you?"

She was right. I'd lost William's trust. I had to get through to Catherine.

"Oh, I think he'll believe me. He's well aware of the dangers of this drug. If I tell him Mrs. Bucheim gave it to you, he'll fire her." I doubted he would, but it was my only card.

Her smug expression faded with her confidence. "It was Matthew. Happy? You can tell William, but he won't fire him. They're like brothers."

Matthew, who warned me that first day not to hurt the missus, had stolen the laudanum from my medical bag and given it to Catherine. Then he put the empty bottle back in my bag to make me doubt myself. And clever, devious Catherine had poured the laudanum into a perfume bottle, hiding it in plain sight.

"You can't take any more of this." I held the bottle toward her. "If not for your sake, then for Hannah's."

"Irene didn't mind," she said, coyly.

"What do you mean?"

"Where do you think I got it? Irene said it would calm my nerves. And it does."

Irene had been giving Catherine a drug she knew would harm her and her baby? I didn't know if I believed her. No competent nurse would dose a pregnant woman with laudanum to calm her nerves.

"Let me help you, Catherine," I said, seeing the escalating panic in her eyes. "I have an herbal potion that will help you wean off the drug."

Her eyes turned feral. "Don't think I don't know what you're up to at night, sneaking around the manor with your pasty face and prim ways. You're just like Irene, thinking you can take my husband from me."

Her terror over losing the drug had tipped her over the edge.

"I have no interest in William. I just want you and Hannah to be healthy."

Unexpectedly, she lunged at me, jerking the bottle from my hand so violently it flew across the room and hit the armoire, smashing into pieces.

"Look what you've done," she screamed at me.

Hannah wailed at the sound of the breaking glass and her mother's raised voice.

I went to Hannah and picked her up, while Catherine stood looking horrified at the shards of broken glass scattered across the Oriental carpet.

Then she stepped around the broken glass, grabbed her fox coat from the bed, and strode out of the bedroom, slamming the door behind her.

"There, there, Hannah," I cooed. Cradling her in my arms, I softly sang a lullaby.

Unless Matthew could procure another bottle of laudanum, that was the end of Catherine's reliance on the drug. I trusted Theo, who claimed to have found the bottle at his cottage when he moved in, not to supply Catherine with any more laudanum. Before I left Ravenwood, I'd do everything in my power to ease her withdrawal.

Once Hannah fell asleep, I knelt down and started picking up the shattered glass, carefully placing the shards on the settee's end table. As I reached for one of the larger shards where laudanum had pooled, Hannah let out a hiccup, distracting me.

I felt a sharp pain and dropped the glass.

A jot of blood oozed from my finger. Reflexively, I put my finger in my mouth. Then sat back on my heels, looking at the now-empty shard resting on its side, its edge glistening red.

It wouldn't have been much, maybe a drop or two, I assured myself. I took a hankie from my dress pocket and wrapped it around the wound, knowing its injection had the sure swiftness of a hypodermic needle.

CHAPTER FORTY-FIVE

"I can't believe Father Quinn is dead, poor man," Mrs. Bucheim lamented as she slopped a suspect stew onto my blue enamel plate. My stomach churned at the chunks of dark meat swimming in the greasy gravy that I prayed were beef, not fresh game hunted by Matthew.

I had no appetite. My brain was as murky as the gravy, clotted with deceptions. If I believed Catherine, Matthew had stolen the laudanum, Irene had sanctioned her usage, and Theo had supplied the drug. A cabal of culprits feeding Catherine's habit, under the guise of good intentions.

I glanced at the windows, dark with night, reflecting Mrs. Bucheim's ravenlike figure, shiny and black. A raven at the window pecking, wanting in.

I shook my head at the image. A few drops of laudanum in my blood and the world had shifted. I wanted to sleep.

Under Mrs. Bucheim's watchful beady eyes, I grasped my fork, stabbed a potato, and put it in my mouth, thinking food would stanch the drug's effects. The starchy vegetable practically melted on my tongue, it was so tender.

"I owe you an apology," I said, putting down my fork and struggling to tame competing emotions–euphoria, irritability, and restlessness. A bead of sweat ran down my back. The kitchen was stifling with its raging woodstove. "I'm sorry for suspecting you of stealing the laudanum from my medical bag. I know you didn't do it."

Mrs. Bucheim finished filling her plate, then returned the iron stew pot to the woodstove before sitting down. Blood smeared her pristine apron and flour like talcum stuck to the sleeve of her black dress.

"What brought this on?" she asked, arching her back warily.

The words tumbled out. "Catherine admitted to me that Matthew stole the laudanum from my bag. She's been dosing herself. That's the reason she's been so . . ." I struggled for the right word, "erratic."

She humphed. "Well, that's explains why the missus left in such a foul mood. You were pestering her with another of your wild accusations."

My apology fell on deaf ears. Of course, she'd defend Matthew, her surrogate son, whose only offense in her eyes was bringing the cur into the house.

You're too honest. Some things should be kept to oneself. My mother's words rang round the room. I ignored them.

"I found the drug in her room. She'd hidden it in one of her perfume bottles." I rubbed my forehead; a headache like a storm was building behind my eyes. "She can't take that drug. It's harmful to her and Hannah." I heard my words as though someone else was speaking them. I wanted to stand up and gaze at my reflection in the window to make sure I was really here.

Mrs. Bucheim tore off a chunk of bread, slathered it with butter, seemingly indifferent to my warning. I was mesmerized by the strength in her knobby, arthritic hands.

"The doc said it was medicine for her nerves. That it would calm her. It wasn't my place to question the doc or what medicine the missus took."

What about Irene? It was important to me to understand this woman whose life had been so cruelly ended and whose shoes I was walking in.

"Did Irene know Catherine was taking the drug?" I looked over my shoulder expecting Irene to be there, urging me on, telling me to clear her name.

"She was her nurse, wasn't she? I don't know what you're nattering on about Matthew taking medicine from your bag. He was only doing right by her. He'd do anything for the missus."

I dabbed at my damp forehead with my napkin, suddenly wondering if he would commit murder for her, or was it Irene wondering that? Had I been too single-minded in my belief that William was the murderer?

"Well, Matthew wasn't doing right. You see that now, don't you, Mrs. Bucheim?" I stared into her dark eyes that seemed to swim away from me.

She grumbled her assent.

"Promise me, you'll tell Matthew that giving Catherine the laudanum was dangerous to her and Hannah." I wanted her to say she would tell him, if only to stop my head from spinning.

"I doubt he'll listen to me. He likes to go his own way. But I'll try."

How little I knew of Matthew, who suddenly loomed as a possible killer.

"Are Matthew and William close?" I asked innocently, as I cut a cube of meat into a tiny piece and put it in my mouth. It, too, melted on my tongue, leaving a rancid aftertaste.

Mrs. Bucheim arched one of her dark eyebrows. "As close as brothers."

That's what Catherine had said. I washed down the unknown meat with a swallow of coffee, heavily laced with sugar and cream. For a moment, it seemed to steady me.

"When did Matthew start working for William?" This raspy voice didn't sound like me.

"Are you feeling all right? You're sweating?"

Her concern felt like the lake's rolling waves, tossing me back and forth.

"I'm tired, that's all. Tell me about Matthew," I persisted. "How did he end up being foreman? He doesn't seem . . ." I paused searching for the right word, "suited. He seems happier hunting. Was it because of his boyhood friendship with William?"

My head was pounding so loud I thought Mrs. Bucheim could hear it.

"Mr. Henry hired Matthew as a logger. That's how he got the bum leg. A tree fell the wrong way. That soured him. Not long after Mr. Henry died, William took over and made Matthew foreman and caretaker. He was none too happy."

She dabbed at her thin lips with the checkered napkin as though the words had soiled them. Was she smiling behind the napkin?

"Matthew?" My mind drifted. I was finding it harder to concentrate.

"No, Mr. William. You sure you're feeling all right? Your face is as red as a rooster's wattle."

That was the second time or was it the third she'd asked me that.

"I'm fine. Why was William unhappy?"

"He thought he'd inherit Mr. Henry's Chicago construction business. He'd been working there for years. But Mr. Henry had other plans. Left the construction business to his other nephew. Gave Mr. William the island and the logging concern instead. Don't ask me why."

So, Henry Thiery wasn't as fair minded as she'd first told me. William had been saddled with a business he had no interest in, sentenced to live on an isolated island, with an unhappy, unstable wife.

"Aren't you going to eat your stew?" she asked, smiling grimly.

I picked up my fork and made another foray into the greasy collage. My brain bounced to Frederick Huber and my suspicion that he knew something about the Harmonites, might even have been one of them. I touched the place where the pendant rested, out of sight under my dress.

"I met Bernie's father this afternoon at the tavern. Do you know when he and Bernie came to the island?"

"How should I know? And what were you doing at the tavern? That's no place for a woman."

What answer would please her? "Theo wanted to know what time Father Quinn had left the tavern last night."

"He should have done that himself." She dipped her bread into the stew and swirled it around before taking a generous bite. "Now are you going to finish that or just move it around your plate?"

I looked down at my plate. The meat had turned a peculiar gray color. "My stomach's a bit off."

"Looking at too many dead bodies will do that," she quipped.

Chapter Forty-Six

The spiral staircase swirled around me as I made my way unsteadily toward the turret room. Dizzy and disoriented, the drug still lingered, though its hold on me was lessening, leaving me exhausted. For once, I welcomed the eerie, drafty room and the hard bed.

When I reached the landing, I stopped and held the kerosene lamp aloft. The door to my room was ajar.

Had I left it that way? In my haste to leave this morning, I couldn't remember.

When I entered the circular room, nothing appeared amiss. The fire glowed faintly; the curtains stood open, the bed unmade, the key still on the dresser beside the ewer and basin.

I closed the creaky door and shoved the chair under it. Then I moved the bed and opened the secret compartment. Everything was still there: Irene's locket, the Moroccan binder, and John Engel's book. I pushed the bed back into place and lifted the mattress. Eleanor's letter was where I'd hidden it.

Breathing a sigh of relief, weariness rolled over me. I kicked off my boots and sat down on the narrow bed, my mind sifting through what Mrs. Bucheim had told me about Matthew. How he'd do anything for Catherine. And how Catherine had accused me of pursuing William, like Irene had done. Jealousy and blind devotion were a lethal combination.

I could see Catherine, her mind swimming with laudanum and jealousy, begging Matthew to rid her of Irene. And Matthew, the hunter, luring Irene into the forest on some pretext, limping behind her, then smashing her head with a rock before burying her in a shallow grave.

Not bothering to change, I lay on the bed, gazing up at the cobwebs swaying above me, then glanced at the dresser, where the portal lay—a cold descent into the cellar, a hunched walk through a dank tunnel, and a trapdoor leading to an altar. Night after night my guilt had conjured an illusion, a presence I was convinced was my mother come to haunt me. And the dead child's dissolved face—was she, too, haunting me? My practical mind couldn't account for it. And that deeply shook me. Was I losing my grip on reality?

My emotions were plummeting as though I was falling off a cliff into a dark abyss. I could sense the presence wanting in, wanting to tell me something I didn't want to hear.

"Go away," I whispered, then turned off the lamp, rolled onto my side away from the dresser, and closed my eyes against it.

❧

Leaves fall all around me in colors so bright my eyes hurt. Matthew limps toward me. In one hand he holds a dead rabbit, in the other a large rock. I try to run, but my feet are tangled in the undergrowth of vines, thick as snakes.

He throws the rabbit at my feet. Its throat is slit. Its fur drenched in blood.

"You ask too many questions. The last one was nosy like you," he says, lifting the rock over his head.

I raise my arms against the blow. "Don't," I cry. "Don't."

❧

I woke drenched in sweat, my hair damp on my neck, my pillowcase smeared with blood from my cut finger that throbbed with pain.

Light was glistening the stained-glass windows, the golden roses, pulsing with color. I stared at the roses as the dream's menace faded away.

Golden roses. *The* golden rose—Huber's words came back to me. He'd recognized it, but when I asked him, he'd been evasive.

"It's gold, ain't it?"

He knew something about the Harmonites. But I needed tangible proof linking the golden rose to the Harmonites besides mere decoration. And if he evaded me again? Then I'd go to Bernie.

My heart thudding in my chest, I got up and pushed the bed aside. With anxious fingers, I pried up the loose floorboard and retrieved the binder. Drawings in hand, I shuffled through them until I located the detailed sketch of the church.

Though I suspected what I'd find, I wanted to be sure. There was always the possibility that Engel's original design had been altered.

The drawing of the church depicted the same rose design I'd seen carved into the church's lintel, which was the same rose in the turret windows, and nearly the same rose as my mother's pendant. Unlike the turret windows and the church's carved rose, my mother's pendant had no leaflets or stems.

I read the footnote at the bottom of the drawing, printed in large, bold letters and heavily inked.

Drawing by Caleb Engel. Below his name he'd written *Door of Promise*.

In the dawning light, the room came into focus. I wasn't sure when Mrs. Bucheim began her morning ministrations. But it would only take ten minutes, at the most.

I knew exactly where to find Caleb Engel's book—*Ideas on the Fate of Man, pertaining to the Present Times and the Second Coming*, which detailed the tenets of his Harmonite Community. Within those tenets, I hoped to find the significance of the golden rose to the Harmonite Community.

In my stocking feet, so as not to wake anyone, I hurried out of the room and down the spiral stairs. If I was right, then as Irene had claimed, a Harmonite had returned to the island. And I knew who that was.

The book was where I'd last seen it. I pulled it out, searched the index for the chapter titled *God's House on Earth*. Quickly, I skimmed the pages until I found the reference.

"I had a vision of the Golden Rose as a symbol for our colony according to the prophet Micah. 'The Golden Rose shall in truth come to you; yea, the divine Holy Ghost, which proceeds from the Father and the Son shall make his abode with you. You will found a colony whose constitution was grounded upon the words in the Acts of the Apostles.' The Golden Rose will anchor our church on earth."

Though the significance of the Golden Rose to the Harmonites wasn't clear to me, it was clear that it was a symbol for their colony.

Was it too big a leap to believe Frederick Huber was the returned Harmonite? His fascination with my pendant, calling it the golden rose, his questions about my mother, and his evasiveness all pointed to him. Whether he was the returned Harmonite or not, he knew something about them. Which meant Bernie knew about them.

But if Huber was the returned Harmonite, would he admit it? He'd kept his identity a secret because, if Irene was right, he'd done something terrible he didn't want known.

"I don't care what you did," I'd tell him. "I just want to know what happened to my father."

CHAPTER FORTY-SEVEN

It was late afternoon before I reached the town. It had been a tumultuous day.

Suffering the effects of withdrawal from the laudanum, Catherine had been beyond reason. To my query about her dinner with William, she'd snapped, "Your reign of terror is over. You have two days."

Even my offer of a sleeping potion was met with resistance.

Panicked, I'd frantically continued my search for the diary, but found nothing in the drawing room or the parlor. For once Mrs. Bucheim hadn't been watching my every move. She didn't even question where I was going when I left Ravenwood. Maybe I was no longer any of her concern, since I'd soon be gone.

The gray undecided sky matched my thoughts, as I hurried past the white church toward the tavern, barely feeling the cold. I'd formulated no strategy for the wily Mr. Huber, who I suspected used his infirmities to run roughshod over people, especially Bernie.

A feeble attempt at a path had been carved out of the snow, leading to the tavern door. When I stepped inside, it was as though Mr. Huber had never moved since my last visit. He sat in front of the hearth in his cane-backed wheelchair, an open book on his lap, a mug on the floor beside him. No one else was in the tavern.

"Come back, have you, girlie?" he said, turning his watery eyes on me.

I stomped the snow off my boots and walked toward him, determined to get a straight answer from the sly, old coot. I grabbed a chair and placed it near him, but far enough away from his steely grasp.

Sitting down, I unwound my scarf, unbuttoned my coat, and retrieved the golden rose pendant. I dangled it in front of him like a taunt.

"You recognized this, didn't you?"

His cloudy eyes roamed my face, then landed on the pendant. "Of course," he scoffed. "Who wouldn't? That rose is everywhere, the church, in them windows at Ravenwood, everywhere."

"It's the symbol of the Harmonites, a religious sect who lived on the island before Henry Thiery." I said Harmonites firmly but slowly, so he would hear me.

"Harm a who?" He cupped his ear, grinning. "You have to speak up. I can't make out what you're saying. Come closer."

I wasn't falling for that trick again. "Mr. Huber, you can hear me just fine. Were you a Harmonite? Did you return to the island after they left?"

"What are you accusing me of?" His eyes glazed with worry, his aged hands clutched the wheelchair wheels so tightly his knuckles whitened.

"I'm not accusing you of anything. I don't care what you did back then. My parents were Harmonites. I just want to know what happened to my father, John Engel." I was frantic with impatience.

His large hands started turning the unwieldy wheels. The wheelchair moved backwards, then sideways, knocking over the mug. Coffee ran across the filthy stone floor but he kept turning the wheels desperate to escape me.

"I promise I won't tell," I begged him, rising from the chair.

"Leave me alone, you she-witch," he said, trying to maneuver away from me, bumping into chairs and tables.

"What's all the racket?" Bernie emerged from the back room, wiping her hands on a rag. "Pa, whatcha doing? Stop moving." She untangled Huber from the chairs.

"Tell her to get outta here." He pointed a shaky finger at me. "She's like the other one. Poking her nose where it don't belong. Asking too many questions."

"I didn't mean to upset you, Mr. Huber," I said, my open hands by my side in a gesture of surrender.

"I think you'd better leave, Nellie," Bernie replied. "Pa is having one of his days."

"I'm not having one of my days," he shouted. "It's her. Talking nonsense."

"I'm sorry," I said, as I shoved the pendant under my dress and made for the door.

When I stepped outside the cold descended with an iron swiftness, making it hard to catch my breath. Humiliated and frustrated, I lumbered down the snowy path toward the road.

"Wait up," Bernie called after me.

When she reached me, she grabbed my arm with such force I felt her crushing grip through my coat. "You can't come to the tavern anymore," she said. "I don't know what you said to my pa, but I don't want him upset. He's a sickly old man."

I pulled my arm away. "I was asking him if he was a Harmonite. They were a religious group who lived on the island before Henry Thiery. Disappeared in the night. No one knows what happened. You said you knew nothing about them. That I should talk to Theo Proctor." Even to my own ears, I sounded daft.

She stepped back as though I'd slapped her. "Is that what you were pestering my pa about? You think he belonged to that group that once lived here, then disappeared? Well, he didn't. And I never said I didn't know about them. Though I never heard them called Harmonites."

"You said you didn't know who lived at Ravenwood before Henry Thiery. Which is the same thing." I knew what I heard.

"I thought you were asking about a specific person living at Ravenwood. What do these Harmonites have to do with you anyway?"

"My parents were Harmonites. I only discovered that after my mother died," I explained, tamping down my desperation. I told her about the photograph and the pendant, and that my father might have died on the island. But I held back about the diary.

"Still don't see what any of this has to do with my pa."

I yanked out the rose pendant and showed it to her. "Your father wanted to know where I got this. He called it *the* golden rose as if it had some meaning to him." I emphasized *the*. "In the Ravenwood library I found a book about the Harmonites. The golden rose was the symbol of their religious community."

"Look, Nellie, I'm sorry for you not knowing about your pa. I really am. But we're from Manistee. That's where we lived before coming here, after my ma died. The land was cheap, and Pa wanted a new start. Me and Pa don't know nothing about golden roses or Harmonites."

I wasn't sure I believed her. Bernie was a devoted daughter and she wouldn't hesitate to lie for her father.

"Maybe you just don't remember." I wanted to give her the benefit of the doubt. Though, considering Bernie was a few years older than me, she would have been six or seven years old when the Harmonites lived on the island. Old enough to remember.

Her concerned expression hardened. "Are you calling me a liar?"

"Bernie, if you and your father were Harmonites, you have to tell me, please," I pleaded.

"I'm no liar and if I catch you near my pa again, you'll answer to me." She shoved me aside as she walked the snowy pathway to the tavern.

⚘

Shaken by my encounter with Huber and Bernie, I trundled down the snow-covered road to the post office. Maybe the letter I'd been expecting from Eleanor, containing the information about Irene, had arrived.

Orr wasn't in the post office. But the woodstove radiated a welcome heat. Like a moth to a flame, I went to it. As I stood warming my hands, I peeked at the cubbyholes. None held mail. On the counter was a gray mail sack. Faded black letters spelling *Domestic* festooned the sack, as well as a trail of numbers that had no meaning to me.

Today's mail had yet to be sorted. Anxious to get to Ravenwood before dark, I called out a hello. No answer.

Thinking Orr might be in the general store, I left the comfort of the woodstove and walked down the short hallway that connected the post office to the store, past the stairs that led to what I assumed were Orr's upstairs living quarters.

I'd never ventured into the store, having no money to buy anything. It was a small store overflowing with various canned goods, dry goods, and sundries, favoring the loggers' needs.

Like the post office, it boasted a woodstove with a pipe chimney that curved to an outside wall. A large silver-plated cash register adorned the shiny wood counter. Rows of boxes lined the top shelf. Several items of clothes hung on a rack. Though worn, the wood floor was swept clean of dirt and snow. Orr was as meticulous as he was observant.

Restless, I returned to the post office. The squat mail sack was too tempting. Before opening it, I went to the window and looked up and down the road. It was empty.

My heart fluttering, I slid open the clip, loosened the rope, and pulled out the letters. Quickly, I riffled through the handful of letters, looking for my name. There was no letter addressed to me. I started to shove the letters back into the sack when I saw the scribbled name. In my hurry, I'd gone right past it.

The letter was addressed to Irene Hayes, Ravenwood Manor, New Harmony, Michigan. I turned it over. Written on the flap was: Chester Docket, Traverse City, Michigan.

I heard the creak of footsteps on the stairs. I crammed the letter in my purse, secured the mail sack, and returned to the woodstove.

"Miss Lester," Orr said, as he bounded into the room. His white hair stood up around his head. "You caught me taking my afternoon snooze. I see Tom left the mail sack."

"I stopped in to see if my letter came." I clutched my purse so tightly my shoulder ached.

"Well, let's take a look-see."

Instead of opening the mail sack, he picked up his pipe from the counter, knocked the spent ashes into a can on the floor, packed the pipe with tobacco from his leather pouch, lit it, took a few puffs, then he spread the letters out on the counter and went through them one by one.

I was so nervous, I wanted to jump out of my skin.

"Sorry. Doesn't seem to be here," he said, taking the pipe out of his mouth.

"Thank you. I'd better be going. It's a long walk back to Ravenwood."

"I saw you at the tavern yesterday morning. Bernie told me you asked her what time Father Quinn left the tavern."

"Nothing escapes you, Mr. Orr," I teased him.

"There's no question it was an accident?" His stare was unnerving.

"Looks that way." I moved to the door, then turned back. "You'll hold my letter when it comes?"

He tapped the side of his hoary head. "I haven't forgotten. Still got my faculties. Tell Mrs. Thiery I'll bring by the christening photographs tomorrow."

The last rays of light hovered over the lake as I started up the road, struggling through the deep, snowy grooves left by the logging sleds. Only the mail boat still bobbed in the harbor. I pulled my wool scarf around my face against the falling snow and gusting wind coming from the northwest.

Like the wind, my mind whirled with a conviction, one I couldn't prove–Frederick Huber was the returned Harmonite. And with that conviction another–the missing diary had been written by a Harmonite.

Despite Bernie's plausible story about coming from Manistee, I didn't believe her. She was covering for her father. His grasping fascination with the gold pendant, his questioning whether my mother had worn it, the way he said, "finely made," as though he had had a hand in its creation.

As I reached the turnoff to Ravenwood Manor, that nagging question at the heart of the mystery returned: What had Huber done that he didn't want known?

And how far would a daughter go to protect her father?

CHAPTER FORTY-EIGHT

"The missus told me you're leaving," Mrs. Bucheim said, uncharacteristically lingering at the table after dinner. She'd waited until Matthew had lumbered away to the caretaker cottage, the cur sniffing at his heels. Sitting next to Matthew during dinner had me on edge. I'd kept looking at his powerful hands and imagining them smashing a rock into Irene's skull.

"Catherine thought it best I leave by the end of the week. She no longer needs my help." Aggrieved, I stared down at my empty plate. Hunger had overcome my aversion to the gamey stew, aided by Mrs. Bucheim's warm honey biscuits.

She shook her head and tsked. "The missus is not herself. I'll talk to her."

Incredulous, I asked, "You want me to stay?"

"Well, I can't handle her and Hannah by myself," she huffed. "That's what I told the doc when he came round to see her after you left. She was madder than a nest of hornets when he refused her that medicine. She threw him out."

She rose stiffly from the table and began clearing the dishes and cutlery. I caught the scent of the rheumatoid salve I'd given her. After she piled the dishes and cutlery in the cast iron sink, she picked up the kettle of hot water and poured it into the sink before sitting down, probably letting them soak.

"Took me an hour to settle Hannah. I'm just too old for this," she said wearily. "I'm starting to think there might be something wrong with the missus."

I hid my shock at her admission. So, she'd finally seen past her loyalty to Catherine and William. It was a small but important victory.

"Is William coming home tonight?" I didn't think he'd rescind Catherine's short notice, but I wanted to convince him that Catherine needed professional treatment.

She shrugged. "Missus seems to think so. Well, I'd better clean up before the water gets cold. And no, I don't need your help."

⸎

As I made my way past the grim ancestors, averting my eyes from the girl's death portrait, I pondered Mrs. Bucheim's change of attitude and concluded it had little to do with me. Aging and burdened with crippling arthritis, she could no longer handle Catherine and Hannah by herself. In the days I'd been at Ravenwood Manor, she'd realized four hands were better than two, even if they were my hands.

Once I reached the turret room, I secured the door with the chair and sat down on the unyielding bed. A slight tremor ran through me as I tore open the envelope and unfolded the letter.

The paper was ragged at the top, probably ripped from a notebook, and splotched with ink where the pen had leaked. It was dated over two weeks ago, before I came to the island, and well after Irene's death. When Chester Docket penned his letter, he'd had no idea he was writing to a dead woman.

Dear Miss Hayes,

I'm sorry for my delay in writing you. What you asked me took longer than expected. I had to see about a job first. I'm working in Manistee on a dairy farm. My ankle has healed, thanks to you and the doc.

Now to George Orr. No one ever heard of him in Lake City. So he was lying about that. But I decided to ask about him in nearby towns. Bingo. One old timer in Cadillac knew George. Grew up with him. Said he was always looking for trouble. Got in a bar fight once and nearly killed an Injun. Beat the brains out of him for no good reason except he was an Injun. Now here's the interesting part. The old timer remembered George leaving over 30 some years ago. He got religion, joined some fool religious group, the old guy said. Changed his name to Jeremiah Strong. Never heard from him since.

So I guess your doubting him was right. Though I always thought George was a harmless old coot, just a little too much in other people's business. I wished you'd shown me this peculiar diary you found. I might have been able to give you my two cents.

Whatever this is about, I'd be careful. A man only lies for one reason; he's hiding something he doesn't want anyone to know.

I can't thank you enough for nursing me back to health.

Sincerely,
Chester A. Docket

George Orr? I read the letter again as though I'd missed some hidden clue, buried in the words of this plainspoken man. I'd missed nothing. Still, I couldn't wrap my mind around it. I'd been so certain Huber was the returned Harmonite and that Bernie had lied to me. But I'd been wrong. George Orr, not ornery Frederick Huber, was the Harmonite who'd returned to the island. George Orr, the easygoing, kind "old coot," who knew everyone on the island and had his finger on everyone's comings and goings.

Then I remembered how surprised I was at Orr's anger when he'd called Abe a murdering Injun bastard. And Abe's claim that it was Orr who'd beaten him. Was there another side to the affable George Orr? And what had he done that he didn't want anyone to know?

My heart thundered. I placed my hand on my chest as if that could quiet it. The returned Harmonite Jeremiah Strong aka George Orr had been living in New Harmony in plain sight.

Jeremiah Strong? Why did that name sound familiar to me? I couldn't put my finger on it. Whatever his name, it didn't matter. Nor did it matter what he'd done.

That was in the past, I told myself. I was a hair's breath away from learning my father's fate.

My tenure at Ravenwood Manor ended in two days. This couldn't wait until morning.

Whatever tiredness I'd been feeling had evaporated. Quickly, I donned my coat, hat, scarf, and gloves, then slipped the letter and the sheathed photograph into my pocket.

As I opened the door and stepped onto the landing, I heard raised voices funneling up the spiral staircase from the first floor: William's indecipherable baritone and Catherine's high-pitched whine. I couldn't make out their words, only their tenor. They were arguing. I stepped back into the room and shut the door leaning against it, considering what to do.

I glanced at the ponderous dresser. I didn't like my other option, but I was too impatient to wait.

The dresser was no easier to move than the first time. As I flew down the stone steps, I thought of my carefully measured life. In my twenty-eight years, I'd never done anything so ill-conceived or so foolish, except coming to the island. But I wasn't turning back.

If possible, the cellar was mustier and colder than before. I pushed open the storm cellar door and stepped out into the harsh clear night.

A crescent moon shared the sky with a dazzle of stars. I took in a deep breath. The air so sharp, it stung my lungs.

In the distance I heard the muffled howl of the cur. I hurried away from Ravenwood Manor, trudging through snowdrifts and looking over my shoulder for the rampant dog.

When I reached the rutted road, I let out a sigh of relief and followed the lumber wagon's runners, grateful for the lighthouse's relentless beam, lighting the night and making it less lonely.

By the time I neared the town, I'd lost feeling in my hands and feet. As I moved past the tavern, where two forlorn horses stood blanketed and tied up, I thought of how wrong I'd been thinking Frederick Huber was the returned Harmonite. I owed him and Bernie an apology.

I picked up my pace and headed to the general store. Though the store was dark, the upstairs living quarters glowed with a soft light.

It took too long for Orr to answer my insistent banging. When he finally opened the door and saw me shivering on his doorstep, he didn't look surprised.

"Sorry to disturb you but I need to talk to you," I said, pushing past him, not waiting for him to invite me in.

He shut the door, turned the lock, and pulled down the roller shade. The sound of the lock engaging gave me pause. But I wasn't leaving.

"What are you doing here? Has something happened at Ravenwood?" A black shiny apron protected his corduroy trousers and red flannel shirt. A chemical odor clung to him like animal musk.

"It's a personal matter that concerns you. It can't wait," I blurted out, looking back at the locked door, my desperation overriding my common sense.

He stared at me with a curious intensity, as though seeing me for the first time.

"Why don't you come upstairs. I can finish the developing process later," he said, taking off his apron and laying it across the store counter.

"I'll make you a warm milk toddy. Then you can tell me what brought you here on such a cold night."

His affability was unnerving, as was the partially opened door and its strange light slicing into the room.

As I followed him up the worn wooden steps to his living quarters, my heart thundered in my chest. I'd been too impulsive. I should have thought this through. Other than Docket's letter, what proof did I have that Orr was the returned Harmonite? And if he was the returned Harmonite, what grim secret was he hiding? What would he do to keep it hidden? I should leave, but I couldn't. I had to know about my father.

The stairs led to a small, sparsely furnished parlor: two rockers, one side table holding an ashtray and a pipe, a woodstove, a brown leather sofa, a bookcase, and a table covered with a white cloth. The room had the feel of a monk's cell. Only the atmospheric island photographs that adorned one wall broke its austerity. The heavy scent of tobacco and burning wood hung over the low-ceiling. I was finding it hard to breathe.

"Make yourself at home," he said, stoking the wood in the stove with a metal rod before disappearing into his kitchen.

While he prepared the toddy, I explored the bookcase. Each shelf was artfully arranged with colorful rocks, Indian arrowheads, and books. A small, tattered book jutted out from the others.

I was about to reach for it when Orr came up behind me. "Hobby of mine, collecting beach stones." He offered me one of the brown earthenware mugs he was holding.

"Those honeycomb-looking ones are Petoskey stones. Named after the Michigan town. They're fossilized coral." He reached across me and grabbed the biggest one.

I stepped back.

"This one's about ten pounds," he said, hefting the rock that filled the palm of his hand. "But you didn't come here to learn about Petoskey stones, did you?"

With care, he replaced the stone. Then he moved to one of the rockers and placed his mug on the side table.

"Please sit. You must be tired after your long walk." He gestured toward the sofa. "Now what's this personal matter that concerns me?"

I wasn't the least bit tired but I sat on the sofa, cupping the warm drink between my gloved hands. Though the room was warm, I was still trembling with cold. I took a generous swallow of the toddy. It flowed down my throat and into my stomach like velvet.

I inched forward and placed the mug on the table, then fished the letter and photograph from my coat pocket. Orr had yet to take a sip of his drink. His keen blue eyes watched my every movement as he rocked back and forth slowly.

Holding the letter and the photograph, I said, "Mr. Orr, I'm sure you've heard of the Harmonites, a religious sect who lived on the island before Henry Thiery. No one seems to know what happened to them. I have proof you were once one of them."

His face was so impassive, I wasn't sure he heard me.

"Is that the letter you stole from the mail sack today? The one addressed to Irene Hayes?" He stopped rocking.

A frisson of fear shot up my spine. "How did you know?"

"Oh, you foolish girl, meddling in other people's business." He shook his white head as if I were a recalcitrant schoolgirl. "Every mail sack contains a sheet of paper with the letter count for that day. Today's count was 14. But there were only 13 letters in the sack. I thought Tom, who brings the mail by boat, had made another mistake. So, I went to the tavern to ask him about the missing letter. When I told him he was short a letter, he mentioned there'd been a letter to the dead girl. When I searched the sack there was no letter for Irene. Since you'd been in the post office right after the sack was delivered, I knew you took it."

My face burning, I took another swallow of the toddy. "I'm sorry. I was looking for my letter and saw Irene's."

"And you decided to take it. That's a federal offense." He grinned. "Hand over the letter and we'll forget about all this. No one has to know."

I wasn't giving him the letter. Once he knew its contents, I was afraid he'd toss it in the woodstove.

"I can't."

I slipped the letter from the envelope and read it to him. When I finished, he was staring through me as if I wasn't there.

Finally, he spoke. "What's it to do with you if I were a Harmonite?"

I rose from the settee and crossed the room, my legs suddenly shaky. The milk toddy had hit me hard. Standing in front of him, I held out the photograph. His eyes flicked over it, then looked away as if the photograph offended him.

"That's me and those are my parents. You recognize them, don't you?"

"Why don't you sit down?"

I wasn't sitting down. He was going to tell me what I wanted to know.

I turned the photograph over so he could read the inscription. "My mother told me my father died before I was born. I'm almost certain the man in the photograph is my father. Do you know what happened to him?"

He said nothing.

Suddenly my body felt heavy with exhaustion. I shoved the photograph and letter in my coat pocket and staggered back to the settee.

I had to make him talk.

"There's a diary. I believe it belonged to a Harmonite. Father Quinn told me Irene had discovered it at Ravenwood. Something in the diary led her to believe one of the Harmonites had returned to the island. That's why she wrote the letter to Docket, and he all but confirmed it was you."

I waited for his denial. His eyes drifted to the bookcase, and then back to me as if calculating the distance.

"I don't care why you came back here. I just want to know about my father. Did he leave the island with the Harmonites? Is that what my mother meant by 'they took John from us?' Or was he–?" I hesitated.

A sly smile crossed his lined face. It was like watching a lizard change colors. "It's your mother's fault your father died."

"What are you saying? That my mother had something to do with my father's death? I don't believe you." He was lying. My mother would never hurt anyone.

He stood and walked to the bookcase. I turned and watched as he pulled out the slim book I'd noticed earlier.

Then he sat down beside me, holding the worn book in front of my face. Its black leather cover was cracked, its spine peeling.

"Do you know what this is?"

When I didn't answer, he said, "It's your mother's diary. The one Irene found at Ravenwood."

My mother was the author of the mysterious diary? I couldn't quite take it in.

Then it hit me like a body blow. There was only one way Orr could have gotten his hands on the diary. He killed Irene.

I had to get out of here. But not without the diary. I lunged for it. He shoved me so hard, I fell backward on the sofa.

I tried to stand but my legs gave way. A wave of panic swept through me. He'd put something in my drink.

A resigned sadness crept into his face. "It's useless to fight it, Anna. I should have recognized you the moment I saw you."

I flinched as he touched my hair, then ran his rough hand across my cheek. "You're so like your father."

Anna, my name is Anna, I thought stupidly.

"John Engel, your father, died here, because of your mother. That evil bitch fooled everyone. Even you."

"No, she was good," I whispered. My eyes were beginning to close. *I can't fall asleep. I have to keep him talking, convince him to let me go.*

Suddenly he slapped my face and all my hope of escape left me.

"Stay awake," he commanded. "Don't you want to hear your parents' sordid tale? It's all here in your mother's diary."

Taking in a ragged breath, he carefully opened the fragile book. The room seemed to dissolve around me. What remained was his angry face and flaming red shirt as if all the light and air resided in him.

As he began to read my mother's words, I heard her voice, rising above his hatred. I felt myself slipping away, back to the island when I was a child. I saw my mother sitting by the hearth, pen in hand, writing, her face quivering with emotions that I didn't understand.

> *"November 1, 1894. They won't tell me where they buried John. There's no fresh grave in the cemetery beneath Sophia's gaze. I fear they've burned his body to punish me for my testimony against Brother Engel. Without a human form, he will not ascend.*
>
> *He died in my arms, his body raging with fever. Anna, a quiet mouse in the corner, heard his last breath and watched his spirit rise. I saw it myself. How he hovered over our marital bed. All pain gone.*

The vision sharp as a knife pierced me—my father's last breath, his spirit leaving us, the emptiness I'd felt.

Orr's brutal slap stunned me awake.

I struggled to speak. "It was a fever that killed him, not my mother."

"A fever I caused," he gloated.

The rustling of the diary pages made me shudder. There was still some horrible secret Orr wanted me to know. Some lethal punishment he'd inflicted on my father.

"Ah, here it is." He tapped the page with his finger. "I could almost thank Sister Gertrude for telling your mother what I'd done to your father. It added to her sorrow. But then it was Gertrude that helped her escape. If only I'd known. No matter now."

His words were jumbled in my head–Sister Gertrude, escape, added to sorrow, what he'd done to my father. My head lolled back.

Orr shook me so hard my teeth rattled. "Wake up, Anna, it's almost over." His voice seemed to come from far away.

I blinked my eyes open. Orr was a wash of color without form. Even his vivid red shirt was fading. Fighting the drug's pull, I bit the inside of my mouth until I tasted blood. I had to know how my father died.

"November 30, 1894. Sister Gertrude came last night to my room after midnight. My persecutor turned ally.

"The brethren mean to make an example of you," she murmured. "As they did Brother John. I overheard Brother Engel and Brother Jeremiah whispering in the library. Brother Jeremiah persuaded Brother Engel to exact the same punishment on you that was meted out on John. The bone whip will be soaked in the steeped leaves of deadly nightshade. I will not abide murder. No matter the depth of the sin."

"They murdered John?"

"They murdered John?" Orr repeated my mother's words in a mocking tone. "Not they, you wicked, Black witch, but me." He thumped his chest triumphantly. "Me!"

Then he closed the diary and stood, looming over me. "Your father felt the ire of my poisoned whip and didn't survive. Nor will you."

And then I fell into darkness.

CHAPTER FORTY-NINE

Snow woke me. Heavy, determined flakes falling fast from a blank sky. I was cocooned in it. No longer shivering, I was beyond cold. I'd never felt so at peace.

"Momma," I murmured. She was hovering over me dressed in her burial clothes.

"Get up," she demanded. "Anna, you have to get up."

I closed my eyes against her plea. Sleep, I wanted the balm of sleep to take away the cold that had invaded my body. A body I could barely feel.

My mind drifted away, my body with it. It would be so easy. No pain. Just a welcome sleep.

Far away a baby wailed in misery. His plaintive cries carried on the wind. What he wanted, only I could give. I was done giving.

I curled into a ball and rolled over. The ground gave way beneath me as I fell like the snow. I landed with a soft thud.

Where was I? All I could see was white. I turned on my side afraid the whiteness would swallow me. Then I saw it–the altar. Where Orr had left me to die.

I was inside the maze.

Words I didn't want to remember returned. "Now justice can be done."

Anger flooded my body and with it pain. As though in a dream, I pushed myself up to a seated position. My clothes seemed to be strangling me. I unbuttoned my coat, tore off my scarf and gloves.

Move. The wind moaned. Move. I put my hands over my ears to stop it. No, no, no, I murmured.

But the wind wouldn't stop moaning. I had to get away from it. I struggled to my feet, staggering, then my legs gave way. I lay on my back, listening to the ticking of my brain.

Get up. Get up. Get up. There was no escaping its insistence.

I crawled to where I'd thrown my scarf and gloves, wrapped the scarf round my face, shoved my icy hands into the gloves, and buttoned my coat. Then I crawled under the altar.

It's going to hurt. It's going to be hard. And still you might die.

Those were my thoughts as I cleared the snow from the trapdoor, as I yanked on the handle, as I inched down the stone steps on my hands and knees, not trusting my legs.

The tunnel stretched before me, long and dark, its earthy smell the way I imagined death. Bracing myself against the wall, I slowly rose and took a tentative step forward, then another, then another. My icy, useless feet dragged along the tunnel's dirt floor. My legs kept collapsing under me. But I kept going, hunched and hurting.

When I reached the tunnel's end, I shoved the barrels aside. Spent, I lay down on the cellar's dirt floor, shivering uncontrollably. Cold, like a shadow, wouldn't leave me. Though the tremors were painful, I knew it was a good sign. My body was awakening.

Only a few more steps, I told myself as I painstakingly climbed the worn wooden steps to the larder door. The door was shut. My stiff hands fumbled with the doorknob. I took off my gloves, blew on my hands, and rubbed them together. Then I turned the knob, but the door wouldn't budge.

On the other side of the door, I heard the creak of footsteps coming from the kitchen. "Help me," I called hoarsely.

The footsteps came closer. The door swung open.

"What the devil are you doing in the cellar?" William asked. His hair disheveled, clad in red-and-white flannel pajamas, he held a mug of what smelled like cider.

"George Orr," I whispered. "Tried to kill me."

CHAPTER FIFTY

Matthew emerged from the town stable, limping toward the sleigh where William and I waited.

"Orr's wagon is still there. It's been out tonight. In the back I found ropes and a blanket. Must have dragged you to that altar. Can't see him carrying you," he said, as he clambered up onto the sleigh's seat.

I'd insisted on coming.

"It was me he wanted dead. He's not talking his way out of this," was all I'd needed to say to convince William and Matthew to let me accompany them.

Grumbling, William shook the reins. The bells jangled as the horse moved down the road toward the general store. The snow had stopped. But the moon was still lost among the clouds. The stars as lost as the moon.

Sandwiched between them on the sleigh seat, I writhed with fury, which had banished the cold from my bones. That and the hot cider William had given me.

Sitting in the warm kitchen, I'd explained everything to William from my discovery of the photograph that had brought me to the island to my mother's diary, which implicated Orr in my father's death, and my belief Orr had murdered Irene to protect his murderous secret, to his leaving me to die on the maze altar.

As I talked, I'd watched William's expressions change from anger to skepticism to determination. When I was done, he'd said, "That bastard's not getting away with murder."

He'd roused Matthew, who grudgingly agreed to come. His distrust of me was as pronounced as his crooked nose.

William guided the horse to the back of the post office near the jail's egress, where there was a lean-to. The area had been cleared of snow. Probably where he'd loaded me into his wagon.

No lights shown upstairs.

"I'll go around the front and bang on the door," William directed. "Matthew, you wait by the jail door, in case he runs out that way. Nellie, you stay in the sleigh."

While William made his way through the snow to the front of the store, Matthew tied the horse to the post, grabbed his rifle from the sleigh, then walked to the door. He looked like a hulking bear as he stood, rifle in hand, his back to me.

I couldn't sit still. It was too cold. Quietly, I stepped down from the sleigh and stood where Matthew couldn't see me, shifting from foot to foot to keep warm.

William's fierce hammering echoed through the quiet town. "George, open up. It's William Thiery," he shouted.

No answer.

His pounding resumed as he continued to shout, "Open up, George."

A light went on upstairs. I watched Orr's shadow move across the shade, then disappear. I held my breath, knowing Orr wouldn't go down easily.

William hammered again. Matthew moved closer to the back door, raising the rifle, anticipating Orr's escape.

The door flew open so fast, it knocked Matthew off balance, causing him to drop the rifle as he stumbled backward. Before Matthew could grab his rifle, Orr shot him. Matthew crumbled to the ground. Spooked, the horse jumped sideways.

In a panic, Orr started to run toward the dock. He was heading in my direction. I knew I should scurry to the other side of the sleigh, so he wouldn't see. But I couldn't let him get away. I had to stop him. I grabbed the whip from the sleigh floor.

When he reached the sleigh, he saw me. Just as he raised his gun, I struck him with the whip. The bullet went wide. The gun fell from his hand. But he kept coming. I struck him again, lashing his face. It didn't stop him.

His body slammed into me, knocking the air out of me. I fell backward into the snow, dropping the whip. His hands went round my neck. Furtively, I clawed at them. The pressure on my throat was unbearable. I couldn't breathe. My eyes started to water. I kept clawing at his hands, at his face, at his eyes. He was mad with hatred. A strange sour taste filled my mouth.

I reached around for something to hit him with. But all I felt was snow. I was dying. And the last thing I would see was my father's killer.

A loud crack sounded. Orr's hands fell away, a look of shock on his crazed face. The top of his skull was gone. He collapsed on top of me.

Repulsed, I shoved him off and rolled onto my side, coughing and choking, gasping for air.

"Are you all right?" Matthew stood over me. Blood bloomed from his arm, darkening his coat sleeve.

I sat up and tentatively felt my neck as I swallowed. Then I gathered a handful of snow and washed Orr's blood and tissue from my face.

"Thank you," I rasped.

"No thanks needed." Matthew held out his hand. I took it, trembling with adrenaline, as I struggled to my feet.

"What the hell happened?" William asked, as he came round the building, tromping through the snow.

"Orr tried to make a run for it. I shot him," Matthew answered, always a man of few words.

"Looks like he got one off before you brought him down." William pointed to Matthew's arm.

"Orr tried to strangle me. Matthew saved my life," I added, wanting to give William the full picture of what happened, how close I'd come to death.

Sorrow swept over me as I looked down at Orr's blasted head and scored face. The whip had lashed it open, the way I imagined he'd whipped my father. Though he'd murdered my father, Irene, and almost murdered me, I'd wanted him to live. His death took away all hope of knowing why he killed my father.

I looked out toward the turbulent lake. Heard the crashing of the waves. The island seemed to be held in its own chaos. I wanted to go home.

William and Matthew lifted Orr's body and hauled it inside the jail. I felt nothing as I watched them lay his body on the hard pallet, where Abe had waited for his lot to be decided. Now it had. Though he had his own sins to answer for, he hadn't killed Irene.

"We'll have to telegraph Sheriff Wilkins," William said, rubbing his blood-stained hands on his trousers. He glanced at Orr's body. "If we can't find someone who knows how to work the telegraph, in the morning one of the men can take the boat to Charlevoix."

"Matthew, let me tend to your wound," I whispered, my throat raw and tight. The blood was dripping down his arm onto the wood floor. "There are probably bandages and antiseptic in the store I can use to treat it, until we get back to Ravenwood."

We went into the dark post office. On the counter was a kerosene lamp. I lit it and walked through the breezeway into the general store, the men trailing behind.

"Take off your coat," I rasped to Matthew. "William, can you go upstairs and fetch me a basin of hot water so I can clean the wound?"

While I rummaged the store shelves for supplies, Matthew waited in the chair by the woodstove. Just as I expected, I found bandages and antiseptic.

After ripping Matthew's shirt away from his arm, I gently probed the wound. "It looks like the bullet went straight through. I'll clean it up."

When William came into the store, he was holding a steaming basin of water. Something was tucked under his arm. He put the basin down on the counter. I dipped the cloth in the water and started cleaning Matthew's wound.

Ever stoical, Matthew gritted his teeth through the pain. After I was done, I put the cloth in the basin, then applied antiseptic and wrapped his arm tightly. "When we get to the manor, I'll take another look at it."

"Thanks, Nellie," Matthew said, with such gratitude, tears rushed my eyes.

"It's me who should be thanking you," I answered, blinking away my tears. It had been a long and dreadful night.

"Nellie," William said.

I turned toward him. In his hand was my mother's diary.

CHAPTER FIFTY-ONE

Though the turret room's hearth blazed, I was shivering with apprehension as I sat on the hard bed. The diary rested in my lap—cracked, worn black leather, small and easily hidden. What pages remained had yellowed.

In my drugged state I hadn't noticed that Orr had ripped out most of the entries, leaving their jagged edges like teeth. I wondered why he'd left these?

Though Orr had crossed through the author's name with heavy ink, as if he could imprison her, it was still decipherable—Mary Engel.

On the inside flap she'd written the year 1894—the last year the Harmonites lived on the island before they disappeared.

I glanced at the dark dresser, half expecting the presence to be there. It wasn't. Maybe if I turned off the lamp. No.

I took in a deep breath and began to read.

March 30, 1894

John returned from the meeting of the brethren in a terrible state. Though he won't say it to me. For him, words are potent. I know he fears the Second Coming is near.

With anguish, he told me we are now to be celibate. Even the married couples are to refrain from all carnal acts. Brother Engel says we must be in a state of grace for Christ's coming.

I think not just of us, but also of Martha, newly married, so anxious to have a child. Just this morning, while we worked the fields, she said to me, "I want a girl just like your Anna. So sweet and obedient."

"Not always," I'd joked. "But I wouldn't trade Anna for the world."

While we sat at the kitchen table, John held his head in his hands; his shoulders slumped. Coming to the island has changed him from an easy man to a man deeply shadowed.

I could kill Brother Engel for what he's done to him. I bite my tongue at my blasphemous words.

If only I could have been at the meeting when he stood before the men, preaching in his booming voice, telling them they are the chosen people, divinely appointed to establish the Kingdom of God on earth after the Second Coming of Christ.

It's a wonder his words didn't turn to poison in his mouth. That God didn't strike him down.

But I am not honest with myself. I would have kept silent. It is my way. It's how I've kept my secret hidden, even from John. Though sometimes I think he knows but is afraid to ask.

On these pages, I can tell the truth. Though no one can ever see what I write.

If only I had tarried longer in the greenhouse on that fateful day. Then I wouldn't have seen them. Light-footed and eager to return to our cottage, I hurried down the path, my basket bursting with lettuce and herbs, eager to make a salad of fresh greens. The day unusually warm.

The laughter stopped me. I knew that laugh. I stepped off the path.

It took a moment for me to understand what I was seeing. Their bodies intertwined, her skirts hiked, her bosoms exposed, his head buried in them.

I didn't need for him to raise his gray head to know who he was–Brother Engel. The keeper of the faith, the prophet of the Harmonites, who speaks for God, was fornicating with Matilda Franks, a woman half his age, as beautiful as a she-wolf and just as treacherous.

John has gone to bed. Anna sleeps the sleep of the innocent. Tomorrow, I'll find a place to hide my diary. No one can see what I've written.

❧

July 10, 1894

Sister Gertrude sought me out today as I rested on the bench in the apple orchard. Every time I see her, she seems to be even thinner. Her checkered dress hung on her, her face sallow as candle wax. Something is eating away at her from the inside.

From the onset, she's never liked me, suspicious and watchful, as if she can see into my soul. As if she can see who I truly am. But no one knows my true nature, not even John. We see what we want to see.

"It is our divine mission to follow the prophet's decrees. Are you being true to them?" Sweetly said, with a drop of vinegar to make her point.

Though only the brethren have sway over us, Sister Gertrude likes to instruct the women in Engel's ways. Being his most ardent follower and his favorite, he looks the other way. No one plays the piano but her and with soulless passion.

There was malice in her question. Her husband lies under the protected wings of Sophia, the Virgin Spirit, tucked away in the woods, where we will all rise into the glory. There is little to tempt her.

Her white bonnet hung low on her head, shading her eyes so I could not read them. But I knew her intent.

"I follow the prophet in all things, as God intended," I answered. What did she know of what John and I did in the night? Though at first John resisted, I told him that we should not turn our backs on our earthly expression of love. I was willing to take the risk, because I know how much he desires a son.

"There is talk among the sisters. Of course, I don't listen to idle gossip and have warned the gossipers," Sister Gertrude hesitated. "But still."

Still hung in the warm July air like a strange bird come to roost in another's nest.

It was on the tip of my tongue to tell her what I saw that day in the forest between Engel and the scarlet woman, as I've come to think of Matilda.

I've told no one, not even John. It is a secret of immense burden. One capable of tearing the community apart. I do not want this to happen. I will not have that sin on my soul when Christ returns to earth.

I touched her hand because I knew no one had in a long time. She let me. In the tree's shade her skin was cool and harsh, the way I imagine a snake's skin.

"Sister Gertrude," I said in my kindest voice, my eyes searching her face. "I follow Christ's commands through the prophet on earth. I fear no retribution on the day of Christ's return."

She slipped her hand from under mine. I felt the warmth go out of her.

"Words are easy," she said. "Actions are true."

She didn't believe me.

It's only a matter of time before John is called to a reckoning. It's only a matter of time before everyone will see how we sinned and are cast out. Pray, they see nothing else.

❧

August 2, 1894

This afternoon Brother Engel cornered me in the barn. There is no other word for it.

In the barn's dimness, his piercing blue eyes held me fast like an insect pinned to his will. Fear shot through me. I've felt that probing look before. Does he know?

This close I was overwhelmed, as I always am, by his vigor belaying his fifty years and his robust tall frame. He was a shadow unto himself. The way I imagine Christ standing before me. Imminent in his glory. But I know Brother Engel is not Christ.

"Sister Mary." His voice was kindly. "Sister Gertrude has come to me with her concerns that you and John are not abiding by our stricture of celibacy. This sets a poor example for our community."

Relief coursed through me as I held the milk pail before me, the looseness of my dress and apron another disguise. My secret is still safe.

"Has not John pledged before the council his devotion?" I asked. The smell of cows and manure dizzied my stomach and lightened my head.

"He has. But someone has witnessed you and him engaging in carnality."

I knew that wasn't true. No one has seen us. It's Sister Gertrude buzzing in his ear. She now lives in his grand house. At night the sound of her playing the piano echoes through the woods. God's music, Brother Engel calls it. "We are calling the Lord down to us."

"Brother Engel, who do you choose to believe? Idle gossipers or your own son?" I dared to touch the sleeve of his fine cotton shirt. He glanced down. I removed my hand.

"Not even my own son is exempt from the laws of God. Did not God sacrifice his own son to redeem us from our sins?" His voice wrung free of kindness sent a chill up my back. I swayed with faintness.

"Are you not well, Sister Mary?"

The barn spun around me. I dropped the pail and the milk rushed around my feet like a white river.

"Let me help you." He grabbed me before I crumbled to the barn floor and led me to the milking stool.

I prayed I would not be sick. The image of his bare buttocks as it thrust back and forth and Sister Matilda's impassive face, peering implacably over his bulky shoulder, intensified my sickness.

He knelt beside me and offered his handkerchief. I took it. It's cool silky richness in contrast to my rough homespun cotton dress.

"I know," I whispered. I didn't recognize my voice, its rich boldness.

He leaned in, his long white beard brushing my face.

"What do you know, Sister Mary?"

"I saw you and Sister Matilda in the forest."

"I take many walks in the forest with members of the community."

A slight throb in his neck betrayed him.

I held John, Anna, and the unborn baby in the palm of my hand. It was godlike and frightening to have such power.

"I saw you and her fornicating."

He pulled back as if I'd spat on him.

"I thought I could reason with you. But I see your sin has turned you from God. The brethren will meet next week. John will be called before them for a reckoning. As his wife, you must implore him to confess and ask for mercy."

"He's your son," I hissed. "We've done nothing wrong. If you speak out against him, I'll bear witness against you."

He smiled and placed his hand on my belly. "For one so thin and small, your belly grows."

Then he stood and looked down on me. "There is salvation if he confesses and vows to never sin again."

"And will you take the same vow?" I struck back, my head and heart beyond reason.

He didn't answer. I watched him walk out of the barn and fade into the bright sun.

I fear for John. For in all things, the punishment falls harder on the man. And even harder on the son of the prophet.

I wish we'd never come here.

October 3, 1894

I know John's body as I know my own. So twined are we.

He didn't need to speak when he staggered through the cottage door. The weight of his pain was in the stiffness of his gait; his feigned smile–telling me it wasn't as bad as it was.

It was after midnight. The coward brethren had left him outside on the doorstep, scurrying away into the night, fearing my sharp tongue.

When John had walked to the main house for the reckoning, I'd busied myself with mending, pricking my fingers repeatedly, until I had to stop.

"You're hurt." I hurried to him and eased him onto the horsehair sofa. His stifled cry shuddered through me. "What did they do to you?"

"Help me off with my shirt." He turned sideways. Blood saturated the white cotton shirt in an angry design of punishment.

They'd flogged him.

At the sight of his severed flesh, I stifled my cry.

"It's best if I cut it away," I said, fearing the fabric clung too tightly to the wounds. That pulling the shirt over his head would release another agony of pain.

From my sewing basket beside the hearth, I retrieved my scissors and cut through the blood-soaked fabric. Gently, pulling the fabric away from the lacerations, too many to count.

John remained quiet, the pain evident in his muscles' tenseness. It would take a long time to heal the lashings. But their memory would remain in the scars until he died.

"I don't want Anna to know. Promise me you won't tell her." His face sought mine in the glowering firelight.

"She'll see you're hurt. The other children will talk." Why was I always the one holding the mirror to John's face? His naïve gentleness a fault.

His head hung down with the realization that his sin would reverberate through the community, as if they didn't already know.

"Why did they beat you?" I asked. "They could have punished you in so many other ways less violent."

"No more than I deserved." His resignation splintered me.

Would he never fault his father? Would he never see through the net he had cast over all of us?

As I cleaned the wounds and applied the salve, I said, "Who did the whipping? Was it your father?" I needed to know where to cast my hatred.

"Brother Jeremiah. He took to the bone horsewhip with vigor. I could feel his hatred in every lash. They tied me to a post in the barn. My hands over my head."

A fury like no other I'd ever felt burst through me. Jeremiah, Engel's adopted son, envious and troubled, must have gloried in the bone whip.

The baby kicked in protest. "Why didn't you testify against your father? Why didn't you tell the brethren what I saw in the forest that day?" Before the reckoning, I told John of his father's sin and begged him to tell.

"Oh, Mary. You've never understood what we're about. It would break the covenant. It would shatter our community. My father's sins are his to confess."

"As yours should have been," I pointed out.

"Help me to bed," he said.

I put his arm around my shoulder and lifted him from the sofa, as best I could. He swayed for a moment, then regained his equilibrium. Slowly, I guided him toward our bedroom. Every step a painful reminder of what was done to him.

"I thought accepting the lash would save you," he whispered, so as not to disturb Anna who slept in the adjoining bedroom. "The coming child has not dissuaded them."

Now I swayed. "What are you saying?" I searched his eyes, all the green gone, leaving shards of brown I could not read.

"You must prepare yourself. The sisters will conduct your reckoning. I'm sure your punishment will be tempered."

He kissed my cheek with resignation. Whatever the prophet had done to him had altered not just his body, but also his soul.

His father had betrayed his rightful son. The lacerations cut too deep for me to forgive.

With a heavy heart, I write this. Somewhere in the forest an owl's lament travels the night, as the scents of the dying flowers waft through the open window, where a moon lodges. Its purity rains down on me. The baby moves inside me.

"I will not be silent," I murmur to him. Already I see his face so like John's, but his hair is black, as are his eyes, like mine. He is both of us and none of us.

⸎

October 14, 1894

Three sisters came for me tonight. Their bonneted faces at my door like a gaggle of hens, clucking and preening.

Only Sister Gertrude spoke, pushing her way into the cottage. "You're to go with us to the church for the reckoning. We'll walk the path with you."

Her words offered no solace, nor did I expect any.

They will not beat a pregnant woman, I told myself.

At their collective knock, John had left his bed, despite my protestations.

Though he raged with fever and his back burned red and oozed a fetid pus, he tried to cajole them with talk of mercy and forgiveness.

It was pitiful to see him this way.

"It's all right, John. Go back to bed," I said, fearful he'd weaken my resolve.

"Mercy is shown to those who confess their sins," Sister Gertrude pronounced, her face a shut door.

"It was me that forced her," John declared.

His lie was a serpent that stung my heart. The venom of it coursed through me. But I said nothing. I would need my strength for later, I told myself, as I tied my bonnet under my chin, then draped my black woolen cape over my shoulders.

Sister Ruth and Sister Helen gaped at my stomach with a gleeful horror. Or had I imagined that?

"You've already received your judgment, Brother John. Now it is Sister Mary's turn." Sister Gertrude craned her neck, looking around the parlor. "Where is Anna?"

"Sleeping," I answered. For the first time, fear mingled with my anger.

"Wake her. She must bear witness."

"No. I won't have it. She's only four. Please spare her," I begged. Children never attend reckonings.

"Brother Engel requested she be there." Sister Gertrude's grim smile was soulless, like her music.

When neither John nor I moved to wake Anna, Sister Ruth walked to Anna's bedroom and fetched her.

"John, stop them," I pulled at his arm.

"No one will hurt her," he said, his fevered gaze directed at Sister Gertrude.

"It's not about that child but the one Mary carries."

At that moment, I didn't know whom I hated more, Sister Gertrude or John.

"Mommy, where are we going?" Anna rubbed at her eyes. To no avail Sister Ruth had attempted to confine her unruly hair in the bonnet. Her reddish curls cradled her neck and face. Her smocked dress hung limply on her small, thin frame.

"We're going to church. Everything will be all right," I assured her, adjusting her bonnet and helping her into her woolen coat.

As we trudged the dark snowy path, I held Anna's hand in mine. The baby stirred as though sensing my distress.

The crunch of our hard boots on the snow was like the church bell that broke the night's silence. Ringing the sisters to church, announcing the reckoning.

"I'm tired, Mommy," Anna said. "I want to go home."

I lifted her into my arms and nuzzled her as we neared the town. "Be a good girl," I whispered. "Whatever Brother Engel and the others say about me, block your ears to it. It's all lies."

"Hush. You are not to talk to the child," Sister Gertrude rebuked me, her white, cratered face as cold as the moon.

The church glowed with light. The black-caped sisters cast a harsh look at me as I walked down the aisle, and then mounted the altar–a reluctant penitent. Sister Ruth guided Anna to the first pew and sat next to her.

As I gazed out at the sisters, I saw a sea of ravens. None of them was faultless. And among the ravens was Sister Matilda, whose sin was more damning than mine.

"Sister Gertrude, please commence," said Brother Caleb. He sat on the altar chair, warmly dressed in his linsey-woolsey coat, blue worsted nightcap, stroking his long gray beard like a golden age Solomon.

And then it began. Some things are worse than lashes across a bare back. I focused on Anna, her pale face, sleepy-eyed and confused.

Three accusations of carnality from three Sisters: Gertrude, Helen, and Ethel–John and I in the woods, near the inland lake, in the orchards.

None of it true. All of it damning.

When they were done, Brother Engel's voice echoed through the church like a prophet newly arisen, come to earth to save us.

My stomach twisted as he spoke.

"You have broken God's tenet. With this sin on your soul, Christ will not accept you into heaven when he returns. The Second Coming is nigh. Confess your sin and ask forgiveness. What do you say?"

In truth, I meant to confess and say nothing more, take my punishment and be done with it. But the wrongness of it was like a worm eating me from the inside out.

Looking out at the black-caped sisters, their eager faces turned toward me, waiting for my confession so that they could go on living in tyranny under the dominion of a false prophet was too much for my spirit.

I found my voice, so silent for so long. "I confess to having carnal relations with my husband. But in my marital bed only."

A communal gasp rippled through the church.

"The place is of no matter. You sinned before God," Brother Engel replied, his thunderous voice ringing to the rafters, another bell tolling.

"I refuse this judgment," I replied to him. "Expressing my love to my husband is not a sin. For if you deem it so, then you must condemn yourself, Brother Engel."

"What nonsense is this?" Sister Gertrude shouted from her pew.

"I testify before God in his house that seven months ago when I was walking in the woods, I saw Brother Caleb and Sister Matilda engaged in carnal relations."

"Blasphemer." Sister Gertrude jumped up from the pew and dashed to the altar.

I feel the sting of her hand on my face still.

"Enough, Sister Gertrude," Brother Caleb said, rising from his seat and striding toward me. I cringed, expecting another blow, which didn't come.

"You should have begged forgiveness, instead of casting aspersions on me. Your lies have condemned you. The brethren will decide your fate."

"It's not a lie. I saw you. Sister Matilda," I called out to her, "speak true."

She ducked her head and remained silent.

My fate was sealed.

As Anna and I walked home, the night's maelstrom swept over me like the nighthawks weaving through the trees, eyes eager for what will sustain them.

When I tucked Anna into bed, she asked, "Why did Sister Gertrude slap you, Mommy? Did you do something bad?"

"No, my darling. She was angry about something I said. You must never slap anyone, no matter how angry you are. Now go to sleep."

It's almost dawn. I await the brethren's judgment.

I pray Anna remembers nothing of tonight.

❧

November 1, 1894

They won't tell me where they buried John. There's no fresh grave in the cemetery beneath Sophia's gaze. I fear they've burned his body to punish me for my testimony against Brother Engel. Without a human form, he will not ascend.

He died in my arms, his body raging with fever. Anna, a quiet mouse in the corner, heard his last breath and watched his spirit rise. I saw it myself. How he hovered over our marital bed. All pain gone. His red hair like the sun rising over the cottage, harbinger of what is to come.

I held him. Told Anna that her father is in heaven with God. Not to listen to the other children who mock him and call him evil. I will not stand for it.

In my rashness, I threw stones at them outside the church. They taunted Anna to tears. They tore her dress and pulled her hair, calling her witch.

And now we must leave the cottage.

There are so few things to pack. The brethren's judgment was swift, led by Brother Jeremiah who now occupies John's place in the church, and in Brother Engel's heart. How quickly a son is replaced with a false one. Anna and I are to live in the manor house until the baby arrives. After that the brethren would not say.

Though silent, I read their thoughts in their long and sour faces. I will be banished. Cast from the island in a boat alone. Left to drift and find my own way. But Anna will remain here without her mother.

Already Sister Gertrude is teaching Anna to play her discordant music. Every day Anna trudges by herself to the manor, her sad, pale face full of sorrow for her father who will not come again. I listen to her hesitant notes that echo through the forest. She has no gift for music. Like her father, she has a gift for birds and other animals, sketches them in his blank sketchpads, her small hand busy with his colored pencils and paintbrushes.

Yesterday, she brought home a bird with a broken wing.

"I'll mend it," she said to me. Gently, she cupped the fluttering bird.

What could I tell her? The bird will never fly.

Now, it sits in a basket. A cloth spun round its wing.

When I am done writing, I'll take it into the forest and set it free.

Only John's sketchbooks left to pack. The ones his father has yet to see and will never gaze on, his hatred so strong.

Has he left John's other books in the library? Or has he burnt them along with John's body? Two nights ago flames flickered the sky. But it did not smell like burning flesh. Brother Engel is a man of many colors and no heart.

Matilda ran away last week with Brother Conrad. A man more suited to her young body and silly heart. Brother Engel condemned her.

When they come for Anna and me, this diary will be close to my heart, hidden from them. They must never find it. There are so many places in the manor to hide a small book. I will find the perfect place.

John, my dearest love, the words I write in this diary will avenge you one day.

❧

November 23, 1894

Blue as stone and just as quiet. The cord like a snake wrapped around his slender neck–our son stillborn. The bonneted ravens clucked at me, as they tried to wrest him from my arms. I would not let them.

"Not yet," I cried, clutching his tiny, lifeless body to my chest.

He was as I dreamed him. Hair and eyes dark like mine with John's square face and dimpled chin; and to my relief, his skin as fair as Anna's.

As the day waned, I sat and rocked him, looking out at the lake. His spirit would not let me go. Finally, I fell helplessly into sleep.

Which sister took him? I don't know. No one will tell me where he's been taken. Is he resting under Sophia's kind eyes? I pray it is so. His body intact, so it can rise again. Despite everything, I still cling to the belief.

Brother Engel came the next day, his gray tangled beard like his tangled soul. His blue pitiless eyes pierced me, as though he could read my soul.

"You must be purified," he demanded.

I pulled my robe over me like a useless shield. What else can he do to me now?

"Where's Anna, your granddaughter?" My way of reminding him of blood and kin.

"Sister Gertrude is seeing to her."

"Bring her to me, please. I am her mother."

"Until the ceremony, you'll dwell in the turret room."

And then he was gone, leaving the air stale and bitter.

❧

I've been exiled to the turret room, high above Eden House, locked in and alone. Somewhere below me, Anna wanders the house.

What have they told her? That I'm unclean? That I'm sinful?

It's been six days since my son, Daniel, died. Six days locked in this dizzying room. Only Sister Gertrude comes. She brings me food I don't eat, cleans my linen barely slept on, and removes the waste bucket.

Today, I asked her what Anna has been told.

"You must eat," she answered, putting the tray of food on the dresser—a magnificent meal of beef stew, baked bread, butter, and stern coffee. My stomach revolted with longing, but I ignored it. The one thing I can control.

"Please," I begged her. "What have you told Anna of me?"

Was it my imagination? But I think she's softening toward me.

"That you are recovering from the birth. That her baby brother has gone to God."

"Does she ask for me?" I'm desperate for any morsel.

"I cannot say." She walked to the rose windows, her skeletal finger tracing their intricacies. Was she deciding whether to tell me of Anna?

I studied her. Something has changed. Her rigid posture replaced by rounded shoulders. Her pristine smock wrinkled and stained.

She said nothing.

I tried another tack. The aroma of the food distracting. "I hear her playing the piano in the afternoon."

"She is much improved." Still, she didn't turn around.

"She needs her mother."

When she turned around, her sallow face was brightened by the windows' light. "Before I came here, I lost a child. A boy. He was stillborn like yours."

Have I judged her too harshly? Was her sternness the only thing, besides her religion, holding her together?

"Then you know my pain. Please, let me see Anna."

"I can't do that. It's not allowed until after the purification ceremony. You must be patient." Her bright face suddenly hardened. The memory of her lost child vaporized.

"What are they going to do to me? Beat me like they did John?" Fear rushed through me.

"Oh, no. Nothing like that." She moved toward the dresser and leaned on it.

"You'll descend a set of stone steps to the cellar. It'll be like descending into the nether regions, a place of darkness. From the root cellar, you'll follow a tunnel, which leads to the maze altar. Once through the trap door, you'll ascend into the light.

The water purification will be performed by three sisters, who'll strip and bathe you before the congregants. But the ceremony can't take place until your blood stops. So you have some time to contemplate your sins."

"Sister Gertrude, you know I haven't committed any sins. And if what John and I did was a sin, then what Brother Engel and Sister Matilda did was also sinful, only more so because their union wasn't blessed by God."

She pushed away from the dresser. "You'll never be purified if you persist in lying. You must denounce your lie before everyone."

"I swear before God. I'm not lying."

She shrugged in resignation and moved away from the dresser. "Your stubbornness will be the death of you. A new sister is helping me with my duties, Sister Sarah. She has Brother Engel's ear. So if I were you, I'd keep my mouth shut around her."

Was there a spark of jealousy in Sister Gertrude's dutiful brown eyes?

"And Anna?" I asked. "Will Sister Sarah be helping with her?"

"No, I'll continue to care for her." It was small compensation.

Desperate, I dropped to my knees in front of her and grasped her hands. "Please, Sister Gertrude, bring Anna to me. If only for a few minutes, I need to hold her, see her, smell her sweetness. You know what it's like to lose a child."

As if my hands were fire, she jerked hers away, went to the door, and walked out. The key turning in the lock was like the air leaving the room.

I sat on the chair by the window and thought about the ordeal ahead. I was to be led from my room down a stone staircase to the cellar, and then through a tunnel to the maze altar.

Where were these stone stairs?

As far as I knew, there was no stone staircase in Eden House. The spiral staircase that led to the turret room ended at the landing and was made of wood, not stone. The staircase must be hidden.

Rising from the chair, I began moving furniture and tapping walls for hollowness. Nothing. Then I looked at the heavy dresser with its wavy mirror.

Sister Gertrude had stood next to it, leaning on it as she told me about the ceremony. I took the tray from the dresser and placed it on the bed.

One by one I removed the drawers, lightening the weight. Then I shoved and shoved against it with my shoulder. Each time moving it an inch or two, feeling the seepage of blood.

Finally, a red wood door emerged. I tried the doorknob, but the door was locked.

From the tray that Sister Gertrude brought, I grabbed the knife and worked around the lock endeavoring to loosen it.

If I could open the door, I could escape the room and the island through the cellar door that led to the outside.

I stopped. Anna. I couldn't leave Anna to Brother Engel's machinations. Maybe I could convince Sister Gertrude to bring Anna to see me. Then we could escape together. I continued gouging around the keyhole and doorknob until the keyhole and doorknob were sufficiently loosened. Tentatively, I opened the door. I saw a short stone landing and stone stairs leading down to the cellar.

Now, I had to pray Sister Gertrude would bring Anna to me.

After pushing the dresser back into place, I ate my food with relish. I'd need my strength.

As I finish writing, the light has left the room. I'll seek a place to hide these pages. The writing has been my salvation.

No mother should lose her child.

November 30, 1894

Anna and I are to leave tonight under the cover of darkness and snow.

Sister Gertrude came last night to my room after midnight. My persecutor turned ally. I feared to question her alteration. That pinched face, muddy brown eyes, dark clothes, and bonneted head still the same. Yet, she has changed.

"The brethren mean to make an example of you," she murmured. "As they did Brother John."

"They're going to flay me?" I asked horrified. No woman had ever been flogged.

"Brother Jeremiah will carry out the punishment in the barn with the bone whip. It is unseemly."

"John died from his wounds," I protested. "Do they mean to kill me?"

She picked at the sleeve of her dress as though it offended her. "I overheard Brother Engel and Brother Jeremiah whispering in the library. Brother Jeremiah persuaded Brother Engel to exact the same punishment on you that was meted out on John. The bone whip will be soaked in the steeped leaves of deadly nightshade. I will not abide murder. No matter the depth of the sin."

"They murdered John?" I collapsed on the hard bed and clutched the quilt to me, its thinness like my faith. His father had sentenced his only son to death.

"Once the house is asleep, I'll bring Anna to you. You'll escape down the stone staircase and out the cellar door. Then you and Anna will walk to the dock. There's a boat waiting for you. A fisherman will take you to the mainland. From there, you'll have to find your own way."

She reached into her dress pocket and pulled out a small drawstring bag. I heard the jingle of coins. "This is all I have." She handed me the bag.

"Why are you helping me?" I asked, not expecting an answer I could understand.

"He brings Sister Sarah to his bed every night when he thinks I sleep. He is a man of many sins, a false prophet." Her voice was laced with disappointment and sorrow.

Her displacement had been as good as murder. He'd murdered her soul.

"What will you do?"

"A worm in an apple spoils the fruit. I will be that worm."

"Be careful. Brother Jeremiah is an indomitable foe, capable of the most dire of God's sins." Why hadn't I seen the canker that grew in him?

"I have no need of care, when I have God on my side. He will not abide an unrepentant sinner in sheep's clothing." That spark still burned in her.

I didn't have her faith. God had let John be murdered under his watchful eye.

She started for the door, and then stopped. "I never told Brother Engel of your deception, though it troubled me greatly. You see, unlike him, I believe we are all God's children. Did John know of your Negro blood?"

I felt the room spin round me. I'd been found out. That familiar fear rose into my mouth, with its metallic taste. I shook my head. "How did you know?"

"As a child, I lived in the south. There were many like you, pretending to be white. I saw one hung for it. The town folk had a picnic afterwards." She took in a shuddered breath. "You broke our covenant. You have much to answer for, Sister Mary."

She gave with one hand and took with the other. "And yet you're helping me escape?"

"As I said, I don't abide murder."

After she left, I realized Sister Gertrude and I were alike in one way. Just as I'd hidden my true nature, she'd done the same.

This is my last entry. I'll leave the diary under the loose floorboard beneath the bed. I want no reminders from this life. Maybe one day, someone will find it and know the truth about the Harmonites.

But I will not be parted from the only photograph I have of John, Anna, and me, and the rose pendant John gave me when first we embarked on this new life, thinking Harmony was another Eden, a path toward heaven we could travel together.

Anna must never know how that path ended in death, despair, and disillusionment. And Anna must never know my true identity.

❧

Below my mother's startling words was Orr's sick scrawl. He'd written his vile epilogue while I lay dying on the maze's altar, still believing in his righteousness, justifying his murders.

I, Jeremiah, have prevailed. God's justice has been served. The daughter of the Black she-devil, Mary, is slain. Left on the sacrificial altar. The adulterous Irene Hayes struck down by my hand. As I once meted out justice to John Engel with the poisoned whip, so now. The path is cleared of all evil impediments. Nothing stands in the way of His Second Coming. The time is nigh. I am ready.

I swiped at the tears coursing down my face.

With such clarity it hurt, I now understood my mother. It all shuttled into place, not just her abhorrence of religion, but why she'd lived in the shadows, had trusted no one. She'd lived with the fear that someone might discover she was a Mulatto.

She'd woven a cocoon around us to protect me, probably watching, praying I wouldn't remember the island or recognize her olive skin, broad features, and thick, curly black hair for what they were–signs of her race. What courage she'd shown in defying Engel and rescuing us from his deluded machinations. What courage she'd shown in living as a white woman in Chicago. Then there was that day on the Chicago streetcar when she'd given up her seat to an old colored woman, knowingly putting her own life in peril to stand up for an injustice.

I glanced down at Orr's twisted words, written in the guise of Jeremiah, the name he'd chosen for his new life as a Harmonite, as if redemption was a matter of changing one's name. He had not prevailed. How it must have rankled him, when he realized Sister Gertrude had been our salvation. How it must have rankled him knowing my mother, the Mulatto, had escaped his wrath.

Justice had been served. George Orr was dead. I took some comfort in that.

I placed the diary on the bedside table, beside the photograph and Docket's letter that Orr had inexplicably left inside the diary. Troubled and unsure, I walked to the rose-patterned windows and looked out. The snow lit the night with a cold light. The windows' chilly draft sharpened my thoughts.

When I turned around, I caught my reflection in the tarnished mirror. I finally knew who I was. The daughter of a colored mother and a white father. The knowledge left me adrift.

I'd come to the island to discover the identity of the man in the photograph. Little did I know that in discovering his identity, I'd discover my mother's.

Weary, I returned to the iron bed, turned off the lamp, and crawled under the thin quilt.

No presence flickered by the dresser.

"Mother," I beckoned.

She refused to come.

But the air in the room felt lighter, that cold heaviness gone.

I turned on the lamp, rose from the bed, and left the turret room. I had to know. In my white nightgown, I was as ghostlike as the ghost I was seeking.

When I reached the dead girl's portrait, I lifted the lamp. My mind refused what I saw. The girl was as before—staring at me knowingly, with her rigid grimace and unformed hands. No one had ever tampered with the portrait.

The presence was gone. The portrait as it once was.

Ravenwood Manor no longer held me in its ghostly grip.

CHAPTER FIFTY-TWO

I ran my hand over the cottage's splintery mantle, while Theo read the diary for a second time. A memory, sharp as a thorn, pierced my mind. This had been our cottage. I was certain. I'd sat here by the hearth on a rag rug, with the broken-winged bird nestled in my small hands. My mother smiling softly at me, as she moved her hand over her pregnant stomach, my father at the window sketching. Or was it the diary that had planted the memory?

I moved away from the memory, away from the mantle, and joined Theo on the patchwork settee. His dead wife's eyes followed me.

Theo closed the diary, his slender fingers resting on it almost reverentially. "What I don't understand is why he didn't destroy the entire diary after he murdered Irene." His inquisitive blue eyes held me. "Why keep the pages that implicated him in your father's murder? He knew there's no statute of limitations on murder. Not to mention his confessing to murdering Irene and attempting to murder you."

Why didn't he ask me the obvious question? Had I known my mother was colored?

I played along. "It's the same reason he didn't destroy it after he left me to die on the altar. I don't think he believed he'd get caught. Why he kept those pages and destroyed the others? I think he enjoyed reading my mother's agony. He was a sick, deluded man."

As was my grandfather, Caleb Engel.

"Quinn, probably in one of his drunken moments, blabbed to Orr about Irene finding the diary. Told him there was something in it, damning someone living on the island. Orr panicked and killed Irene," Theo speculated. "But why did Irene believe George Orr was Brother Jeremiah?" He was probing as though after a story. That's how I needed to think of him.

I shrugged. Another question, I had no sure answer for.

"This is only speculation. But when I first read Docket's letter, the name Jeremiah Strong seemed familiar, but I couldn't place it. Then it came to me this morning. It was etched into one of the gravestones at the Harmonite cemetery."

On my way to Theo's cottage, I'd stopped by the cemetery to make sure.

"One of the gravestones read Abigail, daughter of Jeremiah and Esther Strong, born 1888 died 1888. Abigail was George Orr's daughter. My guess is Irene saw Orr at the gravesite, maybe praying or putting flowers on the grave. Combined with the diary, she figured it out. Maybe she wrote to Docket for information to be certain. When Catherine fired her, she had to leave. And then she met her fate. She never saw the letter."

"Irene should have confided in me and not Quinn. I would have protected her," Theo retorted.

"Do you really believe that, Theo? That you could have protected her?" He still believed he could atone for his wife's lonely death.

"I would have tried." His eyes shifted away. "Orr must have killed her when she came to purchase the boat ticket. Then moved her body to the woods, so the blame would fall on one of the loggers."

"We'll never know," I said, wearily, tired of the dead. How they haunt you and won't let you go.

"At least he was caught. Thanks to you, Nellie. And now you know what happened to your father. He sounds like a good man."

"I wish I could have known him." In a way I did. He'd be with me always in spirit and in my heart.

"Are you sure I can't get you something? You look like you could use a stiff drink."

He didn't wait for my answer, went to the kitchen, and returned with two glasses, a finger of whiskey in each.

I took the glass, raised it, and clinked it against his. "Hair of the dog," I joked. The whiskey prickled my nose and burned my throat.

He looked at me quizzically. "Ah, Orr's milk toddy." He took a generous swallow of his whiskey, then put the glass down on the crate.

Before I could react, his quick fingers unbuttoned my top two dress buttons, pushed the fabric aside, and gently touched the bruises that ringed my neck. Where Orr's fingers had marked me.

"Don't," I said, pushing his hands away.

"That son of a bitch." He pulled me to him and held me. His scent more intoxicating than the whiskey.

"Theo, I'm leaving tomorrow," I whispered.

He let go. "Tomorrow? Why? I thought William asked you to stay on?"

There were too many reasons to name. I chose the easiest. "I want to go home."

"Are you ready to go back to the trenches? I read that the flu's still raging through the city." If he was hurt, he hid it well.

Despite matron's threat that I could never return, I knew the city hospital would take me back. Nurses were in short supply. But I wasn't sure if I wanted to return to fourteen-hour shifts and watching patients die. But I didn't want him to know that. Whatever I decided to do had to be my decision alone.

"I can't stay here." What I wanted to say was, I can't stay here, because there's nothing for me here. To test him, to see if he would say, "I'm here." But if he did, would I stay?

He picked up his drink, swirled it, and drank it down. I waited into the silence. Finally, he said, "At least, now you know."

"Know what?"

"Who you are, Anna Engel."

The name sounded nothing like me. "Anna Engel stays here. Nellie Lester is going home," I said disappointed. I glanced at his wife's photograph. He was still tied to her. He wasn't going to ask me to stay.

"I should go." I stood, feeling the loneliness return.

"Hold up." He took my hand and pulled me onto the settee. "I want you to know I don't give a damn what your mother was. It changes nothing between us."

"Why are you telling me this?" I held my breath, as I studied the contours of his face, the mesmerizing blue of his eyes, the small scar that scissored his eyebrow. I wanted to reach out and touch it. I wanted to lie down beside him. My desire so strong, my body felt alight.

"I'm telling you this, because–" He ran his fingers through his blond hair. "Because maybe it's time I go home too."

For a man who once made his living with words, he was suddenly at a loss for them.

"But I thought New Harmony was your home." I had to be sure.

For a brief moment, he glanced at his wife's photograph. "I'm done with running."

He leaned in and kissed me with such tenderness, my heart ached. When he pulled away, I slowly stood and took his hand. He didn't have to show me. I knew the way to his bedroom. The fire crackled, snow pelted the windows, and our clothes fell softly to the floor.

EPILOGUE

Snow flurried around me, as I stood on the deck of the Mersey, watching the island disappear into the horizon, until only the dark, undulating waves remained. Large ice chunks bobbed in the water. I gripped the icy railing, as the boat rocked and a large wave tumbled over the deck, saturating my boots and the hem of my dress. I'd become so accustomed to the cold I barely felt it. I was headed home. The island could no longer touch me.

Before I'd left, I'd gone to the tavern to apologize to Bernie and her father for my accusations, fully expecting to be told to leave.

But Bernie had grabbed me in a tight hug and wished me well.

"It must have been terrible for you, almost dying, and Orr killing your Pa like that," she'd said, her brown eyes warm and forgiving.

Fred Huber had piped in with his usual prattle. "Still got that room upstairs for you, girlie."

There'd been no bear hug from Matthew. Instead, a welcome promise that once Sherriff Wilkins's investigation was over, he'd personally deliver the diary to me in Chicago.

"Can't trust the mail," he'd said straight faced.

I heard a shrill cry and looked up. The sky was as blank and gray as the water.

Must be Hannah waking from her nap. I should go inside. But I didn't. It was going to be hard untangling myself from her.

The crisp air helped keep me rooted, invigorating me, making me believe I could heal. That I could eventually sleep through the nights, and one day forget how close I came to dying at the hands of the man who'd killed my father. I felt my bruised neck through the wool scarf.

Let Mrs. Bucheim see to Hannah. Let her see to Catherine, who was slowly emerging from the drug's hold, thanks to my herbal potion and William and Mrs. Bucheim's intervention.

It had come as a shock, William's insistence that Catherine leave the island and seek treatment in Chicago for her *nerves*, as he called it. To my surprise, he'd didn't have to convince Mrs. Bucheim to accompany her and Hannah. She'd stood in the great room, her spine as ramrod straight as an andiron, saying, "I'll see to the missus if Nellie has other obligations."

Maybe she, too, was done with the island and its strange pull that sucked you under.

William had nodded sadly. For once, his money couldn't buy him what he wanted: me as Catherine's nurse. When he'd seen I couldn't be persuaded to remain on the island, he'd offered me an enormous sum to be her private nurse.

I had no other nursing obligations. But I'd waved Eleanor's letter at him as proof of another commitment, knowing he would never read it. That had satisfied him.

Eleanor's letter had touched the tender places I carried like open wounds. Her praise of Irene Hayes left me saddened. "One of my most promising nursing students, with the exception of you," she'd written. "Her only fault was she was too trusting, if that can be considered a fault."

In the end Irene's trusting nature had led her down a flowery path strewn with William's promises. I still stood in her shoes–the other nurse. If not for Irene, I would have never known my father's cruel fate or my mother's true heritage.

A lone raven cawed, drawing my attention away from my thoughts. It circled the Mersey in a dance of its own making.

An omen of ill luck, sailors believed.

I don't know if I believe in omens. What I do believe in is that a mother's love lives on, even after death. How else can I explain the presence that visited me in the night?

I heard the cabin door slam behind me.

"Come inside, Nellie. You're shivering." Theo wrapped his arms around me.

I leaned back against his broad chest. "Can't we stay like this just a little longer?"

"If that's what you want." His arms tightened as the Mersey rocked us toward home.

ACKNOWLEDGMENTS

I'm deeply indebted to my friend and colleague, Nancy Cirillo for reading several drafts and helping me shape the character of Nellie Lester. I'm most grateful to my literary agent, Jill Marr, for pointing me in the direction of a Gothic mystery. Many thanks to Liz Leutwiler who led me to the 19th century Harmonite religious community, a central element in the book. The team at CamCat Publishing is owed a big thanks for allowing me a voice in the decision making process from cover art to editorial to the voice over talent of the audio edition. Last but not least, I want to thank my husband who was my sounding board for plot ideas.

About the Author

Gail Lukasik is the best-selling author of *White Like Her: My Family's Story of Race and Racial Passing*. The book captured national attention and led to her appearances on *The Today Show*. She also starred in the award-winning documentary film, *History of Memory*. Her articles about coming to terms with her mixed-race identity were published in *The Washington Post, Mic.com, Independent.co.uk,* and *The Daily Beast*. This is Gail's fifth mystery novel. She lives in the Chicagoland area with her husband.

If you enjoyed Gail Lukasik's
***The Darkness Surrounds Us*,**
please consider leaving us a review
to support our authors.

And check out Terry Friedman's
paranormal mystery
***Bone Pendant Girls*.**

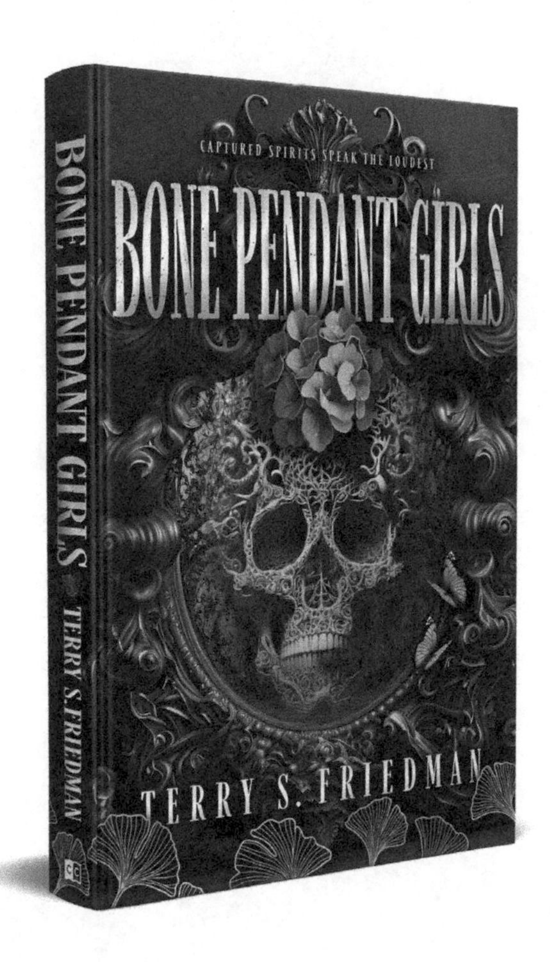

ANDI

2022

Ginkgo leaves drifted down like butterfly wings outside the gem show. They made a yellow carpet on the walkway to the boarding school's gymnasium. Within the swirling leaves, Andi heard a voice. Hollow metallic vowels rustled like leaves in gutters. Consonants scratched and thumped like animals trapped in heating ducts. When the frantic skittering of syllables merged into words, a ghostly plea slipped into her consciousness. *"Trapped . . . help."*

"You'll find your way to the Other Side," Andi whispered.

Some days, the spirits refused to leave her in peace. Turning off spirits' voices was like trying to keep a snake in a bird cage. The Shadows had been with her since she was four. Her mother had sent those spirits to watch over her. But the voice she heard today was not the Shadows. They rarely spoke.

"Please . . . help."

Andi opened the door. "I'm not the one to help you," she told the young voice. "I attract bad men."

The ticket ladies took her money and stamped her hand. She scanned from one end of the gymnasium to the other. So many vendors. Where to start. Left, past the fossils, to a station called P&S Lapidary. They always had unique pieces.

"Please . . . ma'am." The whisper had a faint Southern lilt.

"Aw, come on. Hijack someone else's head. Go see my ex-husband. Convince him to give me all his money." Andi looked left and right to make sure no one had heard. No need to worry. Odds were good that at least one other person in the crowd talked to herself.

Andi made her way through thirty stations. Through bargain-bound women rummaging in bins of clearance beads, through vendors taking orders to set stones, through miles of bead strands, she searched for the perfect happy, shiny piece. Twice around the gym, and that whispering voice drilled its way into her conscience again.

"Please . . . Buy . . . me."

Cripes! The urgency of that sweet young voice. She heaved a sigh. "Hope you're not expensive. Where are you?" Her feet ached and the place was stifling hot. "Where?"

"Over here!"

She couldn't see a damn thing through the shoppers lined up two people deep at the stations. Up on her toes, down, from foot to foot sideways. A tiring, annoying dance. Andi shivered despite the stuffy gymnasium.

"Here!"

Easing her way through shoppers, she peered into a glass display case. Malachite beads, a red coral branch necklace, two strands of ringed freshwater pearls, and one pendant with a cameo style face etched in bone.

The vendor with a bolo tie looked like her ninth-grade geography teacher. "Let me open that for you. The face pendants are going fast. Only two left." He lifted the hinged glass cover.

"Me!" A loud whisper from the carved pendant with a girl's face.

Andi looked intently at it. Like most cameos, the face was a side profile. Tendrils of the girl's curly hair escaped an upswept hairdo, framing her face. At first, she appeared to be asleep. Then the girl's face studied her too, eyes blinking as if she'd just awakened. Andi shivered. In the spirit world she'd inherited from her mother, voices whispered. Images in jewelry didn't move.

What now? She spoke silently. Subconscious to subconscious.

"Hurry, ma'am! Buy . . ."

A woman, who reeked of Chanel No. 5, snatched the face pendant from the case.

"Excuse me," Andi said. "I came here to buy that piece. It called to me." There now, she'd admitted she was crazy. She gave a lopsided grin and a shrug. "Please, could I have it?"

"Sorry, hon. I got here first." A condescending glance at Andi, and the lady wrapped her bratwurst fingers around the pendant.

"Not to worry, ladies," the seller told them. "I have another like this." He pushed the tablecloth aside, reached under the table, and pulled out a second pendant. "It's stunning with Namibian Pietersite accents. I could let you have it for the same price."

"No . . . me." An adamant voice.

"I don't want the other pendant," Andi said. "I came here for the one in her hand." At the next booth, a woman holding a jade jar stopped talking and stared at her. Andi blushed, knowing she sounded like a petulant child.

Suddenly, the woman gasped. "Ouch! Awful thing cut me. It has sharp edges." A thin line of blood welled on Chanel Lady's finger, and she dropped the pendant as if it had bitten her. Andi caught it before it hit the floor. The silver bezel felt ice-cold. A young girl's eyes gazed up at her and blinked. *"Thanks, ma'am."*

She stared at the pendant. Her mother had warned about spirits attaching to people. If spirits attached, she'd said, terrible things could happen.

Chanel Lady cradled the darker pendant. Not a word uttered from it. Maybe the tea-stained piece believed in being seen and not heard. Its bone face was younger. Pietersite in the top bezel had chatoyancy, a luminous quality. Thin wavy splotches of browns, blacks, reds, and yellows swirled through dark stone like tiny ice crystals in frozen latte.

"Yes, I like this one better. Excellent quality Pietersite," Chanel Lady said.

"If you don't mind, I'll take her payment first." The seller probably wanted to send the woman to another station before she started a fight with his customers.

"No problem. Is this ivory?" Andi asked. Whether vendors called it mammoth bone or not, elephants didn't deserve to be slaughtered for jewelry.

"Absolutely not. Wouldn't sell it if it was. Cow bone," he assured her.

A triumphant smirk aimed at Andi, and Chanel Lady made her way through the crowd. Subduing an impulse to give her the middle finger, Andi turned back to the pendant. She studied the heart-shaped face, turned it over, and winced at the tiny price sticker. Was she insane? Andi couldn't afford that; she'd lost her teaching job.

"I'll need your address and email." The seller handed her a clipboard.

She'd fought over it and won, no changing her mind now. While he charged her credit card, Andi filled out the information for his mailing list. Then she weaved through shoppers to find a quiet corner by the concessions stand.

What the hell. The pendant was a dose of credit card therapy. Unzipping the plastic sleeve, she lifted the piece by the bail. Two bezels set in silver. One disk held labradorite, a luminous blue stone with black veins, and in the second bezel, a face carved in bone. She shifted it in her palm, studying the details. Had light played with the image, making it look like the girl moved? That sweet innocent face seemed at peace now. It would warm at the touch of her skin.

Once more around the gym, and she left the show, slogging through the grassy field toward her car, wondering how a whispering girl had convinced her to buy a pricey pendant. Yet, she had a sense that something other than her credit card bill had changed.

An arctic gust tried to snatch her cap. One hand on her hat, the other holding a bag with the talking pendant, Andi shook off a chill. She remembered the invisible friend who had first spoken to her when she was four and stayed her best friend until middle school.

"You can't go around talking to yourself," her father had scolded. A teacher later suggested Andi might be autistic. Infuriated, Father took her to a psychologist. The tests had shown nothing worse than a high IQ. On the way home from the doctor's office, her mother admitted, "Great Aunt Bertha had *the gift.* More a nuisance than a gift, really."

Andi brushed back an unruly strand of dark hair and tugged her cap down over her ears.

After crunching through dead grass, she tossed her handbag and the pendant onto the passenger seat and cranked up the CD player. "Go away with me," the singer crooned.

". . . to . . . park, ma'am."

She glanced sideways at the small bag. Sleep deprivation, her father would say, but he'd never been invited to tea parties with ghosts. That was a secret she'd shared with her mother. Father thought Andi's invisible friends were imaginary and the Shadows with yellow cat eyes were nightmares. Her mother knew better. "The voices will always be there," she'd told Andi. "You must learn when to turn them off." Over the years, Andi had discovered stress and lack of sleep made the "off switch" harder to control.

Cheer up, she told herself. Maybe hallucinations came next, and Elvis would show up at the Wawa and buy her a cup of coffee.

"Please . . . park," the plaintive voice whispered.

"It's winter in Pennsylvania. You are obviously not–why am I talking to a bag? Turn the voice off." But the girl was so polite, and she was curious about why the pendant chose her. Okay, it might not be so cold in the park. Yeah, and maybe gas prices would plummet to a dollar fifty-nine overnight. Not likely, but fresh air might clear her head. She bought decaf at a convenience store, glad that Elvis wasn't there, and drove to Franklin Township Park.

Finding a parking space was no problem. Andi shared the lot with a white plastic bag that blew from empty space to space like a kite loose from its owner, spiraling, then tumbling down, then lifting again. Like a wisp of memory, nagging, then burying itself for a while.

"Talking pendants," she muttered, staring out the windshield. Frost had washed the green from the grass, turning the blades to bristly stubbles like a blond buzz-cut. Sepia November. Crusty brown mud puddles. Empty asphalt paths. Purple-gray trees with branches like bony arms reaching for the clouds. Not even a die-hard runner around. Here was a great place for answers to mysteries of the universe. One foot out of the warm car, and she wondered if her sanity had flown South for the winter. She slammed the door and stuffed the small brown parcel into her pocket. "A nice Southern girl with manners wouldn't bring me out here to freeze to death."

No voices now. Maybe Southern spirits had a freezing point.

Andi found a bench under some pine trees and sipped steaming coffee, warming her hands on the cup. Two playground swings squeaked out a seesawing harmony on their metal chains. It reminded her of winter in a beach town and metal store front signs tossed by wind, of a foghorn wailing in the night, of Lewes, Delaware, her hometown. She hadn't been home in years. Guilt and shame had festered like a wound that wouldn't heal between her mother and father. If only she hadn't been so eager to get into a stranger's car.

A man, a free puppy, and a tattoo. That's all Andi remembered about the kidnapping. Unfortunately, she couldn't forget the pain when her parents tried to have the tattoo removed. No, she would not return to a psychiatrist, not even for divorce counseling. Some memories were better left buried.

All this damn solitude must have turned her brain to scrapple. Andi stamped the numbness from her feet. "We're at the park like you wanted. So, why'd you choose me?"

Wind rattled the treetops. A single gingko leaf landed on the toe of her sneaker. No ginkgo trees in sight. This time of the year, she'd know if a gingko tree was nearby because the fruit smelled like vomit.

"Why the silent treatment?" she asked.

No answer. Angry gray clouds slid across the sun. "Okay, I give up." She pitched the cup into a trash bin and started back. When she slipped the pendant from its protective sleeve, a raindrop fell on it. Another drop. Another. Whispering, a different voice, a younger girl's voice.

"Key in lock, rattling, rattling. Remember?"